ABOUT THE AUTHOR

T. W. HOWIS (he/him) is an Australian writer living in Wadawurrung country. He enjoys conducting interviews with artists, writers, and creatives and makes regular contributions to Aurealis Magazine, Jimmy Hornet and more. He loves watching British crime shows, reading fantasy books, and making marmalade. He is involved with several writing projects including a comic book.

Broken by Magick is his first novel.

www.twhowis.com

facebook.com/TWHowis
instagram.com/twhowis

BROKEN BY MAGICK

T. W. HOWIS

First published in Australia in 2026 by
Ellstone House Publishing
PO Box 5178, East Geelong VIC 3219, Australia

Copyright © T. W. Howis 2025

T. W. Howis asserts the moral right to be identified as Author of this work. All characters and events in this publication, other than those in the public domain, are fictitious and any resemblance to real persons, living or dead, is purely coincidental.

All rights reserved. No part of this book may be reproduced, stored in a retrieval system, or transmitted, in any form or by any means, electronic, mechanical, photocopying, recording, or otherwise without prior written permission of the author and publishers.

 A catalogue record for this book is available from the National Library of Australia

ISBN (POD): 978-1-7641322-0-6
ISBN (EBook): 978-1-7641322-1-3
ISBN (Paperback AUS): 978-1-7641322-2-0

Without limiting the author's and publisher's exclusive rights, any unauthorised use of this publication to train generative artificial intelligence (AI) technologies is expressly prohibited. Ellstone House Publishing also exercise their rights under Article 4(3) of the Digital Single Market Directive 2019/790 and expressly reserve this publication from the text and data mining exception.

www.ellstonehouse.com.au

This book would never ever have been possible without the love, support, patience, and amazing editing skills of the love of my life, my darling Rebecca.

1

All Detective Inspector Brighton wanted to do was go home to his family.

'Time to pack it in,' said Brighton, looking around the operations room at his weary brain-dead crew, all slumped around their computers.

Some were even asleep. Brighton didn't blame them. For two days they had searched for Anna Bolton, a missing child believed to have been kidnapped, and some like himself, hadn't left the station since being assigned to the case.

'But guv,' said Detective Sergeant Jimmy Griffiths, 'we're still nowhere near to cracking this. The geezer that took her left us nothing. We have to find something on him.'

'I appreciate that Jimmy, but at this rate I doubt we will find anything much tonight. We haven't even confirmed that she's been taken. We still haven't found any witnesses.'

'I know that, but the fact that nobody has seen her and there weren't sightings of her on CCTV suggests foul play. Don't it?'

'Look. I get what you're saying Jimmy, but for all we know she may have fallen in the canal, or a narrow boat's picked her up. That's happened before, remember that kid that stowed away on one as a lark and surprised two pensioners that time? The best we can do is come back tomorrow and start again with fresh eyes. Let's hope that Jeanie in forensics comes up with something to help us. Now come on you lot. Surely some of you must still have families to go home to. I know I have.'

His team didn't need much prompting and soon the room was deserted, except for Jimmy who waited around so that they could leave together.

'You're learning Jim,' Brighton said as they walked down the stairs. 'If the others see that you're not dashing away before them like some people do, you might get some more respect out of them. You'll need that when you're running the show.'

The younger man looked at him.

'Thinking about moving on now guv? We're not getting too dull for you, are we?'

Brighton smiled.

'Nah Jimmy. The missus wants me bound to a desk.'

'Geez,' said Jimmy with a cheeky grin. 'Lucky I'm single innit.'

'Sir,' said the desk sergeant, interrupting with a hint of a smirk at stopping his superior in his tracks just inches from freedom. He motioned to the phone. 'It's for you.'

'Did they say who it was?'

'No sir. He just wants to talk to you. He sounds a bit strange to be honest.'

Brighton tried not to roll his eyes as he walked over to the desk.

'DI Brighton.'

'Ahh,' said a curious voice 'Be ye William Brighton?'

Brighton froze when he heard the name that he despised more than the woman that gave it to him. The man's voice sounded cruel, and as ancient as time itself. A harsh rasping, almost medieval accent that sounded like nothing he'd ever heard before, except for maybe Worzel Gummidge ordering a cup of tea and a slice of cake.

'Who am I speaking to please?'

'Meet me at the witching hour. Near the statues of the beast and fountain and the knave on the pillar.'

What the hell is he talking about? Brighton thought for a minute.

'Hang on. Are you asking me to meet you at Trafalgar Square?'

'Aye. At the last hour of this night.'

Brighton rolled his eyes. Great. That's all I needed, he thought.

'Midnight then. Is this about the missing girl?'

'Aye the little ginger girl. She cries for her rabbit.'

'What's your name? I can send...'

The phone went dead, and Jimmy watched it take Brighton's smile along with it.

'Who was that guv?'

'The kidnapper. He wants a word.'

'You're joking right? What makes you so sure it's him?'

'He mentioned her rabbit.'

Anna's favourite toy rabbit had not been disclosed to the media, but Brighton had his doubts. It might be related to the case, but then it could be one of his old snouts, completely unrelated. His gut told him otherwise, and that a five-hour wait until midnight was worth it. He hoped so.

'You're not serious are you guv?' said Jimmy, as Brighton turned around and flashed his security pass. 'You've been stuck here for days!'

'Yeah and as you said Jimmy, we're getting nowhere.' He turned to the desk sergeant. 'Please tell me we taped that.'

'We did sir. I'll pull it up and send it right to you.'

'Thanks for that... Don, isn't it?'

'That's right.'

'You did well. That might be a good lead.'

Jimmy ducked back through the security door.

'Well, if you're staying guv then so am I. Do you want me to call the rest of them back? Bet they're just over at the boozer anyway.'

'No, it's okay. I've got this.'

'You sure?'

'Yeah, I think I can take on one old man if he's the real deal. He probably won't even show. You know these hero types we deal with. Go home Jimmy. Please.'

'Are you sure?'

'Yeah, I'm sure. See you tomorrow.'

'Alright then. Thanks boss'

As Brighton watched Jimmy walk back towards the door, he remembered that he'd made a promise to his daughter. Of all the nights to get a lead on this case.

'Hey Kerry, it's me.'

'Hi ya Will. Where are you? Emily's on in forty minutes.'

'Yeah, about that.'

'Oh no. You're not coming, are you?'

'Nah.'

'Something's come up,' they said in unison. Kerry knew better than question him.

'I've got to meet someone in five hours.'

'Is this related to the Anna Bolton case?'

'You know that I can't talk about it.'

'Why did you marry me then, Will Brighton, when you knew full well that I'm a leading crime reporter? I'm bound to ask you questions. My editor is pressuring me for an inside scoop on this case.'

'Hey, you weren't a crime reporter when we met. Remember? You were getting coffee for the lonely-hearts advice woman. Delores, wasn't it?'

'You'll be a lonely heart if this keeps up Will. So, what do you want me to tell Emily?'

'Tell her the truth.'

'She'd be terrified. One of her friends knows the missing kid.'

Crap, thought Brighton, remembering that London wasn't such a huge place after all.

'Sorry, I had no idea. Just say I'm at a silly meeting.'

'You've had a lot of them lately.'

'That's not my fault.'

'I know that. It's just...' She tapered off mid thought, deciding not to continue.

'Just what?'

'Well just for once it would be nice to go out and do something as a family, and not have your employer throw cold water over our plans all the time.'

This had been coming for a while, Brighton knew he deserved it.

'It's not my fault that someone decided to go out and kidnap a little kid.'

4

'So, it is the Anna Bolton case.'

'No comment.'

'Hang on. Did you say you're meeting at midnight?'

'Yeah. In town.'

'That gives you loads of time to get here. You could still be here on time.'

'Sure, I could probably make it but there's no time to get back. Track work starts tonight. Then there are the buses, and I might as well forget about trying to be back in time.'

'You could get a cab.'

'We can't afford that right now, and work won't pay for me to finish my shift and just come back whenever I want to. They sure won't pay the cab charge. Remember the last time we tried to claim that?'

The deep sigh on the other end of the phone suggested that she did.

'Alright. I get it. Will you be home later? I'm beginning to forget what you look like.'

'Yeah. I should be. But I can't make any promises. It depends on the lead I'm following. I'm sorry.'

'So am I,' said Kerry and hung up.

Brighton felt bad. How am I going to make it up to them this time? he thought. This was his reward for always putting the job first. Always had, and he warned Kerry about that when they first started dating. So had her father, though as a High Court Judge, his perspective on career coppers like Brighton was positive and fresh.

'When he's a Detective Chief Inspector he won't have to be completely hands on,' he'd told his beloved daughter eight years ago. 'After that he'll have a lot more time.'

Trouble was that Brighton liked being a Detective Inspector and was too good at it to be promoted up the chain. For now, London needed him rightfully where he was, cracking major cases and keeping the public safe; even if that meant keeping his family together with a mangle of frayed threads and broken promises.

A curse on this place, thought Zaliel the wizard, sniffing the putrid air near Nelson's Column, and wondered if William Brighton would indeed show up. For his sake, he had better.

Since making the call, Zaliel had received pity coins from the charitable, ridicule from teenagers, and was asked by some clueless family from Iowa where something called the Eyeful tower was. He only knew of one tower in London. He had escaped from it a long time ago by reciting a spell carved in the wall, disguised as an astrological chart.

Through the stench of rotting rubbish, his nose pricked up when he detected the scent of something dying not that far away. He stood up and went looking for it. Sure enough, he found an ancient pigeon huddled up against a drainpipe halfway down a nearby alley.

'There, there old one,' he said, as he picked it up with little fuss and put it in his sack. 'Now my cats will have something to play with for their breakfast.'

When Zaliel returned to Nelson's Column, he found his seat occupied by a professional beggar. His hungry glassy eyes looked up from his new iPhone and scowled.

'Oi, Wot you looking at? This is my spot. On yer bike.'

'Nay. I have no bike.'

'Wot?'

'I have no bike.'

'Do you think you're funny or sump think?' The middle-aged man huffed and puffed and made strange grunting sounds like an amorous sea lion as he lifted his heavy sagging body up from the pile of old rags and newspapers. He glared at the stranger and clenched his fists.

'I said get lost you old twat!'

At first glance the mighty wizard tapping his ancient fingers against one of the lions looked like a fellow beggar, until he drew his wand from his belt.

'Nay. You move along swine. Or ye'll regret it.'

'Ere wots all this then? Eh? Wot you call me?'

'I called ye swine. Tis what thou art and what thou shalt be.' He waved his wand. 'Estne porcus!'

A flash of green light hit his enraged opponent with such a kick in the guts that it knocked the huge man to the ground where he lay quivering and gasping for air as the magick surged through his body transforming his DNA. When the spell ended, the beggar jumped up and squealed, attempting to balance while trying to understand why he had four legs, and his body was covered in a hideous coat of coarse black hair. His missus wasn't going to like this one bit.

'Now go pigge! Leave me be!' Zaliel shouted as he zapped the boar on the bottom, sending it squealing away into the dark.

Zaliel's eyes narrowed as his twisted wrinkly face grinned at this little victory. For the first time in years, he felt satisfied, for the magick he'd acquired made him powerful.

There was a time not so long ago in the Magical Wooded World when everyone scurried away in fright at the very sight of him. Whole villages would go into lockdown until he passed by. All children whether goblin, elf, gnome, or dwarf were told to behave by their parents, or the wizard would surely take them.

Everything in his world was perfect until little Anna Brighton came along and ruined his life and reputation. The only reason he had returned to London was to find her and destroy her; and take back what was his.

Finally, he thought, hoping that the young man scuttling towards him had the information he needed.

'WILLIAM!' he wailed, like Golem had just stepped on Legos.

'That's DI Brighton to you.'

His unease with his own name surprised Zaliel.

'Aye no matter,' he said without apology.

'So, you're the guy that called?' said Brighton, scanning around the ancient bloke for a possible weapon.

The huge square, usually popular with locals and tourists, was deserted at this hour. This made it an ideal spot for a hit on a bleak night, and the Detective Inspector had many enemies.

'Well?'

Zaliel stared up. His yellow eyes glowing in the soft neon city lights.

'Aye, from the small red room that stinks of goblins piss.'

I wonder if you've smelled yourself lately thought Brighton, taking a step back as he examined the old boy's costume. The hooded cassock and sandals made him look more like a medieval monk than just a bum in the street.

'So why did you call me? Do you have information about the disappearance of Anna Bolton?'

'It may be that I do, and I shall tell thee if ye tell me where thy mother is in return.'

Brighton's skin crawled. He despised his mother more than his name, but what if this crazy old man knew where the missing girl was? What if he had taken her?

'Where is thy mother?'

Brighton rolled his eyes. Everyone except him wanted to know where his mother was. This wasn't the first time that a fan had managed to track him down and lure him out under false pretences, but it still upset him. He'd given up a night with his family for this waste of time.

'Look I really don't know okay. I haven't spoken to her for years. Where is Anna Bolton? How did you know about her rabbit?'

'I shall tell thee and more if ye tell where Anna Brighton is.'

'Are you deaf? I just said that I don't know where she is.'

'I don't believe thee.'

'Look mate, I don't know who you are but I'm in no mood for this. Good night.'

Zaliel growled as he grabbed something out from the belt in the rags he wore.

'You dare walk away!'

Brighton looked the old man up and down. A part of him pitied the fool, but he was having none of this. Even he had limits.

'That's enough mate. You've had your fun. Now either you clear off or I'll march you down the nick and charge you for wasting police time.'

'Be thou sure?' said the wizard pointing what looked like a skinny stick square at Brighton's chest.

'What are you going to do with that? Turn me into a toad? Look I get that you're just some daft plonker that's watched too much Harry Potter, and that's not your fault. But I'm too tired for this shit so I'm going home. And if I so much as catch you trying to follow me, I'll have you nicked.'

'Percello!' said the wizard waving his wand.

Brighton saw a brilliant light and felt the heat from a shaft of energy that knocked him to the ground, before it bounced off his chest and hurtled away into the night like an errant meteor.

What the hell was that? Brighton thought, scrambling back to his feet. A ruddy wand taser? He'd seen it all now.

'That's it. You're under arrest for assaulting a police officer,' he said, pacing back to the glaring wizard.

'It cannot be!' said Zaliel with a gasp, clenching his fist with so much anger that he nearly snapped his wand in half. 'I know not how you live, but no matter.'

Before Brighton could apprehend him, the wizard waved his wand. This time there was no mistaking the beam of bright magickal light streaming towards Big Ben as it struck the witching hour.

'Expergiscere, o leo fortis et impetum.'

The bell struck twelve times as normal but then for the first time in its history, Big Ben chimed again. At the thirteenth chime, a beam of warm light surged out from the ancient clocktower and washed over the four giant lion statues in a sparkling wave.

The light mesmerised Brighton like a moth. What the hell is that? he thought, trying to remember any notes about new light show rehearsals in the city. Was it some kind of laser pointing taser or children's magic trick? There were plenty of toy wands around. Maybe this guy is just some kind of next level fan.

'That's enough,' he said, moving towards the wizard with his handcuffs at the ready.

Before Brighton reached Zaliel, one of the lions towering over them stretched as it stood up and shook its majestic metal mane. A puff of warm foggy air exhaled from the lion's mouth followed by a roar that echoed through the deserted streets. The other three lions stood, arched their backs and roared like a movie was about to start. Together, they glanced down past the sneering wizard and glared at their intended target.

Some people freeze when confronted by danger, and some who are either very brave or very stupid decide to step in and resist it. Brighton legged it.

'Shit!' he yelled, lifting his legs high as he leapt over the bollards, and ran off into the night in full flight with the four bronze lions chasing him in earnest pursuit.

Brighton tore off in the direction of The Mall because he knew it would be abandoned at midnight, and he hoped to lose them in the Kensington Gardens. The last thing that he wanted was chaos in the streets. He ran past Horse Guards Road, with the lions' heavy metal legs clanking away as they gained up on him. They started roaring as they closed in. Then Brighton heard a siren. Glancing back, he saw a police incident response vehicle roaring down The Mall, gaining on the lions.

One of the bronze beasts turned and jumped onto the car with a loud bang, crumbling the roof in like a packet of stale biscuits and burst both the front tyres, sending it spinning out of control. Before the car splashed into St James Park Lake, the lion jumped away and joined its pride.

Brighton kept running towards the building that the Royal Family called the office.

'Stand back from the King's Guard!' said a sentry guarding the palace, training his rifle at the exhausted policeman.

'Detective Inspector Brighton. Scotland Yard,' said Brighton, wheezing as he doubled over to try and catch his breath.

'What's the meaning of this? You're not supposed to be here.'

'I'm not the one you should be worried about.'

Brighton pointed and the guard turned to see four huge bronze lions charging towards them. He pressed the button in his sentry box for help.

Then he sank to one knee and fired a round from his rifle. The tiny 5.56mm bullet just ricocheted off one of the lions. He may as well have thrown a rock. The guard fired three more rounds before retreating back behind the gates of Buckingham Palace, as the other seven members from his section raced over to join him.

As the giant lions surrounded Brighton, the guards all opened fire at them. Two lions charged the wrought iron barrier, tearing it to shreds as the guards kept firing. As the third lion drew near, it saw a large feral pig and broke away, chasing the squealing pig all the way home. Its squeals were replaced by high pitched alarm bells ringing all around the sleepy palace as lights throughout the building flickered on.

The remaining lion padded closer to Brighton, with its head down and glowing red lifeless eyes burning with the anger of its animator. It strained its jaws and pushed out a menacing metallic roar. Brighton made no effort to move. He had no energy left to outrun his aggressor, whether he believed it was real or not. This is just a dream he thought, as days of straight shifts with little sleep caught up to him.

He yawned and when he opened his eyes, found the lion's paws in front of him. He looked up into the face of the victor and felt like the mouse he found his cat playing with when he was a boy. The cat had no idea what it was doing and neither it seemed did the lion. It stared down at him and then as if urged on by the strange old man in Trafalgar Square, it raised its right paw in the air and brought it down to rip Brighton apart.

Brighton never felt the lion's blow. As soon as the bronze paw touched his skin, everything changed.

Have you ever wished that you could rewind the ratty day you've just had. That you could get some of it back and delete the rest?

That's exactly what happened. Brighton stood up, bent over, lifted himself back up and ran backwards down The Mall. The fence was repaired, the alarms all stopped, and the guards were all back at their posts. Brighton ran after the lions as they sprinted home towards Trafalgar Square. He watched with wide disbelieving eyes as the police car drove back out of the St James Park Lake and repaired its roof like a Transformer, before driving off in the direction of Kensington.

He sprinted backwards into Trafalgar Square, jumped over the bollards, and found all four lions were sitting in their correct positions. Their eyes dulled back to an earthy bronze. In his peripheral vision, Brighton saw the old man climbing into a heavy hessian sack.

'Hey you!' said Brighton.

Zaliel paid him no heed and as Brighton came closer, the wizard drew the sack over his head and said 'Home.'

With his last remaining energy Brighton grabbed at the bag in a spear tackle as the heavy sack and struggling wizard lifted into the air and started spinning around. As it spun, a green mist swirled up and around the sack before it burst into a shower of bright sparks and green smoke. Brighton fell down like an outsmarted coyote onto the mound of rags and newspapers left by the wizard, hitting his head hard and sending him to LaLa land.

He lay there for a long time, trying to process what had happened to him. It must have been a dream he convinced himself. I showed up. The guy wasn't here. I must have slipped on some rubbish and knocked myself out.

His hands were already shaking as he began to lift himself up, then he heard a loud bang above him and scrambled for cover. A rolled piece of parchment tanned with age, fluttered down through a bright green mist and rested on the ground with the grace of a feather. His stomach sank. Whatever that was, it was not going to be as easily dismissed as a dream. Big Ben chimed twice as he walked back to the station.

~

Back in his office, Brighton donned a pair of plastic gloves, opened the scroll with care and read:

> William,
> Tell me where thy mother is on this parchment and burn it. I will get the message directly. If ye do not do this by sunset, little Anna will be no more. Canst, thou live with that? Z

Brighton took several photos of the disturbing document with his phone and started writing up his report about the night's curious events. He made sure not to include the lions, Buckingham Palace, nor any mention of the mysterious floating sack, because he knew that they'd have him sectioned for sure.

It was seven in the morning by the time he'd finished a draft he felt comfortable submitting. He stumbled down nine flights of stairs, grabbed two hot cups of tea in the downstairs caff and headed out to search for his own wizard.

2

There is no way this is right. There has to be something wrong with the data. Jeanie Boswell looked down at the evidence in front of her and tried to flick her hair out of the way. For some reason it seemed extra red, extra bristly, and extra frizzy this morning.

Before she could even think about how to process the data, she heard a familiar voice say 'knock knock' at her door.

It was the man she called her guvnor, more out of respect than obligation, standing there with two styrofoam cups. She guessed that one was for her. How did he know that this was exactly what she needed?

'Morning guv.'

'Alright Jeanie?'

'I am now,' she said as he passed her one of the teas.

'Ta for this. I really needed some tea.' Then she saw the evidence bag tucked away under his arm. 'Is that for me?'

'Yes. It's evidence for the case. Potentially from the kidnapper himself would you believe? Could you send it off for prints and analysis?'

'Sure thing. Wow this looks really old,' said Jeanie examining the paper. 'From the weight and look I'd say it was some kind of parchment, possibly medieval but this is in amazing condition. Where did you get it from?'

'I might have run into the alleged kidnapper last night. Before you ask, he managed to get away, but he left this behind. The writing's been done with an ink that looks like something from the Middle Ages, so there may be a way to track him down through rare suppliers.'

Writing? She gave him a funny look.

'What are you talking about? There's nothing there.'

He frowned and took the old paper back.

'Quit playing around Jeanie. It's right here. See?'

Have you lost the plot? she thought, not liking his tone one bit. He looked drained and she wondered how long he had been awake for.

'I'm not playing around guv. There's nothing there. Well, nothing that I can see anyway.'

'But it's right there in front of you.'

'Okay, but why can't I see it?' she said, deciding to remain logical.

Though it puzzled him, Brighton believed her.

'That's a good question. Tell me, can you see it now?' He showed her one of the photos he'd taken earlier.

'No way!' she gasped as she read the message.

'How is this even possible Jeanie?'

Jeanie crossed her arms. Brighton felt like she knew the answer but seemed reluctant to say anything.

'Is there something you'd like to tell me?'

Jeanie felt bad. She felt almost certain that she knew what the Z stood for but didn't want her boss to think she was crazy.

'This reminds me of something I read about once, but it can't be. This guy you met last night was he an auld fella by any chance?'

His eyes widened for a moment, and he stared back at her like he'd seen a PTSD induced apparition.

'Where'd you get that idea?'

'I'm right then, aren't I? The guy you saw last night was an auld fella.'

Brighton nodded, hoping she wouldn't dig deeper.

'I went back down to the scene the day after the kidnapping and worked the whole area again with that new M-VAC system we bought.' That went right over your head, didn't it? she thought, looking at his blank expression like he was lost. Typical. 'M-VAC guv. It's a vacuum machine designed to extract DNA from both porous and rough surfaces.'

'Really? Is it any good?'

'Yeah, it's been cracking open a few long abandoned cold cases and because we had nothing, I thought it was worth a shot.'

'Please tell me you've got something.'

'I found two good samples on a rubbish bin lid and Anna's rabbit. These matched each other. When I ran them through the database, the DNA matched several known child abductions.'

She watched a glimmer of his face light up like a fox near an open henhouse door before adding 'But this presents a whole new problem.' The fox disappeared.

'So, what's this problem then?'

'As you can see there were quite a few hits.' Jeanie handed over the printout of the names and cases. 'The first known cases are from 1917. The next are child abductions from World War Two. Those were only added to the database for training. It doesn't make any sense guv. The kidnapper would have been at least ninety years old and then some.'

He didn't respond.

'Guv?' Jeanie noticed Brighton was too busy staring at the next entry. 'I see you found the other Anna Bolton.'

'How can there be another missing kid called Anna Bolton?'

'This one's a bit different. Anna was eight years old when she went missing in 1976. She's the only survivor that's been found. The others are missing or dead.'

'We need to find her. Do you think she'd still be alive?'

'She changed her name to Anna Brighton after she married and became a very famous author.'

Brighton's face turned as red as a baboon's ass. He didn't know that his mother had been kidnapped. Another secret she'd kept from him. He wanted to say that this was bullshit, but instead he stared at the floor hoping it would all go away.

Oh shit, now I've done it, Jeanie thought, realising that if he hated being called by his first name that he must despise the woman that named him. It never occurred to her, and she wanted to know why he seemed to despise her so much, but now wasn't the time.

He looked like he was going to flipping lose it, but he never did. He breathed deeply. His shoulders slumping back down as he exhaled.

'How long have you known about this?'

'That your mum's The Anna Brighton? Oh, I've known for ages. It was easy to work out.'

'Don't tell me you're a fan?'

Jeanie nodded and smiled.

'I've been reading *The Magical Wooded World* since I was a kid.'

She wasn't ready for a look of distain, like her guv had just lost his shoe in a pile of elephant shit.

'Bit old for that now, aren't ya?'

'Not really,' she said, stepping back. 'She writes well you know, and I read her books every year.'

When he folded his arms, she realised he couldn't give a tinkers.

'But still, that doesn't link Anna to this girl. She was never a Bolton.'

Jeanie noticed how he called his mother Anna, and he felt more comfortable using Anna than mum.

'That was her maiden name.'

'No that's not right. It was Marriot.'

'Marriot's an alias guv. As far as I can tell, she must have bought it in a pub in Mansfield in 1986. After that Anna Bolton just disappears without a trace like a character in one of her books.'

'Regardless, there are tonnes of Brighton's around.'

'That's true, but she named her son William and there's only three William Brighton's and two of them are long gone. That's how I worked out your connection.'

Check and mate.

'Okay you've got me, but please don't ever call me William. I hate it. I don't even like my wife calling me that.'

'Yeah, I've heard that around but never understood. That's why I didn't really want to say anything. You're not upset with me, are you? For being a fan?'

He shook his head.

'No, it's fine, as long as you know that I am not a fan of hers or her work. I'll need you to keep this to yourself for the time being.'

'The bit about your mum or the bit about you guv?'

'Both.'

Jeanie frowned. No way was she going to let this slip through her fingers. She had to challenge him.

'Why should I do that? This is a big discovery for me and for the case and for your mum. It means we are getting closer to finding her kidnapper! Do you know what that will do for my career? For us fans it's huge! Kind of like finding out who Jack the Ripper was.'

'Yeah, I get it. You get all that glory. What do you think it will do to my career? My life will become a media circus for a start. Everyone I love will be under the microscope. I can see the news headlines. Estranged son comes out of the woodwork. Then I'll get taken off the case and that's just for starters. Look Jeanie, everything about Anna Brighton causes trouble. She's like a curse that won't go away. I've managed to avoid all that since I left home, and I plan to keep on doing so, okay? So, for the time being all I ask is that you please keep this quiet.'

'Okay I will for now. But promise me that when this is all done and dusted, and we get the guy, that I can have some credit.' That's all I ask.'

'Okay. You're on.'

~

'You should have let me stay with you. We might have caught him guv,' said Jimmy Griffiths after Brighton gave him his official brief about the previous night's encounter.

'I don't think so Jimmy. Jeanie may find something we can use but in the meantime head up to Trafalgar Square. I want the newspapers and rags that the old man sat on. Search the whole site for forensics. And bring everything back to her. I want the statues tested as well.'

Who knows if there was any trace from making the lions alive, but Brighton wasn't taking any chances. He was keeping this to himself and the whole wizard thing; but now he knew that Jeanie was a fan of his mother's writing it was only a matter of time until she worked out that magic was involved.

'And make sure that we access footage from every single CCTV camera and security camera for eighteen blocks. That includes the tube station and all buses that may have been in the area. Go door to door as well. Someone might have seen something.'

Griffiths nodded.

Brighton's acting boss, Superintendent Armitage didn't quite know what to think of the situation. The septum of his pointy little pixie nose stiffened, and his brow furrowed as he thought, reminding Brighton of one of the Winkie guards from the *Wizard of Oz*.

'So, you're telling me that this character managed to evade you and then later you found a note that threatened your mother and indicated that he may have Anna Bolton?'

'That's right sir.'

'I'd like to see it.'

Brighton showed him the photos from his phone.

'If the ink on the paper is gone, why did you bother?'

'Sir?'

'I don't understand why you decided to show me this when you could have deleted the photo. This could potentially incriminate you if she is found dead.'

'It's the right thing to do sir. I have a responsibility to be honest even if it's not in my best interest.'

Armitage sighed. Of all the coppers in London, trust him to find one with morals and ethics. Your funeral, he thought.

'Alright, as long as you know what you're getting into. So, we will run this like we have a potential person of interest for the kidnapping of Anna Bolton. Are there any other leads so far?'

'DS Griffiths and the rest of the team are up there now. I should get an update in a few hours.'

'Okay. Have you contacted your mother?'

'Sir?'

'Have you contacted your mother and told her about the potential threat?'

'If it's all the same, I'd rather not do that.'

'Why on earth not?'

'We're estranged sir. In any case I've no idea where she lives.'

'Really? I'm sorry to hear that. We should get word to her though just to be sure, and to the local police. If you give me her details, I'll put them through the system and reach out to her.'

Brighton fidgeted in his seat; a small bead of sweat formed on his brow.

'That's not going to be easy. She doesn't have a car sir. She won't have a TV License either. I doubt she even has a personal bank account. If you must make contact, you'd need to go through her agent, her lawyers, or her publishers.'

The superintendent's brow creased, and his eyes narrowed as he processed this odd revelation.

'Publishers? That's a strange thing to say. Is she an author or something? There can't be too many Brighton's in...' He paused and took a sharp breath as he watched his subordinate cringe.

'Wait a minute. Don't tell me that your mother is THE Anna Brighton?'

'Yes sir,' said Brighton as the cat jumped out from the bag for the second time.

The intriguing revelation made Armitage want to ask a barrage of questions, but he saw that his junior officer was in no mood to chat about her. His face looked downcast as if he hoped that the floor would swallow him whole.

'Please sir. Nobody knows about this. Not even my wife. I'd rather it be kept that way,' said Brighton deciding not to tell Armitage about Jeanie's revelation.

Not even your wife? thought Armitage. What did Anna Brighton do to you to deserve being shunned like that? He thought about Brighton's request.

'That's not going to be easy now considering the circumstances, is it?

It may even have a bearing on the case. I won't make this public knowledge for the moment Detective Inspector, but I can't promise that it will stay a secret. In the meantime, find the girl and your mother.'

Brighton nodded, leaving Armitage to ponder the young DI's extraordinary predicament.

3

'Sir.' said Probationary Constable Milly Draper, 'There's a woman downstairs at reception for you. Claims she's a witness.'

Brighton looked up from his desk. He wanted to scream. His team were still in the field and Draper and a couple of newbie staff fresh from the academy were holding the fort. He still couldn't understand how these spoon-fed newbies thought. Surely, she could demonstrate enough initiative to take a statement before the witness changed her mind.

'Well go and see what she wants.'

'But she's asked to speak to you sir.'

'She asked for me?'

'Yes sir.'

'What did she say exactly?'

'I'd like to speak to Brighton about the case he's working on.'

Might be an old snout he thought. That made sense.

'Alright. Thanks PC Draper.'

By the time he got to the reception counter, there was nobody there aside from a crazy beggar man squealing to the duty sergeant.

'I'm telling you the old bastard turned me into a ruddy pig!'

That would be somewhat of an improvement surely, thought Brighton. He'd had enough curious conversations to last a lifetime and the last thing he needed was to be held up by this porcine chap. Judging from his face, so had his colleague.

'Sergeant was there a woman waiting for me down here?'

The desk sergeant looked up.

'Oi I'm talking here. He made me into a pig! I can prove it.'

'Quiet you. Yes guv. Early thirties, 5'9, thin and long black hair. You've just missed her.'

'What's she wearing?'

'Jeans, baggy black shirt, suede coat and a green scarf.'

Brighton thanked him and ran out the front entrance, scouring the streets for his elusive witness. He couldn't see anyone at the bus stop, so he set off for the nearest tube station.

'Spare change?' said a voice he once knew a long time ago.

Looking down he saw a woman sitting on a suede coat. Her green scarf waving in the early autumn breeze. She smiled at him.

'Hi Will, or do you still insist on being called Brighton?'

'Marta?'

She nodded. 'Yes, little brother. It's me.'

Brighton wasn't sure what to say to his estranged sister.

'Has it really been eight years?'

'Yes. Time flies when you're not having fun. But you seem to be doing alright for yourself.'

'I came back for you that day that I found you under the dragon near Temple. But you'd left and I haven't seen you since.'

Marta looked at him with playful young eyes, but her lifestyle choices had aged her beyond her years.

'Did that really happen? I thought it was a dream.'

'I'm not surprised. You were in quite a state.'

She blushed like an indignant octopus, both offended and embarrassed at the same time.

'Well, I'm clean now if you must know. I have been for a while.'

'That's great to hear but I really don't have time for family reunions right at the minute. Did you leave the station just now?'

'Yes. I came to see you.'

'Why? I mean why now after all this time?'

'I might have something that could help you find that missing girl.'
Brighton folded his arms.
'What could you possibly know?'
'Is that any way to speak to me? You'd be surprised what I know, but hey if you're not interested.' She started getting up.
'All right. Go on then, tell me.'
'Okay, but you need to understand that this might sound a bit strange. All right?'
'Try me.'
'I've been having these dreams for weeks. Visions of the girl being held by Zaliel. Remember? The wizard from her books? I've seen him around too and I think he's been following me.'

At first his gut told him that she sounded genuine, but he reminded himself that this was only because she probably believed her own bullshit. He'd seen people lie so well because in their hearts they wanted what they were saying to be true, so much so that they believed themselves.

Brighton wrinkled his nose, reached for his wallet, and pulled out a few notes.

'Look I don't have time for this. What do you really want eh? How much do you need?'

Marta looked horrified.

'I don't want your money Will,' she said, pulling out a small book from her coat pocket. See for yourself. It's all here. It's all in her book. I'm not lying.' She pulled out an old copy of their mother's first book.

He flinched at it for a brief moment, like a vampire seeing a stake aimed at it.

'Is that the copy she gave you?'
'Yeah. Have you still got yours?'
'Nah. Sold it ages ago.'
'All good. Borrow mine. Please.'

She tried to give him the book, and he backed away from her as if repelled by kryptonite.

'I thought you said you were straight.'

She looked cross and pulled up her sleeves.

'For God's sake Will I'm clean. Look!'

'Sorry but I don't believe you.'

'But I have proof,' said Marta, raising her voice as he turned away. 'Listen to me. I'm your sister!'

That was too much for Brighton. It was bad enough that two people knew about his secret never mind this rubbish.

'You're nobody to me Marta. Don't you understand? You stopped being my sister when you up and left me there. It took me two years to save up and get away from Anna Brighton on my own.'

'I'm sorry OK! You know what she's like. I just couldn't take it anymore.'

'That's what I mean. You only care about yourself. Always have, always will. Just take the money and go.' He threw the cash on the ground and stomped back to the station.

'Will! Wait! Please!' Marta scooped up the cash and her jacket and ran after him. When she gained up to her brother, she thrust the book at him. 'Please look at the book. I'm telling you. It's Zaliel. You need to find him. Zaliel is real.'

Brighton brushed her desperate hands away from him, making her drop the book in the process. His jaw tensed.

'If you don't walk away this instant, I'll have you up for harassing a police officer and wasting police time. You've got your money. Now leave me alone. Alright?'

As her brother strode away, she called after him.

'I'm just a worthless junkie to you. Aren't I William?'

This time Brighton didn't turn back.

Back in the Magical Wooded World, Zaliel watched the argument through his obsidian scrying stone. He felt relieved that Brighton hadn't listened to his sister, but she was meddlesome and had to be dealt with. He drew his wand and prepared his travelling sack.

4

'What do you call this Jimmy?' said Brighton a little later, looking up from Griffiths' report on Trafalgar Square. 'No witnesses, and not much of anything for forensics!'

'But guv the altercation happened late at night. If anyone did see anything they ain't talking, except for a dosser who claims he was turned into a pig! There's not much CCTV because there was a power outage bang on midnight. Didn't help that the old boy sat in a blind spot. Believe me I looked everywhere and we're lucky we got what we did. Just beat the cleaning crew and they were none too pleased to see us n all.'

'Alright then. Go and grab some refs.'

He looked through the available footage hoping for a break but found there wasn't much to play with because the angles were tight. For fifteen minutes he tried to find a potential image with no luck.

'Alright guv?'

Brighton looked up as Griffiths placed a paper bag and a bottle of water on his desk.

'Thought you could use a break. Roast beef and pickles. It's all I could find.'

'Thanks Jimmy.'

'You're welcome guv,' said Griffiths looking over Brighton's shoulder at the screen. 'Is that some of the footage?'

'Yeah. I was trying to see if I could use the reflection from the fountain to get an image of the guy.'

Griffiths looked impressed.

'That's a brilliant idea!'

'Cheers, but save the accolades. It's the wrong angle.'

Griffiths looked at the screen and thought for a minute.

'See that van there driving past? Have you tried looking at its rear vision mirrors? They're tiny but you might get lucky.'

'You're an absolute genius sometimes Jimmy. Good work!'

Jimmy smiled and gave his boss some space.

Zooming into the driver's rear vision window gave Brighton a front row seat. Sure enough, there was the old man cursing and waving his arms at the dosser he saw downstairs earlier. A peculiar cloud of green smoke came out of nowhere and the dosser disappeared. He didn't run out of the smoke. There were no alleys to slink away into and there were no manholes for about a block. The smoke drifted away revealing a pig!

What the hell is going on? thought Brighton. He threatens me with a wand, leaves me a crazy message and disappears in a puff of smoke. The only way that this makes any sense is if Marta is right, but that puts me in a right corner.

He rewound the footage, took a video on his phone, and looked down at his watch. Anna Bolton was running out of time. No time for that sandwich now.

'Any luck guv?' said Griffiths, walking past.

'None, but tell me did forensics swab the walls around where the old bloke was sitting?'

'I'm not sure.'

'Well find out. If they didn't Jim, get them back out there.'

'They won't like that boss.'

'Serves them right for not doing the job right the first time. It's not like they have to trudge out to Willesden Green. When they have the samples, make sure that everything goes straight to Jeanie.'

'There weren't none around that I saw but I'll find out.'

'Cheers. It's grasping at straws, but it's all we've got.'

On his way up to see Jeanie, Brighton thought about warning Anna Brighton about the threat. He imagined her laughing and then blaming him for ruining her afternoon of writing.

'Hi ya guv!' said Jeanie, snapping him back into the present.

'Hey Jeanie. Any luck with that parchment?'

'Early days I'm afraid. No prints, but I've sent a few samples off and hopefully they'll...'

'We're running out of time,' he said, cutting her off. 'What about the newspapers and the rags found at the scene? Any luck there?'

'We might have something. There's a couple of hairs that Alex is testing for DNA right now. Hopefully not animal. There's also some loose threads. Some that look like they're jute and there are a few that I'm sure are very old linen.'

The robe and bag that the old man sat on, thought Brighton.

'Good work. Was any trace found on the walls?'

Jeanie raised her eyebrow.

'Funny you should ask that. We've identified some sort of residue, but I haven't a clue what it is. I got old Roy Gupta from down the hall to have a look at it, and he's never seen anything like it neither.'

'Keep trying. In the meantime, may I have the parchment back?'

That threw Jeanie a little.

'You're not thinking of burning it are you?'

'Damn it. I should never have shown you that photo.'

'But guv. That's just mental. It's not scientifically possible for starters.'

'Just like it's not possible for me to read a message that you still can't see? A girl's life is at stake Jeanie. She's my daughter's age for Christ's sake!'

'I know guv. Don't you think that we're doing everything we can to save her? Because we are! And so are you! When was the last time you were home, or slept for that matter? I've never seen you like this before. The fact that you're even thinking about burning evidence or even thinking that magick is real tells me that you're fatigued, and I've got to report it guv. You're not right. You're not fit to be on the case.'

He frowned.

'So what are you saying? Do you think that I'm not fit to lead anymore?'

Jeanie stood up from her desk.

'Tell me something. What would you do if your boss confided in you that he thought that magick was real. You'd have them sectioned in an instant. Wouldn't you?'

'Under normal circumstances I'd agree. But this case is strange Jeanie. I've seen a lot of weird things in my short career but never anything quite like this.' He leaned in towards her and held out his mobile phone. 'I'm about to show you something that you cannot tell a single soul about. Okay.'

'Okay,' she said, hoping it wasn't a dick pic.

Instead, she watched a man turn into a pig.

'What the hell was that? A street magician?' Despite the evidence in front of her, she still held a firm grip to reality through the one thing she trusted: science.

'Where's he gone?' said Jeanie looking at the footage again.

'We don't know. There's no manhole cover, no alleyway and nowhere for him to go. He literally turned into a pig. He was downstairs earlier trying to convince the duty sergeant.'

'It's just impossible.'

'I know that, but I had to show you because you think that I've lost the plot.'

'Are you trying to tell me that our prime suspect is a wizard?'

'My sister seems to think so. She thinks it's the wizard from Anna's books. She came all the way here to warn me. Thinks he's following her too.'

'She thinks it's Zaliel? That's mental.'

'I thought the same thing, but the guy wrote a message for me on a scroll that you can't read, so you tell me.'

'That's where I thought I'd heard about this before. Your mo... Anna's books. The characters write private messages called OFYE, Only For Your Eyes. But it's just a story!'

'That's why I think that burning the parchment may be our only chance. It's the only way we have to get to him; it sounds crazy but that's all we've got.'

She saw the desperation in his eyes, pleading with her to help him save little Anna.

'May I have it please?'

'Alright. But I need you to sign for it, for the chain of evidence,' she said, looking all flustered, but handing it over all the same.

Brighton signed the register as the sun set in the distance, temporarily darkening the room before the lights automatically turned on. He took the parchment out from the evidence bag and scribbled his mother's address in Dartmoor down on the back.

'Have you got a lighter Jeanie?'

Jeanie's hands shook as she gave him a box of long safety matches.

'I've never destroyed evidence before.'

'Me neither,' he said, lighting the bottom corner of the parchment.

His words burst into a cloud of green smoke in an instant, startling him as the ash fell into wastepaper basket. The cloud seemed to become alive; it flicked and circled around them like a predator shark before slithering up the nearest ceiling vent.

'You're lucky that's metal,' said Jeanie, dousing the strange smouldering remains.

'I just hope it doesn't set the smoke detectors off.'

'Oh, it won't. We're always setting things on fire here, so we should be fine. I'm more worried about getting caught?'

'Leave that to me. I know it's a long shot, but I had to do it. If anybody says anything, tell them that I ordered you to hand it over. Okay? This is on me.'

'Oh, I know that. Let's just hope for your sake that it worked.'

5

Brighton stared down at the little girl who shared his estranged mother's name and prayed that she hadn't suffered.

The coroner had pronounced her dead, now Jeanie was by her side examining the body for evidence. What do I say to her family? he thought, knowing from the moment they learned the terrible truth, that they would become as broken as his own.

Nothing made any sense. Who on earth leaves a body at the National Archives in Kew? A staff member found her on the way in to work and raised the alarm, after warding off a hungry fox.

He knew just by looking, that Anna's body had been staged with great care and that the murder took place somewhere else. The clothes she wore were not the same clothes she'd been taken in. They looked pretty retro, as did the braids in her hair.

Despite the head curator's protest, Brighton sealed the Archives off so that evidence would not be further compromised. He watched his team scour the area and kept people back as far as they could to preserve the scene. The CCTV was taken away for scrutiny later, but a fierce storm had plunged the complex into darkness last night and he figured that it happened around the time that Anna's body was placed in the grounds. It looked like the modus operandi of a wizard.

'He's back guv,' said Jimmy.

'Who?'

'That head curator bloke. He wants another word.'

'I bet he does.'

As the face of the investigation, Brighton handled both the public and the media, something he found most challenging. Instead of pandering to the head curator, Brighton strolled past the row of journalists. When he saw his wife Kerry in the crowd, he pretended to ignore her and she pretended to be upset at being snubbed, as he made his way over to Nora Jennings, the senior crime journalist from the BBC. Her eyes lit up as he spoke.

'Hello Nora. Would you mind doing me a favour.' He leaned in. 'See that silly git over there?'

'The one turning into a beetroot?'

'Yeah. The head curator.'

'Right?'

'He wants us to pack up and go. He doesn't give a toss about little Anna. He's more worried about losing revenue from all those pensioners sitting in the buses over there.'

Nora gasped. 'No way!'

'Said as much earlier. Got all hot under the collar too. Money means more to him than a little girl's life. Can you believe it?'

'You're kidding. He's just a bloody public servant for goodness sake.'

'I know right and he's laying it on really thick. Do you think that's something your viewers would like to know?'

'Absolutely. They'll be livid.'

'Could you make that happen for me?'

She nodded. 'Sure thing. May I have an exclusive update in return?'

'Of course.'

'Thank you. Appreciate the heads up.'

The play wasn't exactly above board, but it would get the loathsome prat off his back, and he needed all the time he could get. He made his way back to the body, while Nora and her cameraman approached the curator and created such an uproar that by midday, the Minister of the Department of Culture, Media and Sport ordered beetroot man to pack his desk up.

Jeanie looked up from her examination.

'She can go now,' she said, barely holding back her tears.

She knew that his daft plan wouldn't work and yet she allowed herself to be talked into helping him, jeopardising her career in the process. Never again, she thought, glaring at him before turning away to pack up the evidence bags.

As the mortuary attendants guided their gurney through the crowd, Brighton motioned Jeanie over to him.

'So, what can you tell me?'

Her brow furrowed as she looked at him.

'I estimate that the time of death was around eleven last night. Judging from her eyes and skin, cause of death seems to be electrocution. But I won't know until we do further tests.'

'Good work Jeanie. Are you okay?'

'Yeah, thanks' she said, without emotion.

'You don't look it.'

'Honestly DI Brighton, you sound just like me dad. Just leave it will you!'

Embarrassed, she turned her back on him to gather up her kit. As the mortuary attendants lifted the little body onto the gurney, Jeanie saw a small book on the ground. Anna must have been lying on it.

'Hey! Get back,' said Jeanie to one of the attendants before he could pick it up.

'What is it?' said Brighton.

'It's a copy of *The Magical Wooded World* by Anna Brighton,' Jeanie said, putting it into a large evidence bag. 'First edition by the looks.'

He winced at the sound of his mother's name being spoken.

'Send it off for prints please.'

Jeanie nodded.

'She alright guv?' said Griffiths, handing Brighton a takeaway cup as he watched Jeanie storm back to her car.

Brighton shrugged.

'Dunno Jim. Ta, what's this then?'

'Tea, bag left in and three sugars. I'm not sure what that bloke was going on about. The caff here's doing a roaring trade.'

'Thanks Jimmy,' he said after taking a long sip. 'I really needed a sugar hit.'

'All good. So, what was the book she found?'

There's just no escaping this one, thought Brighton.

'The first copy of *The Magical Wooded World* by...'

'Anna Brighton? Hey, you wouldn't believe it, but they have a big exhibit here with some of her original manuscripts and the artist illustrations and all.'

Brighton gave his DS a hard stare worthy of Paddington Bear.

'You're shitting me, right?'

'No. Go and see for yourself. My kids love her. What about your Emily then? Wouldn't it be funny if she were Emily's granny?'

Brighton tried his hardest not to show his discomfort.

'What else is happening here?'

'Nothing, there's only that exhibit. I reckon she's a national treasure.' Jimmy saw the look of distain on his boss' face. 'I can see why you're not happy guv. I hope the media doesn't catch on and link you to her either.'

Brighton squirmed in his boots. The last thing he wanted was the media calling the tragedy a Brighton Mystery. One Brighton was enough thanks. What did his mother do to upset this guy enough to make him kill a little kid? What's this all about? All roads led straight back to her.

'Good pick-up Jim. Let's get them out of here. Call the press conference in five. We'll do it over near the car park, as far away from the Archives as we can. The BBC might hang around longer. Just make sure Nora has the best spot in the house. And Jimmy, don't say anything to anyone about that book. Okay?'

'You've got it.'

He thought of the parting words of his old mentor, Pete McKenna.

'Always remember young Brighton. Find the motive and you'll find the killer.'

Zaliel stood hidden from view on the flat roof of the Archives, watching his nemesis enter the media swarm.

'That's what you get for lying to me,' he muttered.

Stepping into his sack, he pulled it over his body and held it over his head, scrunching it tightly together from within.

'Home!' he commanded and disappeared in a cloud of bright green smoke.

∼

Jeanie noticed the smoke swirling in the autumn wind. It reminded her of the footage Brighton had shown her days earlier. Grabbing a few swab kits, she hurried to the roof, hoping to find enough residue to link to the murder.

Brighton put on a set of headphones for the guided tour and entered a winding maze of glass cabinets, framed photographs, and mementoes from a life of writing. The exhibit started with his mother's childhood. Much to his surprise, he knew very little about her.

'Born in 1968 near the small village of Princetown, Anna Bolton was the oldest daughter of William and Trudy Bolton.'

So that's where the name came from, he thought, looking at a photo of his estranged grandparents, and he wondered if their lives had ever crossed paths. He moved on, listening to the narrator talk about her schooling and home life. There was nothing out of the ordinary that he could point to and link to the case. Until she started writing, her life was pretty normal.

Much to his relief, the exhibit did not mention her marriage, name change or her children. Instead, it focussed on her career and Brighton found himself reading an open page from her book.

'This is the original manuscript of the first book of The Magical Wooded World series written by Anna in 1998. The book went on to be a best seller,

cementing Anna's reputation as a firm favourite for generations of British readers.'

Boom! he read.

My spell knocked Zaliel from his broom and sent him hurtling down into a ravine. I can still see that nasty scowling face and the beads on his bristly beard as he screamed and tried to counter the spell. He landed with a whump and a bump in a twisted cruel lump and I had him right where I wanted him! How exciting!

'Mountain tremble, mountain wake! Please great mountain, make no mistake. Keep this nasty wizard prisoner for me and don't let him go until for a hundred years I am free!'

There was sound like an earthquake. Rocks exploded. The mountain woke up and sat on Zaliel, covering him completely. I'd done it. I was free at last. Or was I? You never know with magicians. What if he escapes?

Even when the mountain finally sets him free, I don't think that he will forget me in a hurry. He shall be back, but do you know something girls and boys? I shall be ready for him. Wait and see!

Brighton knew that what he had just read was at best a poorly written story, but all the same, being buried under a mountain would be motivation enough to track her down and extract revenge. Was that what she'd been running from her entire life? Before he could even give it a second thought, Jimmy tapped him on the shoulder.

'Guv you've got to see this.' Brighton followed Jimmy back to the first photo collection of Anna's childhood and pointed to a small black and white photo.

'Guv? Does this look like the dress the victim's wearing?'

Sure enough it was his mother when she was a child wearing the same dress Anna Bolton was found in. Brighton felt like kicking himself. Why hadn't he seen it? But he lightened up. He'd brought Jimmy along because he had an amazing eye for detail.

'Sure looks like it. Go and ask for a copy for me.'

Their exchange attracted the attention of a young woman hovering nearby. She reminded Brighton of Jaws in a suit. All that was missing was a dorsal fin.

'I'm afraid you can't have a copy of that picture. It's very old. I won't allow it.'

'We'll see about that. And who might you be?'

'I'm the curator of this collection.'

'My apologies. I thought you were one of her fans. I'm Detective Inspector Brighton,' he said, flashing his badge. 'I need the copy for a murder investigation.'

When she caught his surname, her attitude changed. She drew closer and looked him up and down. As curious as a cat with a new toy.

'Brighton you say? Not William Brighton, by any chance?'

He looked down.

'I prefer DI Brighton or just Brighton, if you don't mind.'

'My,' she said, as her dark almond eyes sized him up through expensive horn-rimmed spectacles. 'Anna said you were hesitant about your name, but I didn't realise the full extent. Cecilia Lemon. I represent your mother's affairs.'

She smiled and watched his discomfort before she extended her hand.

She's enjoying this, he thought, noticing a strange mark on her right wrist as she dropped her business card on the table. He read Cecilia Lemon in a swirling text with Legal Affairs and Curator underneath. Lemon alright, he thought. What a sour piece of work. No wonder the old bat signed up with her.

He looked behind her to see that Jimmy was back and judging from his expression the front desk hadn't been very accommodating. Brighton changed tact.

'So, you look after all this...' he said, struggling to find the appropriate words. 'History.'

'That's right. I manage everything.'

'Then perhaps you could tell me more about this book I found,' he said, winking at Jimmy as he led her back to the manuscript.

As soon as the coast was clear his offsider snapped a dozen well focused photos of the picture with his mobile phone. It was an old school diversion routine, yet he still marvelled at the way his boss executed it, always lowering the mark's defences. Grinning, Jimmy put his phone away and popped back down to the cafeteria.

Cecelia Lemon looked at Brighton with a puzzled expression, trying to understand the enormity of what he'd just said.

'So, you really don't know who Zaliel is?'

Brighton nodded.

'Not really, only what other people have told me. I never read her books you see, and she never read them to me either.'

Cecelia looked almost traumatised.

'I don't believe you. Surely, she read them to you.'

'She never read to either of us. Look it sounds like you don't know the first thing about her Miss Lemon.'

The muscles around her high cheeks flexed as she wrinkled her nose and squinted at him with anger and indignation.

'I've worked with Anna for the past three years.'

'I don't doubt that for a moment, but how much do you truly know about her? You only know what she allows you to see. Please don't be offended. I know what we could do,' he said directing the focus back to the manuscript. 'You tell me all about this Zaliel geezer and I'll give you a few home truths.'

Cecelia thought about it.

'Very well. Zaliel was the wizard that captured Anna when she was about eight or nine years old.'

'In the book, right?'

She ignored him and continued.

'He took her back to the Magical Wooded World.'

'That's near Bournemouth, isn't it?'

Cecelia glared.

'Do you want my help or not?'

'Yes of course. Sorry but it's hard when the subject is possibly the most least favourite thing to me. Look I get the general gist. She escaped from this Zaliel character. He went after her and she buried him under a mountain, right?'

The fact he'd committed the pages in front of him to memory satisfied her.

'That's right.'

'So, what happened to him then? He's still under there?'

'Nobody knows. Your mother never wrote about him again. Fans still send her requests asking what happened to him and her standard response to them is that for all she knows he is still under the mountain to this day, and she hopes he stays there.'

So much for that then he thought. I knew this would be a waste of time. At least we found the dress.

'And these fans are fans of his?'

'Yes, Zaliel has quite a following. Some are quite dedicated.'

'Are there any of these dedicated types that might be a bit fanatical then?'

'What do you mean?'

'I don't know, I'm just wondering. Are there any that you can think of that you've got concerns about?'

'Are you talking about Anna's safety? Oh yes, she's had a few death threats in her time, mainly harmless but there were one or two that went a bit far.'

'Could you let her know that we have received another threat and to be careful?'

'What do you mean? Does it have anything to do with all the commotion outside?'

'The dead girl? Yes. We tried to get a message to her through her publishers, but nobody has responded.'

'Don't worry. I'll see to it that she is warned, but I can't guarantee she'll do anything about it.'

Jimmy wandered back with a coffee just at the right moment.

'Guv. The examiner at Royal London's ready for you.'

'Thanks Jim. And thanks so much Cecelia. You've been a great help. Are you in London for a while?'

'Yes, I am. The exhibit finishes in a few weeks. Now about your side of the bargain.'

Crap thought Brighton. He didn't want Jimmy to know anything about this. Not yet, and he wanted to keep his secret as well.

'Yeah, about that. I may need you to come and help us with our enquiries at Scotland Yard. DS Griffiths here will set it up.'

6

'Ms Boswell was almost correct. The subject died from a sudden blast of energy,' said the forensic examiner to Brighton, later that afternoon.

'Like an electric shock?'

'Well, yes. In a roundabout way but the energy source from this shock is somewhat different,' said the young man crinkling his forehead as he tried to find the most logical response.

'A normal electrical shock has a central contact point even if you put a toaster in the bathtub. In this case however, I couldn't establish where the contact point was. There's not a single external mark or bruise other than a few scratches, most likely from the fox that found her, and they're not really relevant to the cause of death. All I know is that the surge caused a massive coronary very quickly.'

'Like a cattle prod or a taser?'

'Good guesses, but unlikely I'm afraid. The energy that fatally killed this young lady completely surrounded her at once. Like a spell from the movies. More Gandalf than cattle prod.' He saw the confused look on Brighton's face. 'Gandalf. You know, the wizard from Lord of the Rings? Tolkien?'

Brighton shrugged his shoulders, making the examiner wonder if the Detective Inspector had even heard of Middle Earth.

Just hearing the word wizard was enough for Brighton to want to end the meeting. The last thing he wanted was a forensic examiner poking his nose around.

'I'm sure there's a logical explanation,' he said. 'But let's leave it to the scientists, eh? Could you please send your report to Jeanie ASAP? She'll work it out. Photos as well please.'

As he neared the exit, Brighton saw the familiar face of old Bert the forensic surgeon, ambling alongside an orderly wheeling an occupied gurney back to the mortuary chambers.

'Well, well, if it isn't young Brighton,' said Bert, his red puffy face grinning. 'Haven't seen you for ages! What are you doing here me boy?'

'I'm investigating the murder of the little girl they found up at the Archives.'

'Nasty business that. I hope you get the bastard.'

'Cheers Bert. Me too. Who do you have there?'

'I guess we'll never know. No ID on her person when they found her in the loos outside Embankment Station two days ago. Heroin overdose with purity that's off the charts. Nothing like I've ever seen before. No needle marks or anything. If there's more of this junk around, we must find it.'

'That's my old patch and I still have a few regular informants out that way. Let me take her picture if that's okay and I'll ask around. Who knows, we might be able to identify her.'

'Go on,' said Bert, 'What about the others I've got back there? Are you going to find their homes too? Reunite them with families that couldn't care less about em in the first place? You're getting soft son.'

'Steady on mate.'

'Oh alright. Sorry Brighton it's been a bit of a day. Go on then.'

As he lifted the sheet, the young Detective Inspector drew a quick sharp breath.

'Do you know her?'

Brighton said nothing for a long time then he nodded, as his tears fell down and onto Marta's face.

'That's my sister,' he said, his lips quivering as he processed his loss and forced his words out.

'Aw shite,' said Bert. 'Are you alright? Is there anything I can do?'

'No. I'll be fine. Just keep her safe for me. I'll arrange to collect her.'

Even hardened Bert looked dismayed as he watched Brighton continue on his way.

Brighton shook as he walked. Each step like wearing lead boots, as he fought both tears and guilt. Considering the way he and Marta parted company, it was too much to bear.

∼

After composing himself, Brighton summoned his team to the briefing room. In spite of his loss, he had a murder to solve and threw himself back into his work.

'Okay you lot, we've got a new lead, and I've got to tell you all something about the case. Our new lead is my mother. The author Anna Brighton.'

'She's your mum?' said Griffiths. 'But guv why didn't you say so at the scene? You knew about the exhibit and the book. You should have said something then.'

'There are a couple of reasons why I didn't Jimmy. The first is that initially there was no confirmed connection between the case and Anna Brighton. The second is personal. I want nothing to do with the woman. We're estranged and I didn't want the publicity or attention, but that's all changed now. This afternoon the clothes that the victim wore were identified as vintage from the 1970's. They have AB embroidered in the name tag. There is a slim chance that they may have belonged to my mother when she was growing up.'

He paused for a breath and looked at his team. Some looked surprised at the revelation and others like Jimmy looked disappointed that he'd kept her a secret. He gave Cecelia's card to his surprised offsider.

'Jimmy, could you call this woman that we met at the museum for me. She's Anna Brighton's lawyer. When you do, see if she can ID the dress. If you can't get a hold of her, try and locate Anna yourself. She's not easy to find so start with her publishers. Use the legal team if you have to coerce them. When you do find her, tell her I need a word.'

Jimmy nodded and reached for his phone.

'The rest of you, I want you to start thinking about possible links with other kidnappings. Jeanie has a list of cold cases that might be connected and DNA. This could be a family operation. We've all seen that before. They may well have tried this in the past, and the investigating officer just didn't see the connection. Okay? Start digging.'

The room buzzed like flies at a picnic. Before he could sit at his desk, Jeanie rang.

'Guv? I need you to see this,' Jeanie said with unexpected apprehension. 'Now.'

'I'll be right up.'

Brighton found Jeanie sitting at her desk cradling her head in her hands.

'What's wrong?'

She turned and looked up at him.

'I need to know what's going on. What have we gotten into?'

'What do you mean?'

'Take a look at the table.'

Propped against a large white microscope stood a familiar piece of parchment.

'Is this some kind of practical joke?' he said, trying hard not to yawn. 'I'm in no mood for this.'

'And you think I am? I watched you burn that thing to a crisp the other day.'

'And you've been upset ever since.'

'What do you expect? You put my job on the line and yours and what did that achieve exactly?'

'Don't you think I know that? I've regretted it ever since! But I didn't want that little girl to die and now she's lying in the morgue. How do you think I feel about that? Well, I'll tell you. I feel like absolute shit! Look I'm really sorry for raising my voice, Jeanie,' he said looking down at the ground, visibly choking up as his shoulders sagged.

'That's fine, really it is. I've heard a lot worse.' She watched and shifted uncomfortably as her boss cried into his sleeve. 'Are you okay guv?'

'No. I've found out just now that my sister's dead. I shouldn't even be here.'

'I'm sorry for your loss guv. I really can't even begin to imagine how you're feeling right now.'

Brighton nodded.

'Thanks, but that's no excuse for yelling at you.' he said, wanting to move their discussion back to the parchment.

'If this scroll isn't a practical joke, then how did it get here?'

'Honestly? I don't know. I just came back from the canteen and found it there.'

That's a bit convenient, he thought, but given the circumstances he decided to give her the benefit of the doubt.

'Alright then, get Jimmy to check the CCTV cameras and make sure that nobody else has accessed this lab. I want to be sure we cover any other possibilities before we consider the occult again, okay?'

She nodded.

'Have you swabbed it for residue?'

'Already done. I'm sending it off for comparisons that we have from Trafalgar Square, the abduction site, and the National Archives.'

Brighton looked surprised when Jeanie mentioned the murder site.

'Why wasn't I told about trace from the Archives?'

'Because I haven't confirmed anything yet,' she said. 'I saw some green smoke just like we found on the CCTV, so I accessed the roof and grabbed a few swabs just in case.'

'Good work. Have you examined the parchment yet?'

'No. I wanted you to see it first.'

They both donned plastic gloves. Jeanie picked up an evidence bag while Brighton held the old document.

'Does it say anything?'

'No. There's nothing here.'

'What about the other side?'

Some days he could kick himself. Turning the old page around he read:

Leogare,

Tis your fault and yours alone that the child has departed this world. If you refuse to tell me where Anna Brighton is, another will share her fate.

Z

'This isn't happening,' he said as fear drained the colour from his face.

'Oh my God' said Jeanie standing behind him. 'Why does he think you know where she is?'

'You can see it?'

'Yeah. I can this time.'

'See? I'm not going crazy. He thinks I know where she is because she's my mother. He doesn't get that we don't talk to each other anymore.'

'No way! Now it all makes sense! Well sort of.'

'What are you talking about?'

'Zaliel and your mother. Duh'

This was the elephant in the room. Zaliel. Since Anna Bolton's death Brighton wasn't game to speak, think, or even contemplate that Zaliel was real. He hadn't given anyone the full details about his encounter in Trafalgar Square for a reason. He still wanted to believe that was all a dream and not reality, even if the evidence suggested otherwise.

'Remember Zaliel? *The Magical Wooded World*?'

'Don't tell me you're beginning to believe this crap is real.'

'What do you mean guv?'

'Zaliel and the Magical Wooded World.'

'Of course not. But I'm not the one that destroyed the evidence, last time. Am I?'

Brighton fumed but let the comment pass. Under the circumstances he felt like he deserved it.

'All I know is that there must be a logical explanation and somehow real or not, Zaliel ties into all this.'

'I don't even really know who Zaliel is.'

'Don't tell me that you haven't read them? You haven't, have you?'

Fancy that she thought, Anna Brighton's own son has never once read one of the most famous books of all time.

He shook his head.

'You're right. I haven't read them. I despise those books as much as I despise her. So, what's the connection?'

'Well, you're lucky they were some of my favourite stories then!' She smiled as her inner geek took the stage. 'It's all about a little girl who's kidnapped by a wizard and held prisoner in a walking tower in a strange land called the Magical Wooded World. She escapes and the wizard comes after her, but she beats him with his own magick and manages to get away.'

'And this wizard. What do you know about him?'

'Zaliel? Oh, he's a wicked wizard guv. He and Glitch, the goblin king's son, sell little kids to other witches and wizards for slaves. I think that the Z is short for Zaliel.'

'This is getting ridiculous. You're saying that a wizard from another world is responsible for Anna's death? Why him then? Were the aliens unavailable this month?'

Jeanie rolled her eyes.

'Sarcasm really doesn't suit you guv. That's not what I'm saying at all. I don't think it's Zaliel but maybe it's someone that thinks he is, or he likes larping. I think he's an older fella and maybe he's been a magician, you know, the rabbit in the hat kind rather than the spell casting variety. Or he's learnt magick at home, either way it accounts for all the smoke.'

Brighton thought about the possibility.

'What's this larping again?'

'Live-action roleplaying guv. There are loads of groups throughout the countryside. There's Sword Quest, steam punks, ninja clans, imperial storm troopers and that's just for starters. A larper that's well organised could have access to all sorts of places.'

He groaned. The things people did for a laugh.

'Including a walking tower?'

'Well maybe not an actual walking tower but you could call a boat or a caravan a walking tower if you were imaginative enough, right? The more I think about it, I think we may have a rogue larper on our hands. This has a really immersive feel to it right down to the dress that the victim wore and if we could find the owner of that dress, we might just prove my theory.'

Brighton felt a wave of cool relief that she'd moved away from the wizard fantasy.

'Okay. I'll run it by the team. Work with Jimmy Griffiths on this. He's trying to contact the author's lawyers. They might know about collectors. Find out if any of them have been burgled. Might have to get you to come down and explain this larping business to them though. I don't think they'd get it. Now did we get any joy from the book?'

'Yes. There are at least three sets of prints. The book belonged to a Marta Brighton at one stage.'

'My sister?'

'Yes guv. Her prints are on the cover, and her name is written on the inside page.'

'How did Marta's book get there?' he said, 'she tried to show it to me when I saw her the other day.' I wish I hadn't brushed her off like that, he thought. 'We'll need to broaden the investigation to include my sister and her movements for the past month.'

'Your mum autographed it too. It's very rare. I think it's a galley print.'

'What's that?'

'Galley prints are prints made before the final proofread.'

'Yeah right. She gave us both the same book one year for Christmas when I was about nine and Marta was fourteen. She'd autographed them too, thinking that we'd be impressed. Neither of us were. I just wanted a football.'

'Do you still have your copy, guv?'

'No. I sold it when I moved to London. It paid my rent for months.'

'I'm not surprised. They're highly collectable. I'd say this copy would even fetch eighty to ninety thousand pounds now.'

Brighton whistled. That would have made a decent house deposit, he thought.

'Cheers. Hey, you didn't happen to find an e-mail or a mobile number? Or an address? Some way of contacting her if the book were lost?'

'Yeah, there's an address written inside the cover for a boarding house in Hackney.'

Hackney? That was a strange place for her to end up, he thought. Must be a rehab or halfway house, though judging by the autopsy, he doubted she'd stayed clean for long. There might be clothes or other possessions there or even CCTV.

'Alright. Is there anything else?'

Jeanie shook her head.

'Can I take the book with me?'

'Sure, as long as you sign it out of evidence and return it.'

'Cheers. Do the trace again on that parchment and that MVAC as well if you like. Whatever you do, don't give it to me again.'

'Yes guv. I'll get onto it.'

'And find out who this Leo Gare is. Sounds like a disco dancer.'

'I can tell you that now if you like. It's not a who, it's a what. Leogare is a middle English word for liar.'

As she said leogare, he shivered like he'd been knifed in the kidneys.

'Did you learn that when you were off larping Jeanie?' he said, smiling to keep his composure, all the while wondering why the killer thought he'd lied about his mother's address.

7

Brighton didn't want to tell Kerry about Marta's death. After reading Emily a bedtime story and tucking her into bed, he sat down on the couch and thought about how to approach the subject.

His wife looked worried.

'What's wrong Will? You've been out of sorts all night. Is it work?'

As a rule, they never talked about his job. Despite being an exceptional investigative journalist, Kerry knew that there had to be some professional boundaries. She promised never to snoop and likewise he was forbidden to ask her about her sources. They both kept everything to themselves. Work stayed at work.

'No. I found my sister Marta at the morgue today. Dead from an overdose.'

Kerry looked thunderstruck. She held her husband as she had countless times before when he'd come home with a tragic experience. But this time it was close to home.

'Oh God Will. I'm so sorry.'

'Thanks. I'll be fine. We hadn't spoken for eight years. Not until I bumped into her the other day.'

'Why didn't you tell me?'

'It was work. Besides I just fobbed her off anyway. That's what hurts the most Kerry. The last time I saw her I wasn't very nice. I wish I had listened to her.'

'That must be terrible, especially after finding her the way you did.'

'I guess so. But if I wasn't there today, they'd never have identified her. She'd have been put in a public health grave with three or four other people and that would be the end of it.'

Kerry shivered.

'I couldn't think of anything worse. Have you contacted your mothe...'

Brighton cut her off at the pass.

'No. I haven't. Besides she won't care, and Marta wouldn't want her anywhere near her funeral.'

Kerry looked shocked.

'Not even to say goodbye for the last time? How could you even know that? This is huge. I'd want to know if Emily died, even if we had nothing to do with each other. She's my daughter.'

'You've no idea what my mother is like.'

'I've been with you for nine years now Will and I don't know anything about either of them, only not to mention them around you. Especially your mum. Do you have any idea what that's like?'

'Sorry Kerry but you don't understand. You don't have a clue!'

'But Will, you left home a long time ago. People change.'

'Not her. She'll never change.'

'I'd like to decide for myself if you bothered to let me. Instead, you chose not to have anyone from your family in our lives! Do you have any idea how strange our relationship is? There was nobody from your family at our wedding or at Emily's christening. It's one big silly secret.'

'That's because I didn't want to have either event ruined by her or Marta. She was a junkie. How could I trust her? And my mother is a monster. Take my word for it. More chance of getting a Christmas card from Golem.'

'But you kept them secret from me and from Emily. We're your family.'

'I did that to protect you. I don't like keeping secrets Kerry and I'm not going to keep them anymore. I love you too much. I'm sorry. I'm sick of all the secrets. It's time you knew the truth.'

Oh no, she thought, as his brow furrowed, this didn't look good.

'What is it Will. What happened? Please don't be an affair. I just couldn't handle it. Anything but that.'

'Never. I'd never cheat on you Kerry. Not ever.'

'Then what is it?' She looked at him as he struggled to find words and knew that he was going into damage control. 'What do you want to tell me?' her voice rose as she prepared for the worst.

'My mother is Anna Brighton.'

'Anna Brighton? THE Anna Brighton? The one whose books I read as a child?'

'Yes. That's my mother.'

Kerry's eyes widened.

'Are you all right?'

'No, I'm not. It's like you just told me that you were related to the Queen or Elton John or something outrageous like that. How could you keep this a secret from me?'

He looked like a gasping fish, stuttering as he struggled to find the right words.

'I knew I shouldn't have said anything. But feeling the weight of all those years of secrets lift of my shoulders feels great.'

Kerry stared at the alien creature that she still didn't know, while soaking in the information like a chocolate Digestive in tea.

'I don't know what to say Will. I'm trying to comprehend all this. It's upsetting, but I know you and there must be a good reason behind all this secrecy.'

Closing her eyes, she tried to think of nothing for a moment. Perhaps meditation could help. Nope. She opened her eyes and looked at her husband.

'I'm glad you told me Will, but you need to know that I feel violated by you hiding this from me like I can't be trusted or something.'

'I'm sorry. I didn't know how to tell you. But I need to tell you something. I do not want my mother in my life. I don't even like thinking about her. And I don't want her anywhere near our Emily.'

'But why Will? Tell me. What did she do to make you hate her the way you do? I've never seen anything like it. Honestly, who could hate Anna Brighton? She's like the Mary Berry of children's literature. She's harmless.'

'That's because you only know of the famous author. That's all a lie. Anna Brighton is just a brand. Like an actor or a singer or a handbag. All she cared about was her work and her image. She didn't care about Marta and me. Just the thought of her makes me want to scream.'

'Darling, I didn't know.'

'She didn't want anyone to know.'

'What do you mean?'

'That she didn't give a toss about us. Writing's all that mattered to her. Day and night tapping away on that bloody typewriter. She may be a famous author and if you believed all the publicity and the interviews you may very well think of her as an exemplary human being. An enchanting and wonderful woman. Nothing could be further from the truth. Marta and I were just an inconvenience. A burden and nothing else.'

'That's horrible.'

'That's not even the half of it. She moved us around all the time like we were on tour. I attended that many schools I lost count. Marta couldn't handle the insecurity. She started taking drugs, and when Anna found out she wanted to kick her out of the house, but my sister grabbed her purse and made a run for it. You know I thought she'd take me with her, but she didn't. It took me ages to leave on my own. In the meantime, though, I was stuck with the nasty old cow. I turned Marta away the other day Kerry and she was trying to help me. But I wouldn't have it, and I blamed her for everything like a selfish twat. Now she's dead.'

Kerry couldn't handle seeing her husband in so much pain. She gripped him tighter.

'You can't blame yourself for that Will. Her addiction killed her. Not you.'

'Oh, that's the worst part. We don't know what killed her for sure. What I do know is that in spite of everything she's still my sister and she's gone. I know we're saving for the house, but I need to bury her Kerry. I can't have my sister sharing a grave with strangers.'

'That's fine,' said Kerry without a second thought, seeing his relief.
'Thanks love. I'll pay it back as soon as I can. I'll get more overtime.'
'No. You're away enough as it is. We hardly see you.'
'I know but...'
'We're your family and we're more important than a stupid house, okay? We'll manage.'

8

'Morning boss,' said Griffiths.

'Morning Jim. Could you grab us a cuppa please? The queue down there is mental.'

'Sure thing. Hey, that woman's here to see you. You know the one from the National Archives.'

'Cecelia Lemon?'

Griffiths saw Brighton's discomfort and nodded.

'Yeah, that's the one. Sour little thing ain't she? I put her in 308.'

Cecelia Lemon gave Brighton a frosty look, raising her eyes as he entered the tiny interview room.

'Finally. I have been waiting here for more than twenty minutes.'

'My apologies.'

'Now let's get to business. I understand you have some items that may belong to Anna.'

'That's one of our theories. If you've come for photos for her to identify them, we could have saved you the bother.'

'Oh, it's no bother at all.'

'Okay I'll go and get the photos for you then.'

Her laugh reeked of sarcasm.

'Detective Brighton I would never dream of bothering Anna with something so trivial.'

'Trivial? That's a poor choice of words to describe a little girl's murder.'

Cecilia rolled her eyes. 'That's not what I meant William.'

'That's Detective Inspector Brighton to you.'

Cecelia yawned.

'There's no need to be so abrasive Inspector. And no need to disturb Anna while she's on sabbatical with such a trivial matter of identifying her own belongings.'

'Okay then. I'll go and get them' he said, escaping from the ice queen as fast as he could.

In the corridor, he saw Griffiths chatting to a pretty young woman from Human Resources, who made her excuses as he approached.

'Oi you! Where's my tea then?'

'Sorry guv, I got kinda side tracked.'

'Yeah, I can see that. I thought you were done with Ciara. Now go and get the little girl's clothes from evidence and bring them over to the interview room for me. Don't leave her alone with them either. I'm going to the caff. If she asks where I am, tell her I'm out on a call.'

Griffiths smiled and nodded.

Brighton headed for the caff, hoping the morning queue would delay him long enough to regain his composure. He couldn't stand entitled people, never mind the fact that she worked for his mother. Twenty-five minutes later, refreshed and with tea in hand, he returned to chaos. Opening the door to the interview room he found the solicitor unleashing a tirade on Griffiths.

'What's going on here?' he said loud enough to silence the jabbering hyena.

'Finally,' she said, giving him her full attention. 'I was just telling your colleague that I'm taking possession of this dress and this book as well.'

'I'm afraid that's not possible. They are evidence in a murder investigation.'

'These are far more important than that. The book for one is super rare. As for the dress, do you have any idea how valuable it is?' She looked at his blank face. 'Obviously not. Well, I'll explain, shall I? This is *the dress*. It's like *the dress* that Dorothy wore in The Wizard of Oz. This is the one that Anna wore in her first book. You know, *The Magical Wooded World*. When she was taken by Zaliel.'

Brighton forced himself to not roll his eyes at the mention of the Magical Wooded World yet again.

'That's just a story Ms Lemon. The truth is that Anna Brighton never journeyed to a far-off fantasy land. She just lived it every day of her life and probably still does to this day.'

The lawyer barely contained her outrage.

'Just you wait DI Brighton,' rising up and hissing into his face like a spitting cobra. 'I shall be instructing your mother to act the moment she contacts me.'

'I don't doubt that for a moment Miss Lemon. Once the case is over, you'll be contacted about the dress and if it's hers, she is welcome to put a claim in for it. As for the book, that's my sister's property. Now if there isn't anything else...' He gestured to the door.

'You know I'm surprised at one thing. The whole time I've been here you've not once asked about her. Did you know she was...'

'Look I couldn't care less about Anna Brighton. I warned you about the crazy fan. That's all I had to do. DS Griffiths will show you out.'

Once she'd left, Brighton lifted the evidence bag with the dress, revealing the book had been turned to the page bearing Marta's address. Great. That's all I need, he thought as he hurried out of the station, hoping to get to Hackney before the brazen lawyer.

9

Stale cigarette smoke greeted him like an unwanted guest as he drifted through the faded curtains and into the foyer of the rundown hostel.

Looking around, he saw that the hostel probably wasn't so dreary once upon a time, but now it waited for the inevitable demolition gang to knock it down and replace it with something even more hideous. Hearing raised voices, he found Cecilia Lemon arguing with a very tired looking caretaker, at the end of a long wooden reception counter.

'I want to see her room. Now.'

'Like I told you, she ain't in.'

'I don't care if she's not in. I just want to see her room.'

'Are you old Bill? You got a warrant or something?'

'No. I just told you I represent her mother. I've been asked to check up on her.'

'That's not my problem. Look if you want to wait for her, you can sit over there with old Freddy,' he said, pointing to a worn-out settee dominated by a huge man slobbering cornflakes from a packet as he watched an East Enders rerun. 'You wouldn't mind some company now would you Fred?'

Brighton watched as Cecelia turned into a pufferfish. All poisonous barbs and bloated ego.

'All right?' he said to the balding caretaker before she exploded. 'DI Brighton. We spoke on the phone.'

'Ah yes Mr Brighton. Am I glad to see you!' said the caretaker, scratching at his dandruff and powdering the front desk in the process.

Jostling past Cecilia, he leaned on the counter just shy of the snow drift.

'What do I owe you then?'

'Two hundred and fifty pounds should cover it.'

Ouch Brighton thought, hoping there was enough credit on his card as he handed it over.

'Room 762, level seven,' said the caretaker beaming as the receipt screeched out of the squeaky eftpos machine.

'Cheers,' said Brighton taking his card and the room key from the caretaker's sweaty hand.

He climbed up the first flight of old wooden stairs held together by a tatty carpet spine from a bygone era. Each floor looked the same. Fading green wallpaper, the same white carpet yellowed by age and memories, each covered in numerous stains and cigarette burns.

'Excuse me,' said Cecelia when she caught up to him. 'Where do you think you're going?'

'I'm collecting my sister's belongings. She's living with me now.'

'That's curious. I was under the distinct impression that she was missing.'

'How the hell would you know? Has Anna put the feelers out for us again?' he said, remembering a time in the distant past when he found a private investigator following him around his beat.

There'd been others, but he'd been super vigilant ever since and always managed to evade them.

'You've no proof of that.'

'Look Ms Lemon. The truth is that Anna Brighton couldn't care less, but I'm sure she'd put the word out about her 'personal family tragedy' and use the occasion as a publicity stunt to launch another book.'

'What an outrageous thing to say!'

'Oh? I read at that exhibition that she did the same thing when my father died. If you're her curator, you should know that.'

Cecelia's unusual green eyes narrowed and blinked.

'I don't believe you. Anna would never do that.'

'I'm afraid you're wrong Ms Lemon, and when you see her next, tell her to leave us be. We won't have anything to do with her or her new pet shrew. Okay?'

Cecilia glared at him and sneered, exposing rows of tiny sharp teeth. This shrew was not about to be tamed.

'How dare you speak to me like that!' she shrieked, shaking her fists at him.

'Know what?' said Brighton surprised by the relaxed tone of his voice. 'You remind me of an entitled teenage girl I nicked once at Harrods for shoplifting. She screamed as I put the cuffs on. She screamed and kicked as I removed her from the store, and when I put her in the back of the car she crumpled into a heap and cried all the way to the station.'

'You won't dismiss me so easily William,' said Cecelia, using his name as a hateful barb.

Brighton looked at her.

'What is your problem? Why are you being so personal about this?'

Cecilia clenched her shiny teeth.

He changed tact.

'Tell me, do you make a habit of shouting at police officers?'

'Don't treat me like a fool. You're not here on police business.'

'You know my sister's book? The one in the evidence bag you decided to open and get this address from? It just happens to have been found at a murder scene. I have just cause to be here and search her room in my current capacity.'

'My what an intriguing concept, but tell me, where is your warrant?'

'I don't need one. She is not a suspect. She reported a break in and that her rare book was missing. It's a galley book as you know. My team isn't very far behind and hopefully we'll get a lead. Now if there isn't anything else, I'm going upstairs.'

He turned, feeling her strange, hateful glare burning into his neck as he continued his climb. Reaching the seventh floor, he looked down and saw with some relief that she'd gone. His legs hurt and he leaned on the banister, taking a minute to get his breath back. The hall lights were out, and as his eyes adjusted to the darkness, he looked about for any clue to find room 762.

The dank corridor smelt of rising damp, dancing in a circle with old fish and chips wrappers. His nose detected a faint wisp of marijuana and fresh cat's piss, as he found his sister's room at the very end of the corridor.

He opened the door and switched the light on, not expecting to find a red bulb. Nor what it illuminated. At first glance Marta's room didn't look at all like a junkie's nest. A small pile of folded clothes lay on a tiny neat made-up single bed. Fading bunches of lavender disguised the dampness.

His mouth dropped when he looked at the walls, they looked like a serial killer's shrine. Every inch of every wall including the ceiling was covered top to bottom in hundreds of drawings. They were all sketched out in lead pencil on art paper, highlighted in colour, circling around the bay window and its heavy drapes, and even plastering three sides of the ancient wardrobe tucked near the door. Zaliel's yellow eyes stared at him from all directions.

What the hell have you gotten into Marta? thought Brighton, taking as many pictures on his phone as he could. Some of the pictures were almost life sized, drawn on large art pad pages stuck side by side and held in place with scotch tape. He opened her wardrobe and gathered up her things. Everything fit in her suitcase, Marta didn't have much.

His gut told him to look under the bed. Crawling under, he used the torch setting on his phone and found a cereal box holding a small book taped to the bed boards. As he grabbed it, Brighton sensed another presence in the room, gasping as the squeaky wardrobe doors shut. Get a grip man, he thought. It's just a draft that's all. He slid back out, banging his head on the bed frame and looked around at the empty room.

He opened the notebook and read his sisters tiny, neat handwriting:

I know Zaliel saw me across the river from him when he took the little girl the other day.

I will never forget his terrifying stare as he climbed into the sack, and they disappeared. I've seen him around here since then. Maybe he's coming for me.

I'm getting really scared, and at night whenever I hear

the boards creaking outside, I worry that it's him. I just know he'll get to me. It doesn't matter what I do.

Wish I could go back to my brother, but he doesn't believe a word of it. Thinks I'm back on drugs and even though it really hurts me, I know why he chooses to think that way.

Marta had just given him a witness account for Anna Bolton's kidnapping that confirmed Zaliel's involvement. If Zaliel knew she was aware of him, he may have killed her.

He opened the wardrobe, looking around to make sure that he hadn't missed anything. Under it, pushed right to the very back, he found her camera and a couple of packets of developed photos. No time to look at these now. Brighton just wanted to get out of there. He'd get Griffiths to come back and get all the pictures later. Who knows, a few might even be useful to the investigation.

A sudden burst of air blew into Brighton's left ear. Jumping like a nervous colt, his flailing arms dropped Marta's camera on the thick shag-pile carpet. As he picked it up, something ripped through the life-sized picture of Zaliel on the wall behind him. Panicking, he rolled forward and crashed into the bed as the wizard stepped through the picture and glared at him.

'Fieri in carcerem' he chanted, pointing his wand at the carpet near Brighton's feet.

The Detective Inspector subsided into the carpet. He tried scrambling out but sank all the way up to his chest. Moving his feet in the space below, he found nothing to stand on. Grabbing at the bed he gripped the sheets, his face sweating in panic as he tried to stop falling through the floor.

The wizard moved closer and looked down at him.

'Where be thy mother, William?' he said, 'Tell me now!'

'I told you before, I don't know. The only place I can think of is in Dartmoor.'

'Nay. She is not there!'

'Then I don't know where she is. Now tell me something. Why did you kill little Anna? Did you kill my sister too? What did they ever do to you Zaliel?'

'So, you know who I am do you?'

'I know who you think you are.'

'Then surely you know why!'

'Not for a moment you psychopath.'

'Your words mean nothing. Your sister was weak. The little one too. I did this to punish ye and if thou do not tell me where Anna Brighton is William, another shall pay!'

'Not if I can help it!' said Brighton.

Grabbing at Zaliel's feet, he tried to pull the struggling wizard down to him, but Zaliel kicked and stomped on his hands until he let go.

'Another shall pay! Pone locum igni!' said Zaliel, waving his wand, and turning the room into a fireball.

'You're mad!' said Brighton as his sister's pictures fuelled the inferno around him.

Ignoring him, the Wizard climbed into the sack. Brighton watched as he shouted 'Home' and disappeared. Green smoke fanned the flames as the embers reached the carpet, turning it into a spiral, swirling hypnotically like a melting Wonka bar.

Brighton grasped the bed, trying to heave himself out but he could not free himself from the powerful grip of the carpet. He let go, falling not into oblivion but into the downstairs bathroom, and into the lap of a rather portly drag queen who screamed when the stranger rudely splashed into her warm rose scented bath.

'Sorry!' said Brighton jumping up and rushing into the hall as the enraged soapy diva screamed 'Get out!'

He ran back up the stairs, hoping to save the camera and the book before the flames devoured them. He couldn't see or smell any smoke, and when he opened the door everything was just the way it was. There was no fire and the picture that the wizard stepped out of was intact again. Then he found the evidence that confirmed he hadn't lost the plot.

Burnt into one of the walls were the wizard's parting words.

Another shall pay!

10

'How could you seriously expect me to believe you?' said Jeanie after Brighton told her about his encounter with Zaliel. 'I mean it's all very well to believe in a magick scroll, that was desperation, but Zaliel climbing out of walls and zapping you with his wand? What am I supposed to think?'

'I wouldn't have believed me either, but look at the evidence.' He opened Marta's bag and started piling her drawings of Zaliel on the table.

'Tell me, does he look familiar? It's the same bloke I saw at Trafalgar Square, and here look at this. Look who he's with!' He rummaged through the pictures and pulled a drawing out of Zaliel carrying Anna in his arms. 'This proves that Zaliel took Anna!'

To Brighton's surprise, Jeanie looked nonplussed and if anything, a little more concerned than she originally had when Brighton arrived unannounced, dripping wet, and spouting nonsense.

'How is this really proof?' she said. 'These drawings, were made by a woman who used to be a drug addict and judging from the pictures and photo's you've shown me, there's a good indication that she may have had mental health issues as well.'

'Or something spooked her.'

'If she was so scared then why did she obsess? Why didn't she get help?'

'I told you already. She did try to get help. She came to me, and I couldn't see past her addiction, so I fobbed her off.'

'That's why I think you're a bit too close to this to have any objectivity. There is another possibility that we've not considered yet.'

'What do you mean?'

'This might not be evidence of Zaliel's involvement at all, but evidence of hers.'

Estranged or not, the suggestion that his sister could be responsible for Anna's death was inconceivable.

'Marta wasn't like that. She'd never hurt a little kid.'

'With all due respect how do you know that? Her book was found at the scene of the crime.'

'That proves nothing. She was dead long before Anna.'

'She may well have been but that does not rule out the possibility that she had an accomplice.'

'Are you saying that she was working with Zaliel?'

'Or someone that's been larping him. We can't rule out the possibility, can we?'

'I knew my sister Jeanie.'

'Did you? And I mean that respectfully.'

Despite the pain he felt from Jeanie's accusations, Brighton knew she was right. How well did he know Marta? The fact was that she was a stranger and had been for years. Maybe the only feelings that he had left were guilt and nostalgia, masquerading as love.

'Okay I take your point,' he said to her relief, 'But let's make this an expert opinion rather than a hypothesis. Let's add her to the equation. Could you analyse her things, and I'll get Jimmy to see if there was any CCTV of her in Angel the day Anna went missing.'

He hunted around in the suitcase and fished out some evidence bags.

'Check these as well. Swabs and samples of the carpet and walls. If we're going to add her to the investigation, let's be thorough. There's this as well.'

Brighton assembled the full-length picture on the table. 'This is the one that I watched Zaliel walk through.'

'Listen to what you're saying guv. Wizards walking through walls and turning carpets into quicksand. It sounds like you were hallucinating or something.'

'Fine. I'll do a full tox screen. Urine, blood, the works. I did smell a bit of grass in the hall near her door, but you're right, it may have affected my senses. I'll get the team to see if there was a well-proportioned drag queen living below her as well. I'm hoping that experience was a hallucination and...'

He paused as the bench between them quivered and shook like there was an earthquake or an angry god heaving up with an almighty force from below. The life-sized drawing glowed in a strange greenish hue that Brighton knew too well.

'What's happening?' said Jeanie.

'No time!' said Brighton, 'Grab that box of matches!'

Jeanie raced to her desk as Zaliel pushed his way up and out of the picture, balancing himself on the bench with his strong gnarled arms.

'You!' he said with surprise. 'It cannot be. I banished you to another world. This time you will pay for your insolence!'

Brighton watched Jeanie rummage through her desk. He had to keep the wizard off guard and give her time.

'I don't get you,' he said, shrugging as Jeanie crept back. 'You have tried to get me twice and failed miserably. What sort of wizard are you anyway Zaliel? I bet you couldn't pull a rabbit out of a hat!'

'How dare you say my name!' roared Zaliel with anger and disgust. 'You will fear it soon enough!'

Brighton saw Zaliel reach back into the void with his right hand while steadying himself with his left. He knew the sorcerer was going for his weapon.

'Now Jeanie!'

Before the wizard retrieved his wand, Jeanie threw a handful of lit matches onto the paper, filling the room with smoke as the picture ignited and crackled.

Zaliel flailed his arms and screamed 'Another shall pay!' He ducked out of view before being consumed in an intense blue and green flame.

Jeanie looked at Brighton in a daze.

'What the hell was that guv?'

'That Jeanie, was proof that we are hunting for a real wizard.'

11

Zaliel peaked out from behind the large oak with anticipation. It had taken years of moving between his world and ours to find any evidence of Anna Brighton's existence. For some inexplicable reason even his most powerful location spells did not seem to work, and she relentlessly moved, always one step ahead, as if she somehow knew that he would not rest until he found her.

That's why she was not paying respects to her daughter he surmised, ducking back behind the tree trunk until the moment was right. No matter. He would strike her son down and then he would find her. The daughter had few belongings and no leads. He was simply fortunate that her brother learnt of her demise. William would have the answers. He would know where Anna Brighton was. Just thinking of the woman made him angry. The humiliation she'd caused him and the pain.

No child had escaped him before Anna. Not only had she managed to evade him, but she'd dared use the magick he'd taught her to send a mountain crumbling down upon him, trapping him, and giving him injuries that took decades to heal. His ego had not healed and neither had his dignity. When Anna beat him, she ruined his reputation of being a terrifying wizard who had defeated demons and robbed dragons. Reducing him to a laughingstock among his peers. Ever since that time he had dedicated his life to finding her.

From his position on the gentle slope above the lonely service, the wizard saw Brighton, the bane of his existence, looking down as the coffin disappeared into the ground. He was not alone. A woman stood by his side, holding a little girl's hand.

The wizard hated the rain drizzling down on his thinning grey hair like the saddest angel, making up for the lack of tears at Marta Brighton's funeral. He had half a mind to use a spell to stop it, but if he did, her brother would surely be aware. Their last encounter had rattled him a little and he'd waited too long for revenge to be worried about a little bit of water.

'Earth to earth, ashes to ashes, dust to dust in sure and certain hope for the resurrection to eternal life through our Lord Jesus Christ.' Father McKinnon finished his last prayer, ending the service and stood silently for a moment out of obligation rather than respect for the woman he did not know.

He hated the rain as much as the wizard did and had a christening and evening services to attend to.

'My condolences again Will,' he said, putting his hand on the young man's shoulder. 'If you need to talk at any time, please know that I'm here for you.'

Brighton nodded and thanked the priest for his time.

Relieved that his job was done, Father McKinnon scuttled off towards the rectory as the heavens opened from above.

Brighton ignored the rain and looked down at Marta, still trying to process the fact that his only sibling was gone, leaving their cold estranged mother as his last remaining family member.

He remembered the day he stumbled across her in London, many years after she'd run away from home. At first he thought it was just another beggar, but he soon realised that the quivering mess, kneeling with her hands outstretched under the dragon that guarded the city of London, was his sister.

She was barely human anymore. A slave to the white powder and she'd do anything for it. Hollow eyes gave a faint flicker of recognition on her starved face when she looked up. While their reunion was brief, he promised to come back and see her when his shift was over, but when he returned she'd gone, and he had no way of finding her.

In the months that followed he made a habit of looking for her and asking for her, but the shady world she lived in treated coppers with suspicion, and he got nowhere fast. When he finally found her, he'd fobbed her off and now was too late.

He wanted to cry. That's what people did at funerals, but his grief had started from the moment he saw her body in the mortuary. He kept it within. He did not want sympathy either. In fact, he felt relief for his poor sister more than anything. As for their mother, he knew that there was no way in hell that Marta wanted her to know, and in honesty the last thing he needed was a conversation with Anna Brighton.

'I love you daddy,' said Emily, squeezing his hand.

Ahh. She is your daughter, thought Zaliel with interest. The wizard heard the strange chiming noise. The Detective Inspector did not want to answer it but knew he had to. Peering around the tree Zaliel was almost blinded by a powerful shimmer of light around Brighton's head as he removed his hoodie and placed the curious device on his ear.

What in hell's name is that? An aura? It could not be. It was no ordinary aura, but a powerful shield only seen by those with magickal eyes that sought to harm him. He hadn't seen it before because the only way to see it was in natural light and from much closer than he'd been in Kew.

Zaliel wanted to scream with the rage that fuelled his hate and desire for revenge. Somehow his target had been warded. Now he knew why his magick failed him. It was useless against his enemy in this world. His plans instantly turned into troll shit. All is not lost, he thought, there is a way. I just need to bring him to my world. There he will be defenceless.

The realisation gave Zaliel hope, and he followed Brighton and his family as they walked away from Marta's grave.

∼

'Well, well, boys look who it is,' said an imposing balding man, laughing and wheezing after a long draw on the stub of an Upman cigar. 'What are you here for Mister Brighton? Come to get a measure of your final resting place?'

The man's cronies laughed at his joke as if their lives depended on it.

Outnumbered, Brighton grabbed Kerry's hand and tried to walk past him without saying a word, only to be blocked by the large group who surrounded Brighton and his family like a pod of killer whales, playing with their food before they dined.

'What's with you Mister Brighton? Can't you handle a joke? Forgotten your manners as well I see.'

'This isn't the time or place Sid,' said Brighton, tensing up.

'Well, aren't you being a big man in front of your family. This is your family I take it. Hullo Kerry. Yeah, I know who you are. Be careful what you write these days. Never know who you might upset.'

'Was that a threat, Sid?' said Kerry

'What if it was? What are you going to do about it? Eh?'

'If you don't mind, we'd like to leave,' said Brighton.

'No one's going anywhere yet sport.'

'Daddy why is he so rude?' said Emily, throwing decorum out the window. 'Why won't he let us past?'

Her outburst made Sid and his crew laugh even more.

'What's wrong Mister Brighton? Need a little girl to fight your battles?'

'You're not very nice,' said Emily trying to break free from her mother's grip like a determined chihuahua.

'Here,' said an older girl, dressed like a tiny fashion model as she stepped out from behind Sid and moved towards Emily. 'Who are you calling my daddy names? I ought to teach you some respect.'

'You don't scare me barbie doll.'

Anna Bell fumed, and Brighton fought the urge to smile and failed.

'Anna Bell Fields, you step down now. I don't need you to fight my battles.'

'But daddy.'

'Be a good girl and go find that priest. Now.'

Zaliel watched as Anna Bell rolled her eyes and stormed off in a huff. He saw an opportunity. Whoever this man was, there was no doubt he and Brighton were at odds.

'Come on lads, let's go and pay our respects,' said Sid Fields. The game was over, and he was bored. 'Good afternoon, William, Kerry, and dear sweet little Emily. Stay safe.' He chuckled and led his crew past them and deeper into the cemetery.

'Who was that?' said Emily once they were alone.

'That was one of the nastiest gangsters in London. Sid Fields,' said Kerry.

'How did he know our names?'

'The man knows everything,' said Brighton. 'I've suspected a leak at the station for a while now, but so far, I haven't proved anything. He's always one step ahead and that's a worry.'

'I'm frightened Will.'

'Don't be. He's sore at me because I'm not on his payroll and he can't get to me. He's not stupid enough to come after us.'

Ahh but maybe he is William, thought Zaliel. Maybe he just needs to be provoked. He retrieved his wand.

'Home,' he said, evaporating in a puff of green smoke as Brighton and his family walked back to their car, unaware that the wizard's scheming would change their lives forever.

12

When the trace from the hostel walls came back the following day as identical to the other scenes, it put Jeanie Boswell in a bit of a quandary. Jeanie the scientist dismissed the notion of magick, as the practitioners called it, to be a load of rubbish. Jeanie the geek who loved reading Anna Brighton books and playing dungeons and dragons, wanted it all to be real, despite the carpet that Brighton swore turned into quicksand having a different trace.

'You are a woman of science,' she reminded herself as she scanned over *The Book of Oberon*, her third grimoire of the day. She wrote down every ingredient she could find. Every incantation had variation. If the magician did a spell on Saturday, they would use frankincense and on Monday myrtle leaves and bay laurel and so on.

She methodically created a table of days of the week associated with each ingredient, factoring in the moon phase and the time of day. Then she added the times and days that Brighton saw Zaliel, the potential sighting of the wizard in Kew, and the day and approximate time that Anna Bolton went missing. Now she had a list of potential trace elements to look for within each sample of trace collected.

'Hi ya Alex,' she said picking up her phone. 'How are you getting along with the samples?'

'Roy and I are still trying to establish definite elements. It's like a biological Rubik's cube. The strangest thing is that we think we've extracted sandalwood from one of them, but I wonder if it came from Roy's car. He loves those joss sticks.'

'Sandalwood you say?' Jeanie looked down her table. That signified a Tuesday which was the night Brighton encountered Zaliel at Trafalgar Square. 'Is that from Trafalgar Square?'

There was silence on the other end of the line.

'How did you know that?'

Jeanie smiled. She loved being right even if her idea was farfetched.

'It's a bit hard to explain but check that sample for aloes and cypress as well. I'll send you a list of what we are looking for from the other sites in a moment. What did you mean by a biological Rubik's cube?'

'It's almost like it's a changing form of living energy or the remnants left by a bio force neither of us have identified. We'd like to send samples and cultures to other agencies.'

'That's a good idea. Send me what you have, and I'll look at it with fresh eyes. In the meantime, check that list. It looks a bit strange, but I think we may be onto something.'

'That's great! Want to team up at quest night?'

Jeanie sighed. You would have to go and ruin the conversation, wouldn't you? she thought, regretting her decision to hang out with him a few weeks earlier when she felt fragile. While they had a lot in common, she just wasn't into men, and he wanted more than friendship. She just wanted a friend that wasn't a cat.

13

Anna Bell Fields stamped her feet and grew tired of waiting for her father's latest conquest to pick her up. Stupid cow's probably forgotten, she thought as she started pacing up and down outside the gates of her exclusive school. This wasn't the first time she'd been left to call an uber and make her own way home, but it annoyed her because sometimes the other girls, like the ones walking towards her now, were cruel and that made Anna Bell angry.

'Forgotten you again, have they?' said a girl from a higher grade, flanked by her two friends.

'No,' said Anna Bell, rolling her eyes, 'They're just late that's all.'

'Are you sure they haven't forgotten you? That happens when daddy has a new pet doesn't it? They forget all about you.'

'Mind your own business, slag.' Anna Bell's menacing tone surprised her older tormentor, and for a moment she wasn't sure what to do and watched in fear as the smaller girl clenched her fists.

'Leave her Britney,' said one of her bored friends.

'Yes, let's go,' said the other, 'I want to go to Selfridges.'

'They're right,' said Britney. 'You're not worth the bother. Silly little bitch.'

The girls laughed and left her. All the other girls and teachers had left for the day, and the place was quite deserted. Anna Bell glared. She wanted to give Britney a roundhouse kick in the guts, but this was her second school this year and she didn't want any more aggro from her old man. Just you wait till I get you alone, she thought, I'll knock that smile out of you.

'Miaow,' said a cute little white kitten that came out from nowhere and stroked her leg.

'Hullo! Where did you come from?' said Anna Bell forgetting all about the toxic Britney and focusing all her attention on the adorable little ball of fluff.

She went to pick it up, but the kitten backed away and dodged round her legs, jumped over her gym bag, and ran across the street where it meowed at her.

Anna Bell decided to give up on the cat and hunted for her phone. She called Stella again; the phone went straight to voicemail, as did her dad's.

She gave in to the kitten's persistence and when she crossed the road it ran a bit further then it came back and stroked her leg again. But as before when she tried to pick it up, the kitten bounded away. You're mine, she thought as she followed the kitten into an alley and then a courtyard where it picked up the pace and bounded over to two full grown cats sitting on an old sack. She didn't notice Zaliel at first. Her focus was on the kitten as it turned into a full-grown cat, transforming from white to mottled brown.

'Ah Grimalkin. You've returned with our guest I see,' said Zaliel, standing up and walking over to Anna Bell who snapped out of it and looked a little scared.

He was the strangest looking old man Anna Bell had seen, and she didn't like the sound of being his guest one bit.

'I was just leaving,' she said and started running back to the alley.

Zaliel waved his wand in the air and pointed it at his retreating prey.

'To me, little feet. To me.'

The effect was like a tractor beam. Anna Bell turned and started walking back to him. Her initial reaction was to scream but she had the smarts to know that wasn't going to get her anywhere. She checked her arms, and she still had control of them. She pretended to be scared, and tie back her hair while loosening one of her little diamond earrings which fell on the ground. Dad will kill me she thought, but it was her way of leaving evidence that she was there. She wasn't stupid.

Zaliel held open the sack, and she climbed in with him and the cats. The sack ponged and the air smelled musty as he pulled it over them and yelled 'HOME!'

Anna Bell felt like she was falling for ages and then landed with a bump on a hard cobbled surface. Zaliel let go of the sack and stepped out. Anna Bell looked around the darkness at her prison. A roaring fire lit an ancient round stone room. She saw a doorway leading to some stairs. The place was littered with cupboards and shelves and looked like an old laboratory from a horror film. What the hell is going on? she thought. Where is this place?

The old man turned to her. 'Get thee out of there Anna Bell.'

'No.'

'You dare refuse me child!'

'Yeah, and for your info I'm not a child.'

'Silence!'

'How'd you know my name?'

Zaliel wasn't used to this sort of behaviour.

'I have been watching you.'

'Yuck. Take me home you old pervert.'

'You are my prisoner!'

'Yeah? We'll see about that.'

Anna Bell sprang out of the sack and ran for the staircase, sprinting up the winding flights until she was puffed out. Why isn't the old git following me? she thought as she caught her breath. She continued her journey up the stairs until she reached a doorway at the very top. Yanking it open, she walked out onto a circular turret and looked over the edge.

Everything was green. The green sky scared her a bit but when she went to look over the edge she gasped. The tower had feet which strained as it climbed up a steep hill. Where am I? she thought, realising the danger she was in. She didn't want to believe it, but she felt like she was trapped in an Anna Brighton book that she hadn't read since getting a phone and Instagram and TikTok. Was the old man Zaliel? Well, if Anna can beat him then so can I, she thought, before walking back down the stairs with her mind focused on only one thing; escape.

∼

Brighton looked around the swanky Leman Street apartment, feeling like an interplanetary explorer in some strange world. It looked far too modern for an old school gangster like Sid Fields. A triptych of horrid artworks that looked like Jackson Pollock had experienced a nasty bout of sea sickness, dominated the grey walls of the huge open plan family room. It turned his stomach just looking at them. To his horror, the furniture matched the art. The rest of the room was glass with views of The Gherkin and surrounds glittering in the morning sun.

'About time you showed up,' said Fields glaring at Brighton and Griffiths from the hideous three-seater lounge he shared with his twenty something trophy wife Stella, and his stoat faced lawyer Joe Martin.

Sitting opposite them, Brighton looked at Stella, noticing a very visible fat lip and fading bruise near her eye.

'Are you alright?' he said.

She twitched in fear and looked down at the oversized glass coffee table.

'Ere wot you on about?' said Fields.

'Your wife looks like she's been assaulted Mr Fields.'

'Oh that,' said the gangster, smiling and winking at Griffiths as he shrugged. 'Stella here bumped into a door last night but she's okay now. Aren't ya love?'

Stella nodded and managed a very unconvincing smile.

'Right. Now that's sorted what are you doing about trying to find my daughter? Old Bull told me you might have something.'

'We've canvassed the area for witnesses and now we are trying to pinpoint where the crime took place.'

'You found any yet? Witnesses?'

'Not currently. It happened late in the afternoon and most of the residents were still at work.'

'That's not good enough.'

'Which is why I'm here. I looked at the report and there are things we need to establish.'

'Such as?'

'Has Anna Bell ever wandered off or run away from home before?'

'What are you saying? Are you suggesting I'm a not much of a father?'

'Not at all Mr Fields,' said Griffiths looking uncomfortable. 'We just need to make sure that she's never done this in the past. That's all.' He smiled and nodded at Fields to emphasise his point.

'All right. The answer is no. She ain't never done nothing like that before.'

'Could you tell us what happened?' said Brighton to Stella, still focussing her gaze on the table.

Fields jumped in.

'Christ we've been through this already. She was dropped off at her school after they came back from an excursion.'

'Do you know where the excursion went?'

'I dunno, Kew Gardens or something wasn't it' he nudged Stella.

'Yeah, Kew Gardens.'

'What's it matter anyway?'

'It gives us a lead. If she was abducted, the unsub might have seen her earlier and followed the bus back.'

'Yeah right. Anyways instead of waiting to be picked up she wandered off, probably because Stella here was about twenty minutes late.'

'It wasn't my fault. I was at the hairdressers. I told you. I looked everywhere for her and then I called you and you called the police.'

'That's right and you lot ain't done nothing since.'

Brighton wasn't about to be intimidated.

'Look Mr Fields, I can assure you that we are doing all we can to find her.'

Fields glared.

'That ain't good enough copper,' he said, clenching his big meaty fists. 'Find my Anna Bell. You hear me?'

'I'll ignore that threat,' said Brighton, 'But how do you expect us to find her when you refuse to help us to establish a motive behind her disappearance?'

Now Sid's stoat like solicitor entered the fray

'That's because your enquiries have no bearing on the matter at hand Detective Inspector,' he said glaring at Brighton through his tiny glasses. 'Furthermore, it is my opinion that this is nothing more than a fishing exercise to gain an insight into my client's private affairs.'

'Forgive me if I'm wrong, but all we have asked is if Mr Fields has any enemies. If he gave us more of an idea who the possible suspects are, then we can start making more enquiries.'

'Ere that's a load of bollocks and you know it. My Anna Bell was taken by that perve wot took that other little girl. You know the one I'm talking about. That geezer you can't find.'

Another shall pay. Brighton shuddered.

Sid smiled at Brighton's discomfort.

'What's the matter? Struck a nerve, did I?'

'And how do you know it's the same guy Mr Fields?' said Griffiths coming to the rescue. 'It's been weeks since her kidnapping. Do you have some information that could help us?'

Fields looked at Griffiths.

'Let's just say I've made a few enquiries.'

'Yes, we're aware that there are at least five men from rival crews in intensive care wards around the city. Was that after you had a quiet word?' said Brighton.

'What are you insinuating Detective Inspector?'

'I'm not insinuating anything,' said Brighton cutting the solicitor off at the pass. 'I'd like to know why you think it's the same person Mr Fields. Do you have some information that can help us to find your daughter?'

'You know I don't. But we both know it's him and if you know what's good for you, you'll find him and my Anna Bell.'

Another threat, Brighton thought. Well, I'm not going to give him any satisfaction. He stood up, signalling that the meeting was over.

'Thanks for your time. We shall be in touch when we have some more news.'

This surprised the thug, who demanded respect and compliance.

'Oi. Where do you think you're going?'

'Why, back to my investigation, Mr Fields. I'm sure that even you can appreciate that time is of the essence.'

Fields pounded the coffee table, cracking the glass and spilling all the drinks. The noise startled Brighton, who froze in his tracks.

'Anything happens to my girl you little bastard,' spat Fields, his every word laced with taipan venom. 'If she's found with so much as a scratch on her, I'll have you and your wife Kerry. Oh, and little Emily too. I know where she goes to school and all. You wouldn't like to see her get all messed up now. Would you?'

Brighton's temperature rose with anger, and he wanted to clench his fists and teach Sid Fields a lesson in manners. Instead, he decided not to react because he knew full well that this was an old trick, the oldest in the book in fact. Years ago, when Brighton was a Detective Constable, Fields tried to pay him off and couldn't believe that the young DC didn't have a price when everyone else did. He wanted something over him and wanted him to react in front of witnesses.

'Let's go DS Griffiths. We'll see ourselves out,' he said with a thin smile, retreating into the relative safety of the stair well.

Anna Bell was last seen in Henriques Street, the same location Elizabeth Stride had allegedly been murdered by Jack the Ripper in 1888. Brighton looked around the narrow street, imagining how hard it would be to get a pizza delivered there. There were no witnesses and no clues where the alleged kidnapping took place.

The area comprised of a school, businesses, and swanky E1 apartments. Brighton and the team kept looking. The car park behind East London Alternative Provision looked like the obvious spot because you could access Back Church Lane from there and disappear onto Commercial Road.

'Let's check that vacant lot across the street,' he said, 'the kidnappers may have taken her through there and out into Batty Street.'

As he led the team through a courtyard behind a Bangladeshi restaurant, Brighton spied a tiny white gold diamond earring on the ground. The first clue. Silly thing to give to a kid he thought, bending to pick it up.

'Over here Jimmy. I'm pretty sure this is hers from the photos they gave us. Get Constable Draper to take it back up to the Fields' place so that they can ID it.'

Within fifteen minutes Draper confirmed that it was Anna Bell's earring and warned that her father was coming down. Brighton cordoned off the whole site, giving strict instructions that under no circumstance were Sid Fields and his crew allowed to further contaminate the scene. To be on the safe side he ordered forensics back to the scene.

'I think it could be our suspect Jeanie. This time take samples of everything. Check for fibres, chemicals, DNA, and everything under the sun that you can think of,' he said to Jeanie. 'And if you could bring that MVAC machine here as well please, that would be great.'

Jeanie smiled. 'I'll go and fetch it. It's in the car.'

Sid Fields watched Brighton's men sweep the area, bringing bag after bag of samples and potential evidence past his prying eyes.

'He wants a word sir,' said a nervous constable approaching Brighton sitting on his haunches staring at the ground in front of him. 'Won't take no for an answer neither the rough old sod.'

Brighton looked up at the young policeman and told him that policemen did not give in to threats or intimidation. The poor constable looked scared shitless.

'Hey copper,' Fields yelled from behind him.

Brighton stood up. He was fed up and decided to show Fields he wasn't scared and wasn't going to tolerate any more intimidation.

'What do you want Mr Fields?'

'I want an update you scrote. That's what I want.'

'I suggest you speak to my DCI then. He's the one I report to. I'm sure that he'll fill you in.'

'That's not good enough. I want it now and you'll tell me what you know. Understood?'

'I'm warning you Sid. If you attempt to threaten or intimidate me, my family, or any of my team again I'll have you charged. Understood?'

Fields glared.

'Well, if you're going to play it that way sunshine, I'd get a patrol car parked outside my house if I were you. You're going to need it.'

His men sneered and laughed. Brighton ignored them.

Fuming about Fields' repeated threats to his family, Brighton stayed at the site until four pm, when the tall lights on stands replaced the sun. Instead of pushing past Fields, he chose to use the other exit and radioed for a car to collect him. Turning left into Batty Street, he saw two of Fields' thugs waiting between him and the car. One was tall and his face looked like a plague mask with his huge nose protruding from his grey hoodie. Brighton knew him as Eric Grimsby, Fields' right-hand man. The other goon he recognised was a Lebanese pimp named Moudi, a swaggering dwarf with an afro.

'Going somewhere?' said Grimsby.

Brighton ignored him and as he squeezed past, Moudi tried to trip him over, but when he did, Brighton rolled and kicked out, sending the dwarf sprawling onto the cobbled street. Brighton looked more shocked than the injured pimp. Maybe I'm possessed by Bruce Lee, he thought.

Before Grimsby could attack, Constable Draper drove up, illuminating them with the car's high beam.

'Just you watch yourself,' said Grimsby, snarling with curled lips, before retreating back into the shadows with the limping pimp.

As Brighton sat down in the car, he noticed his pants were ripped and there was a gash on his left knee.

'That's a nasty cut sir,' said Constable Draper as they turned down Commercial Road.

'I'll be fine.'

'Why didn't you arrest them?'

'Because I have decided to show restraint.'

Constable Draper looked uncomfortable.

'But they assaulted you.'

'Did they? Did you see anything constable? The light is pretty bad.'

'Not really sir. But I saw you fall down, and I reckon it was that little fat geezer what did it too.'

'My point exactly. You didn't see anything. That's why I let it go. Their brief will just blame it on the footpath. The council has been letting them go for years. They'd have the charge dropped in no time. Those guys were trying to provoke us. Trying to get us to act and do something rash so that we play into their hands. Remember that constable, because they'll try that on you one day. Besides, I did manage to defend myself,' he said with a grin.

~

Back at the station, Brighton patched his knee up and changed into a spare pair of pants he kept in his locker. Now he wouldn't have to add to Kerry's anxiety when he arrived home.

Before finishing her shift, Jeanie Boswell reported to Brighton about what they'd found at the abduction site.

'At first there wasn't much we found that was of interest. The fibres found near the earring were identified as hair from three cats, and hessian, the same material used for sacks.'

The sack fibres looked promising. Anna Bell wasn't tall, and the perpetrator could have bundled her up and carried her for a short distance without attracting attention, longer if she'd been drugged.

'Do you think we could identify the sack from the material?' He said, trying to think outside the square.

'It's a real long shot. I doubt that each manufacturer has unique identifiers, and the sacks have so many uses from sandbags to hauling tobacco and coffee. I'll schedule some further tests just to see if we can identify anything on the fibre. There's something else.' Jeanie paused to draw her breath and smiled 'I swabbed around the walls and cobblestones near where the earring was found.'

'And...' said Brighton, too tired to be impressed by her showmanship and trying not to be rude at the same time.

'I found the same residue that we found at the Bolton scene, the laneway, Kew, and your sister's lodging house. It's not in any databases that I can access. We're examining the chemical make-up but it's going to take a while. I'll say this though. The stuff covered her. We've found trace on the earring, walls of the buildings around her, and the cobblestones for about a twelve-foot diameter.'

'So, she disappeared in a puff of smoke?'

Jeanie tried hard not to roll her eyes.

'You're a real tough gig sometimes,' she said. 'Every now and then it would be good to get positive feedback for the hours of work I've put in. Come on. Give me something.'

'Jeanie it's not you, so please don't take this personally. We both know who it was. It's Zaliel. My sister knew that. It's a pity the photos in the camera never turned out, but we have her drawings, and I've seen him three times now. We have to try and find him even if we both think it's mental.'

'Agreed, but how do we prove it?'

'Have you compared the other forensics for the Anna Bolton abduction site?'

'Not yet.'

'I want to know if there are any similarities between them. If I remember, Anna Bolton's body was covered in scratch marks that the examiner dismissed. They may have been made by a cat. Check everything again for cat hair.'

'I feel like a proper idiot,' she said face palming. 'We didn't pay much attention to the scratches at the time because he thought it might have been a fox.'

'That's okay. Just keep me updated. I want to know as soon as we have more on this strange chemical.'

'Will do guv.'

As Jeanie turned, he called to her.

'Hey Jeanie.'

She saw the faint glimmer of a smile on his face.

'Well done. That's good work.'

'Thanks guv,' she said breaking her poker face as she scurried away to her lab. OMG, she thought, did he seriously give me a compliment? About time.

There was one last thing to do before home time. Brighton had to report the multiple threats to his family. Detective Superintendent James Bull looked past Brighton to the clock on the wall behind him. When he saw that his retirement party commenced in ten minutes, he decided to make his move.

'Look Brighton. I respect your concern, however what do you propose we do about it? We can't arrest Fields even if we wanted to. From what you have told me, there's no evidence. It's a pity you didn't adhere to procedure and have the interview recorded.'

'We were at his home sir. You requested me to go there. Remember? Mr Fields made a threat to my family. DS Griffiths witnessed the whole thing. Fields knows my daughter's name and where she goes to school. Given his history, I request that either my family are moved to a secure house or that a patrol car sits outside our home until the investigation is over.'

'That's out of the question. You know we don't have the budget, and besides we don't know for sure that he'd do anything.'

'I'm sure we'd find the money if it were your family in danger. Sir,' said Brighton watching as Bull's face turned red and prepared himself for the charge.

'How dare you. I'm in no mood for your little games.'

Ever the matador, Brighton continued egging him into a bullfight that Hemingway would be proud of.

'But it's true sir and you know it. I'm just an honest copper doing my job and if I get struck down nothing happens. Nobody, not even my senior officer gives a toss. I know that. But I'm not talking about myself sir. I'm talking about my family. They mean the world to me. If something should happen to them. Sir.'

'You dare threaten me Brighton? I'll bust you back down to constable for this.'

'I wouldn't think so sir.' Brighton changed his tone as he revealed his sword. 'After all, you wouldn't like the press to learn where the funds came for that luxury holiday to Greece or that big house in the country now would you? You won't just be a disgraced ex copper. You'd be a jailed ex copper with no pension, and that's after your assets are seized as proceeds of crime.'

The revelation stopped the Superintendent in his tracks. In three sentences he lost both his advantage and the moral high ground. How could a junior officer know anything about his shady dealings? For the first time in his career, Jimmy Bull caved in.

'Alright I'll see to it. Now get out of my sight.'

On his journey home, Brighton smiled. His bluff worked and he couldn't believe how the old bastard fell for it hook line and sinker. Half the station knew about the holiday and the house. Bull's secretary loved a good gossip, and nothing escaped her eye. If you wanted to know about anything going on at the station all you needed to do was sit within earshot of her at the canteen. All he did was put two and two together. It wasn't hard, considering the high standard of living in the city, and there was no way that even a senior officer could afford to make such plans unless they'd been supplementing their income. Besides thought Brighton, the old git would be gone tomorrow, and any threat perceived or otherwise along with him. He wouldn't dare make a move. Though meagre, the pension and his 'integrity' were all that mattered to Jimmy Bull now.

'Is that you Will?' called Kerry.

'Hi ya,' he said, navigating down the narrow hallway lined with Kerry's paintings from art college.

While she had the talent and still dabbled, Kerry used her keen eye and investigative skills as a side hustle to help an art curator friend confirm the sometimes-tricky provenance trail of selected works before he committed to buying them.

As he neared the kitchenette, he smelled beef stew and his stomach rumbled, reminding him that he hadn't eaten a thing for hours. Thank goodness for the slow cooker.

'Daddy!' squealed his little princess, running down the stairs wearing fairy wings and a huge grin. He scooped her up into his arms and hugged her.

'Guess what Daddy? We did painting today and Mrs Marsh gave me a star and put my reading level up. I'm at level six now. I'm reading Paddington. He's ever so cute!'

She chattered away, telling him all about the day and what she'd done, chirping like a hungry baby bird all the way to the kitchen.

'Go and sit down you,' said Kerry to Emily as Brighton hugged his wife.

'How was work?' he said.

'Really good and I finished early to go to the gallery. Johanne gave me a sneak peek at the Whiteley exhibit that arrived today. You should see it. The man was a genius. They haven't hung one single frame yet and already there is a huge amount of interest for the auction.'

'That's great I can't wait to see it.'

'Neither can I! Evelyn the art critic at the paper is jealous that we have tickets to the launch party this week. She didn't even get a look in.'

Damn. He'd forgotten all about it. The last couple of weeks he'd walked on eggshells at home. After Anna Bolton's death he made an effort to be home more, but this new disappearance threatened him on a number of levels that he needed to tell Kerry about.

'Why don't you go and wash up Emily. I need to talk to mummy for a moment.'

Emily nodded. He waited until her little feet clattered up the stairs.

'What's wrong?' She said as the bathroom door slammed shut above them.

'We've got a bit of a situation. A gangster's daughter has gone missing, and he threatened me today.'

'Who was it? The gangster?'

'I'll tell you if you promise not to report it.'

'Okay. Now who threatened you?'

'Sid Fields'

'Christ. We only saw him the other day. This is more than just a bit of a situation Will. Are you okay?'

'Yeah, but that's not all. He's threatened our family. He knows where Emily goes to school.'

Kerry shivered and he hugged her. Despite her bravado, the investigative reporter knew how dangerous Sid Fields was.

'What are you going to do? Have you pressed charges?'

'It's not that simple I'm afraid.'

'What do you mean? You just told me that he's threatened us! He can't do that.'

'Come on Kerry. You know that his sort can, and his lawyer would make it disappear anyway. He'll say he was worried about his daughter or something like that. Anything to wiggle out of it. Ask your dad, he knows all about it. He's no stranger to Fields either.'

Kerry's dad, the Honourable Jacob Maloney, was a retired Judge and Police Prosecutor and familiar to threats his entire working life.

'I didn't think I'd have to go through this again Will. Do you think he's serious? Are we in danger? Is Emily?'

'We should be fine. A police patrol car will be parked out the front for a few nights. Nothing's going to happen.'

'How did you get old Jim Bull to agree to that?'

Brighton smiled.

'Let's just say Mr Bull is focussing on his retirement.'

'Well, that's a relief. Do you think that we could still go to the opening party?'

Brighton thought for a moment.

'I don't see why not. It should be fine. Besides, I've been looking forward to seeing Whiteley's work. The patrol can look after Emily and the babysitter until we come home.'

'Will they be doing this every night?'

'Yes. Until the girl is found. There's no point in taking any chances.'

'I agree,' said Kerry looking relieved.

After putting Emily to bed, Brighton plonked down in the settee and searched for his book *The Crow Trap* by Anne Cleeves. Even in his own time, his mind was on the job in some form or another. He wanted to call the station and get a patrol car sorted for tonight but doubted that Fields had the nerve to make his point straight after their encounter. Kerry walked over with two steaming mugs of tea.

'She's fast asleep. I don't know how she does it. I wish I could do that.'

As Kerry put the cups down and walked over to her side table, a brick smashed through the bay window, filling the air with shattered glass as it thudded onto the faux wooden floor.

Brighton jumped up and ran to Kerry and hugged her.

'Are you okay?'

'Yeah,' she said struggling to breathe as her anxiety kicked in.

Brighton fished around in his bag with frustration until he found a pair of gloves. There was a piece of paper wrapped around the brick and secured with kitchen string.

He undid the knot and unfurled the paper to read:

If anything happens to her, you and your family are dead meat. Remember that.

Brighton growled with anger. He wanted to drive down to East London and drag Sid to the station by the scruff of his neck. He wanted him to pay for threatening his family. Instead, he called it in because he knew that Fields, his lawyers and his dodgy alibi would always beat the truth.

In his heart he knew that Zaliel had Anna Bell and that the reason he was so agitated was down to one person and one person only. So, he decided to pay his mother a visit.

14

Brighton felt anxious, like he'd just entered the lair of the medusa and wished he had a sword and a polished shield. Considering the way his last encounter with Cecelia Lemon ended, her office in Plymouth was the last place on earth he wanted to visit, but he had little choice. He sought an audience with Anna and the only way to get that was to negotiate with her pet Gorgon.

Glancing around her office, he found it stripped bare aside from a glossy white Nelo study desk, and three replica Eames office chairs in a white faux leather finish. Apart from her degree and the business incorporation documents, the walls were bare. No plants, no graduation photos. He found nothing to tell him anything about her. For now, she remained a mystery.

Cecelia kept him waiting for twenty minutes. Payback for London, he thought. She sauntered in without a word and sat down, ignoring him as she rang her receptionist.

'Reschedule my twelve pm and where is my coffee? I don't care, just get it now.' She slammed the phone down and gave Brighton her full attention, narrowing her eyes and giving him a look that could turn him into stone.

'What do you want?'

'Is civility out of the question?'

'Hmm. You tell me. You're the one that dismissed me the last time we met.'

'You were out of line, and you know it. I could have charged you with evidence tampering, but I didn't.'

'You haven't answered my question. What do you want?'

'I need to speak to Anna.'

His answer startled her, and she tilted her head and laughed like a piranha being told a joke.

'Why? Don't tell me that you're here to reconcile?'

'No. This is about the case I'm working on. One of her fans has lost the plot. He's larping one of her characters Zaliel. He's kidnapped and killed one little girl. Now he's kidnapped another.'

'And what does this have to do with Anna?'

'She may be able to shed some light on his identity.'

'I doubt that.'

'Really? You told me that there were threats made to her before.'

'I did?'

'Yes, at the exhibit. There's a possibility that the person I am looking for has threatened her in the past.'

'I don't think she had any direct dealings with these fans.'

'Well, we need to rule that out and the only way to do that is by talking to her.'

'That's not possible. She is on sabbatical and has given me strict instructions that she is not to be disturbed.'

'Even by her son?'

'Yes, even by her estranged son. She doesn't even want me disturbing her.'

I wonder why, thought Brighton rapping his left fingers on the desk as his patience ran out.

'What if I was to tell you that the new victim's father is a London gangster named Sid Fields. Last night he put a brick through my window with a threat to my family if his daughter is harmed. I have an eight-year-old daughter named Emily. Do you think that Anna would want her young granddaughter to be hurt or worse?'

'Of course not,' she said, unhappy that he played such an emotional card because if she refused, she would make Anna more heartless and colder than Brighton cared to remember.

'Good. Then call her and ask if I can see her.'

'That's impossible. She has no phone, not even a mobile even though she's staying in a remote location. She has no internet, and the nearest post office is a long walk which she can't manage now that she's had her second knee replacement.'

'Then how do to you speak to her?'

'I don't. I wait for her to call from the village and if I don't hear anything I deliver her groceries.'

'When was the last time you went up to the cottage?'

'Last week as it so...' She paused realising he'd trapped her. 'Damn. How did you know she was at the cottage?'

'I am a detective remember?' Duh he thought, trying not to smile. 'Also, the post office gave it away. I remember the distance. She had me walk there after school every day to collect and post her mail. Thanks for your help anyway.' He rose from his chair, glad to finally be out of there.

'Stop. You can't just go up there on your own. I won't allow it.'

He smiled at her discomfort.

'It's a free country Miss Lemon.'

She looked alarmed and if any more colour drained from her pale face, she'd be transparent.

'Please. Let me go with you. It will be easier for everyone, because if I don't go and she finds out I led you to her, I'll lose my only client.'

'Alright you can come along. I'm not going to sabotage your business, even if we don't like each other. I'm not that kind of person.'

The drive to the cottage took no time in Cecelia's cramped Maserati. Brighton had to nurse the bags of groceries which contained all kinds of things that he never thought his mother would like. There were pork scratchings, Penguin biscuits, Lays Crisps, Branston's Pickles, Bovril, and twelve cans of cider. The Chocolate Digestives and Chicken flavoured instant noodles, two cartons of cigarettes and the bottle of Polish vodka on the other hand were for the woman he remembered. He marvelled at the cigarettes. The old bat must have cut down he thought. No way this would last a week.

When they arrived, Brighton didn't want to get out of the car. The two-story cottage was exactly the way he remembered it when he left home, and for a moment he felt as if nothing had changed. What was he going to say to her after all these years?

'Are you coming in?'

Brighton nodded and climbed out of the car, carrying the bags of groceries. He watched as Cecelia knocked on the door. She knocked several times but there was no answer. Typical mother he thought, looking up and seeing movement in the curtain in her bedroom. She'd played this game before, pretending not to be home when she had visitors.

'She's definitely there. I saw the curtains in her bedroom move.'

Cecelia opened the letterbox and called through.

'Hello? Anna? It's Cecelia. Could you open the door please?'

Suddenly she stopped calling. Cecelia hunted in a frenzy through her tiny handbag and retrieved a set of house keys.

'What's wrong?'

'I think there's been an accident.'

'What do you mean?'

'Anna? Anna are you okay?' said Cecelia, ignoring him and fumbling as she put the key into the lock, and opened the front door.

Brighton followed her, as she ran to the crumpled body of his mother lying on the stairs. Cecelia screamed as he turned his mother over. Judging from the fly larvae cavorting about in her eye sockets, Anna Brighton had been dead for some time.

Cecelia gasped and fainted in shock. Gagging at the pungent sweetness of rotting flesh, Brighton grabbed her before she fell and walked her back outside.

'Best we wait here until the police arrive.'

She nodded and quivered, still in shock as she sat down on one of the chairs on the patio.

After he made the call, Brighton went back inside and looked down at her body for a very long time in silence as wave after wave of emotion surfed through his mind. He felt himself choking up the same way he did when he found Marta. Despite their estrangement, and all the terrible things she did to him, there was an overpowering feeling of loss. She was his mother. Now there was no possibility of reconciliation and that left him feeling empty, his feelings unresolved. He felt angry because she never tried to reconcile with him either.

Then he remembered what he had done and felt the dread of impending doom sink in his stomach like a horse swallowed by the swamps of sadness. Not once, but twice, he had told the man who wanted to harm her where he could find her without a second thought. If Zaliel murdered her, it meant that he had technically aided and abetted her killer, and Jeanie knew all about it. That made him feel worse. He turned his phone torch on and looked down at her torso.

'Excuse me! What do you think you're doing?'

A tall athletic woman with long wavy hair that ran down past her shoulders stood in the doorway.

Her partner shuffled behind her. He looked like a tubby reject from The Peaky Blinders. His shifty dark eyes looked Brighton up and down with distrust.

'DI Brighton, Scotland Yard,' said Brighton extending his hand.

'I'm DCI Sharpe and this is DS Charamboulos,' said the woman with an air of authority. 'Step away from the body please.'

'Why are you here?' said Charamboulos with a tone of hostility as the three walked outside. 'This is a local matter.'

Not too bright are you mate? thought Brighton.

'Actually, I'm not here in an official capacity. The deceased is my mother.'

'You're Anna Brighton's son?' said DCI Sharpe taking an interest. 'Why didn't you say that when you called it in?'

'I didn't think it was relevant Ma'am.'

'Really? I would have thought it was. And who is this?'

'I'm Cecelia Lemon, Anna's lawyer.'

'So why are you here?'

'If you really must know,' said Cecelia in the tone Brighton knew only too well, 'I was dropping off supplies and bringing her son for a reunion.'

'Reunion?'

'We lost contact some time ago,' Brighton explained. 'Besides I wouldn't call it a reunion. The purpose of my visit is related to a case I'm working on. There is a possibility that it's connected.'

'That may be, but if you think that I am handing this case over to you then think again.'

'I wouldn't ask you to.'

'Doc's here,' said her sidekick, as a bored middle-aged man dressed more for a dinner date than examining a corpse sauntered through the front gate and stopped in front of them.

'Where is it?' he said, sounding aggrieved and inconvenienced.

'Do you mean my mother's body?' said Brighton surprising himself with unexpected anger. 'Through the door on the landing. Just follow your nose.'

The doctor snorted with contempt as he walked in, and emerged a few moments later, looking a little green in the gills.

'She's dead,' he said, walking back to his car.

Now the circus commenced. As the pathologist and the scene of crime officers filed past, DCI Sharpe continued her questioning.

'So how did you lose contact with your mother?'

'I left home and decided I didn't want to see her anymore.'

'Why is that?'

'It's a long story and quite personal, but the short of it is that I didn't want her in my life.'

'So, you didn't like her?'

'No, I did not.'

'Did you hate her?'

Brighton thought for a moment.

'At first. But I would say I loathed her more after a few years and as time moved on, I had no feelings towards her at all.'

'You don't seem surprised that she's dead,' said Charamboulos.

'What's that supposed to mean? Am I a suspect?'

'We can't rule out the possibility.'

'That's ridiculous. I haven't been here for years. Check my office and ask my wife.'

'Yes, but you might have paid someone to do it. Arranged a hit.'

'Do you know how ridiculous that sounds Detective Sergeant?'

'Who else would benefit from her death? Do you have any other family?'

Benefit? The thought of Anna's estate hadn't even crossed Brighton's mind.

'His sister Marta,' said Cecelia, putting him into an even more uncomfortable predicament.

'Yes. I did have a sister. But she died two weeks ago from a heroin overdose.'

DCI Sharpe gave Brighton a hard stare that he did not like the look of.

'I'm sorry to hear that,' she said, before walking into the cottage.

Cecilia glared at him, realising that he'd deceived her that day in the hostel, but to his relief, she said nothing.

'Did you get along with your sister?' said Charamboulos.

'No. We were estranged.'

'So, you didn't get along with either your mother or your sister?'

'That's right.'

'And now they're both dead.'

Before Brighton could respond, DCI Sharpe returned.

'Our pathologist thinks that the victim might have slipped on the stairs but won't know until she's done the autopsy.'

Brighton waited for the clumsy DS to accuse him of pushing her, but it never eventuated. Instead, it looked like he took his cue from a Midsomer Murders episode.

'We'll be in touch,' he said, with a pathetic impersonation of DCI Barnaby's disparaging look before he and Sharpe walked back to her car.

'Can we go soon?' said Brighton, watching as the ambulance drove away with his mother's body.

Cecilia looked surprised.

'Did you want to stay for a moment? We have permission to go inside.'

'Not really. It's getting late and I've got a long drive ahead.'

'But your mother has died. Surely you can get personal leave? Bring your family here?'

'No thanks.'

Cecelia didn't know what to think. She prided herself with being emotionless but had never seen anything like this before.

'Don't you want to stay and make arrangements? You know, for the funeral and everything.'

'Not really. I have an urgent case in London that can't wait.'

Brighton just wanted to be alone.

'Of course. I understand. But you need to realise that there's a lot to get done and I will need your approval for things. Then there is the estate to consider.'

Estate? thought Brighton. He didn't care less about his mother's estate and all he wanted to do was get as far away for this miserable cottage as possible.

Other than remembering that she'd left the groceries at the house by accident, Cecelia was silent all the way back to Plymouth. Brighton didn't mind, he sat staring straight ahead, all the while processing his mother's sudden death.

15

Brighton's phone woke him from his first deep sleep for weeks. All the overtime, not to mention the drive to Plymouth and back, took its toll on him and he'd crashed on the sofa after dinner. The Met took Sid's threat seriously and kept a squad car parked out the front of their home at all hours, and for the moment, he and Kerry felt a lot safer.

The call was from a silent number, but he answered anyway, thinking it was work.

'Brighton.'

'William finally.'

'What do you want Cecelia?' He rolled his eyes to Kerry. 'It's after nine o clock.'

'I've been trying to get a hold of you for the past two days. Didn't you get any of my messages?'

'I'm sorry but with the investigation, I don't have a lot of time.'

'I see. Have you at least read the will?'

'The will?'

'Don't tell me you haven't received it? I sent it two days ago.'

'I'm not sure. I've hardly been home. And besides, I'm not really interested in Anna's affairs, and could you call me Brighton please? You know I don't like my name.'

'My apologies for upsetting you,' said Cecelia noting his terse tone, 'But you should be interested in your mother's estate. Like it or not, you're her sole beneficiary.'

'And what if I don't want any of her things? Have you considered that?'

'I understand how you feel Will...Brighton, but please don't make any rash decisions until you've thought about it.'

Did she just call me Brighton? he thought. She sounds more like she's my lawyer than Anna's.

'Now regarding her funeral.'

'I told you already. I'm not going.'

'But you're her son. You're expected to go.'

'By whom exactly? Her adoring public or the press? Let's get one thing straight. I'm not going.'

'Please think about it and get back to me.'

'There's nothing to think about Cecelia. If you want to make the arrangements, that's fine. You can throw her into the sea for all I care.'

Brighton hung up. As soon as he put the phone down, it started ringing again.

Kerry saw the frustrated expression on her husband's face.

'What was that all about?'

'She keeps going on about the funeral.'

Kerry looked at him, a little worried.

'You're really not going, aren't you?'

He shook his head. 'No.'

'But Will, she's your mother.'

He looked sad for a moment but felt nothing. There were no tears. No emotion. His attachment to Anna Brighton was just a ring where a bath had once been. Empty void didn't even begin to explain how he truly felt. The truth was that he didn't really want to feel anything. The whole business made him feel trapped and nobody but he understood.

'I can't. I just can't. Okay? I said my goodbyes a long time ago.'

'That's a bit extreme, isn't it?'

'Maybe to an outsider, but that's how I feel.'

'Is that what I am to you? An outsider?'

Brighton sighed.

'I didn't mean it like that. I meant you won't understand.'

'What won't I understand Will? The poor woman's dead.'

'Poor woman?' He scoffed. 'This is what I was saying. You don't know what you're talking about.'

'Well maybe if you hadn't kept her such a big secret from me, I would.'

As Kerry raised her voice, he knew he was in trouble.

'I'm sorry, I wish I'd never told you about her.'

'What a terrible thing to say.'

'It's the truth. I didn't want her in my life and now she's back, the press will be all over this. Is that what you want? Those people are sharks.'

'I'm surprised they haven't picked the story up.'

'Oh, they will and when they do, that's when the fun will start. Now you can understand why I didn't want her at our wedding or anywhere near Emily. She'd have brought them as well.'

Kerry looked alarmed.

'I hadn't thought about that.'

'I have, and if we go to that funeral they'll be camped outside the house for months. Now can you understand?'

'Why didn't you say that before?'

'I was getting to it. Has anything come in the post for me?'

'Sorry, I forgot. This arrived yesterday,' she said, handing him a legal envelope from under her side table.

Brighton took out a thick sheaf of paper and skimmed over it.

'It's her will. It looks like the cottage and her book royalties are all tied up in a trust. They'll be mine when I retire from the force.'

Kerry looked stunned for a moment and was surprised to see how pained her husband looked. She gave him a hug.

'That's fantastic news! How do you feel about it?'

'I don't feel anything. I don't want a single penny. I'd rather give it all to universities and turn the house into a writing retreat or something. That's your world more than mine. Would you be able to ask around for me?'

'Don't you think that's a bit rash? There are loads of good things you can do for others, but we are your family. I'm not saying that I want a

Ferrari or anything stupid, but we should think about our future. We could finally buy a house of our own. We could use the cottage for holidays.'

'Okay. Let me think about it. But I'm not going back to her cottage. Especially not for a holiday. There's way too much baggage.'

'I know where you're coming from. I wouldn't want to go back there either. Not after finding her the way you did.'

His big brown eyes showed Kerrie his appreciation as he reached over and gave her a kiss.

'Thanks for understanding.'

Then Kerry remembered something, and she looked uncomfortable.

'There's something you should know. Before you told me about her, I bought some of *The Magical Wooded World* books for Emily's birthday. But now I'm not so sure. I can put them in a bag for the charity shop if you like.'

Brighton sighed.

'I don't mind if Emily reads them. If I said no, it would be like depriving her of Harry Potter, and I'm not one of those parents. All I ask is that I don't have to read them, and we don't tell her about her famous grandmother until she's old enough to understand.'

'That's fair,' said Kerry. 'I'm still taking everything in myself to be honest. When it rains, it always pours with you. What's going to happen next?'

16

Anna Bell Fields cried, holding on for her life as she whizzed through the skies above London, the wind whipping through her hair. I'm not getting caught again, she thought, struggling to stay awake. When I get home everything will be good again and daddy will strangle him and get me a Big Mac and a strawberry thick shake. Anna Bell didn't see Zaliel's arm reach out until he grabbed her broom and shook her off. She grabbed onto his arm, screaming as her broomstick fell out of sight.

Zaliel held her in mid-air relishing her fear before he let her go, watching her claw into space, plummeting through the air, and thumping down on the bonnet of a five-year-old Audi sports car. The force of the impact and its noisy alarm smashing through the early morning serenity.

She lay there, staring up at him through lifeless eyes. Blood cascading from her mouth soon turned her pretty white coat into a red wet mess, like a slaughtered baby harp seal. Nearby residents milled out of their homes to investigate, and as he flew away, the screams of those first to see her body echoed through the waking streets.

At three in the morning Brighton's mobile phone rang. Yawning, he tried opening his eyes while fumbling around for the phone.

'Sorry to wake you guv,' said Griffiths 'But we've found Anna Bell Fields. She's dead.'

That woke him up. Lifting himself out of bed he stumbled into the kitchen.

'We're sure it's her?'

'Yes sir. One of the responders recognised her picture from the briefings.'

'Good work. Text me the details. I want the whole area cordoned off. Get forensics down there ASAP and wake the family liaison officer up. Wake Jeanie up. I'll be there shortly.'

He kept a set of clothes on his bedside table for times like this so he wouldn't have to turn lights on or keep Kerry awake by rifling through draws. Before he neared the door, his wife groaned.

'Don't I even get a kiss?' She knew the call was work and wanted something for the inconvenience, even if it was just a peck on the lips. He kissed her and hugged her tight.

'Don't forget about tonight,' she said. 'The Whiteley exhibit. Remember? It starts at eight.'

'Okay, I'll try to be back by seven, let's take Emily out of school for the day. I think we should have her stay up at your parents for the night as well. Is that alright?'

'Why? What's happened?'

'We've found the missing girl's body. Sid Fields will be furious, and I'm worried he'll take it out on us. She'll be safer at your parent's place in Highgate.'

'Okay, can we have the police car there as well?'

'Yeah, I'll sort it. Stay safe darling. I love you.'

'Love you too.'

He dressed in the hallway and by the time he'd put his shoes on, his phone buzzed with the address.

Brighton descended into absolute chaos. There was an ambulance and twelve patrol cars, all with their lights flashing. A van of police dressed in riot gear arrived and started dispersing the crowd of tired and angry residents shouting at the police manning the cordon. The media circled like hungry wolves and needed containing as well. Spotting Griffiths speaking to one of the constables, he motioned him over.

'Morning Jimmy. Get this cordon extended please. I want the whole street sealed off. Get those people out of here, especially the media and if they put their drones out, have them pulled.'

The department recently bought several electronic devices that looked like bazookas, designed to shoot drones down by shorting their circuits.

'Yes guv' Griffiths nodded.

'And Jim. You're aware how sensitive this case is. Tell the team that when Fields and his crew shows up, I don't want him anywhere near me, or the crime scene. If his crew gets heavy, I want them sorted out. Including him. Okay?'

'That's a bit excessive innit guv? I mean his kid's just been murdered right?'

'Do I have to remind you Jimmy that we are the police and no two-bit crim like Sid Fields is going to get heavy with my team. Understood?'

'Yes guv.'

Brighton stood alone looking at the dead girl. Where did she fall from? How did she get there of all places? I need to find out fast, he thought, calling the team over to him for a quick briefing.

'Morning everyone. I want you to search all the properties near the scene including the home of the owner of that car. Ask for permission first. If they refuse entry, then get their details, and put uniform outside the front and back of the property until we get warrants. Nobody leaves here or enters without my say so. Jimmy, I want the lane sealed off as well. That goes for the other side of the street. Get all spare bodies looking for any evidence on the ground. Look for anything unusual that may be tied to the case.'

As Jimmy delegated the work, Brighton saw a dark green Honda Civic pull up, waving when he recognised Jeanie Boswell at the wheel. If she was upset about being woken at sparrow fart, it didn't show. She suited up, put her gloves on, and tucked her frizzy red hair under the plastic hoodie.

'Morning guv,' she said, as she strolled over to the Audi.

Looking down at Anna Bell, she took several photos from different angles and noted the indentation in the bonnet. Brighton did not want to waste his time asking about the cause of death.

'So where do you think she fell from?' he asked after a while.

Jeanie looked around.

'There aren't any buildings or trees around here. Just this brick wall that forms a part of the alley behind us and it's nowhere near high enough. I'm guessing that she may have been pushed out of a helicopter. It's the only plausible explanation.'

Brighton nodded, yet there was something different about this case and he could not put his finger on it.

Fields and his crew arrived twenty-five minutes later. Sid left diplomacy in the car and tried to push through the cordon. Eric Grimsby and his other henchmen formed a second front and threw bottles and bricks. When a bottle smashed close to Brighton, he'd had enough.

'Arrest the lot of them,' he yelled.

The riot squad cordon surged forward, outnumbering, and disarming the surprised crims, though a few took two officers to overpower them. Brighton saw Eric Grimsby push through and walk straight for him, gripping a piece of lead pipe in his hand.

'Don't do it Grimsby,' he said standing his ground, protecting both Jeanie and the scene.

Before Grimsby struck, his face contorted like he was having a shit, and he sank to his knees. Behind him stood young Constable Draper, charging the taser in her hand again just in case. She smiled at Brighton before cuffing the semi-conscious muppet, and bundling him off to the crowded Ford Transit Van.

Fields hadn't been arrested. Either he hadn't made a fuss, or the cordon team weren't quite sure what to do. Brighton strolled over to Fields and his minders, two walking wardrobes that took more steroids than a former governor of California.

'I wanna see her,' said Fields without any niceties.

'You may Mr Fields. But first I want your men out of here. Stand them down. You may see her as soon as they've gone. Understood?'

Fields' face flushed red like he was holding his breath, livid with Brighton for having the audacity to give him orders in public. He whistled and the remnants of his crew stopped what they were doing and dispersed. Fields turned to his bodyguards.

'Hop it you two. There's a caff called Mandy's about a block from here. Take the car and wait there. Go on.'

The two big goons drove off in his Bentley and when they were out of sight, Brighton motioned him through the cordon.

Jeanie looked up and saw Brighton and Fields walking towards her and the scene. She wasn't impressed but knew not to question Brighton, so she retreated back to her car, hoping that the coffee she'd picked up at the twenty-four hour McDonald's in Kensington was still warm.

Brighton watched Fields shake when he saw the state of the Audi. When he recognised the body of his little girl he jolted from surprise and shock.

'No!' he screamed.

Brighton held him back.

'That's as far as you can go Sid.'

'Fuck off Brighton. Let me go. I need to see her.'

'You can do that as soon as...'

'No. I want to hold my little girl. Now. Understood?'

Brighton tightened his grip.

'Listen to me Sid. Do you want us to find the people responsible for this? Well? Do you?'

Fields nodded.

'Of course I fucking do.'

'Good. Let us do our jobs. I can't have you holding her yet. Okay?'

'Alright. Let me go.'

When Brighton let him go, the old gangster punched him hard in the nose. No luck could save him this time. Crack! His septum snapped and he tasted the blood pouring into his mouth.

'That's what you get for touching me copper,' yelled Fields sizing him up.

Gritting his teeth Brighton moved in fast, dealing out a barrage of blows before tripping Fields' legs out from underneath him and throwing him to the ground. He cuffed and restrained the surprised thug before Griffiths arrived to assist him.

'Sid Fields, I'm arresting you for assaulting a police officer. You do not have to say anything as it can be used against you in a court of law. Take him away,' he said to Griffiths who marched the struggling criminal over to the nearest patrol car.

'You're a dead man and your family is history! You hear me copper!' Fields screamed as he was bundled away.

Brighton winced and held his head while clamping his nose with his finger and thumb.

'That's nasty guv,' said Jeanie. 'You need medical assistance.'

'I'll be fine. Do you have a first aid kit handy?'

She nodded and retrieved her personal kit from the car.

'Sit still for a moment, I'll fix you up.'

'Cheers. Just focus on the case. Don't worry about me,' he said inspecting the damage through a mirror.

No point in going to hospital, he thought, thankful that his septum hadn't broken through the skin. He dressed the wound with a couple of cotton balls and plasters to cover his nose and stem the bleeding. He wasn't about to leave the scene either.

The sun rose. Commuters gawked as they drove past. Brighton took a couple of painkillers and soldiered on. He halved the team manning the cordon, moving them back to the curb to lessen the impact for the morning traffic. At six o clock he requested updates from the search parties.

'Everyone in the block cooperated guv,' said Griffiths. 'A few were upset about the inconvenience, but when they found out it was Sid's daughter, they all complied. Nothing turned up except for a big bag of weed at the Audi owner's home. It just wasn't his lucky day.'

Brighton changed the focus of the team.

'Good work everyone. We need to get the screens set up to hide the scene from prying eyes. Halve the cordon and leave a few people at key points.'

While his team set the screens up, Brighton sent a few members from uniform to get refs for everyone, and during breakfast he gave his team an idea of what to look for.

'We're looking for animal fur and hessian. Swab all ground for chemicals. Everything goes to Jeanie.'

Brighton called Griffiths over.

'Jim, could you take a quick look in the laneway please, just past where the cordon is. I'll meet you in the middle from the opposite end.

'Yes guv,' Griffiths said and trotted off.

As Brighton passed Jeanie's car, a journalist snuck through the cordon and ambushed him, hoping for a scoop.

'That looks nasty DI Brighton. Did Sid Fields do that to you?'

'No comment,' he said, signalling to two uniformed officers who were having an unofficial break. 'Hey you two. Come here please,' he said pointing at one of them as the sheepish constables shuffled over.

'Sorry for disturbing your extended tea break but could you please direct these members of the media away from the area. And you,' he said to the remaining loafer, 'You're with me.'

He moved towards the entry of the laneway, smiling as he listened to the feigned rage of the journalist and her emotive diatribe about her rights being infringed. When they arrived at the entry point, he told the constable to wait and guard the entrance.

'Don't let anyone in or out unless it's one of us, and unless you want to join the police archives, do not leave this space until I call for you.'

The young copper didn't need to be told twice.

Following the proceedings of the investigation from afar through his obsidian scrying mirror, Zaliel saw the broomstick in a pile of leaves, safe for now from the prying eyes of those pesky humans.

'I must get it back,' he muttered and prepared for a quick return journey. Grabbing his travelling sack, he produced a piece of green chalk from a pocket in his robe, drew a large circle around himself, and four magickal symbols each at compass points. Then he climbed into his sack and secured it to his rope belt.

'Salomay, Dalomay, Adonay! I call thee elemental spirit guide, the guide of the air to do my bidding in the name of the father, the son, and of the Holy Spirit and all most holy Virgin Mary. I command you to appear before me!' he said three times, his performance drifting into Latin until a powerful green light hovered above him. 'Element of the air! I command you to help me and stay whilst my bidding is done. I compel you by the father and the son and the holiest of spirits to stay. I bind thee in the name of the archangel Michael.

The green light appeared to bow in his direction, pleasing the wizard a great deal.

'On my command oh mighty one of the air, send me to the place I desire and when I say 'Home,' I command you send me back here to this tower at this time. Now send me on my way!'

The elemental of the air bathed the wizard in a shroud of green light. After a flash and a blast, he disappeared.

Griffiths looked around the alleyway for anything strange and out of place. There was nothing untoward except for an ancient syringe. His neighbourhood used to be pretty rough, but now there were cafes and croissants, and strange bearded types that rode bicycles and paid a fortune for cereal. There was even a group of steam punks that met every month at the library, a repurposed slaughterhouse from the early nineteenth century. Things were very different.

He wouldn't be caught dead in this alley five years ago, and while Fields' gang tightened its grip on the neighbourhood, they'd also given it a makeover.

The last thing Sid wanted here was a ghetto. This is where his property development arm was. Everyone at the division knew that. What they didn't know about, was Griffiths relationship with Sid.

Griffiths kept a low profile and managed to keep it from the whole station, but when Sid found out that he'd passed his sergeant exams and was privy to all sorts of juicy titbits, he didn't waste any time in reacquainting himself and putting Jim on his payroll.

When his daughter disappeared, Sid wanted regular updates and told the Detective Sergeant to get all the information he could on his boss.

That wasn't too hard for Griffiths, he feigned interest in an old flame in HR, getting into her knickers just to get a peek at Brighton's file. That's how Fields knew so much. He knew where Brighton lived, he knew where his wife worked and where Emily went to school. Jimmy felt guilty about betraying his guv'nor but his family's safety and the extra cash were a bigger priority.

Griffith's phone rang and when he saw the number he decided to answer.

'I told you guys not to use this number.'

'Do you think Sid gives a flying fuck sport? What he does give a fuck about though, what he really wants to know, is where Mr Brighton is going to be tonight. So, tell me or something bad might happen to your sister at school today. Wouldn't want that now, would ya?'

'Alright. He was going to some Aussie art exhibit with his wife. In St Johns Wood. I don't know if he'll be going still on account of Sid breaking his nose.'

'Is his kid going?'

'Doubt it. They have a sitter. Should be home by ten. Hang on a tick. I'll call you back', he said, noticing an ancient broomstick lying in a pile of leaves.

Where did that come from? he thought, looking at a strange row of glowing purple bands around the wood where the bristles were. Definitely not something you'd find at Tesco. As he picked it up, a sack appeared out of nowhere in a flash of blinding green light and made him jump. Zaliel climbed out and stared at Jimmy with hypnotic glaring eyes, reducing him to a paralysed mess, too horrified to say anything.

Before Jimmy could run away, Zaliel pointed his wand at him.

'Nunc Moriatur!' he said without hesitation, sending a bright green pulse of light from the wand, striking Griffiths square in the back, and shutting his body down. The last thing Griffiths did as he collapsed into a dying heap was break a twig off the end of the broom before Zaliel snatched it.

'I'll take that,' said the wizard and stepped back into his sack. 'Home!' he commanded in a booming voice and disappeared in a cloud of green smoke.

The alleyway twisted left and right winding round an old beggar's back, so Brighton didn't see what happened. He didn't hear Zaliel say the deadly words that killed his sergeant, but he did hear someone yell 'home' from further down the laneway where Griffiths was supposed to be. He picked up the pace and through the dissipating green smoke he saw his young offsider sprawled on the ground.

'Help! I need help here,' he shouted. 'Officer down! Officer down! Call an ambulance!' He turned Griffiths over on his back and found a weak pulse.

Griffiths opened his eyes and looked at Brighton as beads of sweat formed on his deep brown forehead.

'It's a wizard,' he said, closing his eyes again as his body gave up and convulsed in Brighton's arms as he died.

'No!' said Brighton trying to revive him, as back up arrived on the scene.

When news spread that an officer died, Superintendent Armitage arrived on the scene.

'You need to get to a hospital DI Brighton. That broken nose looks nasty.'

'I'll be fine sir. I need to work the scene.'

'It's okay Brighton. I'll take over for the moment, and this is not a request. It's an order.'

Brighton decided not to argue. By the time he returned to the scene, it was after four o'clock. The bodies of Anna Bell and Griffiths were at the morgue, the cordon was gone, and most of the team had left.

'I didn't think you'd be back guv,' Jeanie said looking at the new plasters on his nose. 'Are you okay?'

'Yes, thanks Jeanie. I'm glad you're still here. Would you please swab the area where we found Jimmy and do the same tests we did when you found that strange chemical? I heard a man's voice shouting before I arrived. And Jimmy said it was a wizard.'

'Are you saying that Zaliel killed Jimmy?' she said looking serious. 'I'd already swabbed the scene after I found fibres which may be from a hessian sack.'

'Well done,' said Brighton.

Jeanie smiled.

'Thanks guv. Hopefully we'll get some more answers from their clothes.'

He nodded.

'Thanks for all your hard work today. I'll see you later.'

Brighton decided to go straight home instead of the station and a flurry of questions from his superiors. They could all wait until tomorrow.

Brighton entered his home, looking like he'd just lost a cage fight. When Kerry saw the state of Brighton's face, she froze with fear, her heart raced and she started hyperventilating, gasping for air like a caught fish before sinking and flopping on the hallway floor.

'Jesus! Kerry,' he said, running over and holding her while trying his best to reassure her as the anxiety attack kicked in.

'I'm okay. Sorry for coming home like this. I should have cleaned up at work.'

She hugged him.

'What happened to your face?'

'Sid Fields punched me,' he said flinching as her hair touched his sensitive nose.

'Are you okay? I knew about the scene, but my editor decided I was too close to the story and sent Greg to cover it. He never told me you'd been attacked.'

'Yeah, it's broken but it's not as bad as it looks. The doctors said it was a clean break. Work will pay for it to get fixed.'

'He broke your nose? Did you arrest him?'

'I did, but knowing his solicitor, he'll be out soon enough. At least I made it home.'

'What do you mean?'

'Jimmy Griffiths is dead. Most likely murdered.'

It was the last thing any copper's wife wanted to hear, whether he was related or not. Jimmy wasn't a stranger in the Brighton house and got along well with Kerry.

'I don't believe it,' she said struggling to keep it together. 'He was coming over for dinner next weekend. What happened to him?'

'I don't really know. One minute he was alive and laughing. You know what he was like. The next I find him in an alley dying and muttering about wizards.'

Kerry looked confused.

'What did he mean by that?'

'I'm not sure yet,' he said, trying not to spill the beans, because he knew from her look and tone that she was instinctively sniffing out a story.

'I'm worried about you Will. I'm worried about us too. Are we safe?'

'Yeah, we'll be fine darling. I'm more concerned about Jim's family. I'm going around there as soon as I can.'

'Surely you're going to take some leave?'

'I can't. The last thing I need is to step away or step aside. I'm going to get whoever did this and if I need counselling in the meantime, I'll get that too.'

That surprised Kerry because the man she knew kept everything to himself, wrapping up his emotions as tightly as a toasted kebab.

'All I want to do now, is just to go out and see that exhibit with you as I promised. I'm really looking forward to it.'

'Are you sure?'

'As long as you're okay.'

'Yes. I'm fine now.'

'All right. I'll go freshen up.'

Brighton showered and changed into the smart black Brioni suit that Kerry's parents gave him for his last birthday. He looked in the mirror. You don't look too bad, he thought, all things considered.

'Are you ready?' said Kerry, hugging his shoulders from behind.

They heard a car honk outside. He turned and looked at the blue evening gown she wore and smiled.

'You look gorgeous princess. I think our carriage has arrived.'

Kerry took Brighton's hand after he shut the front door, and they walked into the night towards the black cab.

It wasn't the bomb explosion that affected Brighton. That was gone in seconds. Nor being thrown to the ground as the force ripped through his home in moments, turning the very fabric of his little family's most precious memories into a broken fiery mess. As the force threw him into the air, Brighton put his hands in front of him like he was catching a wave at the beach. Considering the intensity of the bomb, he was relatively unscathed aside from cuts and bruises on his hands, and a ripped suit from surfing bitumen. The lingering noise upset him the most. All he could hear were electric pulses of meaningless sound buzzing around in his mind, like a startled horse with a wasp in its ear that refused to leave.

Getting up, he felt pain in his knees and his left ankle. He blinked and tried wiping the brick dust out from his eyes before he found Kerry sprawled out on the pavement nearby. She must have hit the cab because there was a sizeable dent on the bonnet and her beautiful brow was cut and bruised.

He wasn't sure if he whispered or said her name in his normal voice. His voice drowned by the sea of inaudible tinnitus ringing in his ears. When Kerry looked up and hugged him, she just felt grateful that they both survived. He carefully lifted her up to her feet and together they walked as far away as they could. After reaching a safe distance, he left his wife and headed back to the cab to try and get the driver out.

A second explosion sent a huge hunk of burning lumber crashing down onto the cab smashing its windscreen and turning it into a fireball. There was no saving the poor bloke.

Shielding himself with one arm, Brighton called out to his horrified neighbours as they emerged to investigate.

'Get back!' he shouted. 'That was a bomb, and it might have damaged the gas main. The whole place could go in any minute, never mind that bloody car!'

Pandemonium ensued as Brighton made his way back to Kerry and held her tight. Thankfully the ringing in his ears slowly subsided, and as the fire engines arrived, he and Kerry watched the only place that had ever felt like home to them burn to the ground. Brighton felt incensed. His gut told him that only one person could be responsible. Sid Fields.

17

Kerry and Brighton received medical attention at the scene, and while the ambulance officers felt it would be wise for Kerry to be admitted for possible concussion, the two refused, feeling it would be safer elsewhere. Brighton looked at himself in the police car as they drove to Highgate. Not even the best tailor in Saville Row could restore his jacket to its former glory but he didn't care in the slightest. All that mattered was that they were all alive and at Kerry's parents' house.

What a sight they must have been, fronting up out of the blue looking like they'd just auditioned for the Night of the Living Dead. Kerry's mother was distraught when he told them what had happened.

Kerry's father, the Honourable Jacob Maloney enjoyed his son-in-law's company. He'd been a no-nonsense Police prosecutor in the 1990's before accepting a position at the old Bailey and quickly cemented his reputation of being harsh with career criminals like Fields. He took Brighton into his study for a drink, and they settled down in his comfortable armchairs across from the glowing embers of the fireplace that Maloney insisted be kept lit at all times. He puffed away on his pipe and looked in wonder as Brighton recalled the day's events.

'He actually punched you in the face and threatened you in front of a crowd of people?'

'That's right Judge Maloney.'

Brighton called his father-in-law Judge Maloney as a matter of respect, much to the old boy's delight and to the chagrin of his wife and daughter. It brought a smile to his face.

He thought for a good while and his brow furrowed as if freshly ploughed by a team of oxen. When he finally spoke, it was with an air of certainty.

'Do you know something young Brighton? In all my years I have never heard of a villain going after a police officer like this, especially so quickly. It makes no sense at all to me. I mean why would he incriminate himself like that? Sid Fields is many things. He's certainly impulsive and he's demonstrated that he's not beyond threatening people, but at the same time he's not stupid. Secondly, a bomb so powerful that it wipes out a whole building takes time to make and to set up. They're sensitive and not something that one would simply knock together on a whim and plant within hours. Believe me I've sent enough terrorists away to know that. So, you have to ask the question. Who else wants you dead?'

'I can't think of anyone off the top of my head but there must be a few people that bear a grudge.'

He thought about the possibilities. There was the Russian Oligarch that he'd sent down for bribing an MP. He had means and motive, but he was happy in his cell in a low security prison, a far better outcome than being deported back to Mother Russia.

He and Jim had done a few operations in the Angel and up in Old Kent Road. Yardies mostly. If his living room had been peppered with machine gun fire, then he'd put them on his list, but bombs were not their usual modus operandi.

'I'm not sure Judge. But whoever it was accessed the property, potentially in broad daylight. How would anyone find us in the first place?' He thought back to his mother's solicitor, Cecilia Lemon. How had she found him?

'Well, I would wager that it's not that hard to do these days,' said Maloney. 'Old school detective work for starters. There are loads of private detectives about, and most of them are former coppers with a grudge. And of course, there's that damned Internet. Nothing is private anymore. Your mobile telephone can be turned into a tracking device with one foul text. But there is another alternative. The information could be coming from someone on the inside.'

'With all due respect Judge, I don't even want to think about that.'

'But you must Will. You must face the possibility that someone you trust or have trusted in the past has ratted you out. I know that the idea of betrayal messes around with you and creates trust issues, but I've seen it time and time again Will. Now, who in your team knew about tonight? More importantly who knew when you'd be leaving? Is there anyone who knew about that? Is there anyone who may have made a real effort in the past months to get close to you and bond with you? Do you know anyone who has contacts in human resources?'

Brighton shook his head, but he realised that Jimmy ticked a few of those boxes. The young DS had been eager to make his mark, and they had spent many hours together in recent weeks. What did he tell Jim? He racked his brain trying to think and remembered that he told Jim about Brett Whitely and Jim told him that Whitley's work sounded like a visit to the morgue. Jim's idea of art didn't venture far from The Beano.

What did he know about his offsider? He struggled to remember, and after a while he had enough suspicion that he decided to make a few discrete enquiries starting with Jim's mobile phone. He thanked his father-in-law and changed the subject by telling the judge about Bull being a corrupt old fart. Old Maloney laughed when Brighton told him about their encounter.

'Ha! I knew that old James Bull was as corrupt as they came. Oh, I'd love to have been a fly on the wall when you put the frighteners on him! He's a lily-livered coward and I don't half doubt that he shit his pants in fear!'

The old judge coughed and wheezed and laughed so much that the door of the study opened, his good wife entered, and judging from the look on her face, she was clearly not amused.

'Jacob Maloney what are you doing drinking at this hour? Here I am, trying to calm our poor daughter down and all the while, you two are having the time of your lives! I think it's time you went to bed, don't you?

You have your examination in the morning and if you think you're going to wheedle your way out of that again you are quite mistaken!'

She slammed the door and went back to Kerry.

Brighton had no idea what the examination entailed, but if it was the one he was thinking about which involved a cold rubber glove and touching your toes, he understood why the old judge was reluctant. He certainly wasn't laughing anymore, and the colour drained from his face like he'd just kissed a vampire.

'Well boy, you heard the voice of reason. I suggest we leave it there and continue tomorrow,' he said putting out his pipe.

'Thanks for listening Judge. I appreciate it.'

'Any time young Brighton and thank you for looking after our girl. She needs all the love she can get.'

Brighton stood and shook Maloney's hand. As he exited the room, he smiled when he heard what sounded like another large whiskey being poured.

Later, Brighton lay next to Kerry on the sofa bed in her mother's sewing room. It took some time and a few sedatives, but she'd finally gone to sleep. He wished that he too could close his eyes and drift away, but his mind was focussed on both work and what the judge had said. How on earth did Sid strike so early? Surely the patrol car would have seen something before they drove to Kerry's parents' home. There was still the issue of the threat that Fields had made against him to his face, witnessed by most of his team. The judge was right. As far as Sid was concerned; Brighton was responsible for his daughter's death, but why would he do something so brash? Brighton knew that Fields was dangerous, but he just couldn't see him making a threat like that and going ahead with it on the same day, even if he had a right to be upset.

He thought about his own daughter. How were they going to tell Emily that all her things were gone and that she'd never be able to go home ever again? How would she feel? Never mind that she'd met the murder victim.

The thought of never going back to their home absolutely devastated him and he knew that Kerry wouldn't be able to cope either. It was too much to ask her to pretend everything was back to normal after something like that. If Emily's life had been taken, there was no telling what Brighton might have done. He couldn't stop thinking about it. He was angry. Everything about his well-ordered life and their modest plans for the future were up in the air now, and it felt as if nothing mattered. He felt like he was a fugitive on the run. Things were never going to go back to normal, and he knew that he and his family would be targets for as long as Sid Fields drew breath. He closed his eyes and hoped that tomorrow would bring a solution to the problem.

18

'What are we going to do with you DI Brighton?' said Armitage as he sipped from his morning coffee.

'Well sir, I'd like to keep working the investigation. We have a lot of new evidence from both the scene and my sister's room and ...'

Armitage shook his head.

'Come on that's out of the question and you know it.'

'Not if we remand Sid Fields, sir.'

'On what grounds?'

'Assaulting a police officer for starters.'

'You and I both know that even if we remanded him in custody his brief would have him walking free in hours. It took no time for him to achieve just that yesterday afternoon as you may well know.'

Brighton knew alright, but the idea of a gangster as ruthless as Sid walking the streets after he assaulted a career copper didn't sit well with him. He frowned.

'Are you suggesting that he gets away with what he did to me?'

'Absolutely not, but we're better off getting him on attempted murder with the bomb.'

'But sir that could take months. We're still combing through the wreckage, CCTV, and witness statements for any evidence that would identify the bomber. Meanwhile Fields remains free.'

'That should be the least of your worries. You know he wants you dead. It's all over the streets. The bomb showed us that he doesn't care if he takes your family out with you either. We must consider your safety.'

'What are you suggesting sir?' said Brighton. 'Protective custody?'

'Well, that's one option. Unless you have somewhere else in mind that's out of London and off the radar.'

Brighton twisted his face in pain.

'I might have somewhere, but I swore that I'd never go back there.'

'Sometimes we have to do things even if we don't like them.'

'Yeah, but this isn't really an option sir.'

'I see. Where is this place if you don't mind me asking?'

'It's an old cottage, just north of Princetown near Wistman's Wood.'

'Never heard of it.'

'It's close to Dartmoor sir.'

'Dartmoor? Hmmm, that's remote enough from London to be off Sid Fields' radar and you'd be able to keep your freedom.'

'I really don't want to go back there. Not if I can help it. And besides, how am I going to work? I can't investigate my caseload remotely.'

'It's close to Plymouth, isn't it?' said Armitage in deep thought. 'A good friend of mine is the Detective Chief Inspector down there. Her name is Hayley Sharpe. I'll call her if you like and put in a good word. We might be able to arrange a temporary transfer until everything settles down a bit. What do you think?'

Brighton wondered about that. He'd met Sharpe at the cottage and wasn't sure if it would work. But he was running out of options, anything was better than protective custody and sitting around some strange house for months. He'd rather be working and living a normal life. Still, there was the family to consider.

'Sir I think that's a great idea, but it's very sudden. I'd like to talk things over with my wife first. It's a big decision for both of us.'

'Alright, but let me know soon. Our budget is thin enough as it is, and we simply can't afford round the clock security for you for much longer.'

Brighton arrived back to his in-laws to find his wife alone in the kitchen.

'Hey babe. Where is everyone?'

'Grampa and Grandma took Emily down to the Heath. Dad bought her a new kite, and she got all excited.'

'Fair enough. Why didn't you go with them?'

Kerry looked at him as tears fell from her beautiful brown eyes.

'Hey, what's wrong love?' He said with concern as he put his arm around her and gave her a comforting hug.

'It's my job. I had to resign.'

'What on earth for?'

'Sid Fields rang my office yesterday looking for me and wanting to know where you were. He threatened my editor Matthew, and Johanne at the gallery as well!'

Brighton liked both men and he felt really bad about them being threatened.

'Are they okay?'

'Matt is. He's used to it, but Johanne is terrified.'

'Then he needs to press charges!'

'He won't. Everything he owns, everything he's built will go up in smoke if he does. They practically told him that.'

Brighton frowned as anger and weeks of pent-up frustration burned deep inside him. He felt guilty that Kerry's career and friends were affected the most and that he was powerless to stop Fields.

'I'm really sorry love.'

'It's okay. I'm not blaming you for this Will. I knew what I was getting into when I was marrying a copper. Dad told me as much, but I never thought in a million years that your job would ever do this to us. I can't believe that we were nearly blown up! I just want this to be over.'

'So do I love, you know that. Armitage just made things difficult for us as well.'

'What do you mean?'

'He told me that we have to choose between protective custody or moving away. The Met can't afford to maintain our security.'

'Well, that's just great! What are we supposed to do?'

'There's only one option and I was dead against it, but it's the only way we get to keep our freedom. We move into Anna's cottage.'

'But that's miles away, isn't it?'

'Exactly. It's miles from here and Sid and his gang.'

'And my parents and any prospect of me getting another real job! What am I supposed to do for work?'

'Armitage is reaching out to a contact in Plymouth. There might be something there for you as well.'

'Why Plymouth?'

'Because it's not far from the cottage. Only about an hour or so.'

'And where is Emily supposed to go to school?'

'There's one in the village not far from the cottage. It's small but at least it's nearby.'

'Well, that's not so bad then,' she said cheering up a bit. 'Plymouth is a bit regional, but there is a decent arts scene there and a few magazines if I remember correctly. But what about you? Could you handle living in a place with so many bad memories?'

'I'll survive somehow. At least the worst memory is no longer with us, and I'd rather be there than having to expose you and Emily to being shut away and moved around all the time. I think we've been traumatised enough.'

Kerry nodded. Both of them were in two minds about the road ahead but knew it was for the best.

'I don't know what my parents are going to say but leave it with me. I haven't even told them about your famous mum yet.'

'I guess we're going to have to,' said Brighton, surprising her. 'It's the only way for them to understand how we knew about the place. Besides I am sick of keeping secrets from everyone.'

'Who are you?' said Kerry feigning a look of surprise with a faux gasp, 'and what have you done to my husband?' she smiled. 'I'm so pleased you said that.'

'That's okay. It's long overdue, I think. Now all I've got to do is call the crazy woman that Anna left in charge of her estate.'

'Please come and see me as soon as you're settled,' said Cecelia Lemon, when Brighton called to discuss the cottage.

Considering the way their previous encounter ended, she seemed genuinely concerned for both Brighton and his family, agreeing to accommodate their immediate needs as a priority.

'We need to discuss Anna's estate.'

'Okay, I'll make an appointment with you shortly. Thanks again for all your help.'

'All sorted,' said Brighton to Kerry as he put his phone away. 'She'll send the keys and get the place cleaned up. With any luck, we should be able to move in by the end of next week. She was really helpful about the whole thing.'

'Well, that's good news, considering what you told me about her.'

'Yeah, that's a bit of a concern to be honest. She's almost too nice if you know what I mean.'

'Yes, Mr Detective,' said Kerry rolling her eyes. 'Honestly, it's like people aren't allowed to be nice. You are her new boss remember.'

'I forgot all about that. Maybe you're right.' Not likely, he thought, trusting his copper's instinct, *I wouldn't trust her as far as I could throw her.*

19

After a long drive, Brighton pulled up outside the remote cottage in darkness. Both Kerry and Emily were fast asleep.

'We're here love,' he said to Kerry, gently waking her. 'I'll go and find some lights. Hopefully the power is on.'

Kerry groaned and stretched her arms as he turned on the interior car light. Grabbing his torch and the house keys, Brighton opened the creaky front gate and walked down the short hedge lined path. He tripped over on the tiny narrow steps leading up to the veranda and went slamming into the black front door. The sound reminded him of the time when his mother slammed it in his face all of those years ago.

'Are you okay Will?' called Kerry from the car.

'Yeah, I'm fine.'

Lifting himself up, he remembered which key in the bunch opened the door and put the key in the latch. The hinges resisted all his efforts and Brighton pushed hard on the door three times to get it open. He started making a mental list of what needed fixing. To his surprise, the air that greeted him smelled fresh, a curiosity considering that his mother smoked more than a pack a day, sometimes two packs when she was writing in the zone. Cecelia must have aired the place out.

He found the hallway light switch to his left and flicked it on. Nothing. Not even a flicker. Great, he thought finding his way down the hallway to the kitchen, where he hoped to find some candles. To the left lay the pantry, a long narrow space with shelves crammed with all sorts of things. His best chance of finding candles or a lantern. Shining the torch around the shelves, Brighton looked in marvel at the space. There was no logic to it at all. A chaotic clutter of dry goods, canned goods, home-made preserves, storage, and cleaning products. Plastic boxes filled with buttons and pencils, and old-fashioned biros collected from hotels around the country when she'd done her tours. His luck changed when he found a jar full of birthday cake candles, some still had remnants of cake icing on them, a box of tea lights, and sure enough, two boxes of old candles. Those will do fine, he thought and took both boxes.

Walking back into kitchen, he tripped over something hard on the ground, the inertia sending him crashing into the dining table. Even though he'd hit his police issue torch hard on both the table and the tiled floor, it still worked fine. The candles weren't so lucky and scattered in every direction. Shining his torch, Brighton found the culprit. He'd forgotten all about the brownie bowl. The little cast iron bowl had been there long before his mother moved in, and possibly for hundreds of years. Whoever had fixed it to the floor put it in a strange spot between the pantry and the hearth, almost in the thoroughfare.

'Are you okay?' said Kerry walking in with Emily in her arms as Brighton lifted himself up. 'That's two falls now.'

'Oh, I'm fine darling'

'That's a relief. What's that thing on the floor? Is that what you tripped over?'

'Why yes. That thing is a brownie bowl, for the house brownie.'

'The what?'

'The house brownie. Folks around here believed in them and some probably still do. They're like guardians of the house and they watch over you.'

As he said that, the strangest thing happened. The light in the hallway flickered on.

'That's a bit freaky!' said Kerry.

'No, it's probably just the old wiring in the place. I bet it's not been maintained for years.'

Kerry found the switch for the kitchen and the light worked straight away. Brighton looked around as the memories came flooding back. The antique table he'd hit was just as he'd remembered. French provincial oak with a gorgeous dark chocolate finish. The matching chairs were big, thickset, and made to last. This was the table of his childhood, and he wondered if his mother had ever found the place he'd carved his initials when he was six. It made him curious to see if they were still there, but that discovery could wait until later.

'There's a note here,' said Kerry picking up a piece of paper with the neatest and daintiest handwriting she'd ever seen.

> Dear Brighton and Kerry,
> Welcome home. You'll find that the house has been cleaned, I have made a few changes and bought some essentials for you, as the nearest shop is three miles away and I doubt it shall be open when you arrive. Rubbish collection is every Tuesday, and I have left the bins in the laneway where they get emptied. I look forward to meeting you both when convenient to discuss your mother's estate.
> Yours sincerely,
> Cecilia Lemon.

Kerry looked up and smiled.

'That was good of her darling.'

'I guess so. I wasn't expecting anything at all.'

'Let's see what essentials she's bought for us,' said Kerry, 'Fingers crossed that there's some tea.'

She put Emily down on one of the chairs and she and Brighton searched through the kitchen together like they were on a treasure hunt.

'I found some milk,' he said, looking in the refrigerator 'And a carton of eggs and a packet of butter!'

'There's a fresh loaf of bread in the bread bin!' said Kerry.

'Brilliant! I found some marmalade in the pantry. We could have that or eggs on toast for breakfast in the morning.'

'Yes!' said Kerry smiling as she held up her prize find, an unopened packet of tea bags.

He hadn't seen her this happy in weeks. Brighton filled the kettle and put it on the gas stove, which lit up when he turned it on.

'Let's go and have a look around,' he said. 'I wonder what the changes are.'

Brighton gave Kerry a full tour. The front room had a lounge suite and was completely lined with bookcases and piles and piles of books.

'There's no tv or stereo,' he explained, 'She couldn't stand either of them. Silence was her thing.'

After he closed the front door, Brighton took Emily from Kerry's sore arms and climbed up the stairs, opening the first door he saw.

'This was Marta's room,' he said, turning on the light to reveal a small pink bedroom with a brand-new single bed, all made up.

All of Marta's band posters were gone and there was not a trace of her to be found.

'What a great space for Emily!' said Kerry.

They tucked Emily into her new bed and kissed her goodnight, making sure to leave the light on for her just in case she woke up. Further down the hall Brighton showed Kerry his old room, which was about the same size as Emily's. He wasn't surprised to find it cluttered and piled with boxes. A makeshift storeroom. Like Marta, everything he'd left behind was gone. At the corridors end stood the door leading into his mother's room. He stood outside for a moment, hesitant and unsure. Kerry saw the apprehension on his face.

'It's okay Will,' she said.

'You're right. Let's get it over with.'

To his relief there was a new mattress on the four-poster bed, made up with new sheets, pillows and a huge doona in a navy-blue cover, which matched the walls and the curtains. The rest had been left the way it was.

His mother's dressing table was French and Art Nouveau. The central mirror was joined by two smaller mirrors on either side that looked like they'd be more at home in Rivendell than Dartmoor. Each had matching borders, two swans with necks that entwined and met face to face at the top like they were kissing each other. The chair had a similar motif.

Kerry looked impressed.

'This is lovely,' she said, admiring the furniture.

'Yeah, well Anna may have been a bitch, but she did have a bit of style, I guess. Possibly her only redeeming quality. I'm just glad we don't have to sleep on her mattress.'

Kerry nodded, equally relieved. She saw that the bedroom veered off to the left in an L shape.

'What's behind there?'

'Oh, that's where she used to write. I'm going downstairs. I think I can hear the kettle boiling.'

This is going to take some getting used to, he thought, walking out the room. Anything to change the subject and not think about being in a place where he felt he was trespassing.

As he left, Kerry snuck a peak at Anna's writing space. She found a decent size nook with an empty antique desk, a typewriter and three new, secure locked filing cabinets. She smiled, thinking about all the possibilities and began making plans for her home office. I really need a project, she thought, and this would be a great opportunity. She started thinking about writing a huge exposé of Anna's work and curating a touring exhibition around the world. Kerry understood the animosity between her husband and his mother, yet at the same time, she knew that Anna was well loved and that her legacy would require careful management. Whether they liked it or not, Anna was the key to their futures.

20

The next morning Emily burst into their room and jumped on the bed.

'Mummy! Daddy!' she said, waking them up with a start.

Brighton and Kerry groaned, and then groaned even more when Emily opened the curtains, bathing the room in the brilliant dawn light. Little pest thought Brighton looking at his mobile phone, which they used as an alarm clock. There were only five minutes to go before the alarm went off. There was no turning back now.

'Wake up you,' said Kerry, giving him a hug as he rolled over and pretended to sleep. 'It's a big day today.'

Brighton had other ideas, he didn't fancy going anywhere, especially to see that psycho lawyer, and when he didn't budge, Kerry gestured to Emily to tickle his feet.

'Wake up daddy!' said his mischievous kid, lifting the duvet and tickling his feet with both hands. He pretended not to feel anything and then grabbed her in his arms.

'Alright Alright,' said Kerry, 'Enough you two. Could you get her breakfast ready while I have my shower?'

Brighton nodded and went down to the kitchen with Emily.

'What do you think of your new home?' he said as they walked down the stairs.

'It's big and there's a garden and everything. Can we grow some flowers dad? Can we go and see the woods? I saw them through my window. They look magical.'

'I guess so. Would you like eggs on toast?' he said, changing the subject as they walked into the kitchen.

'As long as you don't burn them like last time,' said Emily, reminding Brighton that the kitchen was still a final frontier for him and that his forte was boiling water.

'Cheeky monkey,' he said. 'Okay. Why don't you supervise me.'

She smiled and nodded. Even though she was only eight, Emily showed a real interest in cooking and sometimes Kerry let her help with making dinner. He wasn't sure if she would be confident cooking on a gas stove and decided that would be Kerry's call.

Emily's new school was at the little village nearby and she was excited to be around other kids again.

'Now, do you remember what I told you?' said Kerry before they left the car.

'I know, I know,' said Emily, impatient to make new friends. 'I promise not to tell anyone about our home or who my mummy and daddy are.'

'Good girl,' said Brighton, giving her a hug and watched as Kerry and Emily walked into the administration building.

The bombing and Sid Fields had been all over the news and neither of them wanted the word to spread back to Sid about where they were. Even though it was unlikely, they still had to take every precaution.

Brighton wasn't waiting for long at the reception of Plymouth Police Station, before a familiar tall woman approached him.

'Well, well DI Brighton. We meet again,' said Hayley Sharpe

He stood up.

'Yes ma'am.'

'Follow me,' she said leading him down the long white sterile corridor to her office.

'Okay,' she said sitting across from him at her tatty old laminate desk. 'Let's get one thing straight. I don't like being called ma'am. I prefer guv'nor or just guv. I run a tight ship, and the team will vouch for that. You'll see for yourself in a few weeks. Now I spoke to your boss, and he told me that you've experience running operations, and you were in the drug squad once.'

Brighton nodded.

'Excellent. You'll be taking over an operation we've been running for some time. Let's go and meet the team.'

'Guv is it okay if I start work tomorrow, please?'

She sighed and looked suitably unimpressed.

'I was hoping you'd start today DI Brighton. That's why I've taken time out of my schedule to see you. This isn't some meet and greet you know.'

'I appreciate that. But the thing is that I only got here late last night and there are things I need to sort out. I can start early tomorrow though.'

Her disappointment was immediate.

'Fine. Start tomorrow morning,' she said thinning her lips as she glared at him. 'When you arrive, I want you to go to the front counter and ask for my offsider Peter Charamboulos. You've met him before. He is now your DS, and he will brief you on the operation. I'm sure you can work the rest out for yourself. Understood?'

'Yes guv. Thank you.'

Brighton turned and hightailed it out of there before the old dragon breathed fire on him. That could have gone a lot better, he thought as he walked back into reception. I'll have to really land on my feet to win her around.

∼

'How did everything go?' said Kerry when they met up outside the office of Cecilia Lemon.

'Hmm. Let's just say that the jury is out for the moment. Best not to judge people on first impressions.'

'Say that to my dad the next time you see him,' said Kerry laughing.

Brighton smiled and wondered how many people the judge had assessed before they opened their mouths. He'd made a real effort to dress up when he first met her parents, and it paid off.

'Ah Brighton, how nice to see you again', said Cecelia Lemon peering at them from her elegant designer Gucci frames, with a twisted fake smile.

She rose from her seat and extended her hand. When he reached over to shake it, Brighton noticed the mark on her right wrist again. It was a curious little brand mark of a decorative letter G which looked like it been there for quite some time. She saw his stare and withdrew a little too soon.

'Thanks for arranging everything at the cottage,' said Kerry, coming to the rescue. 'That was very kind of you.'

'Oh, you're most welcome,' said Cecilia, 'I left the provisions we bought a few months ago and got the cleaners to pick up a few essentials from the village.'

Brighton couldn't recall seeing any of the things in the pantry including the booze and put it down to the builders Cecelia hired to refurbish the house. He decided to let it pass.

'Now I guess you'd like to know more about Anna's will.'

Brighton nodded. Cecilia opened her laptop and read aloud.

'The last will and testament of Anna Brighton.

To my son, William Brighton, I leave my home to live in as he wishes and to come and go as he pleases. If he decides not to live in the property or to visit it, or that he wishes to sell the cottage then I shall bequeath the property to the University of Plymouth to be used as a writer's retreat and writers in residence.

The property shall remain in the management of my fund until such time as it is dissolved. The offices of my solicitor Cecilia Lemon or her successor will manage my fund, known as Anna Brighton Investments. The fund manager shall receive a fee of twenty-five per cent per annum passed on performance. The fund will be dissolved on the retirement of my son from the police force. Should he be unfortunate not to live until retiring age, then the fund shall pass to his daughter and shall be accessible to her at retiring age or her children etc. If the fund is not dissolved and there are no surviving beneficiaries, the fund will automatically transfer to my solicitors.'

No wonder she's making an effort to be nice, thought Brighton as Cecilia continued.

'Fund Access. There shall be no access to the fund unless there is a dire emergency involving threat to life, family, or unforeseen hardship. Cecilia has been given strict instructions on determining these instances and has been given discretion to act accordingly.'

Cecilia looked up at them, half expecting disappointment, particularly from Brighton, but instead she found disinterest. He didn't have to tell her that he didn't care about his mother's estate whatsoever. It was written all over his face. He was not happy that the old bag had completely disinherited his sister.

'That's why I cleaned the cottage up for you and arranged everything,' she explained. 'Under the circumstances I felt it needed to be done. I've had the fittings inspected and the wiring will be completely redone, as it's not as safe as it should be. There are a hundred and one things to do and I'm glad that you're living there.'

That makes one of us, Brighton thought. Then Kerry spoke and sent him off kilter.

'I have a question regarding Anna's work and the cottage. I'm a journalist and also helped a gallery manager recently.'

Cecelia nodded.

'I know,' she said, 'I did some research before you both arrived. I hope you don't mind.'

Brighton was not surprised. After their last encounter, he'd searched for her online as well and hadn't found as much as he'd hoped. There wasn't much on him either. Neither of them used social media and aside from a few academic papers, Cecelia barely existed.

Kerry didn't seem to care at all.

'That's okay. As you know I've had to leave my job and there seems to be a cloud hanging over Anna's legacy. There's work to be done. Work that I'm more than capable of doing. Her biography, her archive, and potential exhibits of her work. I was even thinking about hosting writers' events at the cottage when we eventually move out again.'

Brighton didn't know what to think. He wasn't happy with his wife's new interest. But he supposed that it would be like a fan of Diana Wynne Jones, or Roald Dahl, or Terry Pratchett, being given an all-access pass.

'As long as I don't have to be involved, I'll support you,' he said. After all he had disrupted her career.

Cecelia listened with interest.

'Wow that sounds great, and it's really very kind of you to offer. I'd need to think about it. I hope you don't mind. I'm not sure about the book. I have someone in mind that specialises in literary biographies, but I am interested in the exhibits and the workshops. The archive is being shipped to the Bodleian at Oxford as Anna had an honorary doctorate in literature there. Once they have documented everything, I'm sure we can plan for an exhibition.'

Kerry tried not to look disappointed about the book or react to the smug look on the lawyer's face.

'Thank you, Miss Lemon,' said Brighton reading the room and going into damage control. 'Is there anything else that we need to discuss or know about?'

'No. A few minor details but I'm sure we can manage for the time being. Do either of you have any further questions?'

'Yeah. Are you able to recommend a good locksmith?' said Brighton.

'For what purpose?'

'For security. I would like to get the locks changed.'

Celia frowned. 'I'm afraid I can't allow that.'

'Why's that then? I'm sure that you'll agree that given the circumstances, we need much better security at the property than there is. We'd make sure that you get a key and the codes for the alarms.'

'Your mother has stipulated that there was to be no change to the premises.'

'Then why did you paint Emily's room?'

'Your daughter's room was originally pink so we could repaint it, but no new colours can be added. No wallpaper and certainly no unsightly security devices.'

'But it's all old hat.'

'Precisely. That front door lock is a heritage lock dating back to the 1800s. I can't have it removed or added to with twenty-first century latches. You're living in a heritage-listed cottage Mr Brighton. It's like living in a museum or staying for a weekend in Sir John Soane's home in Holborn.'

Kerry nodded and Brighton was glad she understood the reference, because like most Londoners he had no idea. Living in a big city full of cultural sites and curiosities was lost on him. Like a lot of people, he wanted to go to the British Museum or The Imperial War Museum, and catch a show in the West End but barely had time to read his book at night, and the weekends were gone in the blink of an eye. Most of his mates finished work, grabbed a curry, and watched Coronation Street, East Enders, and Big Brother if they were up for it. Or it was down the pub and chat on Facebook messenger over pints posted on Instagram.

'I really don't care,' said his favourite server Karen at the canteen when he asked her if she'd been to the Tower of London one afternoon. 'I mean seriously I get that it's a part of history an all but I ain't no history buff and it's just too far from Kilburn for me to care really. I'd have more fun going on another cruise to Jamaica and St Kitts. Know what I mean?'

21

'Settling in alright boss?'

Brighton looked up from the pile of files on his desk to see his offsider Peter Charamboulos back from yet another break of some kind.

'Yeah, I guess. Where have you been?'

'Oh, you know. Just stepped out for a bit like. Old Matt didn't mind that.'

'Oh right. Well, I'm not old Matt, so in future could you ask me before you go running off somewhere please.'

Peter's perplexed look and curled lip indicated that he didn't know what to make of that. Rather than push the envelope, Brighton changed the subject.

'Tell me what we know about Billie Brown and Darren Rocco.'

'Not much to be honest. They're not exactly master criminals and they would have stayed off the radar if they hadn't trod on their rival's toes.'

Brighton knew what Peter was talking about. For some inexplicable reason, Billie and Darren seemed to have acquired really good intel on all their competition, that good that it could only have come from the Met.

'Who do you think they get their inside knowledge from?'

'I don't rightly know boss. They just seem to know everything,' said Peter, twitching with discomfort.

Brighton knew he had to be careful about how to move forward. His predecessor had suddenly retired, and he had a sneaking suspicion that someone paid him off to keep shtum.

'Fair enough. Look I think that the best way forward is to start from scratch. We'll use some basic information and then build the case by compromising their organisation and coercing one of their employees to inform on them.'

'Hey that's a great idea,' said Peter looking somewhat relieved.

'I'm glad you agree. Now do you have any possible candidates?'

'Well, there is one that stands out. Helene Henderson's her name. She's been a small-time dealer for them on and off for some time.' Peter rummaged through the files and pulled out a photo. 'This is her.'

Brighton knew just by looking that it wasn't going to be easy to get her to grass on anyone. She looked as nasty as a Rottweiler's ass with haemorrhoids. Her face was harsher than solar keratosis and looked more masculine and well older than a woman barely in her thirties with a small child.

'Helene's got a sheet going back to when she was caught standing over her entire form at school and menacing them for money.'

'Sounds like a right character,' said Brighton reading her file with interest, noting that she was only fourteen then.

Multiple expulsions later saw her in and out of juvenile detention until she stole her former principal's car and smashed it into his home because he'd assaulted her. That saw them both jailed. She went away for five long years and moved back in with her mother upon release.

'I reckon prison gave her the education she missed out on boss, and her new mates sent her knocking on Darren Rocco's door for work.'

While others may have read the file and seen a hard ass, Brighton saw a woman with a wasted and institutionalised life. A single unsupported woman with an elderly mother and a young son to care for. That to him made her vulnerable.

'I dunno Peter,' he said, playing his cards to his chest. 'Hey, go grab some more of those files and let's try to find a couple more candidates in their organisation, before we make up our minds.'

On the way out, Brighton reported to Hayley Sharpe and gave her an idea about his plan.

'For security purposes, let's keep it between ourselves for now. The less people that know the details the better.'

Sharpe was anything but supportive. In fact, she looked insulted.

'Why? What's the idea of having secrecy? Don't you trust my team DI Brighton?'

'Guv, I don't know the team well enough to trust them and I don't know you either. But it's obvious just reading about Rocco and Brown, that they are receiving information that could only have come from the Met.'

'You're insinuating that someone on my team has been compromised!' she said raising her voice, 'Do you have any idea how hurt that makes me feel?'

'It's not an easy thing for me to say guv. I've been here for five minutes, and I don't know anyone. This isn't new to me either. I've seen it before in London.'

'It's a serious allegation Brighton.'

'It's more of a potential risk than an allegation guv. I'm not saying anyone is bent. I'm not asking to investigate a leak or sending anything to internal investigations. I'm asking that we work together to minimise the risk of this operation being compromised.'

Hayley Sharpe smiled and slowly clapped her hands, catching Brighton off guard. He didn't know what to think.

'Well done,' she said, 'Armitage told me you had a pair of balls, and it takes balls to come in here and say what you just did. I like that. Tell me, do you think I don't know that there might be a leak? I felt the same way after my old DI retired. I thought that he was the rat, but he wasn't. I told you I run a tight ship, and I notice everything. I'm the first in and the last to leave. I look at desks. I audit phone accounts, emails and messaging. I've searched and I haven't found a thing. Now if you can include this in the investigation and we can draw the poison out, even better.'

Brighton nodded. Her whole pantomime had just been a test to suss him out.

Over the days that followed, Brighton came to know Helene

Henderson by sight and had her phone bugged for good measure. Surprisingly she wasn't using a throw away and kept every text.

'What's this woman like?' said Sharpe when he gave her an update on his observations.

'She's like a wild animal guv. Protective, suspicious and looking out for herself. Her biggest flaw, other than not using a burner phone, is her routine. She sees the same people, on the same days, at the same places.'

'That's interesting. Are there any good spots for an obbo?'

'Most are too open but there's one that has potential. It's a walled cemetery not far from my place, and a long way out from the city. The drop takes her a good two hours and a few buses to get to. It's remote but surveillance isn't unfeasible.'

'Okay, so how would you run it?'

'Well, the bus stop is outside the main gate near the car park. She gets off the bus, walks into the cemetery with a cheap bunch of flowers and comes straight back out again. A fat geezer, her punter, walks out with that same bunch of flowers not long after. He goes past the bus stop and down the lane without a care in the world.'

Brighton showed Hayley Sharpe some good photos of Helene and her buyer.

'Okay this looks good,' she said. When's this going down again?'

'Tomorrow guv.'

'You'd best get cracking then.'

The next morning Brighton left home earlier than usual.

'See you later love,' he said hugging Kerry and lifting Emily up for a big hug and kiss.

'Don't forget we're playing monopoly tonight daddy,' she reminded him.

He feigned shock. 'Not monopoly! Nooooo!'

'You promised!' she giggled.

She'd been wanting to play the game for a while and so he picked up a new set, themed with her favourite cartoon series as a surprise.

'Okay, okay,' he said. 'I'll try and be home early.'

~

That afternoon, Brighton called the team into the operations room and walked in behind them carrying a large cardboard box.

'Good afternoon,' he said, handing the box to Peter. 'I'm going to brief in a moment for an operation we're running today. But before I do, I'm starting a new policy. I want all of you to take out your phones. Both your work phones and your personal phones and put them into this box that Peter's going to walk around with. We're going directly to the vans after this and there won't be any time to grab personal items or go to the toilet. His team looked at him in shock.

'You're joking right?' said Clara Tyne who was one of the police constables drafted to the operation. She had a look of worry on her face 'One of my boys is sick and I need my phone to check up on him.'

'I'm afraid not Clara. But if you need to go and tend to your son, then by all means do and we'll find a replacement.'

Clara was about to respond when a gruff older sergeant spoke up.

'I've got this Clara,' he said, frowning at Brighton. 'What you're requesting boss is over the top. You're infringing on our rights and as the union representative I object to what you're doing. I won't be giving you my phone. Neither will anyone else here.'

Brighton was having none of it and was not about to give in to a few objectors.

'Right then. Sounds like that's two replacements we'll need Peter.'

'Hang on a minute. You can't do that!'

'But I can sergeant, and I don't care if you voice your opinion to the group, but you can do so respectfully. Okay?'

'May I ask why you are doing this?' asked Clara Tyne. 'It would help if you told us what was behind it all.'

'Okay. Fine. I want to minimise the risk of information getting back to the target and jeopardising this investigation.'

'So, now you're suggesting that there's a leak here?' said the sergeant. 'That's just insulting!'

'What did I just say to you about showing respect? I'm not suggesting that any of you are leaking information, okay. All I am doing is minimising risks to the operation and integrity of this team. Now those of you who would like to join the operation please put your phones in the box as it comes around' said Brighton, putting both of his phones into the box in plain sight.

Not a single member of the team disobeyed him. Even the sergeant and PC Clyne put their phones in. Peter brought the box back to him.

'That goes for you too Peter,' said Brighton before Peter turned to take his seat.

Peter looked shocked and Brighton saw his reluctance as he put his own phone in there as well. Relieved that there was no further opposition, Brighton locked the box in Hayley Sharpe's office.

A while later, Brighton sat with Peter in his car, waiting for signs of life at the bus stop outside of the cemetery. He didn't like stakeouts. It was bad enough that he had to endure Peter tucking into what must have been the whiffiest kebab in all of England, but the deal was about to go down, and he didn't fancy stepping out and ruining the whole operation. The smell of garlic sauce intertwined with the spicy meat and onions and rang through his nasal hair like church bells. But Brighton hated heroin dealers even more, and he hoped that the operation would end sooner than later.

'Fancy selling smack near a graveyard,' said Peter, squashing the paper bag and the remains of his lunch into a tight ball and tossing it under his seat.

Brighton hid his disgust and reminded himself to get Peter to clean out the car before he went home. He felt sorry for Peter's poor wife whose sleep that night would definitely be broken judging from the borborygmus churning sounds Peter's body made.

'Surely you'd pick a cheerier place.'

Staring into the rain, Brighton's sharp eyes detected movement.

'Shhh. I can see something.'

Peter squinted.

'You're like fox you are.'

Sure enough, a small fat man in a dark blue windbreaker, clutching a bunch of flowers waddled out of the gloom to sit down in the bus shelter about three hundred metres in front of them, without even giving the two coppers a second glance. It might have been a different story if the weather was clear thought Brighton, watching Helene Henderson acknowledge her punter, tapping on her watch as if to say *you're late mate*. Fatty shrugged, reached into the inside pocket of his windbreaker, and pulled out a small wad of cash, which he handed over to Helene. When he saw the exchange Brighton, lifted his walkie talkie to his mouth and said 'Go, go, go.'

At once the trees around them came to life as ten uniformed officers burst out, all running towards the bus shelter.

'Pigs!' Helene screamed, scarpering back into the graveyard while fatso dashed in the direction of the car as fast as his chubby little legs could go.

Brighton grabbed him by the scruff of his jacket, pinning him to the bonnet of the car.

'No! Let me go!' said the punter struggling to break free.

Peter patted the prisoner down and extracted the packet of heroin.

'I'm arresting you on the suspicion that you are possessing a class A drug,' said Brighton cuffing his prisoner, 'you do not have to say anything, but it may harm your defence if you do not mention when questioned something which you later rely on in court. Anything you do say may be given in evidence.'

Together the two officers walked the sobbing man over to the approaching panda, and then joined the others hunting in the cemetery for Helene Henderson. Helene wasn't so easy to catch.

'Come on Peter!' said Brighton running towards the direction of the screams.

He hated graveyards, particularly this one, and with good reason. His mother was buried somewhere in this maze and despite his wife and Cecelia pressing him, he hadn't found the time or inclination to pay a visit to her final resting place.

Sprinting past a row of Victorian era crypts, Brighton saw Helene dash through a row just ahead of him, with three of the team in hot pursuit.

'Circle round! Circle round!' said the sergeant, waving his arms to direct the others. 'We'll have her cornered in a minute!'

Brighton and Peter split up. Brighton back tracked a few rows before racing to intercept her. For a moment, his view was impeded by large monuments to the dead until he got a quick glimpse of her familiar harsh face ducking behind a huge angel.

'Over here!' he called.

Helene stood up warily eying off her opponent, her eyes glared at Brighton, flickering with the desperation of a cornered rat.

'Out of my way pig,' she said, walking towards him in a move that surprised him.

Brighton stood his ground.

'I don't think so Helene.'

That threw her. 'How'd yer know my name?'

'We know more than that. So why not save yourself the bother and give up.'

Helene drew a small blade.

'I don't think so.'

Brighton looked at the pocketknife and was just glad that it wasn't a 9mm as he moved into a karate stance with his right foot forward and left tucked behind, ready to take her on.

'What's all this then?' she said 'Are you going to kick me? Wax on, wax off?'

'No. I was just distracting you, Helene. I don't actually do martial arts.'

Behind the surprised dealer, PC Tyne shouted 'Drop the knife on the ground! Stand still.'

Helene wasn't going without a fight. As she charged forward with the knife raised in hand, PC Tyne whipped her legs out from underneath her with a well-aimed blow from her ASP baton, dropping the startled dealer to the ground with a loud thump. The knife fell out of Helene's hand as she landed on the ground with a plonk, like a lump of meat on a barbeque, screaming in pain for all she was worth.

'Me ankle!' she cried, writhing about and clutching her foot.

'Well done, Clara,' said Brighton to the smiling constable.

Before the others arrived, Brighton picked the subdued prisoner up from the ground.

'Now read Helene her rights and arrest her. She's to be charged with dealing a class A narcotic, affray with a deadly weapon, and resisting arrest. This is Clara's collar, you lot,' he called out as the others milled around. 'See you back at the nick.'

22

As Emily Brighton watched her mother prepare dinner, she wished she were older.

'Can I help mum?' She said again.

'There's not much to do now,' said her mother Kerry, looking up from cutting potatoes for the mash she planned to serve with the thick pork sausages she'd bought in the village that morning, and fresh garden peas and carrots. Still, she knew that look. Emily was insistent and when she became that way, she became grumpy, and that was the last thing Kerry needed.

'Why don't you take these scraps and put them in the bin for me?'

'Aww mum,' said Emily, 'That's not what I meant. I want to help with dinner.'

'Tell you what. If you take the scraps out for me, I'll let you help me make an apple pie for dessert. Is that okay?'

'I love apple pie,' said Emily, 'That's my favourite,' she said with a big smile.

'It's your dad's favourite as well. Now off you go.'

Emily nodded as she picked up the bowl of scraps. She walked out the back door, through the yard, and went out the side gate that led to the laneway where her dad had put the bins out for collection.

When Emily turned into the laneway, she saw a strange old man poking through their rubbish bin with a stick. He wore raggedy clothes and a grey hat like she'd seen wizards wear in those old Harry Potter films her mum liked to watch sometimes. His feet stood in an old hessian sack like he was about to enter a race. What's he doing? She thought. Then she saw three mottled cats, all with the lightest green eyes, circling the man in the sack like sentries keeping watch.

Before she could run and tell her mum about the stranger, one cat saw her and chirped like a chaffinch. The old man looked up from his rummaging and stared at the girl, smiling with his ugly wrinkled face and cruel yellow eyes. Emily gasped with her mouth wide open like she'd just seen a wolf. Dropping the bowl, she turned to run back to her mum, but she wasn't fast enough.

The old man waved his stick in the air and said with urgency in a raspy gasp 'To me little feet. To me.'

Poor horrified Emily found her feet turn and change direction. Each step she took was not back to safety but towards to the creepy old man, and she couldn't stop as he made her walk closer and closer, nearer and nearer, and there was nothing she could do about it. It frightened the poor little girl and as the old man reached out to grab her, Emily took a deep breath, opened her mouth, and screamed for her life.

Kerry heard the scream and dropped the knife. Without a single thought, she ran straight out the door. By the time she reached the laneway, she saw Emily standing next to the man in the sack. She ran towards them, curling her hands into fists.

'Get away from her!' she said with the furious anger of a grizzly bear separated from her cubs.

The old creep waved his stick.

'Prohibere silentioum,' he said, freezing Kerry in her tracks, mid step.

Unable to speak, she watched the old man's cats climb into the dirty old sack and saw him pull it over both himself and her hysterical daughter. As the sack drew shut it disappeared in a flash with a bang and a cloud of green smoke. The magick holding her also disappeared. The momentum sent her skidding and slipping on the hard cobblestones, skinning her shins and the palms of her hands. She could not see either of them at all.

Ignoring her pain she swiped the clearing smoke, finding no trace of her daughter or the strange old man. The horror of having her daughter taken and being powerless to protect her child rose through her tormented soul, driving her into the ground and turning her into a sobbing howling wreck.

Brighton didn't realise that Peter had taken a short cut back to the station, until he looked out the passenger window and saw his house and a cloud of dissipating green smoke behind it.

'Pull over Peter.'

Peter looked surprised and a bit annoyed but complied with Brighton's sudden request.

'Come on guv,' said Peter, 'I need to get home. I've got football practice tonight.'

'Sorry Peter but that's my place, Brighton explained, 'I need to see what's happening. Take the car back to the station and pick me up tomorrow morning.'

'No worries. Hope everything's alright.'

Me too thought Brighton, waving Peter off before he ran as fast as he could to the laneway. A heavy downpour started as he rounded the corner, where he found his wife lying on the cobblestones screaming with her knees and shins bleeding.

'Hey, it's okay I'm here. What's happened?' he said as he sprinted over to her.

Kerry shook with anguish and shouted unintelligible gibberish.

'Man! Man took Emily!' before writhing in his arms, completely inconsolable.

Brighton had seen her panic attacks, but this was next level. He gulped as his gut sank like a stone all the way to the bottom of a deep pond. Emily was missing, and there was no doubt this was down to Zaliel. A thousand questions flooded his mind, but he knew he had to help his wife first. He lifted her up as one of his neighbours popped their head around the corner.

'Oi you what's all the racket? Did you hit her?'

'No, I did not hit my wife. I just found her here.'

'I don't believe you. I've called the police. They'll sort you out.'

'I am the police. Why don't you mind your business?'

He turned his back on the nosey old sticky beak posing as a good samaritan, picked Kerry up in his arms and walked back into the house. Once he sat Kerry down, he looked at her knees and went hunting for plasters, in his mother's Aladdin's cave.

As he opened the storeroom door a curious smell greeted his nose. Cigarette smoke. The smell was very faint, but he smelt it all the same because after years of living with his mother, his nose was very sensitive to tobacco smoke. Why could he smell it in the storeroom? Had Kerry started smoking again? She quit as a favour for him after they'd first met and even though the past months had been hectic, he dismissed the idea. Kerry wouldn't put a nicotine hit before Emily's health. She was a great mum. He found a few plasters in an old box full of medical supplies, some well past their use by date. A quarter bottle of disinfectant as well. He bundled everything in his hands and walked back out to the kitchen. His wife had calmed down a little bit but wasn't saying anything. He ripped off a piece of paper towel and soaked it in disinfectant, applied it to her wounds and then covered them with the plasters.

'That should be fine. Just wait here a moment, I'll go and see if I can find Emily.'

There was always a chance that nobody had taken her, and she was off playing somewhere unaware of all the commotion she'd caused. That's what he hoped. He searched everywhere he could think of, even the nearby woods because she said she wanted to go and explore there, but he'd not found time to take her yet. No luck. As he walked home Brighton saw two police cars and an ambulance outside. He had a bad feeling about this.

Before he reached the entrance, the front door opened, and Kerry walked out in handcuffs flanked by two uniformed officers that stopped when they saw him.

'Hey, what's all this then?' said Brighton to one constable, still surprised and processing the scene in front of him.

'This is police business, now get out of our way or we will arrest you as well.'

'I'm Detective Inspector Brighton. This is my house and that's my wife you've just arrested, so why don't you tell me what's going on.'

The rookie constable shrugged and looked like he couldn't give a toss. The revelation meant nothing to him.

'We were just wondering when you'd get back… sir,' he said with more than just a faint hint of sarcasm. 'Best you have a word with the boss. She's inside. Come on Charlie.'

The two constables brushed past with Kerry in tow towards one of the nearby pandas.

Brighton looked at Kerry as she walked past. She said nothing. Her eyes looked strange and desolate as if they were glazed over, she looked straight ahead, without even acknowledging him.

'It's alright love,' he said, 'We'll sort it out.'

Kerry didn't respond. She's just in shock mate, he thought. You've seen it plenty of times, haven't you?

He opened the door, hoping to see Emily run to him and give him the biggest hug in the world. But she wasn't there.

'Through here DI Brighton,' said a familiar voice.

He walked into the kitchen to find Hayley Sharpe sitting at his table smoking a foul mini cigar and sipping tea from one of Kerry's new cups.

'Hope you don't mind,' she said, flicking her ash into a saucer as he opened the kitchen window, hoping the acrid smoke cloud hanging in the room would clear.

'No guv, I don't mind at all,' he said, deciding not to make a scene. 'Could you please explain to me why my wife has been arrested? What's going on?'

'This is the second time I've been here in a couple of months. First your mum was found dead at the bottom of stairs and now your daughter is missing. Care to explain why you haven't reported it?'

'All due respect what are you insinuating? I was just out there looking for her!' he said as his cheeks flushed red with exasperation. You know as well as I do, that in these cases every second counts. I was going to call in once I'd scoured the area.'

'You can lower your tone.'

'Really Ma'am? Well, if it's going to be like that then I'll remind you that I am off duty, and as you are in my home you can bloody well put that cancer stick out thanks.'

Hayley Sharpe hadn't expected him to be so assertive. She widened her eyes, stubbed the cigar out, reflected on what he'd said and gave him a look that would melt plastic.

'I thought you said it didn't bother you?'

Brighton gulped as she continued.

'At four pm today your neighbours found your wife outside in the laneway in a state of hysterics and phoned the police. She's been delirious. Kept talking gibberish. Has she done that before?'

He looked at her, trying not to frown.

'No DCI Sharpe. Kerry's not like that.'

'Is there a possibility that she might have harmed your daughter?'

'Never. She loves Emily.'

'Is she taking any medication that you're aware of?'

'No,' said Brighton, knowing from years of detective work that his boss was going to reveal something he was unaware of.

'That's strange. Are these yours then?' she said, showing him a packet of tranquillisers, 'Only we found them in the drawer by her bed.'

Brighton stared at ten nasty yellow and green capsules and wondered where the bloody hell they came from.

'I've never seen them before, but considering the shock we've had recently with the bomb and everything it would not surprise me that she's seen someone about it. Even so, what does that have to do with Emily going missing?'

'Come on man. Think. Pretend for a moment this is one of your cases. Wouldn't you find it strange that the husband did not know that his wife was medicated? Now there's only two tablets missing, and the prescription was filled weeks ago. That tells me that your wife is off her meds. Meds she's hidden from her husband. Now can you see why there's more than a possibility that she is quite unstable.'

Brighton nodded. You're a heartless bitch for saying that about my wife, he thought, but whether he liked it or not, Hayley was spot on. Now he was even more worried for Emily.

'Why has she been arrested?'

'She hasn't been arrested. She's been sectioned though as I deem her a threat to herself and others. We're moving her to Mortlake House for the time being. When she's settled down you can see her.'

'I don't think it's her. We need to speak to Superintendent Armitage and fast. Sid Fields might have taken her.'

'Don't you think that the thought hadn't crossed my mind? I've spoken to him already. According to Armitage, Sid has enough strife on with the Met and a rival gang on his heels. So, the timing isn't right.'

'That's never stopped him in the past.'

'Are you second guessing your superior officer?'

'No, but it seems like you're not prepared to cover all the angles either.'

'I'll have you know DI Brighton that we are and that's all you need to know. You're not to drive back to London and confront him. Is that understood?'

Brighton nodded, but underneath he was worried for Emily's life and didn't want Sid anywhere near her, or Zaliel.

'Good. Now think hard. Is there somewhere that Kerry might have taken Emily? Is there somewhere she used to go to as a child? Is there a secret place she might have shown you?'

'None that I can think of. Kerry isn't from here. She's from London. She might have taken Emily down to the woods for a walk, but she'd have not gone far.'

'Alright,' she said, 'We'll start our search there.'

23

'Emily, Emily!' called Brighton, walking through the woods with a large search party of police and volunteers.

'Break!' called Detective Constable Dunbar and the party stopped their search and looked around for places to sit and have a rest.

Out came the water bottles, the flasks of tea and the packets of sandwiches issued to everyone at the start of the day.

'I'm famished,' said Dunbar settling down next to Brighton and devouring his sandwich in four huge chomps. He drank a mouthful of water from his canteen and searched his bag for another snack. 'Damn I must have eaten my apple earlier.'

'Here Dunbar,' said Brighton tossing him his cheese and pickle sandwich.

Dunbar looked at it with interest.

'Are you sure boss?'

'Yeah, I'm not feeling hungry.'

Brighton watched as Dunbar attacked the sandwich with enthusiasm.

'Mmm Great pickles. Is it Branston?'

'No, I think it's something my mother made or bought at a village fair.'

'Well, whatever it is, it's good.'

'You're welcome. Tell me, have you been on a search like this before?'

'Yes I have. Last summer, it was two kids went camping in the woods without telling anyone they were going. That's them over there,' he gestured to two boys wearing their scouting uniforms. 'You'd think they'd know better being scouts, but oh well, they know now, don't you boys?'

The two lads went red in the face and pretended not to hear him.

'Has a search ever been unsuccessful?'

Dunbar closed his eyes and thought for a moment.

'Not to my knowledge. Come on you lot, let's get moving. It will be dark soon. Don't worry boss, if she's out here, we'll find her.'

Brighton nodded, putting on a brave face, yet behind it all he wasn't convinced. They'd hunted high and low for Emily for three days straight, scouring everywhere they could think of. Nothing had turned up, and he was worried sick.

When Brighton came home later that evening, he noticed the house seemed cleaner than he remembered leaving it.

'Kerry?' he said a few times, before searching the cottage, hoping his wife was back, but she wasn't. She was still sectioned. Still sedated and still the prime suspect in their daughter's disappearance. He wanted to see her and hold her, but he wasn't allowed to. His whole world became this strange emotionless and depressing void. No Kerry. No Emily and nobody to talk to. His phone rang and he saw it was Judge Maloney.

'Any news boy?' said the old man in a gruff voice, his usual demeanour.

'None. We didn't find a thing today.'

'What about the media release?'

'Apart from a few dead ends, nothing concrete.'

'Well keep searching man. You can't give up.'

'Do you honestly think I will? This is Emily we're talking about.'

'How would I know? You certainly gave up on my daughter.'

Brighton breathed, trying to control himself and not let his emotions get the better of him.

'That's not fair. You know I can't do anything about that. I can't even visit her. The first thing I did was call you and you couldn't get her out either.'

'So, what are you doing about it then?'

'You know full well that as long as she's a suspect, and as she has been deemed a risk to herself and others, there's nothing I can do. Your wife giving her prescription medication certainly didn't help things either.'

'Leave Deidre out of this. She's not to blame.'

'And I am? I was at work when this happened. I came home found my daughter missing and my wife being sectioned after she was found in possession of tranquillisers that I knew nothing about. Yet here you are, blaming me for all this?'

'Really? You're the copper with a price on his head, aren't you? Not my Kerry, so yes William, I think you're responsible!'

'I'm sorry Judge but I can't deal with this right now. Not if you're going to talk to me like this. Good night.'

Brighton ended the call and slammed the kitchen table hard with his fist in frustration. Stupid old bugger. What does he want me to do about all this? Wave my magic wand or something?

The thought of magic wands made him think about Zaliel and Marta and little Anna and Anna Bell and Jimmy and those lions and his rotten mother, it really wound him up, burning him with guilt until he realised how hungry he was. He scoured the kitchen when he remembered that he hadn't had a thing since breakfast. Looking around the pantry, he found nothing that he could turn into a meal in an instant. There were no baked beans and yet he swore that Kerry had bought a few tins last shopping day. There was a scrap of bread in the bread bin and five rashers of bacon in the freezer which he defrosted and fried together with the two remaining eggs. He made himself a hot cup of tea and blessed his luck that the milk hadn't turned.

As he took the milk back to the sink for his tea Brighton remembered the brownie bowl on the floor and dodged it just in time. It was still empty, and he remembered his mum filling it with milk and a scrap of bread every day. She told him that the brownie cleaned up and watched over the home like a guardian. At the time he thought it was just a load of old bollocks because the housekeeper came around twice a week to do all the work. The only reason that the bowl was ever empty was because she emptied it before he and Marta were out of bed in a silly game to try and fool them. Bollocks or not, I need all the help I can get, he thought as he filled the bowl with milk, broke the scrappy crust of bread into it and added his dishes to the growing pile in the sink before he went to bed.

His mobile phone woke him up around six-thirty in the morning.

'Brighton,' he said, trying to open his weary grit encrusted eyes.

'Sorry to wake you,' said Hayley Sharpe, 'But the search has been called off.'

'What do you mean? I don't understand.'

'We just don't have the resources to maintain this line of enquiry.'

Despite all his years as a front-line copper, Brighton never thought that he'd hear a stock standard response like the one he'd just heard to describe a situation which affected his own family.

'We'll be questioning your wife today at twelve. Informally of course. Now do you want me to tell her the news, or would you like to?'

'So, I can go and see her?'

'Of course. You could have gone yesterday. Didn't Peter tell you?'

'No. I haven't heard a thing.'

'Sorry about that. I thought you knew. Oh well you do now.'

I'll sort that skiving bastard the next time I see him, thought Brighton trying to keep his cool. He felt lonelier than ever and more desperate. His gut told him Emily was alive and somewhere out there, and probably with Zaliel. It crushed him not to have a clue where she was. He couldn't think straight and the only way he could cope was to work the case in his own time.

'I'll tell her guv.'

'Okay, but after we're done interviewing her. If she thinks we've given up looking, she may suspect we're onto her and we don't want her to go and lose the plot again, now do we?'

'Understood. I'll go and see her around three then.'

Brighton ended the call, hoping that he wasn't too abrupt. Even though she was a bit of a harpie, Hayley had been accommodating with leave, staff services and support. But there were limits, and he knew that she'd expect to have him back on duty soon.

He dressed, grabbed his laptop from the nook his mother used to write in and walked down the narrow stairs to the kitchen. He didn't notice that the dishes weren't in the sink until he reached for his mug and looked when his hand touched nothing. His mug and all the dishes were washed and standing in the drying rack. Must have done them after all, he thought as he put the kettle on. Out of curiosity, he looked down at the small silver bowl his mother had kept for the brownie. It was empty, and he reminded himself to buy a couple of rat traps on the way home. The last thing he needed was vermin.

24

Mortlake House had been a grandiose mansion for the Mortlake family until they lost everything after the American War of Independence. Since then, it had been turned into a sanatorium, which changed as the years went by to a secure facility for people with serious behavioural issues, drug dependence, self-harmers, and violence. Brighton had been there once before to interview an old man who swore that fairies set his house on fire, stole his wallet, and emptied his bank account.

After showing reception his warrant card, Brighton left his personal items at the counter.

'Okay follow me,' said the huge muscle bound Tongan male nurse whose bulk reminded Brighton of a lumbering refrigerator with feet as he walked to the ward.

Outside the visiting room Brighton was met by PC Clara Tyne.

'Hi ya guv,' she said trying to be cheerful. 'Sorry but I have to make sure that you're not carrying anything illicit. It's procedure.'

'That's alright Clara,' he said as she patted him down as fast as she could.

When Brighton saw Kerry sitting in the tiny room at one side of a metal desk, he felt as if her life force had been sucked from her body with a giant spiritual vacuum cleaner. She looked gaunt and while sedated, not at all at peace. Deep down in her mind, he knew she was troubled.

'Hello love,' he said, choosing not to hug her because he knew that Clara Tyne would report everything he did straight back to Hayley Sharpe.

Kerry looked past him, straight at the white wall.

'Kerry. It's me. Will.'

He saw a faint flicker of recognition from her eyes before they fixed back on the wall.

'I need to tell you something. It's about Emily.'

As soon as he said Emily, Kerry changed. It was like he was a hypnotist that had said the word that would transform her into a chicken. Kerry banged her hand on the table and stared at him.

'MAN took EMILY. SACK. CATS. THREE CATS. STICK... FROZEN... BANG! GONE. She's gone Will. She's gone. He took her! He took our baby!' she shrieked.

'Hey, calm down love. Listen to me. Calm down before they come back here and give you another shot, okay?'

She nodded and sobbed. He wanted to hold her and stroke her hair; dry her eyes and tell her it was all okay, but he could not make personal contact like that.

'Is everything alright in there?' called PC Tyne from outside.

'Yeah thanks,' he replied. 'Now Kerry. They've called the search off. Nobody's looking for Emily anymore.'

'No, no, no, NO!' she said, burying her face in her hands.

'Sweetheart I know you didn't do anything to her. But they think you did. Tell me something. Please? What happened? Who took her?'

Kerry looked up.

'MAN took EMILY. SACK. CATS. THREE CATS. STICK... FROZEN... BANG! GREEN SMOKE. GONE.'

Green Smoke. Her description confirmed his worst fear. Zaliel had Emily. His eyes hadn't played tricks on him after all. He'd seen the man in the sack himself. Now how could he ever prove that, never mind locate him? He needed to be sure.

'What did he look like? This man that took Emily?'

'MAN took EMILY,' she tried to explain but he cut her off.

'Hey! I know that Kerry but tell me about him. What did he look like? I want to know. Do you remember his face? Was he an old man with yellow eyes and a scraggly beard?'

But it was no use. Kerry was on a loop. Brighton tried again and again to question his only living witness and each time he'd get the same response. Who knows what those drugs are doing to her, he thought. When he gave it one more go, she stood up and shouted the same words at him so loudly that the door opened and the giant Tongan entered with an exhausted looking doctor.

'That's enough for one day,' said the doctor slumping as she swabbed Kerry's restrained arm and gave her an injection. Brighton watched his struggling wife as the Tongan escorted her back to her room.

'Excuse me,' he said to the doctor before she left, 'What's happened to my wife? What are you doing for her, other than pumping her full of drugs?'

The doctor looked at him.

'Are you insinuating that she's not being cared for?'

'No, but I want to know what you're doing for her. Nobody's spoken to me or explained anything.'

'Mr Brighton, your wife is in shock. She can't think. She can't talk coherently, and she can't switch off. She needs time and she needs rest and then we shall see. I recommend that you don't visit her again for at least two weeks. Three would be better.'

'That's ridiculous. What about the police?'

'That's out of my control, I'm afraid. Perhaps you should get a lawyer to organise a temporary order for her not to be disturbed, because as you can see, she's unfit for questioning. These orders are quite common. Now if you'll excuse me, I must get back to my patients.' She said, leaving him alone in the room.

A lawyer he thought, I have no time for them. He only knew one anyway, the woman who managed his mother's affairs.

'That's dreadful,' said Cecilia Lemon, after Brighton told her the news, 'I heard that there was a missing child, but I had no idea that it was your little girl, or I'd have called you straight away. What can I do to help?'

'I'm not sure,' said Brighton, 'I mean there's no way I can afford your services. Even on my salary.'

'Aren't you forgetting something?' she said, reminding him about the trust. 'These are what one would call dire circumstances Will...' She trailed off before saying his full name which she knew provoked him.

Brighton looked reluctant. He wanted to do this on his own with no help from his mother, but he had no choice.

'Thanks Cecilia. So, what do you suggest we do?'

She thought for a moment.

'I suggest a good criminal lawyer to set the police straight.'

'But I thought you'd take care of them.'

'Me?' Cecilia laughed, 'I'm afraid that I'm not that sort of lawyer. I deal with trusts and estates and now thanks to your mother, literary rights. No. We shall contact the Honourable Timothy McGregor.'

'Good choice,' said Brighton. 'I know him by reputation.'

McGregor was called The Bulldog because he ripped the seat off the pants of every prosecuting lawyer and copper he faced. The police hated his meticulous work, his pig-headed stubbornness and fastidious knowledge of the law. Once he gripped on, The Bulldog did not let go. He was exactly the kind of lawyer that Kerry needed.

25

Brighton surprised his colleagues when he came straight to work after seeing Cecilia. He needed to get back, mainly for appearances, but he also had an ulterior motive.

'DI Brighton? A quick word please,' called Hayley Sharpe as he passed her office door.

Sitting on the small black lounge chair, Brighton nursed his takeaway coffee with both hands.

'We weren't expecting you back today. Are you sure that you're okay to work?'

'With all due respect guv, now that the search has been called off there's not much that I can do. I don't see how me traipsing around the woods on my own is going to make much difference when…'

'When what?'

'When I know in my gut that she's not out there.'

'How would you know that? Have you spoken to your wife?'

'You know I have,' he countered. 'PC Tyne would have reported in by now. You also know that she's drugged up to the eyeballs and not making any sense. No, this is my copper's instinct if you will. I'm beginning to believe her story guv. I believe that she's telling the truth.'

'Of course. It's only natural Brighton, with you being her husband and all.'

'That's not what I meant. I know it's best not to discuss it now either. I just want to get back to work if that's okay.'

'That's fine, provided you stay away from your wife's case and leave us to find your daughter. Can I trust you to do that?'

'You know you can. I won't go anywhere near the op's room, and I won't talk to anyone on the case. Just let me do my job please guv. That's all I ask.'

'Alright, but if it gets to be too much let me know. You have a stack of personal leave sitting there so you may as well use it.'

Brighton nodded and plodded back to his desk where he found Peter waiting for him.

'Alright?' he said to his offsider.

'Alright,' said Peter with a guilty look that Brighton picked up on straight away.

'Look Peter, I'm not bothered that you forgot to tell me I could go and see Kerry, okay? So, let's get on with it. How's the Rocco case going?'

'Darren Rocco's been seen with his old mate Billie Brown. They went to school together.'

Brown was a low life waste of space that had recently moved back into town, allegedly after being turfed out of Liverpool.

'I remember you telling me that before. Do you think Billie's dealing?'

'No way. He's not smart enough. He's just a dull prick. If anything, he'd be muscle.'

'We don't know that for sure though, do we? I mean if he caused enough drama to be turfed out of Liverpool then there could be something in it. For all we know he could be our ringleader. Get on to our colleagues Merseyside and see if they know anything. What did Helene say about him?'

'I was just getting to that. She hasn't said a word. She's lawyered up as well. She has The Bulldog looking after her.'

Perfect, thought Brighton. That's all I need. Of all the lawyers to choose, she goes out and gets him.

'No way a two-bit smack dealer can afford the likes of McGregor. Are we still holding her?'

'Barely. The judge has only remanded her till the trial because of the weight involved. The stupid bint had 0.5 of a gram over the maximum weight for personal use, so technically she has a trafficable amount. As for the client, old fatso's singing like a canary. He's on remand too but Sally the prosecutor's going for leniency as he swears it's for personal use. He was a teacher and all, but the board of education dropped him like a sack of shit when we told them. No wonder too. I wouldn't want a smackhead teaching my...' Peter stopped when he realised what he was about to say and turned the conversation back to Henderson. 'So, when do you want to interview her then?'

'Let's go and have a chat with Sally first. If we're up against The Bulldog, then she might help us with strategy. Maybe we could offer Henderson a deal if it gets us close to Rocco and Brown.'

'Okay, I'll ring her and see if she can fit us in today, then I'll call Liverpool.'

Peter went off to make the calls, and Brighton went to the secure cabinet, grabbed the case file, and read it until Peter returned.

'We're in luck guv. Sally can fit us in for a coffee between court sessions in an hour.'

By the time they returned, nearly everyone had gone for the evening. Brighton pretended to go back to the file and as soon as he was alone, he went to work.

'Sir,' he said, calling Armitage. 'It's DI Brighton. I was wondering if I could please have my sister's belongings sent to me?'

'Why on earth for? Don't tell me you're back on the case man.'

'No of course not. I'm sure that the new DI has ruled out any involvement on her part and is exploring other avenues as we speak.'

That part was true. He'd kept in touch with Jeanie after the move and she kept him in the loop. Even though he was a seasoned copper, Brighton felt dismayed at the complete change in styles and approach.

'You've really got your ear to the ground,' said Armitage. 'Alright as long as you are not interfering in the case, I'll arrange for them to be released and sent to you first thing tomorrow.'

Next, Brighton wrote down all the words his wife said earlier in the left column of a piece of paper.

Next to *Man* he wrote: *Male perpetrator*.
Next to *Sack*, he wrote: *Forensics, Modus operandi: Confirmed by forensics found at both scenes in London*.
Next to *Three Cats* he wrote *as above* and a mental note to ask Jeanie about the cat hair again.
Next to *Stick* he wrote *wand?* and *modus operandi*, remembering his encounter with the wizard in Marta's room.
Next to *Frozen* he wrote nothing, though he was tempted to write horrendous children's film.
Next to *Bang and Green Smoke,* he wrote *forensics and modus operandi. Confirmed by forensics found at both scenes in London*.

He'd seen the smoke firsthand at the scene. It had to be the same guy. What the hell did he do to Kerry? The more he thought about it, the more it sounded like what she'd seen had all the hallmarks of a classic kidnapping, even if magick was involved. Lucky she wasn't turned into a pig or something. But why would Zaliel have been waiting for Emily? What was he doing? How could he have known that Emily would go outside at that very moment? Nothing made sense, and everything felt suspicious and far too convenient for his liking. He knew Hayley Sharpe was having none of it, because no forensics was done in the laneway. She didn't believe anything Kerry had said.

I'll have to remedy that, thought Brighton standing up. As soon as it's light tomorrow, I'll investigate the scene myself. Before he left, he grabbed gloves, swabs, tweezers, a few evidence bags, and containers. Everything he needed to be completely thorough.

Another sleepless night turned to dawn and by seven in the morning the day looked glorious and sunny. Starting with the rubbish bins. Brighton dusted the lids, handles and rims and took several good prints that he hoped were not his, Kerry's, or the garbage collector's. Then he examined the rubbish bag, and found the sides full of little round holes, indicating that someone had a good look at the contents. What were you hoping to find you creep? he thought. Brighton thanked his lucky stars that he shredded all their old bills and letters and dumped the contents into the security bins at work. He did not want the chance of crims finding out where he lived or trying to steal his ID. He'd seen it happen before.

Seeing that the bins had been disturbed gave Kerry's story credibility, but he needed more than that to convince the likes of Hayley Sharpe. He processed the scene like a bloodhound on the scent, just like he used to when he was in the murder squads in London and Greater Thames Valley, where he had developed a reputation of having a hawkish eye for detail.

It took just over forty-five minutes on his hands and knees, scanning inch by inch before he found something. Fibres caught in the sticky leaves of a creeping thistle. It was hair, most likely from an animal and far too fine to be from a dog or a squirrel or rodent. He extracted a second and much darker sample moments later, stuck in a patch of dried mud. His excitement grew and then out the corner of his eye, he saw something waving at him, caught in the missing grout in the brick wall. He grabbed his tweezers and latched on to a long thin brown fibre. Coarse like in appearance, he instantly knew it was a strand of hessian. Hessian from the sack that someone took his daughter away in. Now he had a piece of sack and fibres from two possible cats but what about the bang and the green smoke? There'd have to be a chemical residue just like Jeanie collected in Kew and the East End, but would it have lasted long enough for him to trace now? Taking no chances Brighton gave the area a thorough swab. Walls, bins, and the ground. If Jeanie could see me now, he thought as he bagged the last of the samples.

His phone rang. It was Peter.

'Hey guv, are you far away? Only The Bulldog's here champing at the bit.'

Damn. In his excitement, he'd forgotten all about the Henderson interview.

'I'll be there soon. Tell him I'm dropping clothes off to my wife at Mortlake House.'

He wasn't lying about the clothes either. He was allowed to drop them off, but as it wasn't visiting hours his wife was out of bounds. It felt satisfying to hear Peter squirming about for a change. Gathering up all his evidence, he went back to the house, dumped everything on the table, grabbed Kerry's clothes and just before he left, he filled the little bowl with milk and bread.

26

'Finally,' said The Bulldog, as Brighton entered the interview room and hit record on the tape recorder.

'Interview commenced at 9:45 am. In the room are DI Brighton, DS Charamboulos, and please state your names for the record.'

'Timothy McGregor KC.'

Henderson was silent.

'Please state your name for the record,' Brighton said to Henderson.

'No comment,' she said, with her face all screwed up and nasty.

'We need your name for the tape please,' he tried to explain, knowing it wasn't her first police interview. He was about to end proceedings when her lawyer interjected.'

'My dear you've watched too much television in your waste of a life. The detective inspector is well within his rights to ask you for your name and a response will not vilify or sully the remnants of your reputation in the slightest. In any case they already know who you are.'

'So, wot you're saying is it's okay yeah?'

'Yes, so come along, be a good girl and say your name for the record.'

'Horse.'

'No, not your thug name or your drug name, the name your mother gave you. Assuming you have one.'

'Yeah, yeah. It's Helene Henderson. And don't say nuthin about me mum you. You're supposed to help me remember.'

The Bulldog rolled his eyes, wishing that his client practiced a form of body hygiene that included the occasional wash.

Brighton continued.

'Before we proceed, I must advise you that this is a formal interview and that anything you say today may be used in evidence in a court of law. Do you understand?'

She nodded.

'For the tape please.'

Helene looked at The Bulldog whose pasty face barely contained the contempt he held for the low life dreg of society sitting next to him. He nodded.

'Yeah, I get it.'

'Do you understand? Yes or no please?'

'Yes'

Brighton wasted no time.

'Please tell us what you were doing outside the Rookwood cemetery around four pm on Monday afternoon.'

'No comment.'

'I find the location that you found my client to be somewhat irrelevant DI Brighton. She was simply waiting for a bus. The fact that the bus stop was outside the cemetery was neither here nor there.'

Brighton hoped that the Bulldog would say that.

'Okay, which bus were you waiting for then? The nineteen or the nineteen A?'

'No comment.'

'Where were you going?'

'No comment.'

'If your client was simply waiting for a bus Mr McGregor, why is she refusing to tell us where she was going?'

'Because that is also irrelevant DI Brighton as you are most certainly aware.'

'I'll rephrase my question. We know you live on the other side of town

Helene and that neither bus was going to take you home. So, what brought you to that place at that time?'

'No comment.'

'I'd like to establish why your client was at the bus stop. Surely that's reasonable?'

'My client chooses not to answer this question because it is irrelevant'

'Okay,' said Peter jumping in, much to The Bulldog's delight, 'Were you there to sell heroin?'

'No comment,' said Helene with a demonic glare.

The Bulldog raised his eyebrows. It was almost as if Peter had just scored an own goal. Before he could say another word, Brighton placed the evidence bag with the heroin they'd retrieved from the punter onto the table.

'I am now showing the suspect exhibit item number 2D2-R, a small bag of heroin weighing just over four grams. Have you seen this bag before?'

Helene looked shocked when Brighton mentioned the weight and was going to say something rash when she snapped back to her senses.

'No comment.'

'Can you tell us why your prints are on the bag?'

'No comment.'

'Can you tell us why the gentleman we caught with this bag told us he bought it from you for one hundred pounds?'

'No comment.'

'I am now showing the accused exhibit item number 5D4-R,' said Brighton, as he placed an evidence bag containing a mobile phone on the table.

'Is this your phone Helene?'

'No comment.'

'It was found in your possession along with this. I am now showing exhibit item number P17-R4, the contents of your purse. Would you care to explain how you came to have one hundred pounds in your possession?'

'No comment.'

'Are you suggesting that my client is not allowed to be in possession of currency Detective Inspector?'

'That's not the point Mr McGregor as you're aware. Are these your things Helene?'

Helene looked at The Bulldog. He shrugged.

'No comment.'

Brighton sighed. This was going nowhere.

'What's your phone number Helene?'

'No comment.'

'Mr McGregor please direct your client to answer the question for the tape.'

'Tell them your number girl.'

'I don't want to. I lost me phone ages ago.'

'When did that happen?' asked Peter.

'I dunno. Last week or something.'

'If you lost your phone Helene, then it won't hurt to tell these gentlemen what your number is?'

Helene gave them a number which Brighton and Peter knew was dodgy from the outset, but they played along. Peter dialled the number and the phone in the bag did not respond.

'Are you sure that's the number?' Peter asked.

'Course it is. I ain't stupid am I?'

The Bulldog rolled his eyes. He knew what was coming next.

'That's okay Helene,' said Brighton, putting two sets of A4 paper on the table. 'I am now showing the accused exhibits 88IG and 88IGA. These are your phone records and your punter's phone records.'

Brighton nodded to Peter who dialled the number on the record belonging to Helene and the phone on the table came to life.

'Now Helene, according to your records, you called the man twice at different times on the day you met him at the bus shelter. On the same day he went to an ATM and withdrew these two brand-new fifty-pound notes, which were later found in your possession along with your missing phone. There are traces of heroin in your handbag and on your phone that match the heroin in the bag found on the gentleman. Your prints were also found on this bag. Is there anything you'd like to tell us?'

'No comment,' said Helene, shaking her head.

Brighton went in for the kill.

'This is your third offence Helene. I understand that you have a five-year-old son. Lucas, isn't it?'

Helene transformed when she heard her son's name.

'You leave him out of it', she growled.

'Look. Normally you'd be looking at three to five years in jail and Lucas would be going into foster care, but you've been rumbled with a weight which will become intent to supply a commercial quantity of a class A drug. You're looking at fifteen to life and never seeing your son again. But if you help us with our investigations into the source of your...'

Now it was The Bulldog's turn. He'd waited patiently enough.

'DI Brighton. What you are doing is borderline misconduct and what you are requesting is not possible under any circumstances. There is only your account that the alleged transaction took place. There is no electronic or video evidence. Everything you have is purely circumstantial. My client is a victim of circumstance. She was at the cemetery to pay her respects to her mother. She found the bag at the bus shelter and the gentleman saw it and took it, leaving the hundred pounds because he mistook her for a dealer. Because she's on welfare and needs to support her son, she took the money. At no time was she aware that the contents in the bag were illicit. As for the alleged calls, my client is dyslexic and often makes repeated mistakes when she dials numbers. It is entirely possible that she accidentally called the other accused several times. Furthermore, my client does not know any drug dealers or any villains that can assist you with your enquiries. Now if there is nothing else, I suggest that you release her immediately.'

'Is that a fact?' said Brighton. 'Your mother isn't dead Helene. Is she? I mean it's hard for her to be dead when she's downstairs with Lucas having a chat with our social workers now isn't it?'

Helene glared at him with her dark beady bug eyes.

'I'll kill the bitch. You can get out of here and all,' she said to The Bulldog, 'I don't need you.'

The Bulldog was unmoved by the outburst.

'I'm not leaving you. DI Brighton, it's obvious that my client is mentally unstable. I request a break to allow her to compose herself. If she knows what's good for her.'

That sounded like a threat, possibly instigated by whoever was paying his retainer.

Brighton didn't think twice.

'Interview terminated at 10:05am. We'll break for twenty minutes,' he said to Helene. 'Would you like a drink or to go to the toilet?'

'Nah, I'm good.' She looked more concerned about what The Bulldog would say to her shortly.

Brighton waited until Peter grabbed the evidence bags and they left together with Peter heading to the evidence room and Brighton to the gents.

As he walked down the corridor he heard 'DI Brighton.' It was The Bulldog.

'Might we have a quick word?'

'What's this about Mr McGregor?'

'Rest be assured, it's nothing associated with Ms Henderson.'

Brighton looked at the older man, trying to trust him when his gut told him otherwise.

'Alright,' he said, ushering The Bulldog into a small interview room and leaving the door wide open.

'Cecilia has told me about your wife's matter. I had no idea that we would see each other today.'

Brighton looked relieved.

'What did she say about Kerry?'

'She told me that your daughter is missing and that your wife's been sectioned. I'm going to get more details today and perhaps go and see her later this afternoon.' He stopped and looked Brighton hard in the face. 'I was wondering if you could fill me in. Help me get a picture of what you know or what you think you know.'

'If you're asking me to get you information about the case then you're wasting your time. I've no intention of going anywhere near the operations room. It's not worth my job.'

'Even for your wife's sake? I must admit I am impressed. There aren't many men who would leave their beloved incarcerated when they had potential means to set them free.' He paused for a moment, enjoying the sight of Brighton shuffling with unease, and smiled. 'Unless of course you have motive to keep her locked up.'

'Why would I want to do that? I love my wife and if I wanted to keep her locked away, I'd have hired a lesser man than you to defend her. I want to help her, I do. But I'm not going to abuse my position to help her, you need to understand that.'

'I do indeed DI Brighton. However, you misunderstood my intention. I have no interest in finding out about what Hayley Sharpe thinks she knows about this case. I want to know what *you* think. You're an experienced officer and it's your daughter that's gone missing. Surely you might have a few ideas about what may have happened?'

Brighton nodded.

'Sure. I have a few ideas. Went over the crime scene myself as it happens.'

'Good, that's exactly what I wanted to hear. Look why don't we catch up another time at a place where we can talk comfortably at our leisure, instead of a tiny interview room that reeks of piss.'

'Sure thing. Here's my card. Let me know where and when.'

Brighton left his card on the table and walked back to the toilets.

The Bulldog waited for him to leave. From his top pocket he pulled out a glove and a sandwich bag. He put the glove over his slippery, slender fingers, picked up the card and put it in the bag.

'Gotcha,' he said as the bag went back into his pocket, and he made a beeline to the nearest exit.

To Brighton's surprise, The Bulldog did not return to the interview room. All attempts to contact him failed. To make matters worse, Helene wasn't saying a thing. Whatever her brief had said when they were alone had changed her. She looked scared. Gotten to for sure, desperate for her kid's security. Yet silent, as if not saying another word was somehow going to save her life and bring everything back to normal. Brighton and Peter could not even get her to say her name for the tape anymore.

'Interview suspended at 12:15 pm,' said Brighton, standing up. 'Remain seated Ms Henderson. A PC will be around to take you back to your cell.'

'Lucas still here? I want to see him. I want to see me boy.'

'Would you like to see your dead mother as well?' asked Peter, unable to resist a jibe at her pathetic lie.

'Shuddup. I just wanna see Lucas.'

'Well, I don't think that's likely Helene. He'll have to wait until you're sentenced or at the bare minimum in remand.'

At the mention of prison, Helene looked at Brighton like a tortured troglodyte.

'Whatcha mean prison? I ain't going to prison! He promised!'

Brighton stared at the strange wailing, flailing creature, and felt like he'd just pocketed her precious magick ring.

'I'm not sure what he's said to you, but I can tell you that it's most unlikely. We had wanted to offer you a way out of all this and if you had cooperated, we'd have made sure that you'd stay with your boy. But he works for your boss Helene. I don't think he'd agree to any proposal we had.'

'But he's me brief!'

'Is he? Paid for him, did you?'

'Course not. Billie did but...'

Helene clamped up again, realising that if her tongue was a boot, then it just stepped in shit. Brighton sat back down.

'Billie?' he said, 'But I thought Darren was the main man.'

'I ain't saying another thing unless youse protect me and me boy. If you can, I've got something better that will get you in the paper. Or get you killed.'

Brighton looked at Peter. Peter nodded and left the room to see if Sally the prosecutor was still around.

27

Brighton grabbed two bags of groceries and an Indian takeaway from the back seat of his car, and after struggling with the front door he went inside. The spicy smell of the curry kept him awake. All he wanted to do was crash out on the sofa and watch Vera on ITV. He enjoyed reading and watching Vera's cases even if they were repeats because her tenacity and energy never ceased to amaze him. He just wished that it didn't need subtitles at the best of times.

His chances of watching telly and a quiet night in evaporated like boiling milk when he remembered that his mother didn't have a telly. Cursing his luck under his breath, Brighton strode into the kitchen and when he turned on the light, he discovered that his evidence bags from the laneway were missing. He stood and stared at the empty table. All that work, gone without a trace. No! this can't be right, he thought.

Forgetting all about the groceries and the takeaway Brighton looked everywhere for them. He looked through the kitchen and tried the rubbish bin and the laundry basket. Nothing. He looked in all the drawers and all the cupboards. Nothing. He looked in his bedroom and in the lounge room. Nothing. Then he went into Emily's room. He knew he hadn't been in there since her disappearance but went in there all the same.

Turning on her bedroom light Brighton looked over to her bed.

Leaning on the puffy pillow that she rested her head on at night was a book that he knew by sight. It was his sister's copy of his mother's *'My tales of the Magical Wooded World.'* How the hell did that get here? Armitage would have barely sent it and besides it should have gone to the station. Focus, he thought. Someone's done this. Someone took the evidence bags and left this book here. His first thought was to go downstairs, grab an empty evidence bag, and call Hayley Sharpe. But then there'd be more questions, and he decided he just didn't need any more heat right now. Whoever left the book on Emily's pillow had done so for a reason. It was like they were reaching out, wanting him to know something. He sat down on her bed and opened it. On the first page his mother had written a dedication.

> *'To all you wonderful children out there. No matter what your parents may tell you, don't believe them. Fairies exist. Magic is real, and after you read this story, I hope you never talk to strangers again.'*

Loopy old bat he thought and opened chapter one.

> *Why he was out there in the laneway that drizzly afternoon puzzles me to this day. I'd gone into the lane to find a tennis ball that sailed over the wall while I was practicing my serve. And there he was larger than life, poking around our dustbins with a long slender stick. Even more curiously he was standing in a sack with his back turned to me.*

Brighton did not believe what he was reading. *Man, sack, stick*, he thought.

> *While he didn't see me, his cats did. There were three of them, walking around and around him like sharks circling a lifeboat.*

Cats. Three Cats.

> *One of the cats saw me and squawked. This strange sound instantly grabbed his attention and when I looked into his cold yellow eyes, I knew that I was*

in trouble. I turned and ran, hoping that daddy had finished work. Hoping that he would save me from this horrid little man.

'To me little feet. To me!' I heard him say and the most incredible thing happened. I stopped running away from him and stood still before I turned back and walked straight over to him. There was nothing I could do to resist, nothing at all. Later I learned that this was a veniunt ad me, or come to me now spell. I wanted to scream; I did but he silenced me somehow. But he couldn't stop me from being scared for my life.

When I drew close enough, he waved his wand and said 'Here', and I stepped into the large sack with him. He whistled three times and as the cats followed me in, He pulled the sack over us, held the opening in a bunch in his hands and muttered a strange string of words. There was a bang and a flash, and we were gone.

Brighton stared down at the page, scarcely believing what he'd just read. Zaliel really did grab his mother when she was a little girl. Maybe that's why she moved around so much. The more he thought, the more he realised that there was a good possibility that Zaliel was responsible for a lot of the instability in his life. Yet he could not comprehend why his mother had never told him about it. He thought about the whole thing again.

What if this wasn't real at all? What if it's just one of her stories, some kind of built in guilt trip? The Zaliel in her story, the guy that took her couldn't possibly be the same guy who took Emily. He'd have to be at least a hundred years old.

So what? his less cynical side said. Magickal people might be able to live for a long time. He wanted to strike the magickal side out, but he'd seen the wizard at work. He knew that Zaliel existed. He knew that Zaliel was real.

Even so, that didn't explain who had been in the house today and stole his evidence. Why would they want to show me the book and take everything else away? He thought about motives and regretted not trusting his instinct and bagging the book in the first place. The evidence in the book and the evidence back in London supported his wife's version of events and put her in the clear. There was only one person he could talk to about this discovery. One person who wouldn't report him to Hayley Sharpe. The Bulldog.

~

Brighton arranged to meet The Bulldog just before lunch at the Slobbering Hound pub, located around the corner from The Bulldog's chambers in the seedy and ramshackle part of town. The Bulldog didn't care about locations as much as he cared about appearances. The Bulldog was rarely at the office and the more that he kept his overheads down, the more his retainer went into his fat little back pocket. Brighton walked up a flight of rickety old wooden stairs and found the imposing barrister in a small private booth, hidden by curtains.

'Ah DI Brighton,' he said, looking up from a huge mountain of mash with four large bangers and a generous side of peas and carrots, 'Care for some food?'

'No thanks,' said Brighton sitting across from the ravenous lawyer and helping himself to a glass of house water. The Bulldog shrugged as if to say your loss and tucked into his lunch.

'So, what do you have for me?' he said between bites.

'Well, it's thin, but I think that the perpetrator is an obsessive fan of my mother's books.'

He told The Bulldog about his visit to Kerry, the laneway search and the curious evening that followed. Brighton noticed that The Bulldog had stopped eating to give Brighton his full attention.

'That is the most positively bizarre story that anyone has ever told me.'

'I know, it's highly unlikely.'

'Just out of interest, who has Kerry's house keys?' asked The Bulldog. 'That could explain things perfectly. Whoever has the keys has the evidence. Does Cecilia have a set as well?'

'I'm not sure. I'll ask her.'

'Oh no need, I'm seeing her later. Now regarding the idea of an insane fan, that all makes sense and you've given me an angle of attack when I ask DCI Sharpe about forensics in the laneway. I can't believe that she completely overlooked Kerry's account from the start. But I'm grateful that she did slip up,' he said, baring his hungry gnashing teeth.

Brighton hoped that Hayley's pants had extra padding.

'Now, I'm going to Mortlake House at two-thirty this afternoon. I expect to be there no longer than an hour. I shall phone you once the interview has concluded and advise you what the next steps are from there. My office people are actively creating a somewhat decent social media campaign, and the press releases are ready to go out.'

Brighton was impressed. It was a little overwhelming for the young man who never thought he'd ever need a lawyer in a thousand years. He'd seen hearts and minds campaigns before. Done correctly, they had the power to change the outcome of the case in favour of the accused.

'Thanks Mr McGregor,' he said trying to remain unmoved.

'Don't mention it. Now before I leave, I must ask you about the Henderson matter.'

Ah, thought Brighton. He'd hoped that The Bulldog would somehow keep everything professional and above board, and not mention his prisoner.

'I'm afraid I can't help you Mr McGregor.'

'But' The Bulldog pouted, 'I'm her legal adviser. Surely exceptions can be made.'

Brighton knew where this was going and he was pretty sure that The Bulldog wanted the satisfaction of knowing that he was no longer Helene's brief, so that he could report back to Billie and Darren, collect his hefty retainer cheque, and be off on his merry way. Brighton also knew that The Bulldog could not be trusted, and that there was a high likelihood that he was recording the whole conversation to bribe him with later should he slip up.

'Let's do that down at the station if you don't mind.'

The Bulldog looked disappointed but dismissive and Brighton knew that deep down The Bulldog didn't give a shit, everything he did was for show, appearance, ego, and above all for his reputation.

'I take your point but know this, if I find out that my client in any way has been unduly influenced to part my company, I shall vigorously and systematically destroy any parties involved. Do I make myself clear DI Brighton?'

And just like that lunch was over. Brighton dismissed the threat, however, he knew that The Bulldog would eventually find out about Helene's deal, but for now he wanted to keep that to himself. They were still waiting for legal and the witness liaison unit to sort out the finer details. Her son and mother would be picked up at her home and whisked away separately, with neighbours thinking it was a raid. That would go down this evening, and he needed to keep The Bulldog off guard until then. Everyone had been told that Helene had been moved to a prison seventy-six miles away. That should get Brighton all the time in the world.

That night he read more of his mother's book, hoping to get an insight into the potential perpetrator and where his daughter had been taken.

The sack landed with a bump on a hard stone floor. I knew that I wasn't in the laneway anymore when the man stood up and let the sack go. As it fell past my eyes, I found that we were in a strange circular room. The room was all stone with cobbled floors. There were no windows and no doors. The only way out was a narrow staircase tucked in the corner, leading up.

The room was quite large and lit by a fire, several candles dotted around the room. Everything looked old and nothing like my own home. It reminded me of Merlin's tower. There were shelves going round the walls crammed with an unusual clutter of jars, books, and pots. There was a small sink, and it looked like this was where he made all his food. Three bowls that must belong to his cats sat on the floor.

There was a nasty smell in the air. The wicked old man and his cats left the sack and sauntered over to a huge roaring fireplace. He plonked down in a tatty blue armchair and picked up a book sitting on one of the arms.

'Fetch me my supper,' he said.

Who was he talking to? I thought. There was nobody there.

'You in the sack. I said fetch me my supper.'

It was at that moment I realised that the nasty creep was talking to me. I didn't know what to do. I was scared out of my wits.

'I want to go home,' I said and began crying with fear.

The man did not care less, and it seemed as if he expected me to cry.

'Listen to me girl. You're not going home. You'll never see your mother and father again. You are my servant now. So go and fetch me my supper. I won't tell you again. There are sausages in the larder over there. Cook them on the fireplace. If you disturb me with your crying, I shall whip ye.'

He scared me. I was only eight years old and until that day I never had a problem in the world. Now my world was gone. No Mummy. No Daddy. There was nobody but me. I knew in an instant that I had to get out of there. I simply had to, even if I had no idea where I was. I decided to wait until he was asleep and then go and see where those stairs went. I dried my eyes and went over to his larder. Sure enough there were four sausages sitting there on a plate. I found a toasting fork, stringed the sausages onto it and slowly walked to the fireplace. The cats all looked up at me and stared. I had to push past one and accidentally stood on its tail. It hissed and spat; I jumped and nearly dropped the sausages on the floor.

'Be careful,' said the man briefly looking up from his book with a scowl on his face.

I'd never cooked sausages on a fire before. Come to think of it, I'd never cooked anything. We had a cook that did all of that and mother never taught me, so I had no idea what I was doing. But I did my best, and soon I could tell that they were done. I carried them back to the sink and found a plate for them and a knife and fork.

'Here you are,' I said walking back to the man.

He looked up and when he saw the plate of sausages a smile appeared on his crusty weathered face.

'Oh good,' he said, beaming with delight before snatching the plate and tucking into them. After a while he realised that I had not moved.

'What are you waiting for? Off you go. To your spot.'

I looked around trying to work out what he meant.

'Over there silly girl.' He pointed to a pile of rags on the floor.

'Over there?' I said pointing at the rags.

'Yes. Go on. Off you go.'

The pile of rags was on the opposite side of the room to the stairwell and in darkness. With great reluctance I sat down on the rags. They stunk and were very dusty. I was hungry and watched him devour every last one of those sausages until they were gone. He put his plate in the sink, fed his cats, and sat back down on his chair and read his book for a long time until at last he yawned and stretched his arms, and I hoped he'd fall asleep at any moment.

Soon he was, and I looked over to the cats. All three were curled up on the floor in nasty little balls. I stood up and quietly, step-by-step tip toed over to the staircase. I wonder where this goes, I thought and climbed up the winding stairs that felt as if they stretched forever. No matter how far I climbed there were more and more stairs. At the top, I found a narrow landing and a big yellow door. I opened it, hoping to run out onto a meadow but instead I found myself on a tiny turret. I looked over the edge. I was miles up in the air. It was night and the largest moon I had ever seen lit the sky in silvery light. I saw all sorts of tiny lights below me and on the hillsides twinkling everywhere. They must be villages I thought. There was also movement in the sky, and I saw lanterns flying around everywhere. A few came close to the tower and to my delight I saw that they were witches on broomsticks and people riding flying carpets just like people I loved to read about in Arabian nights! I thought about calling to them but there was no way of telling if they were good, or bad like the man downstairs. Where was I? Then the marvel of being in an exciting and strange land turned to dread when I realised that even if I could somehow escape from this tower, I had absolutely no idea how to get home. With a heavy heart I slowly climbed back down the stairs.

Well, that gave me nothing, thought Brighton. A magick tower in a magickal world? Give me a break. Where the hell is this supposed to be? Skegness? Still, he wrote down tower and medieval in his notes. Tomorrow he'd do a Google search that he hoped would help him to pinpoint possible local locations.

28

After the morning section meeting, Brighton sat down at his computer and looked for leads for any castles or towers in the area. When he searched for castles, he found that most of them were jumping castles. Still, he wrote them all down because owning a jumping castle may still fit the profile. In the car he had a revelation about the cat angle. Someone with three cats would have food to buy and registration and veterinary bills. He found the details of everywhere that sold cat food in the area, including supermarkets and delivery services because it would be unlikely that whoever had Emily would leave her on her own. He added every veterinarian to the list and reminded himself to get a list of every retired vet in the area as well because they often moonlighted to earn extra cash after their retirement. When it came to towers, there was a lighthouse, a Norman ruin, and a company called Tower financial planning.

'Another busy night guv?' said Peter, sitting down, 'You should have seen the place.'

'Did you get Helene's family out okay?'

'Yeah, and legal said that her deal should be cleared with the magistrates by now.'

'That's a relief. Any issues last night?'

'Nah. We got there about ten and without too much fuss. Whole thing took about an hour. The council will remove their things today and put them in a storage facility.'

'Good work Peter. Did you see much interest from her neighbours?'

'Nah. The locals didn't seem to care but you and I both know that Billie and Darren will find out eventually and The Bulldog will come knocking for sure.'

Brighton began to wish that Cecelia had recommended another lawyer.

'Are they alright?' Helene said, as Brighton and Peter sat down in the interview room. Brighton noticed that Peter didn't even look remotely tired, which was strange as he'd have been awake for most of the night. Must be that crappy coffee machine coffee, he thought. It was so strong and thick that you could stand a pencil in your cup, and it would stay in place when you removed your hand.

'Your mother and son are fine Helene, and in good care. If you cooperate as per the terms of our arrangement, you can see them later.'

The legal arrangement had basic terms and was written by Sally the prosecutor so that it could be easily understood by a five-year-old. Brighton hoped Helene knew what she was getting into.

'Do you understand what will happen?'

She nodded and looked at him with weary eyes.

'Yeah. Youse will drop the charges and move us somewhere safe if I help you get Billie and Darren locked up. I never thought I'd be a grass. Ever. And now I've got to watch me back because they'll be coming for me, I know they will and if they don't their little mates will.'

'Would you prefer fifteen years to life imprisonment? Being an informant isn't so bad. You might even be able to offer young Lucas a normal life. That's what you have to think about here.'

He was glad she'd already signed the document because he heard the regret and the fear in her voice.

'Okay, now let's start from the beginning. What is it about Billie that you'd like to tell us? What's he up to then?'

Helene looked at Brighton and Peter, not knowing where to start.

'I dunno. Look you're not going to believe this. Not a bloody word, but I swear I'm telling youse the truth... about six or seven months back,

Billie went down to Liverpool, and his car broke down not far from here. So, he gets out and starts walking back to the nearest petrol station because he can't even get a signal on his mobile. Anyway, off he goes. It's pitch black and he can barely see the road. He walked for about twenty minutes and then something happened. Now I swear this is what he told me and if it weren't Billie telling me this, I'd tell who ever to fuck off and see a shrink. He seen lights in the forest and thought it were people with torches that were out and about and thought they could help him. So, he goes to have a look and as he gets up to the light sure enough but it weren't people that he saw. It was... brownies.'

'What did you say?' said Brighton, thinking this was a bad dream.

Peter was having none of it.

'We've just arranged your deal Helene and you're seriously going to give us this horseshit in return? Might as well rip it up now eh guv?'

'Let her finish DS Charamboulos.'

Peter rolled his eyes and looked like Brighton just slapped him in the face. Why was his boss tolerating this nonsense?

'Go on Helene. Tell me what happened next.'

When she saw that Brighton was taking her seriously Helene didn't hesitate.

'He sees these brownies. Little men with pointed little hats all sitting on toadstools around a fire talking like they were having a meeting. He stays out of sight and just watches them. They didn't seem like they was armed or nothing.'

'What were they talking about?'

'I dunno. He never said. The next thing he hears a noise like all the bushes around them are coming to life and out come these other things. Big nasty ugly critters and they attacked them. He watched on. Wasn't his fight, see? He told me they was goblins, like on Lord of the Rings, and he watched the goblins kill the lot of them.'

'What do you take us for Helene?' said Peter who'd clearly heard enough to know that they were wasting their time.

Brighton turned off the tape.

'A word,' he said to Peter, and both exited the interview room.

'Look Peter,' he said when the door closed. 'I know you think that this is just a load of old bollocks. And it might be. But a good detective knows that somewhere in the story there might just be an element of truth no matter how crazy or unbelievable that story might appear to be. Now we have Helene in that room without The Bulldog and with a deal signed. Do you not think for a moment that I'm not going to turn the conversation back to Billie and Darren's heroin racket? Because as far as I'm concerned that's all I've brought her in for. That's all I care about, so let me do my job. Sit there, say nothing and maybe you might just learn something. Okay? Detective Sergeant?'

Peter wasn't used to Brighton talking to him like that and reminding him who was boss. He shrank away.

'Yes sir.'

'Good, now go and get us some tea.'

Brighton opened the door and turned his back as Peter slunk away to the cafeteria with his tail between his legs like Wiley Coyote.

'Sorry about that. My colleague has a distinct lack of imagination. He shall be back shortly with some tea. Now let's continue.'

Brighton struggled to ask the next question, scarcely believing that he of all people would be asking it. He knew that if Sally the police prosecutor heard this tape, her loud horse like laughter would undoubtedly be heard in the next town. This would never come out in court. He knew that he was treading on thin ice and the last thing he needed was a scandal or to be made a fool of.

'Okay. Now what happened after the goblins killed the brownies?'

It sounded like an R rated Rupert the Bear adventure. Rupert and the Brownie Massacre.

'Well Billie see, he tries to sneak off real quiet like, but they get him and take him over to their leader who's throwing dead brownies on the fire. Now they ain't tied Billie up or nuthin. But he's real scared like, and their leader sees that, and Billie swears that he made a sign with his hand. Like this.'

Helene gestured a classic knife across the throat sign.

'Well Billie knows that this could be the end and remembers he has his old Russian pistol. Next thing he knows he's shot the goblin's boss between the eyes. And the rest of them start freaking out. But they ain't pissed off or nothing neither. Turns out they hated the bastard. It was like Billie had freed em or something.'

'What type of gun did Billie have?' said Brighton trying to focus on what he considered the true aspect of the case.

He wrote down goblins and brownies on his pad and gang names next to each with a big question mark. For all he knew this could be a gang and a new alliance being formed between Billie and this gang of goblins. There may even be a murder site to find.

Helene thought about his question.

'I dunno. Only seen it a couple of times. All I remember is that it sounds like one of them tennis players, don't it? Matracock? Marrakov?' Something like that.

'Could it be Makarov?'

'Nah I remember now. He had a Makarov but swapped it for a Desert Eagle he pinched from some scrote in Poland.'

Brighton wrote *Billie has a .44 magnum Desert Eagle* on his jotter.

'That's good Ms Henderson. Now did he tell you where this ambush was? Has he been back to the site recently?'

'Oh yeah. He goes back there all the time I reckon. They're his mates now. He's always going out there at night to meet them.'

'Do you know why?'

'Because they swap stuff. He gives them shooters and drugs, and they give him something better.'

'And what's that?'

'They tell him things, don't they?'

This interested Brighton. He wrote hackers next to the word goblins and put a circle with a question mark around it. A hacker turf war? Maybe he could find goblins on the dark web. He knew for certain he'd find brownies in one form or other.

'What sort of things?'

'All sorts. Sports results before they happen. Dog races and the ponies. Football. They know everything.'

'Are they fixing races and sporting matches?'

'Nah. Nothing like that. They just know who's going to win, that's all.'

He wrote match and race fixing on the page with a question mark next to it, just to be safe.

'Then Billie and Darren wanted to know about the other dealers. Who their banks were, where their cash was, and where their gear was. The goblins told em. Billie shut them down. He took their cash. The goblins took the gear, and you put them away.'

Brighton thought back. There had been a few good anonymous tips lately and a few wanna be Mr Bigs and their crews had been taken off the streets for good. The informants always delivered the intel by courier, on a spotless usb hard drive.

'But the last couple of weeks there's been shit going down between Billie and the goblins. They wanted something big. I mean this was like next level shit and Billie clammed up. Told em to sod off but they weren't having it. He reckoned they said that if he didn't help em out, that they had information to sell about him, his network... everything.'

'So, you're telling me that Billie Brown is being stood over by goblins?'

'Yeah, that's right.'

'That's crazy. You know that don't you?'

'You don't believe me. Do you?'

'Well in all my days of policing, I've only ever heard one more thing loopier than this. I interviewed a guy once who came to the station wearing a bicycle helmet covered in tinfoil. He swore that the CIA put spiders in his ears that transmitted all his thoughts to them via satellite.'

'I ain't no plonker.'

'That's not even half of it. He then told me that a terrorist cell had infiltrated the Tory party, disguised as women. He claimed that one of them was a member of parliament at the time.'

'That's funny,' said Helene, rocking back and forth in her chair, snickering.

'Now imagine how I feel about this goblin story you're telling me.'

Helene stopped laughing.

'That was real but. Every word. I can prove it.'

'What do you mean?'

'What if I take you there? I ain't been in the woods, but I know where it happened. You can see for yourself.'

'Are you sure?'

'Course I am. Hey where's that bloody tea?'

She's right, he thought. If Peter's slacking off, I'll...

Then he heard the door to the interview room open behind him.

'Where the hell have you been?' he said.

Helene panicked and gasped for air.

'You're in a world of trouble DI Brighton,' said The Bulldog. 'And as for you skank, you'll be dead before morning.'

'McGregor' said Brighton, rising to confront the intruder. 'Who let you in here? You need to leave. Now.'

The Bulldog rolled his eyes.

'You're forgetting that she is my client.'

He stared at Helene with his ruthless piggy eyes.

'Aren't I slag?'

'You stopped representing her when you left the interview yesterday.'

'That's right,' said Helene, folding her arms. 'Piss off, you dodgy old tosser.'

'What did you say to me? You'll regret that.'

'I will ask you again to leave, Mr McGregor. If you refuse, I'll have you charged with threatening a witness in protective custody. We still have a full house from last night, so it may take a while to process you. Do you fancy eating dinner with Albie the wino?'

Helene laughed.

'Not that old fart what stinks so bad that he scares the seagulls away!'

The Bulldog's face turned red.

'You've just made a very grave mistake.

'I very much doubt it,' said Brighton. 'Now on your bike before I add threatening a police officer to the charge sheet.'

Helene gave The Bulldog the finger and stuck her pierced tongue out at him before he slammed the door behind him.

'What am I going to do now? When he tells Billie and Darren, I'm fucked.'

'Sorry Helene. I don't know how that happened. All I know is that you're all safe. Only I know where you're staying and nobody else from this division.'

Helene nodded, but Brighton knew she didn't trust anyone but herself. He saw Peter ambling towards him, carrying takeaway cups of tea and a bag of sandwiches.

'Where the hell have you been?'

'Sorry guv. The cafeteria's shut, so I went across the street.'

Brighton looked at his offsider, wondering if he'd warned The Bulldog about the deal.

'Sorry to eat and run,' he said to Helene. 'Under the circumstances I'm going to take you to the safe house.'

'What do you mean?' said Peter. 'I thought she was staying in the nick.'

'That's not your concern DS Charamboulos. While you were out, we had a visit from The Bulldog. Somehow, he knew we were interviewing Helene and managed to get past security.'

'I didn't know,' said Peter with an unconvincing nervous shake in his voice.

He didn't fool Brighton for a moment.

Helene grabbed her coat and her tea and glanced at the sandwiches that Peter put on the table.

'Do you want some for the drive?' Peter said.

'No thanks. I'm gluten free.'

'I've got a job for you while I'm out Peter.'

'Oh right. I thought I was coming with you.'

'No. Besides, this is more important. Find out how The Bulldog got in here. I want whoever let him through put on notice. And get me the files of every dealer we've shut down in the last six months. We have some digging to do when I get back.'

Peter decided not to protest and skulked towards his desk.

As they drove to the safe house, Brighton asked where the goblins were.

'Could you take me there?'

'Okay, but it was dark when I went. The scrote left me in his piece of shit car without a heater and all.'

'Did he use a Sat Nav by any chance?'

'Of course he did. He's bloody useless. Now I remember. We took a left from Timber Creek Road and drove down Dumpty Lane for a couple of miles. Mind the dip in the lane. It's dangerous.'

'Cheers. I know where I'm going now. I'll drop you off first.'

Soon they arrived at a cute, whitewashed cottage, almost hidden by the forest. A familiar figure emerged to greet them.

'Hello boss,' said PC Clara Tyne, looking about as intimidating as a labradoodle. If Brighton masked his disappointment, Helene did not.

'Who's she supposed to be? My security detail?'

'Don't worry Ms Henderson, we have three armed officers in positions around the property.'

Helene looked over the pretty thatched roof and a sea of the greenest ivy growing on the wall.

'Isn't it cute?' said Clara. 'It looks like the three bears may have lived here once.'

Helene shrugged. 'Where's the telly?'

Clara tried not to grimace at Helene's priorities of security and television.

'In the lounge. We arranged for cable TV just like you asked.'

Helene climbed out of the car.

'I'll pick you up around ten in the morning,' said Brighton.

Helene shrugged as she set off to find the television with Clara on her heels.

29

The sun had disappeared long before Brighton found the dip in Dumpty Lane. He flipped his headlights to high beam and slowed down to control the sharp descent. His tyres crunched over shattered windscreen glass and broken pieces of taillight of a less fortunate driver. He saw tyre tracks where a car had parked a few times, judging from the wear in the ground from the tread. Brighton turned the engine off and searched the glove compartment for his ASP baton. Who knows what's out there he thought, putting a few things in his bag before melting into the darkness.

He found a rough track through the ancient oaks, packed between birch, elms, and pines all stunted from lack of sunlight. It had been a long while since Brighton had looked at a tree in detail. Who did any more? Several of the twisted trunks had faces with huge hollow eyes that looked ready to open and stare at him. A set of tracks led down a steep trail.

An owl screeched, scaring Brighton half to death. He jolted forward and tripped on a rock, cursing as he tumbled through the darkness until he slammed into an ancient log.

'Damn it,' he muttered, feeling a burning pain in his left foot. He gave up trying to stand and wriggled over to his shining torch. The sweet stench of death wafted through his nose. It reminded him of the decomposed dementia patient he found when he was a bobby. His hand sank into something wet and squishy, like a forgotten tomato sandwich.

Torchlight interrupted the feasting of thousands of maggots pulsing around a lifeless arm like coral polyps. He looked up and stared into the face of a dead goblin.

'No way. This isn't real,' he said, wiping his grotty hand on some wet grass. 'It's a dream or something. Has to be. I hit that log pretty hard. Is this a concussion?'

But his nose did not lie, and neither did his eyes. Like Zaliel, goblins were real. The strange horned creature's rotting face seemed to sneer at him. In the centre of its skull, he saw a large bullet wound. Judging from its gaping mouth, the last emotion that this goblin experienced was surprise. Helene had told him the truth. He used his phone to take pictures of the corpse. Then he extracted the bullet with his tweezers.

'I might not get you for murder Billie,' he said. 'But I can prosecute you for firing an illegal firearm in public.'

The round might link the weapon to other crimes. The goblin itself had nothing of interest. Its rings, shoes, and valuables were gone. Its big purple ears had chunks of skin hanging off where earrings had been ripped out.

A twig snapped nearby. Brighton flicked his torch off and lay still. The dead goblin was four feet tall. As a pack, they would be formidable, but he still had his ASP. What if there were more of them? What if they see him? He crawled away and found a thick branch that supported his weight to use as a cane. He grasped the torch with his free hand and followed several smaller footprints into a clearing. Scattered about were the charred bodies of eight or nine brownies. They were much shorter than the goblins. A few had heads missing. Others had limbs ripped out of their sockets. The goblins had attacked one with a frenzied force that painted its intestines in the tree above it like savage tinsel. The crows and scavengers had picked the remains clean. He shuddered. Had Stephen King co-written one of his mother's books? He stared in disbelief, not knowing whether to think he was in a crime scene or a video game. He took more pictures and gathered evidence.

Adjacent to one of the dead, he found a strange little charm that glowed in the dark. As Brighton picked it up, he heard voices coming in his direction. He turned off his torch and hid behind the bushes at the foot of a tree. The last thing he needed was a goblin toting an AK47 with a bump of meth in its system. To his relief, the creatures were not goblins. Judging from their height and wings, they were not brownies either. They were fairies. Both held glowing wands at the ready.

When they saw the mess, both went into high states of alertness.

'Now we know what happened to Mr Tickle Whiskers,' declared the short muscular male. 'Aldercy must learn of this at once.'

The tall stocky female with the blunt bob hair cut ignored him. Her pointy, slender ears moved about, listening for danger like a cat on a hunt.

'Back me up Kip,' she said, moving towards Brighton, her wand pointing at his chest. 'You there. Yes, I can see you, so there's no point in hiding. Stand up.'

Brighton had no choice. It took two goes for him to get up. His size alarmed her at first, but she stood her ground.

'Put that down, human. Then put your hands behind your head,' she added for intimidation.

'I can't do that,' he said. 'I've…'

'Put it down or I'll freeze you.'

'Are you guys cops?'

Kip and Eddie glanced at each other.

'Silence creature,' said Eddie.

'May I speak? Please?'

'No, you may not. Know your place.'

Brighton ignored her and spoke to Kip.

'Look. I sprained my bloody ankle and if I put this down, I'll land flat on my face.'

Eddie stared at him like he was a freak show oddity.

'What are you talking about? Your ankle is not bloody at all. Now drop it.'

There was no point in arguing. He fell face down, rolling on the ground writhing in pain, grabbing at his ankle with both hands.

Kip raced over to help.

'Move your hands,' he said, holding his wand near the ankle to examine it. 'That's a nasty twist,' he said, 'But I'll soon mend it.'

Kip closed his eyes. The light from his wand turned from orange to a calming blue, cooling his ankle. The pain swirled and disappeared like water down a drain.

'Thank you,' he said when Kip opened his eyes again.

'You're welcome. Now get on your knees and put your hands on your fucking head.'

Brighton put his hands behind his head. Kip put his handcuffs on. They were super tight, and he couldn't budge an inch. Eddie patted Brighton down.

'What's this?' she said, removing his ASP.

'It's a weapon. Like a baton.'

'What do you need a weapon for?'

'Judging from what I've seen, it's not very safe around here, is it?'

She kept looking through his pockets and put his torch next to the ASP.

'Here's confirmation that he's a human, Kip. He's got one of those fake light things. That would explain his stupidity.'

Kip nodded as he rifled through Brighton's rucksack. He pulled out the evidence bags.

'What are these for?'

'I'm a police officer. They're for a case I'm working on.'

'Ha! A likely story,' said Eddie as she finished frisking him.

'Please, it's true. My bag has a side pocket. My ID and warrant card are there.'

Kip fished around in the pocket and found them tucked down at the bottom.

'He's telling the truth, Eddie. What do we do now? Should we release him?'

'No way. I say we take him in for questioning, and if he's lying, we'll lock him away for murder.'

Brighton didn't like the sound of that one bit.

'What if there's another way? What if I helped you guys? If you are the police. I'll give you everything I've got and in return, I want you to let me go.'

'Pah,' said Eddie. 'What do you think we are? Pixies?'

'Okay. I'll give you the first piece of information for nothing. Close by is a body of a dead goblin. He was the leader of the gang that killed these brownies. He's got a big hole in his head. A human shot him.'

'I don't believe you,' said Eddie. 'Take us there, but if you're leading us into a trap human, I'll turn you into a steamy pile of owl shit.'

'Charming. Where did you do your rapport building training? Burger King?'

'Shut it,' said Eddie, hauling him up from the ground. 'Lead the way.'

Kip put everything back in the bag. Then the two elves marched their captive through the clearing, following the tracks that he'd found.

'There,' said Brighton with triumph in his voice, pointing to the goblin's body.

Kip gasped.

'Eddie! That's Glodprog the goblin king.'

'Are you certain? They all look the same to me.'

'It's him alright. See? He's lost that finger from his fight with Torook, the dwarf. He's missing two toes from frostbite when he was on the run in the Byfic Mountains.'

'Okay. Take one of his fingers back. We'll get one of the witches to do a spell to confirm it's him.'

Brighton watched Kip turn green at the request.

'Does it need to be a finger? I've got his DNA in my bag, and the bullet that killed him.'

'Is this it?' Kip pulled out a bag with the bullet head and the shell.

'Yeah, that's it.'

The bullet intrigued Kip.

'How does this work?'

'It goes with this shell. We call it a bullet. A gun fires them. In this case, a .44 Desert Eagle.'

'A gun? Where's yours?'

'Our police force only has a few guns. I don't have one. That's why I have the ASP.'

'Do many humans use guns?'

'Yes. But not so much in England. In America, everyone has one.'

Eddie looked at the empty shell.

'I've seen these at an attack on the Wizard Drinkalot's walking tavern. Now we know what they are, we must warn Aldercy.'

A walking tavern? thought Brighton. That sounded dangerous and he could see loads of drunk and lost fairy folk in all kinds of trouble.

'What about me?' said Brighton. 'Can I go now?'

'No. You're coming with us.'

'I don't have time for this. I'm looking for my daughter. She's missing.'

'A likely story,' said Kip, 'We found you at the crime scene.'

'And you showed us where another body was. For all we know, you put that bullet in Glodprog's skull.'

'And you removed evidence that may link you to the crime.'

'Good job Kip. Well done for learning your instruction manual.'

There was no reasoning with them. With Kip behind him, Brighton followed Eddie back through the clearing, where they arrived at a great ancient oak tree. Eddie snatched up a handful of acorns and thrust them into a hole in the tree trunk. A bit of bark shone, and when she pushed it a wide portal opened, revealing sunlight and an immense green sky. She motioned to Brighton.

'Move on. It won't stay open for long.'

Brighton peered through the door.

'Where are we going?'

'Why the Magical Wooded World silly. Haven't you heard of it?'

Brighton looked pale.

'Hell no. I'm not going in there.'

'Yes, you are!' said Eddie.

Together, she and Kip pushed him through the portal and into a realm that until now, he'd assumed was just the product of his mother's imagination.

30

'No!' said Brighton, struggling to get free as the portal closed, trapping him in a place he never wanted to read about, never mind visit.

'Stop it,' said Eddie, pointing her wand at him.

Brighton sank to his knees and broke down as days of anxiety and stress overwhelmed his mind.

'Let's face the facts. I went into the woods alone. I fell, twisted my ankle and I've banged my head too. This must be a dream. I'm going to wake up in the morning covered in squirrel crap with an enormous bruise on my head,' he told himself.

'What's wrong with him?' said Kip.

'I've seen it before, it reminds me of some strange furry naked humans in the woods the last time I was there. You should have seen their long hair and scraggly ball sacks bouncing in the breeze when they ran away from me.'

'He'd better snap out of it before we get to the station. Aldercy will have a fit.'

'I know Kip. Come on! There's no time to waste.'

Eddie grabbed Brighton's arm and dragged him along a rough, cobbled path through a forest of enormous oak trees.

'Lead the way, fairy woman,' he said, adjusting to the pale light of the sky from a distant green, glowing sun. Wherever I am, it isn't home, he thought. It has to be a dream.

The path soon emptied into a huge clearing, dominated by a high grassy hill. The party continued straight up the steep and difficult slope. I might escape if I roll back down, Brighton thought.

Kip prodded Brighton's back with his wand.

'Try anything and I'll stun you into next week.'

'What are you talking about?'

'Don't be silly. You're wearing elvish cuffs. I can hear everything you think about. Hey! That's not very nice! I am not into that sort of thing at all!'

Brighton grinned.

'Enough talking. Put your back into it,' said Eddie.

When he reached the top, Brighton looked down at the valley in wonder. The pale emerald sky brimmed with traffic, just like his mother had written in her book. Under a massive mountain, he saw a vast metropolis of purple toadstool houses with antennas on the rooftops and windows adorned with pots of orange and blue geraniums. Some larger mushrooms had decks, and balconies. To his surprise, he even saw one with a built-in swimming pool. Scattered among the mushroom houses were cute little thatched cottages that looked like they'd fallen from the pages of storybooks.

Beyond the houses, he saw a medieval town square teeming with life and dominated by two larger buildings that reminded him of beehives. The huge modern cylindrical structures had layer after layer of intricate windows and shades wrapped around them, both looking more science fiction than fantasy. In the centre of each flat brown roof flew imposing blue flags adorned with a crowned oak tree surrounded by golden symbols that he couldn't make out. What is this place? he thought.

'That's Elfhame,' said Kip, reading his mind.

An angry gnome armed with a spear hopped out in front of them on a giant frog. He frowned at Eddie.

'About time you came back. Why have you brought that... thing here? Have you forgotten the rules, Edilyn?'

Eddie rolled her eyes.

'Of course not. Calm down Gruffy. I'm bringing him in for questioning. Glodprog is dead.'

The gnome shrugged and gave her his best get fucked look.

'And this creature is responsible?' said Gruffy. He glared at Brighton with his beady black eyes.

'No, but he might know who killed Mr Tickle Whiskers.'

Gruffy reminded Brighton of the gnome in the Maloney family garden, and he imagined him with a fishing rod trying to catch Koi Carp from the pond. He bit his lip to stop himself from laughing at the idea.

'Tickle Whiskers is dead? Told him not to go to that wood. What's wrong with the prisoner? Is he drunk?'

'For fuck's sake, what do you expect Gruffy? He's a human. It's not like they're known for being intelligent creatures, are they?'

'I suppose so. But tell him to stop staring at me. Okay? It's not polite.'

'You heard him prisoner. Don't stare.'

Satisfied, the surly gnome hopped back down the hill to his post.

This is one lucid dream, thought Brighton. I must have hit that branch hard. He was so busy gawping that he walked straight into the path of a dwarf.

'Oi you!' the dwarf yelled as the sky above them darkened. 'Watch where you're going, or I'll shove my axe right up your...'

Brighton never learned where the dwarf planned to put his axe.

'Ddd...' said the dwarf, his hand shivered as he pointed into the sky, shitting his brightly coloured little pants as he turned and ran from the massive purple dragon above them.

Trees shook as the dragon landed with a mighty thump. It flicked the dwarf into the air with its tail, roasted him in a ball of brilliant orange flame and swallowed him whole. Shitty pants and all.

'Turn dragon!' said Zaliel pulling the beast around with a thick set of reins looped through a ring in its nose.

Brighton's eyes locked with twin yellow balls of hate.

'Come here William,' said Zaliel. 'Or you shall never see Emily again.'

'Where is she?' said Brighton without a second thought for his safety. 'Give her back to me you bastard!'

'Stop being such a fucking idiot!' said Eddie, grabbing at his arms.

'He's got my daughter. Let me go!'

Brighton wrestled free from Eddie's grip, but he didn't get three paces before a sharp jolt surfed through the adrenaline and sent him falling to the ground. Eddie looked across to Kip, who had his wand pointed at Brighton's prone body.

'How many times have I told you,' she said, 'warn people before you zap them and lower that bloody setting!'

Incensed, Zaliel reared his steed up.

'Kill them!'

Standing on its hind legs, the dragon drew a deep breath.

'Quick Kip,' said Eddie.

Grabbing Brighton's arms, the fairies flew towards Gruffy's checkpoint with flames licking at their feet.

'He's too heavy Ed!'

'Keep going! Keep going!'

The two fairies skimmed over the grass. They dumped Brighton on the ground like a sack of shit before they turned to face the dragon riding wizard. Gruffy sat poised on his battle frog, ready for a fight as other gnomes and fairy folk warriors milled around him. Horns blasted, rousing the citizens of Elfhame, and they came running out of their homes armed with anything they could find.

'You there,' called Zaliel. 'Give me the human and I'll spare your life.'

'Why don't ye fuck off, Zaliel,' said Gruffy, 'Before I get angry and throw ye in the cells.'

The dragon landed near one of the mushroom houses dotted about the place. Its sheer bulk scared the eager villagers back a few paces.

'Come out William!'

'Hey, you up there!' said Eddie, 'He's not going anywhere with you. He's our prisoner. Now unless you want me to take you down for the murder of Grumpy the dwarf, I suggest you f...ly off.'

Zaliel glared at the rude little fairy bitch. Before he replied, someone threw a tomato at him, and soon it was raining plates and ladles and rocks. The dragon grew uneasy.

'Be still,' said the wizard, as his scaly steed reared up.

A window above him opened.

'Get the fuck off my lawn,' said Old Hannay, a gnome with many knots in his long, white beard.

He threw the sloppy brown contents of a chamber pot at Zaliel's head and smiled when he scored a direct hit. The wizard seethed with rage as lukewarm gnome shit dripped down his head and his neck and into his shirt collar. The overpowering stench of the little gnome's protein rich diet made the dragon launch itself the hell out of there, dragging the screaming wizard with it.

Thundering applause and laughter echoed all around and the people of Elfhame hurled every insult imaginable at Zaliel as he disappeared over the distant mountains. As the crowd dispersed, Eddie and Kip returned to their prisoner.

'Why did you do that?' he said. 'He kidnapped my daughter!'

'Get it right, I didn't zap you, Kip did,' said Eddie. 'You're our prisoner and if you knew anything about Zaliel, you'd appreciate what we just did. We did you a favour William.'

'Please don't call me that. It's Brighton. Okay... Edilyn.'

'What the fuck did you just call me?'

'Let's be on our way,' said Kip, smirking at his superior's discomfort.

'This is the central policing station,' said Kip, as they arrived at one of the large beehive buildings. 'We take care of the crime investigation and law enforcement for the entire country.'

'He's not here for a tour, Kip. Come on.' Eddie took them through a revolving door onto the ground floor.

This is just like the station in Plymouth, Brighton thought, noticing a secure counter manned by folk dressed in the same uniforms as Eddie and Kip. The powerful aromas of piss, vomit, and all manner of filth greeted his nose like an old friend. Smells like it too. Nobody in the waiting room or at the counter gave him a second glance.

'Someone stole all the gold from my cellar!' said an angry witch to a bored looking fairy, who scribbled down notes on parchment with ink and a quill with a huge pink feather.

'My neighbours ate the brand-new chocolate coated digestive window shutters I bought from Cookie Land' wept a life-sized gingerbread man 'I know it was them!'

Brighton saw lost children, lost property, and a seriously wasted dwarf woman twerking her chubby little ass in his direction from the drunk tank.

'No thanks,' muttered Brighton, looking away and hoping that Eddie didn't plan on leaving him with her.

Instead, she marched him to a clear security door and knocked three times. A tall witch stood up from her chair and raced over.

'Eddie!' she squealed, hugging her friend after she let the three into the secured zone. 'You're back! We were so worried about you! Well, except for Gruffy. I wanted to search for you, but Aldercy wouldn't allow it.' She looked at Brighton. 'Who's this?'

'Just a human we found near a crime scene. Is Aldercy around?'

'No, he's briefing a search party. You know O'Corra the food critic? He's gone missing.'

'I'm not surprised. How many people has he offended with those reviews now? There'd be a few hundred. When Aldercy shows up could you let him know that I'm waiting in interview room two if it's free.'

The witch shook her head.

'I'd use room five. There was an accident in two. The cleaning gnomes haven't mopped it out yet.'

'Thanks for the warning, Vera. Let's catch up after shift ends.'

'I'd like that. Drinks at the Wilted Toadstool!'

'Oh, great idea! Around seven?'

'You're on.'

Brighton wondered what the Wilted Toadstool was like. Judging from their tender embrace, it potentially had a select clientele. The door opened into a huge candlelit room which had the menace and feel of the Spanish inquisition.

'Sit over there,' said Eddie, motioning to a piece of furniture in the centre of a pentagram painted silver, in a red chalk circle. Strange golden magick symbols floated around the perimeter as if on guard duty.

'I don't think this is a good idea,' said Kip.

'Mind your business, or I'll have you demoted back to Probationary Constable and put you on permanent night patrol. Would you like that?'

Kip gasped and left the room.

'Now you,' Eddie said, turning her attention back to Brighton, 'Get in that chair.'

'How about saying please?'

'What do you mean?'

'I mean, you've been rude to me since we've met and for no reason. I've done everything you've asked me to do, and you have not even asked me if I needed a toilet break or if I was hungry and you haven't even told me what I've done wrong. You just took me prisoner by force and have not offered me any legal counsel. You're not much of an officer.'

Eddie blinked and scowled. She drew her wand, ready to strike him, when the door thrust open and an older statuesque elf sauntered in.

'Nice to see you've returned Edilyn,' he said with a hint of warmth in his fatherly voice as she put her wand away.

'Mr Brighton, I presume?'

Brighton looked at him and nodded.

'You must be Aldercy.'

'How astute of you young man,' he smiled. 'Do take those handcuffs off our guest, daughter. They do look somewhat uncomfortable.'

Eddie obeyed without a word of protest. Brighton rubbed his sore wrists, grateful to be free again.

'Now, I think everyone could do with a hot cup of tea. Don't you?'

Aldercy clapped his hands twice and the interview room transformed into a space that looked like the office of a professor of philosophy. An open journal sat on a small oak desk cluttered with papers, quills, and ink. The journal slammed shut when Brighton peeked at it. Crammed bookshelves lined the windowless room, sharing space with crystal balls and an assortment of curious occult bric-à-brac. Old rugs and copper vessels hung in the gaps. To his surprise, Brighton heard the soft melancholic voice of Julio Iglesias playing from an ancient gramophone.

Aldercy sat in a low sitting armchair and bade Eddie and Brighton to join him. A round door opened, Kip entered carrying a tray with a tea set with four little green cups and a large teapot hidden under the most hideous bright patchwork tea cosy Brighton had ever seen in his life.

'Ah thank you Kip,' said Aldercy as Kip put the tray down on a low coffee table and joined them.

'I hope you don't mind PG Tips,' he said to Brighton as he poured the tea. 'I'm quite fond of the monkey.'

'Thank you,' said Brighton picking up the dainty cup while trying not to spill any tea.

'Now tell me daughter, why have you brought Mr Brighton to our world?'

'We found him when we found the bodies of Mr Tickle Whiskers and his associates. I think he has something to do with it.'

'Tickle Whiskers is dead you say? That's sad to hear. He had strong ties to England and despite my warnings, he'd often venture back, taking others with him. A very reckless brouny. Much like his son.' Aldercy said with a sprinkle of spite.

'Glodprog's gang murdered him. Glodprog is also dead. Killed by a human.'

'Not by Mr Brighton, I hope?'

'I don't know for sure, but the prisoner did lead us to him. That's why we've brought him in.'

'There's something else,' said Kip, not seeing Eddie's eyes roll when he opened his mouth. 'A strange device killed Glodprog. We didn't know what it was, but we've seen them before, haven't we Eddie? Remember? At the Walking Tavern?'

Eddie gave him a dismissive glance and nodded.

'That's true. We'd seen them before, and the human told us about a weapon called a...'

'Gun? Yes, I have seen a gun, Edilyn. But I was not aware about the Walking Tavern incident though, nor about any strange weapons. Perhaps someone will get back on top of her paperwork sooner or later and report it to me.'

Aldercy let Eddie squirm for a while and brought his attention back to Brighton.

'Kip told me you are also involved in law enforcement.'

'That's correct. I'm a Detective Inspector.'

'I'm impressed,' said Aldercy. 'I'd love to learn about new policing methods. Have humans moved away from truncheons yet? Are you using robots like Robocop? Oh, I do like your Hollywood movies.'

Brighton smiled, even though he'd not seen Robocop since he was a child at a friend's house.

'When was the last time you saw one of our police officers, Mr Aldercy?'

'Oh, just call me Aldercy. That's my first name. It's a little rare these days, I'd expect. I first visited your world just over two hundred years ago. Your police officers were called Peelers, I believe. Fascinating people.'

Brighton looked at the elf in wonder.

'Geez, I thought you were only fifty or something, a lot younger looking than my mum was.'

Aldercy smirked.

'My family does come from good stock,' he gave Brighton a strange glance, 'well most of us are.'

Brighton wasn't sure what to make of such an offhand comment, it made him feel uncomfortable, so he sedged back to the police force.

'I would say much has changed since you last visited. Our uniforms have changed for starters. Most of us do not carry guns. Only the armed response units do. The rest of us carry ASPs.'

'Snakes?' said Aldercy. 'Humans must be braver than they used to be.'

'No, not snakes. I'll show you.'

As Brighton reached for his bag, Eddie pulled it out of his reach.

'That's not a good idea,' said Eddie. 'He might try to harm you.'

'I don't believe that Brighton is a threat, Edilyn. I don't believe that he killed the brounies or Glodprog either.'

Brighton noticed the absence of mister. He must have read my mind, he thought.

'Now let him have his bag.'

Brighton opened it and withdrew the small metal ASP.

'Oh, that strange little stick,' said Eddie.

But when Brighton stood and extended it out, she drew her wand at him.

'Put it down. Now! Before I zap you into next week.'

Aldercy raised his hand.

'Oh, stop being so protective, Edilyn. I can take care of myself. Besides, I asked to see it, didn't I?'

Brighton passed the ASP over to Aldercy, who examined it and admired the workmanship.

'What an ingenious invention! So much better than those primitive truncheons. We might have to place an order.' He gave the ASP back to Brighton. 'I suppose we should talk about this gun issue.'

Brighton told Aldercy why he'd gone into the forest and a little about his case and suspects. Aldercy thought for a moment.

'Interesting. Do you know how long they have been trading?'

'I'm not sure. I don't know what the goblins are asking Billie and Darren for either. They never told my witness.'

'Do you have any ideas?'

'No, I'm still trying to deal with the fact this world is real to be honest.'

Aldercy smiled.

'That may take a while. In the meantime, we should work together to stop the goblins before it is too late. Edilyn, you will work with Brighton and be the liaison between our worlds. What's wrong dear? Do you need to use the lavatory?'

Eddie tried her best not to scream.

'I'm fine,' she said, trying to compose herself.

'Good,' he said, enjoying her discomfort. 'As you will be working with us, I shall make you a cunning man.'

What is he talking about? Brighton thought. The term meant nothing to him, but it made Eddie explode.

'But father!' she said, 'We can't trust him. We know nothing about him.'

'But Edilyn, I do know him. I helped his mother escape from Zaliel, the sorcerer.'

'I'm sorry. You did what?'

Brighton thought he'd lost the plot. His mother really had been here. Her *Tales of the Magical Wooded World* were true.

'I helped your mother escape from Zaliel. When you were born, your mother contacted a very clever woman and asked that I give you a charm which would protect you against Zaliel in your own world. He had been close to finding her, and she was scared. I gave our associate instructions to make a small tattoo on the back of your neck. It's so tiny that nobody would ever notice. From that moment, Zaliel could no longer harm you in your world. The last we heard, he had just stopped hunting for your mother.'

'She died a few weeks ago.'

Aldercy looked sad. Or did he? There was something about the look on his face that Brighton felt was not entirely genuine.

'My condolences.'

'The bastard has my daughter. I need to find him.'

'Yes, Kip told me all about your encounter. You're lucky he landed near old Hannay's house. Zaliel isn't easy to find you know. He lives in a wandering tower, cloaked from all detection.'

'We've never tracked him down,' added Eddie.

'But you're magickal.'

'Yes, and so is he. Even more so. His tower is undetectable. No magick can ever find it.'

'Could you help me find him?' said Brighton to Aldercy.

'I will assist you with this goblin case and anything else I can help with. From what you have told us, it's a direct threat to our world. However, once we've shut the goblins down, we shall help search for your daughter. I can't promise that we will find her, but we will try.'

Eddie and Kip looked surprised.

'But that's a fool's errand,' said Eddie. 'There's no possible...'

'Silence. I've told Brighton that we shall help him and help we shall. Making him a cunning man is the first step.'

Brighton's eyes followed Aldercy as he ambled over to a little cabinet cluttered with all manner of bottles and jars.

'What's a cunning man?' Brighton asked.

'Oh, that's easy,' said Kip, 'A cunning man is like a wizard.'

Confused, Brighton looked at him.

'Huh? You're going to make me magickal?'

'Sort of,' said Aldercy, returning with a vial of shimmering deep blue liquid in his hand. 'Once you drink this, you can heal, recover lost and stolen goods, identify criminals, and speak to the dead.'

Brighton looked at the little vial. He was unsure about drinking it.

'There isn't time to waste. It won't harm you. I promise.'

The very sweet drink made Brighton gag.

'I'm sorry, but the urine of a unicorn cannot be diluted. Otherwise, I'd have added butterscotch schnapps.'

As the world spun around him, Brighton felt dizzy. Did he say unicorn piss? How much acid had the unicorn consumed?

'Contact us when you find out something. You can ask the brouny in your home how to do that.'

'The what?' said Brighton.

'Brouny. I forget that you incorrectly refer to them as brownies. His name is Thundershack, and he is expecting you. Until next time,' said Aldercy, waving as Brighton closed his eyes and fell into darkness.

31

Brighton woke up on a soft mound of pea green moss that covered everything in the dreamscape forest of ancient oak trees, dressing them in a well-worn tweed. The forest looked magical, and he didn't realise that he'd left the Magical Wooded World until he saw the sun peeking through the branches above him.

'I'll never drink unicorn pee again,' he muttered, rubbing his sore head.

He found his bag nearby and cursed when he looked inside. His phone was missing and with it the evidence of the dead goblin and brownie massacre. He started climbing up the deep gully. The slippery moss made it a little more difficult than he'd hoped. He grabbed the outstretched boughs of the ancient trees and hauled his way out of the woods. When he reached the road, his car was nowhere to be seen.

'Damn!' he said and made his way to the safe house to get a lift back to the station.

Tall pines replaced the oaks along either side of the narrow dirt road and Brighton took his time in the enveloping fog, keeping an eye out for any sign of traffic. He walked in silence through the mists, wondering if he'd woken from a dream or a spell. Until now, his life had been bound by the confines and constraints of normality. He struggled to grasp that any of the events he'd experienced were real.

'I must have slipped on that moss and knocked myself out,' he said to himself as he checked the back of his head for any unexplained lumps.

While it sounded like a reasonable explanation, there was no evidence, and his headache reminded him of nights on the town in his younger days, more than a wound of any kind. Maybe there was something in the moss that induced hallucinations. By the time he reached the safe house, he'd found nine plausible explanations for his experience, including exhaustion, sleep deprivation, and a potential allergic reaction to fungus. After he negotiated his way past the armed guards, he went to the safe house door and knocked a few times.

'PC Tyne, PC Tyne. Are you there Clara?'

'Detective Inspector Brighton?' said Clara as she opened the door. 'Where have you been? You were supposed to be here days ago. The entire station's been out looking for you ever since we found your car.'

He decided not to say anything to Clara about the night's peculiar events.

'Where is my car now?'

'It's down at the station. The last I heard, the evidence boys finished with it today.'

'What do you mean the evidence boys had it? What were they doing?'

'Looking for clues about your disappearance. You've been missing for two days.'

Two days? he thought. I only spent a couple of hours in Elfhame.

'Are you okay? You look shocked.'

'I'm alright,' he said.

Helene walked in.

'Hey Clara, you wouldn't have a spare lighter, would you? Only someone dunked mine into the teapot.'

Her son poked his head through the doorway and blew a raspberry at them. She laughed until she saw Brighton.

'Oh, nice of you to turn up innit? Gave me a right scare you did.'

'Nice to see you too, Helene. I'll be back tomorrow sometime. We'll talk then, okay?'

'Yeah sure. Ain't like I'm going anywhere. Can I have that lighter?'

Clara hunted in her handbag and gave Helene a small green lighter.

'Cheers,' said Helene, walking back into the sitting room.

'I'd better call in and let everyone know you're safe,' said Clara, putting her phone to her ear.

'Hello Sergeant Peters, PC Tyne here. Oh, I'm good, thanks. May I speak to DCI Sharpe please? It's about DI Brighton. Yes, I've found him.'

She looked at Brighton.

'He's putting me through now.'

There was a long pause and Brighton figured that Sergeant Peters was summoning the courage to call her.

'Good afternoon guv. Yes... I...'

Brighton heard the arctic blast from where he was standing and prepared for the worst when Clara handed her phone over.

'She wants a word.'

'Where have you been?' said Hayley Sharpe, sounding like a Hogwarts Howler.

'Good afternoon, guv... Well, I've been undercover. An opportunity presented itself and I took it.'

'Why didn't you tell me first? For God's sake. Half the force has been out searching the bloody woods for you.'

'Sorry guv. There was no time to warn you. If I had, your reaction would not have been genuine and the people I was with would have seen through it.'

Brighton's bluff worked, and he was glad he'd watched those old Beverly Hills Cop movies when he was a kid.

'I've got some good intelligence on a crime syndicate linked to the Henderson case and evidence that may incriminate Billie Brown.'

'What evidence?'

'Shell and casing fired from a Desert Eagle. It's from Billie's pistol. We'll charge him for having an illegal firearm and for discharging it in public. That should be enough to secure a warrant.'

'That won't do. Our prosecutor is more pedantic than that. Get a better statement from the witness protection girl in the morning. Focus on what we can use, the guns and the drugs. If she doesn't want to cooperate, tell her that we'll cut her loose. Think you can do that?'

Brighton never mistreated and bullied his witnesses; but he knew people like Hayley Sharpe took a dim view to anyone who didn't bow to her will, and so he played the game.

'Of course, guv. You can count on me.'

His response had the desired effect.

'Good work. I want a full report by tomorrow afternoon.'

Brighton winced as Hayley slammed her phone down.

'Are you alright?' said Clara. 'DCI Sharpe can be very confronting.'

Like a shoal of piranha, thought Brighton.

'Oh, I'm fine, thanks. Hey, could you give me a lift down to the station? I need to pick my car up.'

'Oh. I'm not going back to Plymouth for a while, boss. I live in Princetown, you see. That's why I took this assignment. It gives me time to get home to my boys and help them with their homework and football training if there's still light.'

'Brilliant. I live near Princetown. Would you be able to give me a lift? Please? I'll get the car tomorrow.'

'I suppose,' she said, 'As long as you sign for my petrol receipts.'

Brighton watched Clara's old Mini pull away from his mother's cottage and tear off down the road. Driving at record speed, she used all her defensive driving skills to dash off to the village store to buy a carton of eggs before it closed. I hope she likes them scrambled, he thought. Stepping through the front door and into the cottage, he was almost happy to be home until he remembered Kerry was still at Mortlake House and Emily was being held by an evil wizard that wanted him dead.

'About time you showed up,' said a gravelly voice.

Brighton looked around. There was no one there. Where had the voice come from? Was it just in his mind?

'No, I'm not in your mind. You can't see because I'm here in the kitchen. Dumb ass.'

'Who's there?' he said, striding down the hall and into the kitchen, where he found an unusual sight.

At the table sat a strange looking little man with a grey Mohawk. His tiny black eyes stared up at him like a cornered rat. The tubby fellow was about three feet tall, and it must have taken him a long time to climb up onto the chair because he was sweating like he'd been working out for two hours.

'Hello,' he said, 'Do you remember me?'

'No. Have we met?'

'We sure have. When you were a kid. I used to use your room as a shortcut to the bog. I could swear that you'd seen me a couple of times, at least because I was loud and once I let one go and woke you up. You blamed your sister for that. Remember?'

Brighton just could not believe that this little man had been living in his house for all this time, never mind that he'd farted in his bedroom when he was a kid. Of all the memories he had growing up, that was one that stayed close to his mind. He smiled.

'Maybe. I think I can remember the night of the loud fart. It was pretty bad.'

'Yeah well, I'm lactose intolerant and your mother insisted on filling my bowl with macaroni cheese a few times because you refused to eat it.'

That made Brighton feel guilty about the bread and milk he'd left in the brownie bowl.

'No, that was Marta. She went vegan and drove mum up the wall. So, you're Thumbletack?'

'No, that's my aunt. I'm Thundershack. Now introductions are out of the way. Could you order us dinner?'

'Yeah sure,' said Brighton. 'So, what do brownies like to eat?'

'Brouny. I'm a brouny okay? Not a fucking junior girl scout,' said the little man with an indignant scowl.

'Okay, okay I get it. What do you want to eat?'

The brouny pointed over to the menu on the fridge door.

'Bring that over, will you?'

'You want a curry?' said Brighton bringing him the menu for the Tastes of Kolkata, a local restaurant, and a delight to Kerry when she found the menu in their letterbox with a five percent off delivery promotion.

'Course I eat curry. I eat whatever you put in my bowl, and it just so happens that your wife put me on to chicken jalfrezi. Let's have that' he said, reading off the menu. 'And seven onion bhaji's and three samosas, a roti, daal, chapati, one of them mango milk whatsits, and sauces. I like the tamarind chutney as well.'

For such a little guy, he sure loved his curry.

'Yeah sure,' said Brighton. No wonder you're so fat, he thought.

'Oi!' said the brouny. 'There's no need to make assumptions, is there? I mean, we've only just met and you're cracking on about my weight and having a little laugh.'

'I didn't say anything.'

'You don't need to. I can read your mind, and I can talk with telepathy if I want to, he said, tickling Brighton's brain.

'Ew, do you mind? Get the hell out.'

'I just wanted to show you what I can do so that you know next time, okay? Now order my dinner before they close.'

Brighton rang the restaurant, remembering his own meal at the last minute.

'Get a couple of beers as well. Guinness will do fine, but if they don't have it, grab a six pack of Magners Irish Cider, anything but that horrid Kingfisher cat piss you had in the fridge.

Had? Brighton went to the fridge to investigate. Sure enough, the six cans of Kingfisher beer were missing.

You stole my beer you little prick! he thought, glaring at the brouny's smirking little face, not giving a shit that he heard him. There were limits and a man's beer was one of them. Brighton finished the order and sat down at the table with Thundershack.

'How long will they be? I'm famished and when was the last time you went shopping sunshine? Now that you know I'm here, I'd appreciate it if you could be more considerate and get a few things for me from time to time. Like Penguin biscuits, Lays Crisps, pork scratchings, Branston's Pickles and Bovril. Living on your scraps ain't much of a life, especially when you haven't been home for three days. Oh, and get a packet of digestives and those instant noodles. The chicken ones. And a carton of...' He stalled for a moment and thought. 'On second thoughts that's it for now.'

Anna ate this sort of thing, Brighton thought, as he wrote them down in his notebook and wondered what the carton was that the brouny decided not to get. It still pissed him off about the beer and to be honest, he wasn't about to go shopping for the little bastard any time soon.

'Get that tomorrow, will ya?'

'Okay, okay,' said Brighton remembering the mind reading trick. 'So, has Aldercy been in touch with you?'

'Of course, he has. Why do you think I showed myself to you? I never show myself unless I'm compelled to, and that bastard knows how to do that. Let me tell you something about Aldercy. He might look all pleasant and endearing like Gandalf, but he isn't, and I wouldn't trust that elf as far as I could throw him.'

'Thanks, I'll keep that in mind.'

Soon the food arrived, and the brouny ate like a machine, shovelling everything into his mouth with both hands, gobbling away like he was feeding an industrial furnace, chugging down the odd mouthful of Guinness between bites.

'Here, that other one you bought. What's that?' he said, wiping his mouth on his sleeve.

'It's a chickpea curry.'

'Ohhh. Don't mind if I do.'

Brighton yanked the curry away from the greedy brouny before he could get his grotty little mitts on it.

'No you don't. That's mine,' he said, not wanting to know where those dirty little hands had been and doubted much that the brouny had ever washed them with soap. 'You've had quite enough.'

'You cheeky sod!' said Thundershack, wiping his hands on his pants. 'Who are ye to judge me? I ought to...'

'Ought to what? You're supposed to protect this house, not threaten its occupants.'

Thundershack looked at him and sniffed indignantly.

'Know about that, do you?'

Brighton nodded.

'When we lived here when we were kids, we thought that rats ate everything in the bowl, but my mother insisted that there was a brouny in the house that would protect us from harm with his magickal powers.'

As soon as Brighton mentioned his mother, Thundershack sank deep into his chair and looked at the ground.

'I'm sorry about your mother,' he said. 'I swear I tried to save her I did, and I almost had that bloody wizard by the balls as well, but I wasn't expecting her to come out and see him in the house as bold as brass. It was too much for her heart and she died, it was all in the report I sent to Aldercy.'

'But when I told Aldercy that Anna had died, he acted like he didn't know.'

Thundershack struggled to hide his contempt.

'I told you, you can't trust him. Aldercy likes to play with the truth when it suits him.

Brighton nodded.

'Good point. Aldercy also told me you'd help me be a cunning man. I imagine that was complete rubbish as well. Let's face it though, you don't look like much of a teacher, do you?'

'Are you saying I can't do magick? You fucking man child!' glared Thundershack.

'No. I said I didn't think you could teach it.'

'And you're an expert now, I suppose? For your information, I used to teach everyone who joined the Elfhame constabulary a thing or two. Before...'

He sagged back down, looking even more miserable than ever.

'Well, I suppose I should tell you. Once upon a time there was a happy and proud brouny named Thundershack who topped his class in the first constabulary test Aldercy devised for us. I made my mark by tracking down the golden griffin, who'd been stealing sheep and terrorising farmers. Over the years, Aldercy promoted me for my good deeds and made me the head teacher of magick, training every new cadet how to use magick to defend themselves, and to investigate crimes in our land. I created a location spell which found stolen property, and a curse which froze criminals long enough to bind them. Then a young goblin worked out a way to enter your world, and found a library where he stole books about science, crime and gangsters, and evil tyrants. His name was Glodprog, and he had a son called Glitch. Glitch used the stolen books to create an empire and became greedy. He despised Aldercy and when Aldercy took down one of his businesses, Glitch kidnapped Aldercy's daughter Ciara as a warning to him and sold her to Zaliel. Aldercy didn't have a hope of finding her. Aldercy was furious and ordered me to find Glitch and bring him in. Problem was that Glitch was onto us from the start and we suspected there was an informant. When I used my location spell, I couldn't find him. So, I hunted for answers in Goblin Towne and made one of his lackeys talk. He confirmed my suspicion that Glitch was hiding with Zaliel. When I asked him how he was running his business, the informant told me all about these small black crystals that Zaliel and Glitch used to send and receive messages at a predetermined time. I found out where he kept the crystal and came up with a plan, swapping the crystal for one of my own, which acted as a conduit, and recorded every message. But Glitch learned about it somehow and set a trap for us. Glitch told his captain to meet him at the Faraway Mountains where Zaliel's tower would be for a few days. Zaliel was setting up an auction to sell Ciara to the highest bidder and there was a great deal of interest from the witches. When I told Aldercy, he summoned the entire force, and we set off at once. After several days of trekking, the lead scout party returned, and their report drove Aldercy to despair. We found evidence that a large gathering had taken place. But the campfire ashes were stone cold and had been sitting there for over a week. Ciara was long gone, so were Zaliel and Glitch. Aldercy blamed me for the mix-up, and everything started pointing to the crystals being tampered with. We never found her. Aldercy banished me to patrol the outer realms of our land until we learned Zaliel was using Glitch's way to enter your world to steal more children. We heard of these children through whispers and rumour, but they'd be long gone and warded before we could investigate. That was until your mother escaped from Zaliel and luck led her to us. We knew he would never cease to be a threat to Anna, and so Aldercy made me leave the fairy kingdom to protect her and her children in case he came back.'

'That's one hell of a story,' said Brighton. 'But why did she run away when she buried him under a mountain?'

'That happened later,' said Thundershack shifting restlessly in his seat.

'I don't understand why Anna didn't tell us anything? I mean, she knew you were here, and she knew all about Zaliel. Yet all she did was move us around the country like lost sheep.'

'She was trying to protect you okay, and she made me promise never to show myself to her children. When we make a promise, it's binding.'

'If that's the case, why haven't you shown yourself to me earlier, then? Anna has been dead for weeks.'

'Well, it's difficult. I felt bad about Zaliel entering the house on the night she died. I felt even worse when I saw him take your daughter.'

'You saw him?'

'Yes, from the window in Emily's bedroom.'

Brighton went from calm to angry in a flash.

'Why didn't you say something before! I've been through hell over the last few weeks. I'm worried sick about Emily. Every moment I have wondered where she is and if she's still alive. I've been searching everywhere for her. My wife has had a nervous breakdown.'

'No, she never. He put a spell on her. A woman walking her dog heard her screaming outside the cottage and called the police and then you arrived. I never had time to run down and counter it.'

Brighton calmed down. He hadn't forgiven Thundershack by a long shot but changed his mind when he realised Kerry could be home in an instant.

'So, you could heal her?'

'I can't promise anything, but I'll do my best.'

That was good enough for Brighton.

'Have you really been here all this time?'

'Of course I have.'

'Tell me, has anyone else been here recently? I had a lot of evidence on the table, but it was gone when I came home.'

'Oh, I remember him. Unless they are barred, whoever has a key is allowed to enter, so I didn't do anything.'

'What did he look like?'

'Big. Tall man. Bald as a piglet's ass. Used the upstairs toilet and didn't flush it. Dirty bastard.'

'What was he wearing?'

'I don't know. A cheap suit and a cheesy purple tie, maybe.'

Now Brighton knew The Bulldog had entered his home with Kerry's missing keys. But why did he take that evidence? It made no sense to him. That evidence had nothing to do with Billie, Darren, and Helene. But he had just brought home evidence that did.

'Thanks Thundershack, you've been a big help.' He pulled out his evidence bags. 'Can you hide these for me? Just until tomorrow.'

'I can do that. What about the strange, mousy woman? She also has a key, and she's been looking through every room, trying to find something. I'm not sure what it is, but she's been here every day.'

That sounded like Cecilia Lemon.

'We'll need to bewitch the locks. Can we do that? Make it so that nobody can enter the cottage again without permission?'

'Certainly, I can do that. Just give me a minute,' said the brouny closing his eyes and bowing before he opened them again. 'From now on, the locks only recognise your keys. Same goes for the windows. Just knock three times before putting the key in.'

'Thanks,' said Brighton.

Then he remembered the strange glowing thing he found at the massacre. He fished around in the pocket and passed it over to him. Thundershack recognised the charm at once.

'What's this thing?'

'Where did you get that from?'

'I found it in the forest. When I came across the brouny massacre.'

'What brouny massacre?' said Thundershack raising his voice in alarm.

'Didn't Aldercy tell you?'

'No. He did not. That's just typical of him though.'

'I don't understand. What's wrong?'

'I'll tell you what's wrong. This charm belonged to my father!'

The brouny stared at the powerful charm in his hand as Brighton explained where he found it and the goblin that he fished the bullet out of.

'If he was the goblin leader, then Glodprog is dead.'

'I could only hope, but Aldercy knew that. He also knew about your father. He said something about another brouny, and that he was as reckless as his son.'

'And that,' said the brouny glaring, 'is why that deceptive little fucker can't be trusted.'

Brighton felt uncomfortable, remembered his police training and knew that Thundershack needed some time out.

'Hey, I'll give you some space,' he said, getting up.

'Thanks.'

'I know I don't know you but if you need to talk...'

'Thanks. I'll be fine.'

'I'll see you in the morning then.'

'Aye,' said Thundershack, not looking up.

'Have the rest of the Guinness if you like.'

'Thanks. I intend to.'

32

Helene was in no mood to talk.

'I gave youse the goblins, didn't I? What more do you want?'

'I know, but we need more information to get a warrant for them.'

'That's not my problem.'

'I'm afraid it is.'

'What you talking about?'

'My boss just told me that if you don't give us anything solid on either their guns or their drugs, then we're to bring you back home.'

Helene looked scared and angry.

'I ain't no grass,' she spat at him.

'But you are Helene. You told me about the goblins.'

'Ha! That's just a load of cobblers they made up.'

'Is it? You believed it the other day when you told me. What if I told you I dug a bullet from a Desert Eagle out of a goblin's skull.'

She looked at him like he was a total knob end and snorted with contempt.

'I'd say get your drugs from someone else because the stuff you took has made you numpty.'

'You're not making this easy for me. Our deal was complete cooperation or jail. So, if you don't want to cooperate then go and pack your bags while I call The Bulldog and tell him that you're free to go.'

She looked at him, unwilling to believe that he'd put her and her family into danger, but the second threat did the trick.

'So?' he said, 'What's it going to be?'

She sighed.

'Okay, what do you want to know?'

Brighton grilled Helene on everything she knew about Billie's drug and gun operation for hours until he felt satisfied that she'd given him everything she knew. He'd taped the interview and printed a statement which he had her read over and sign. For a two-bit dealer she knew way more than anyone would have thought, mainly because she'd been Darren's bit on the side and spent a long time with them. Helene looked relieved and went outside for a smoke.

He motioned to Clara.

'Okay Clara. I want you to gather up all of their things and move them to the second safe house.'

'But guv, they haven't even been here a week.'

'That's alright. I have something planned, and given that she's just landed Darren and Billie in strife I want to make sure her safety isn't compromised. Could you go and get the officer in charge of security for me so that I can brief him?'

Clara nodded and walked outside.

Brighton didn't like hiding his intentions at the best of times, but he had an idea. The incident with Peter and The Bulldog a few days back was too coincidental for his liking, so he decided to trap them. He planned to spend his afternoon with Kerry at Mortlake House, so when Brighton returned to the station, he went straight to Hayley Sharpe's office to drop the information off.

'I think you'll find that we've enough here for several warrants guv,' he said, putting the brief and a USB of the interview on her desk. Sharpe looked over the typed dossier, her eyes and expression hinting to Brighton that she was not at all impressed with the amount of effort he'd made.

'Good work,' she said looking up at him when she'd read it. 'We'll see what the prosecutor has to say. What about this bullet? Where's that then?'

'I dropped it off at ballistics,' said Brighton remembering that he'd left it with Thundershack. They said it would be a few days, and we won't have anything conclusive until we locate the weapon.'

'Fair call I suppose. Just make sure they check it against the Gwynne Turner murder.'

Gwynne Turner was an albino Welsh rent boy wannabe gangsta, whose body had been found under a bridge a month ago. He'd only been identified by the Boy George tattoo on his ass. His ratty little head, feet, and hands were missing, and his torso had been hit multiple times by a cricket bat, cracking his ribs almost to a paste. Someone decided to put three huge bullets into the mix, and the perpetrators had yet to be found.

'I'll do that right away,' he said.

'Good. I'll let you know as soon as I've heard about the warrants. I suggest that you go and prepare your team and come back first thing in the morning.'

'But guv,' he said 'you gave me permission to have an early afternoon off to see my wife. Remember?'

'Well, that will have to wait I'm afraid,' she said. 'Now we have some evidence to work with, taking these guys off the street must be our main priority.

She expressed the very sentiment that he had lived by throughout his career. Job first. Family second. He was getting sick of it, but now was not the time to argue.

Brighton nodded and scuttled off out of her sight.

'Hi Boss,' said Peter looking up from his desk. 'Glad to see you're okay. Where have you been?'

'No time to explain Peter. Could you please go and get everyone together for me in the briefing room. There's been a development.'

'Does this have anything to do with that nutter witness of yours?'

'You'll know when everyone else does. And could you bring me the Turner file on your way back.'

Peter looked a little anxious, adding to Brighton's suspicion that his offsider was indeed a rat. All Brighton wanted to do was let his team know that an operation was in the mix.

'We need everyone on board for the next week or so. All leave and training are cancelled,' he said, holding the Turner file up. 'We may have located a bullet similar to the ones we dug out of Gwynne Turner, and new intelligence we've just received suggests that we may have identified the gunman.'

The revelation stunned the room, especially his DS.

'Now I want you all to go home and get a good night's sleep. Keep your phones on because this is an on call no notice job. Expect a call at any time. Understood?'

A chorus of groans echoed round the room.

'Look I know it's inconvenient and that you'd all like to have a better picture about what we're doing but I want you to trust me. I'm doing this for a reason, and all will be revealed later. Any questions?'

'What about my holiday?' said one of the detectives sitting nearby. 'I booked it months ago. What am I going to tell my family?'

'I'm afraid this is the job we've all signed up for people. Being a detective means that we require commitment from you at all times. My wife is at Mortlake House. I was supposed to see her today, but I can't. But hey, if you want to be transferred back to uniform so you can have your holidays please see your skipper here and we'll organise it.'

The affected officer looked more frustrated.

'I'll be going to the union about this.'

Brighton looked at him, paused and took a deep breath.

'Look, I understand you're upset. So would I be if someone tore my holiday plans up and that's happened to me a few times. I've no issue about you going to the union either but be sure to bring your contract and workplace agreement with you because you'll find that while it's not the done thing, it is above board, and that's from a former union representative with six years' experience. The thing you'll learn about me is that I will try my best not to inconvenience anyone in the team, but if I do it's for a reason and again you have my apologies.'

The officer nodded but was far from happy. Brighton made a mental note to follow him up later for a one on one. There was a time and place for everything, and he had to rein the team in. Nobody else had comments or questions and Brighton dismissed them, sending everyone back to their desks to scramble for their bags and head for the door.

'DS Charamboulos,' he called to Peter before he could join his colleagues. 'A word please.'

Peter followed Brighton back to his office closing the door behind them as his superior sat down.

'Yes boss,' said Peter not knowing whether to stand or sit down.' Brighton didn't indicate for him to sit making Peter feel even more uncomfortable.

'Okay two things. First, I want you get that detective transferred back to uniform. Today. Make sure he keeps his leave. Let him know that as far as we're concerned, he can take his holiday.'

'That's not fair boss. I've known Tommy for years and...'

Peter stopped when he realised that Brighton was just staring at him.

Brighton shrugged.

'That's an order. It will calm him down eventually. There's no more drama about his holiday and it sends the team a message about commitment and that I expect one hundred per cent from them. Okay?'

'You're the boss,' said Peter.

Brighton ignored the comment.

'The second thing concerns our witness, Helene Henderson.'

Peter sighed.

'What's she said this time? Is it about the Loch Ness Monster?'

'No, she's changed her story, but that's not what I wanted to talk about. I'm concerned about where she is. It's remote and I'd like your opinion about it.'

Brighton looked at Peter's face hoping to see a glint of recognition but saw nothing.

'If you'd kept me in the loop, I'd have told you boss. So where are we keeping her?'

Brighton gave Peter the address and he appeared to think for a moment, unsure what to say.

'Yeah, I know the place. Didn't know we still had a lease on it though. It's a pretty good position. It's off the main roads and the only access isn't sealed which means that you can see traffic from the dust in the day and by the noise and the solo set of lights at night.'

'What about the pastures that adjoin it? Would they be vulnerable?'

'Not if our people are wearing night vision goggles and are doing regular sweeps which is what they should be doing. Who's in charge of security? Watkins or Dunbar?'

'Watkins,' said Brighton.

'Okay. He's a decent chap but not quite a night owl. From what I've heard he's fallen asleep once or twice.'

'Thanks Peter. I'll get you to go around tomorrow and make sure that the arrangements are up to scratch.'

'Can't boss,' said Peter quickly. 'That's my day off and I have a dentist in the morning. Getting rid of a cracked tooth from Henderson when we nabbed her. I'll be in Lala land all day from the sounds of it.'

'You didn't say anything about your tooth to me.'

'Yeah well, I just get on with it. We all do around here. I'll be fine but it does me head in every time I bite down. I reported it and booked leave with DCI Sharpe while you were away. I hope you don't mind.'

'No that's fine. See to it when you come back. Is twenty-four hours long enough for you or would you like two days off?'

'Cheers boss, but one day's enough. I'll just sleep most of tomorrow.'

Brighton nodded and looked down at his in tray, signalling that the meeting was over.

'Anything in here that's important?'

'No. It's been pretty quiet.'

As soon as Charamboulos exited, Brighton rang a number on the new phone he'd bought before work.

'Hello Dunbar? It's DI Brighton. The trap is set, and I expect you'll have company tonight. How are your searches progressing?'

Before he left the office, Brighton checked in with Hayley Sharpe to see if the prosecutor had made any recommendations. She hadn't as yet, but had been told that it was a priority job.

He found his car and drove to Mortlake House to see Kerry, only to be told that visiting hours were over for the day. He felt bad that he hadn't been to see her for a while and remembered that she was trapped under a spell. It still felt too far-fetched to him.

He didn't want to believe he'd spent most of the night chatting to a flatulent brouny either, but remembered Thundershack's request and stocked up on Penguin biscuits, Lays Crisps, pork scratchings and Bovril on the way home, along with enough food for a week, new batteries for the torch and snacks like sherbet lemons, jelly babies, and tiny tins of baked beans to take with him if he had to go camping in the Magical Wooded World for an extended period of time.

It was late by the time he arrived home. He only remembered that the brouny had put a spell on the door when it refused to budge. He tried again, this time knocking three times first. The lock clicked open. Thundershack was nowhere to be seen, so he put pork scratchings into the brouny bowl and left a note

'We need to talk ASAP.'

Days and days of being on the go were catching up. He ran a bath and poured half a packet of Epsom salts into the water before sinking in and closing his eyes.

'Ahem,' said a familiar gravelly voice.

Brighton peeked out from behind the shower curtain to see Thundershack perched on the toilet seat nibbling on a big piece of pork scratching. Thank God that his pants are up, thought Brighton.

'Of course they are you pervert'

'Thundershack stop reading my mind. What are you doing here anyway?'

'You called me, didn't you? Why did you call yourself a sap for?'

'I didn't. It stands for as soon as possible'

'Is that so smarty arse? In case you've forgotten, I'm not a human. Remember? So how would I know what a sap is? It's not something we use, and your language is so bad we call it the language of shite as it is. Any culture that adds twerk to the fucking dictionary and makes brain rot the word of the year deserves to fall on its ass.'

'Okay, you have a point. But could we catch up in an hour or so?'

'I suppose we could, but I'm going to need you to get out of that tub.'

'No way,' said Brighton, 'I just climbed into the damn thing. We can talk later.'

The rumble from Thundershack's flabby belly shook the room.

'Get out while you still can!' he said, dropping his pants. 'I can't hold on for much longer!'

Brighton was out of the bath faster than a five-year-old running after an ice cream van. Grabbing his towel, he'd barely shut the door before an explosion from Thundershack's ass shook the house and nearly took the bathroom door off its hinges. His phone rang. In his rush to leave, Brighton left it sitting on the lid of the cane laundry basket. Taking a deep breath, he tried to open the door, only to find it pushing out towards him. A small arm illuminated by bright green gas held his phone.

'It's for you,' said Thundershack.

Trying not to breathe, Brighton grabbed his phone and answered it as he ran down to his bedroom, making a mental note to fumigate his phone, his hands and his ear afterwards.

'Brighton,' he said as he shut the bedroom door and felt game enough to draw breath, hoping that the stench hadn't followed him in.

'Sorry for the late hour Brighton but I need you down here now,' said Hayley Sharpe, 'An army convoy's just been attacked.'

It only took Brighton thirty minutes to drive to the scene of the crime, on the border of the Dartmoor national park, opposite the woods where he first met Eddie and Kip a few days ago. The long road was not a great choice for a sensitive military operation, and he was surprised that anyone would consider driving through a remote location flanked on both sides by rocky crags and ancient trees. Brighton arrived at the scene of what looked like a very one-sided battle.

Firemen hosed out the remnants of two security vehicles and an armoured car. Burnt remains lay strewn on the ground like discarded Jawas. Brighton looked at them and knew at once what had happened to them. Everything made sense now that he knew about the link between Zaliel and Glitch. The truck had several tires blown out and its strategic cargo was nowhere to be seen.

'Finally,' said Hayley Sharpe looking away from Peter and rolling her eyes at him. 'Where on earth have you been Brighton? I called you nearly an hour ago.'

'I don't know this area guv. I'm still new. Remember?'

He was in no mood for her bullshit at that moment and his terse tone came as somewhat of a surprise to a woman who demanded respect.

'We'll discuss this later. Find out what you can from the driver, and I want a report every thirty minutes. Understood?'

Brighton nodded.

'Do what you do best. I don't care what you do or how you do it. Find the people who did this. I must go back to the office and brief MI5.'

MI5? he thought, as he watched her snake her way around the scene to her car. He saw Peter Charamboulos chatting to one of the uniformed officers and called him over.

'Thanks for coming out tonight Peter.'

'Had no choice, did I?'

'How's the tooth?'

'I'll be right.'

Brighton looked at his offsider and wondered how much he knew about the ambush.

'Okay I'll do my best to get you out of here as soon as I can. In the meantime, I want you to move as many of these people away from the scene as possible. If anyone questions you, send them over to me. You're my 2IC so I need you on point. You'll be doing the reports to DCI Sharpe so approach me every half hour. Got it?'

'Yes boss,' said Peter.

'Where are our forensics people?'

'Not here yet.'

'Good. Call them now and tell them to get back to bed. Then I want you to find a police helicopter that can land in Sloane Square in twenty minutes. Think you can do that?'

'I'll do my best.'

'Good man. Get onto that chopper first. I want it in the air ASAP. Any dramas, get them to call me directly.'

Brighton needed help and hoped that his call would not go to voicemail. The phone rang a little longer than anticipated but he smiled when he was greeted by a sleepy Liverpudlian.

'Guv? Is that you?'

'Hi Jeanie. Sorry for calling you so late, but I need you on a case of national importance.'

'Of course guv,' she said with her usual unbridled enthusiasm.

'Thank goodness. I owe you one.'

'Yeah, I know.'

'Okay I owe you more than one. But I'll make it up to you. Grab your kit and come to Sloane Square for us? Call me back when the chopper arrives. No, I'm not joking. I'll see you soon.'

While waiting for Jeanie, Brighton walked under the tape guarded by two grim faced PC's and over to the shell-shocked army driver smoking a cigarette as he stared at the ground.

While he was not in the defence force, Brighton had seen plenty of action as an armed responder and had a good idea what the guy had been through. He'd lost three of his closest colleagues on a raid in Old Kent Road when a meth addled Yardie opened up on them from a stairwell with a Heckler and Koch MP5, remembering the fear and the terror as he fought to return fire and get a clear shot.

'Hi,' he said, 'I'm Detective Inspector Brighton. Is there anything we can get for you? Would you like something to eat or drink?'

The driver looked up at him.

'I think I'm okay thanks.'

'That's good to hear. The medics will be around soon to have a look at you. But I don't need a doctor to tell me that you've been through hell and back tonight. Are you up for telling me what happened?'

'Dunno if I should tell you anything. You won't be in charge for long but, not when they realise it's gone missing.'

'And what's that Sergeant?' asked Brighton looking at the man's stripes.

'Sorry but that's classified. All I can say is that they'd better find it.'

'I need to know what we're looking for, and I need to know what we're up against. Under the national security protocols, I have the necessary clearance.'

'Okay,' said the weary soldier, not looking that convinced. 'They stole a missile. A D5 UGM-133A to be precise.'

'Alright,' said Brighton, feeling as if he was finally getting somewhere. 'What's that when it's at home?'

'It's a bloody Trident with a nuclear warhead that's what.'

Brighton stared at him for a moment and inhaled a short breath.

'What the hell is a Trident missile doing in the middle of Dartmoor Forest?'

'It's a short cut to HMNB Devonport. There's a submarine waiting for her that's just had a refit. We've done this before and never had a problem. Not until tonight.'

'So, what happened? Who attacked you? Did you see anything?'

'I saw enough to get me locked up in a bloody loony bin for the rest of me life.'

Brighton realised that there was potentially more to this story than domestic terrorism. This could be the weapon that Glitch the goblin wanted. The thought of a nuke blowing up the world where his little girl was held prisoner was too much for him to deal with. He had to know what he was dealing with and fast.

'Try me,' he said. 'Was it a great big dragon and a heap of goblins armed with AK47's?'

The driver looked at him beyond disbelief.

'How the bloody hell did you know that?'

'Let's just say nothing surprises me anymore.'

As Brighton strolled to Peter his phone rang.

'Jeanie? Is that you?'

'No guv. This is DC Dunbar. We just apprehended a party of five men armed with automatic weapons attempting to access the cottage.

'Is everyone alright?'

'Yes sir. We completely surprised them, and overpowered them without firing a shot. They were shocked to find us waiting for them.'

'Good work,' he said to Dunbar, 'Take them down the station and put them in the cells until I arrive. Under no circumstances are they to make a single call. Is that understood?'

'You two. Over here with me,' he said to two bored looking constables, and they followed him back to Peter.

'Hey boss. I did it. Chopper's in the air now.'

'Good work, but I'm afraid I am arresting you for providing sensitive information to a third party not in our employ. You have the right to remain silent. Anything you do say, may be used against you in a court of law.'

'Ere what are you on about boss?' said Peter, his eyes widening as the two constables approached him.

Brighton ignored him.

'Take his phones off him and bring him to the station. Put him in a cell until I can interview him.'

'Turn around please,' said one of the constables, wincing with discomfort.

'Naff off Charlie,' said Peter brushing him aside, 'I ain't going nowhere.'

'Did you just hear me you two? I said take him in. That's an order.'

Brighton's warning did the trick, and the two constables cuffed his former offsider.

'Don't do this! I'm innocent! I haven't done anything! he said, trying to talk his way out of it.

A while later Brighton made a call to Hayley Sharpe. Despite the hour she answered in seconds.

'About time you called. What's this I hear about a helicopter landing in Sloane Square? Have you gone mad? Do you have any idea how many complaints have been made in the last hour?'

'No guv. But considering the circumstances, it doesn't matter. I needed the best forensics officer I know right away, and you said I could do whatever it takes. Believe me there's a good reason and I'm sure the budget will be reimbursed.'

He told her about the Trident, choosing not to disclose anything about Peter's treachery just yet. The Trident was far more important than a rogue cop, and Peter could sweat it out until the morning. The approaching noise from above drowned his explanation out and he made his excuses, as a happy forensic scientist jumped out of the helicopter, waving when she saw him.

'Thanks for coming out here, Jeanie. Sorry for the short notice.'

'No sweat guv. I've packed for a few days. Me mam's visiting and she'll take care of the cat so it's all fine.'

She frowned when he told her about the missing missile and went straight to work.

Brighton worked the cordon, directing the few staff he had left to be vigilant, while his mind thought about the magickal perpetrators and their stolen Trident. How did they get the missile out of here? he thought. Did they use the dragon or an army of goblins? Stepping past the disintegrated soldiers still clutching melted weapons, Brighton looked around the heavily wooded terrain, searching for prints or evidence of disturbed ground. Nothing he saw gave weight to either of his theories.

Maybe they used a spell to clean up, he thought. That made sense to him. This wasn't like the brouny massacre at all. That was completely different because they did not count on humans finding the scene or even caring about it. There must be something.

'What happened to those trees guv?' said Jeanie joining him.

Brighton could have kicked himself. He'd been too busy looking at the ground to notice that several pine trees on the ridge above them showed recent signs of damage and their trunks were split wide open.

'Can you see now why I called you Jeanie?'

Jeanie blushed.

'You'd have spotted them sooner or later guv. I've checked over the bodies, and they've all been killed with the same intense heat that melted their bones into the bitumen. It's like nothing I've ever seen before. Possibly a new type of flame thrower, but even so they'd be using a highly combustible gas that's not normally used by the military. I'll know more when we get them to the lab, and we'll need something to dig them out.'

'Okay, thanks for the update. Do you need any help?'

'Yeah. I'm nearly done but if you could help me get a few samples from those trees up there that would be great.'

Brighton nodded. He was exhausted but he couldn't refuse her, considering he'd woken her up. As they walked up the hill, Jeanie gave Brighton her thoughts about the ambush.

'My guess is that a military helicopter with enough power to lift the Trident up and fly away with it took the convoy out with a new weapon, possibly a flame thrower. Then ten or fifteen shooters came out of the woods to stop that truck. About three hundred rounds have been fired at it and I'm amazed that the driver wasn't killed.'

Jeanie stopped walking and stood silent and still.

'What is it Jeanie?'

'Scratch that helicopter theory' she said pointing at the huge footprint near the splintered trees.

They stared at the print for a few minutes. Jeanie looked at Brighton and to her surprise she saw that he was pretty relaxed about the whole thing.

'Is there something you're not telling me?'

'What do you mean?'

'Come on, I can tell you've seen this before. You know what that is.'

He nodded.

'There's no fooling you is there?'

'It's a dragon, isn't it?'

'Yeah, and a pretty big one too.' He told her everything; Thundershack, Zaliel, Glitch and the Magical Wooded World. She squealed like all her Christmases had come, she'd won the lottery, and Taylor Swift had finally proposed to her, all at once.

'OMG it is all real. I wanted to put Zaliel down to the chemical fumes in the paper your sister drew on. You have to show me!'

Brighton wasn't sure of that.

'I'd need to check first. There might be protocols, but I promise I will ask for you.'

She nodded, and the pair separated to search for evidence. As Jeanie walked away, she felt her heart lift. She felt excited about everything. Her favourite place in the world was real!

Unlike Brighton, Jeanie had devoured every single word his mother had written. She was an uber geek. Someone that went to fan events, Q&A's, and once she even attended a lecture conducted by Anna herself.

She knew everything about every creature in the world she thought Anna had created, especially goblins. Now she was familiar with the goings on in Plymouth, she bet that the shooters were all goblins.

Her eager eyes picked out a faint blood trail. Looks like the army got one of them, she thought, as she followed the trail deeper into the woods and down the gentle slope of a gully on the other side of the ridge. She walked with care, looking for more evidence, her powerful torch lighting up the forest as if it were daylight.

Goblins don't like daylight. They despise it. While they don't turn into stone pillars, it's still a nasty experience for them. It burns their skin and tortures their noses much like when your partner farts in bed after a curry.

'Stop it!' said a croaky little voice in the bushes to her left.

Jeanie whirled around in fright. Through the bracken she saw a three-foot goblin, clasping an AK47 assault rifle on his hip at her. She was a little wary of the weapon but more curious about the creature holding it. She stared for a moment.

'You're a goblin, aren't you?'

'Shut up.'

The goblin struggled out of the bracken and as he raised his assault rifle to his shoulder, Jeanie saw the bloody bullet wound through his blue overalls.

'Let me see that.'

'Off with the nasty light!'

She turned the torch off.

'I can help you.'

'Silence you.'

'Jeanie are you there?' Brighton's voice startled them both.

Jeanie saw Brighton's torch light moving closer above her and heard the goblin cock the rifle. She thought fast.

'What was that? Are you okay?'

'Yeah sir, I'm fine. I found one of the weapons. Looks like they had Russian assault rifles.

'Okay good work. I've been called back to the station. If you need anything just call me. This is your scene and you're in charge of it. When you're ready, get someone to drive you down to Plymouth. In the meantime, I'll call Armitage and explain why I poached his best forensics officer.'

'That'd be great. I'll see you later sir.'

Jeanie watched the light move away. I hope he picked up me calling him sir, she thought. He knows I'd never do that. She listened for movement but heard nothing. Maybe he's hiding. Hope I've done the right thing, she thought, as the first pinkish hue of the approaching dawn frolicked on scattered clouds. I don't fancy his chances against a gung-ho goblin like this, but I don't fancy being his prisoner either.

'Come on. We're moving. The sun is coming!'

The goblin prodded his prisoner and lead her down into a dry creek bed at the bottom of the gully, where she saw the outline of a wooden door with its frame crudely fixed to the side of the escarpment. Thirteen more lay broken in twisted bundles on the creek bed floor like they'd been scrunched up.

'Get in,' said the goblin motioning his prisoner toward the door.

'This is a portal isn't it!' squealed Jeanie in delight.

Despite being a prisoner, she felt remarkably excited.

'I've read about these. Goodness, I wish I had my books. They'd be a great guide to...'

'Shut it and get in,' said her captor bringing her back to reality. 'I won't tell you again.'

As he spoke, a smooth river stone sailed through the air and smacked the ugly goblin clean in the hand holding the Russian rifle.

Jeanie didn't see Brighton come running out from behind the bend. She didn't hear him scream as the goblin dropped the rifle and pushed her into the door, diving in just before the frame exploded in a flash of green smoke. When it cleared, Jeanie and the goblin were nowhere to be found. All that remained was the rifle and the goblin's little green hat.

33

Just after nine in the morning Brighton arrived back at the station, hoping that he could delegate his work. He had to find Jeanie and warn Aldercy about the missile. He was running out of time.

As he stepped into Hayley Sharpe's office, he found Peter arguing with DC Dunbar.

'What's going on guv?'

'Ah here you are. Perhaps you could tell me why DS Charam…Peter has been arrested and why I haven't been told about this?'

'I have good reason to believe that DS Charamboulos has informed another party about the whereabouts of our protected witness.'

'That's rubbish', said Peter 'You've no proof of that whatsoever. I want to make a formal complaint about this lump of a man here guv. He has been on my case ever since our witness made ridiculous claims, and I said she should be locked up and not protected.'

'I don't have time for this,' said Brighton, not allowing emotion to get the better of him. Time to draw the rat out into the open, he thought. 'If you're no grass then how do you explain The Bulldog arriving while you went out for coffee? How do you explain five armed men going to where we had kept the witness, the same night that I told you where she was?'

'That's circumstantial. Even you should know that.'

'I agree. That's why I had a few checks done by DC Dunbar. Would you care to tell DCI Sharpe what was found?'

'Yes sir. We did checks on his work phone, his mobile phone, and bank account. About six weeks ago he bought a new phone at a cash and carry in town. That phone was located in his locker here at the station and a series of text messages have been exchanged all with the same number. He gave details of the safe house location, and that the witness was at the station, along with a few other sensitive titbits. Peter sank into his chair.

'You should have wiped your phone memory Peter,' said Brighton, 'Or at least bought a new SIM card.'

'Shut up. I want a lawyer. I want The Bulldog.'

'That suits us. We want a word with him too. In the meantime, DC Dunbar here will escort you back to the cells.'

For a moment, Peter thought about doing a runner, but Dunbar grabbed him by the scruff and walked the rogue cop down the corridor in a half nelson locked by his stout muscly arms.

Hayley Sharpe struggled for words.

'I had no idea,' she said, 'I've trusted him for years. I made him a Detective Sergeant.'

'Which he's used to his advantage guv.'

'Yes, I can see that. Why didn't you tell me about your concerns? If you knew he was no good, you should have come to me.'

'I wanted to, but an opportunity presented itself and there was simply no time to get everyone on board,' he said with diplomacy. 'Dunbar was the only one who knew everything.'

'Did Peter seriously organise a hit on the witness?'

'I'm not saying he organised the hit guv, but his information did. I'm about to find out the specifics, but I'd like a few things first. Dunbar has done an exemplary job. I'd like him to replace Peter as my second in command as Acting Detective Sergeant until he can take his exams. I want him working on this case involving the hit men while we transfer Peter over to internal affairs.'

'Okay. That sounds reasonable. So, what are you going to do in the meantime? I'm handing the missing Trident over to MI5 and National security.'

'I'll oversee the handover and Dunbar. In the meantime, I have leads of my own to follow up. I'd like permission to do that and report back when I can.'

'Don't go slinking off for days again without reporting back to me okay. You need to keep me in the loop.'

Brighton nodded.

'And Brighton. No more helicopters in Sloane Square again. Ever.'

When Brighton told him about his promotion, Dunbar smiled like he'd just won a meat raffle.

'Thanks guv. I appreciate this I do.'

'You're welcome, but there's something I need you to do for me.' He told Dunbar about his most pressing task. 'A part of your daily duties will be to report to DCI Sharpe on my behalf. I'm going undercover for a day or two. Now all you need to do is tell her that you've heard from me each day, and that there's nothing to report at this stage. Okay?'

'Sure guv. The less I know the better. I've done this before.'

'Good then you're set. I want you to make sure that the prosecutor is sitting in with you when you interview Peter and the hit men.'

'Aye I will. I know that The Bulldog can be heavy at times.'

'And you're fine with that?'

Dunbar gritted his teeth like he was about to plunge a blocked lavvy.

'Bring it on,' he said noticing the colour in Brighton's face drain. 'Are you okay guv?'

Walking towards them were two burly officers escorting one of the hit men to an interview room. The suspect was a tall bald bloke with a familiar long crooked nose who gave Brighton a twisted smile when he saw him.

'Ahh look who it is. Dead-tective Inspector Brighton,' said Eric Grimsby sneering at him with delight at the panic and discomfort he was causing. 'We was wondering where you'd gotten to.'

Brighton stood silently as they bundled Grimsby away, and continued his walk with Dunbar in tow.

'That toe rag was Eric Grimsby. He works for a London gangster named Sid Fields, and if Fields finds out I'm here there'll be hell to pay.'

He briefed Dunbar on The Bulldog, his links to Billie and Darren and now a potential link between them and Sid.

'I doubt it's going to be Billie and Darren. They're just not big enough to interest Sid or dare to contact him. The Bulldog on the other hand probably knows a slew of crooked London based lawyers with interesting clients. I can't have Sid finding out I'm here just yet so here's what we're going to do.'

By the time they reached his car he'd nailed out a plan to put Grimsby out of reach.

34

This time Brighton remembered the charm and knocked three times.

'Thundershack!' he called 'Come out please, I need you. Urgently.'

The upstairs loo flushed, and he heard a loud string of curses followed by the patter of little feet on the wooden landing.

'That you Brighton? Hope you have a decent plumber. The upstairs is blocked solid.'

Brighton sighed and made a note to call Cecelia.

'This is more important than a blocked toilet Thundershack.'

'If you say so,' said the brouny, 'but I'd be careful up here if I were you. Nasty business floating about.'

'I doubt I'm going to forget that in a hurry. Now could you come down please?'

The brouny stomped down the stairs.

'You'd better hope we can clean that,' said Brighton, pointing at the antique rug that Thundershack had walked on with wet shitty feet.

The brouny shrugged.

'I doubt it.'

'Well try and find a spell that can. Now can you get me back to the Magical Wooded World?'

Thundershack nodded. Reaching into his pocket he pulled out a strange little key.

'Okay, but I'm not coming with you. Now listen. In the back garden there is a hedge. In the hedge is a door and this key will open it. Walk through and close it after you. Once you're through you'll see a narrow path. Follow that to the mushroom circle. There'll be about twelve of the things. Big orange mushrooms. Find the one that's had bits pulled off it and grab a bite for yourself. Now it tastes like shit but make sure you eat all of it or the magick won't work.'

'Are you suggesting that the only way to experience the Magical Wooded World is by eating magic mushrooms?'

'Of course,' said Thundershack, completely oblivious to Brighton's drug culture reference, but judging from the stupid look on his face he knew full well that something was up. 'How else would you expect to fucking get there?'

Brighton thanked the brouny. Finding his gym bag, he grabbed his torch, his ASP, and his childhood penknife that he carried everywhere if he was walking in the countryside. It had a few interesting attachments that may come in useful.

The door wasn't easy to find. After much trial and error, dropping the little key on nearly every attempt, he opened it, and followed a normal looking yellow brick path right to a large mushroom circle. Stepping into the circle he felt each orange mushroom rise up to his knees. Their purple gills whispering together in the wind like tripping hippies. He examined each one until he found a mushroom with many small chunks taken from around the cap. He didn't particularly like the idea of eating it but tore off a piece, sat in the circle, closed his eyes, and chewed a fungus that closely resembled the taste and texture of used kitty litter.

Nothing happened at first. Then his body melted like a sugar cube in his mouth. It was the strangest feeling as his hair, his skin, his bones, and his clothes; even his shoes melted into a bright white fizzy liquid, seeping into the deep green grass and consumed by the thirsty dry earth.

Brighton woke up underground and in darkness. Turning on his torch, he explored the musty tunnel, hoping to find a way out. Every now and then he'd find a cute blue door, illuminated by a dull yellow light.

Each had a small brass plaque. One read *Dr Strangewart: Curator of exotic funguses*. Not going there for a cuppa thought Brighton, plodding on. There were many others including an invisible enchanter, a fairy dentist, and finally *Mrs Thundershack*. Brighton nearly knocked on her door, but when he saw the end of the tunnel he decided to press on. Climbing up a set of steps, he walked onto a path bathed in familiar green light. As he walked, the path became smaller and narrower, and he wished that he'd chosen to walk the other way.

Soon there was no path, and he was surrounded by a herd of mystical oak trees closing in around him. Maybe if I climb up, I'll be able to find the way out, he thought. It felt like a good idea. He climbed up the closest tree, using the burrs on its trunk as rough steps. As he hauled himself up into the highest boughs, he saw a large branch and grabbed hold of it, not seeing what looked like a huge blue beehive glued into the highest part of the branch until it sagged down to him. Several tiny winged creatures flew out to see what was happening.

'Drop the branch' said one, 'Or I'll stick my spear in your eye!'

'Hey! Sorry little man I didn't know you lived there.'

'Well now you do numb nuts so drop it.'

'But if I drop it, your home might fall off.'

'Do as he fucking says' said the other pissed off pixie, jabbing his arm with a hard thrust.

'Ouch!' said Brighton letting go.

The stored energy of the bent branch brought it swooping up with such a force that when it stopped, the inertia freed the hive from its moorings sending it flying into space and smashing on to the ground. Brighton skidded down the tree and ran towards where the track ended, getting a decent head start, before the stunned pixie hive mobilised and came after him in an angry swarm. All Brighton could do was run as fast as he could into the bracken, scratching his face and hands. The pixies sensed his fear and swarmed with renewed vigour, gaining on him. Brighton knew that he'd be overwhelmed in moments until a bright yellow beam shot past him and into the swarm.

'Go home pixies!' said Eddie, stepping onto the path in front of him. They hovered in one spot, baying for Brighton's blood.

'I said fuck off you little shits. This human is with me.'

'Look what he did to my castle!' said a furious plump pixie female with a dented crown. 'We're going to roast his nuts on an open fire.'

'Have I not made myself clear? Now flutter off fatso or Aldercy will be pissed, and you don't want to piss Aldercy off do you? I said, do you?'

At the mention of Aldercy's name, the angry pixies flecked off back to the remains of their castle, but not before a few spears found their mark on Brighton's unprotected ass.

'Where the hell have you been?' said Eddie. 'I've been camped in this miserable crap hole for ages waiting for you to come out of that tree.'

'Nice to see you too Eddie. How did you know I'd be here? I only just left my world.'

'Did you come by mushroom?'

'Yes. Not the best way to travel might I say.'

'The mushroom alerts us with spores when you break a piece off. I knew about this yesterday.'

Crap it had happened again. He must have been passed out in the tunnel longer than he thought.

'Bloody mushrooms. I'm starving' he said. 'Have you got anything to eat?'

'Yeah sure. I have a three-course meal for two and a seriously good bottle of vintage 1994 dandelion wine in my backpack just waiting for a moment like this.'

'You know something Eddie? Sarcasm just does not suit you.'

She glared at him and rummaged in her bags.

'Here,' she said, throwing him a strange looking chunk of bright pink cured meat. 'This should keep you going for a while.'

'Thanks,' said Brighton breaking off a piece and putting it in his mouth. Whatever it was, it tasted good. There was a sweetness and purity to it that somehow relaxed him and expanded his mind at the same time.

'Do you like it?'

'Yeah, it's delicious. Thank you.'

Eddie laughed and he felt his conscience say uh oh.

'What did you give me?'

'Mon Cat. You're eating Mon Cat, a flying feline pest that lays eggs everywhere, rips all of our furniture to shreds, and turns our gardens into toilets. People swear that they were introduced from another planet. We discovered something about them by accident when curiosity made one of them walk into a pizza oven. They taste divine.'

To her surprise, Brighton was too hungry to spit out the sweet feline delicacy, and he kept chewing as he followed Eddie out of the woods to the familiar meadow with the steep hill. Before they put their backs into climbing the hill, he told her about the Trident missile that he suspected had been stolen by Glitch, with the help of Zaliel. She turned around and he followed her for a distance as she walked back into the woods and down a rocky track.

'Hey, where are we going?'

'Goblin Towne. From what you told me, if Glitch has his hands on a super weapon, then there is no telling when he'll use it.'

'Wait,' said Brighton stopping. 'Shouldn't we be warning Aldercy?'

'There's no time Brighton!'

'Are you suggesting we go and find Glitch without any support? That's insane!'

'Listen to me human. We don't have time to raise the alarm. We'll simply have to find Glitch ourselves and the quickest way to get answers isn't in Elfhame.'

'You can go if you like. I'm going to go and find Aldercy.'

'Good luck doing that on your own Brighton. You don't even know where you are. It's getting dark and you can't even climb a tree without upsetting people. Even if you did find Elfhame, it may be too late. Come with me to Goblin Towne.' She looked at him with just a glimmer of a smile that disappeared in nanoseconds. 'I could use your help.'

This put him off guard. It was the closest thing to please he'd ever heard from her, but he wasn't fooled for a moment.

'Yeah, alright I'll go with you. Tell me something Eddie. Have you ever considered a career as an actress?' he said, laughing at her.

'Go fuck yourself Brighton,' said the elf, turning her back on him as they descended into goblin country.

〜

In contrast to the bright sunshine he'd experienced climbing up the hill to Elfhame, the road to Goblin Towne was a twisted, unkept and dangerous track, spiralling down into darkness and impenetrable doom of a haunted abandoned mineshaft. No light penetrated down into the depths of this dismal place and soon the pair found themselves in pitch darkness. Brighton turned on his torch.

'This should give us light for a few hours. I just changed the batteries.'

Eddie had no idea what batteries were and was not interested enough to ask. She was just happy she didn't need to waste her magick. The torch served them well, giving them two metres of visibility all the way down to the bottom. Looking around, Brighton noticed that nothing grew except fungi. The trees were all dead and all he could smell was decay. It was like walking into a necropolis. Strange luminescent blue and pink mushrooms dotted a landscape straight from the mind of Hieronymus Bosch.

'What are they like?' Brighton said, growing tired of the silence.

'Who? Goblins? Well, they're tricky for starters. They say that they're the spirits of earthly politicians and financiers, but I think that's rubbish. Not many of them are smart and you'd have to be pretty gullible to believe what a goblin tells you at the best of times. Watch your valuables because they'll pick your pockets clean if they get a chance.'

'Are they violent?'

'That's a good question,' said Eddie with a rare hint of respect. 'But the answer isn't straight forward. Normally goblins are just low-level criminal scum. They mainly do burglaries and the like. There are a few of course that have gone straight and run pubs like the Wilted Toadstool and the Wandering Tavern. Most of them aren't violent. They're not built for it. But that was before Glitch came along. They're getting bolder and it's all about packs and strength in numbers. Crimes have been going up all over the land. Thankfully they don't like daylight or otherwise we'd be in trouble.'

Brighton saw several dim lights up ahead as they passed a rickety wooden sign pointing to Goblin Towne. They continued on in silence. The air became thin, dry, and fetid, making it difficult for them to breathe and they saw nobody approach them or pass them in the gloom. Just before they reached the outskirts of Goblin Towne, Brighton had a feeling that they were being watched and flashed the torch to the left of them, illuminating an old goblin woman weathered by time, wheeling a pram. She looked like something from a Victorian freak show. When the light hit her, it woke the occupant who screamed like it had been slapped. The old woman glared and hissed.

'Now look what you've done! Get that light off me copper.'

Brighton put the seething old hag back into darkness.

'Sorry,' he said as they continued their journey.

'Why did you apologise to her for?'

'I woke her baby. I was only being polite.'

Eddie laughed.

'You don't know anything do you? She's a sentry and the baby is most likely a warning spell, not a real baby silly.'

'How was I supposed to know that?'

'How many old women walk babies alone in the darkness in your world? How do you think old goblins earn a few bob when they need it?'

Brighton didn't know what to say. He didn't see her eye roll but heard the deep sigh.

'Follow me,' she said, leading him to the nearest building. To his surprise it was a tavern, and he hoped they'd have something better to eat than Mon Cat jerky.

'Welcome to the Rotting Ewe,' Eddie said opening the door. 'The roughest tavern in town.'

The Rotting Ewe was packed with all kinds of folk, mainly goblins. Other than a few hard stares, nobody gave Brighton and Eddie a second look as they weaved their way around the establishment until Eddie found a table with a drunk lying underneath it. She signalled over to a somewhat slovenly goblin waitress whose huge purple boobs strained against the tiny filthy bodice she wore. When she saw the mess, the waitress blew on a metal whistle, calling two huge trolls. One dragged the drunk out and threw him through a nearby chute in the floor. The other swabbed the bare floorboards, cleaning up the vomit and the blood. The waitress came back as they sat down. She threw some menus at them and hovered, waiting to take their order. When Brighton looked at her, she glared.

'What?' she said, which infuriated Eddie but not Brighton, who'd lived in London for many years and was so used to zero customer service experiences that he felt right at home.

'Do you have any salad?' he asked

'No! That's revolting.'

It's not like I asked you to clean your teeth, he thought, as she leaned into him. Her rancid breath burnt his eyes.

'What we've got is mutton chops, cat schnitzels, and fish.'

'We'll have two Schnitz,' said Eddie, 'Can we get turnip chips with them? And a couple ciders.'

The waitress grunted, farted, and disappeared like a bad smell wafting into the crowd.

'Damn,' said Brighton, 'I was hoping for a change from cat.'

'Knowing goblins, it's probably not cat. The mutton probably isn't mutton and the fish definitely ain't fish. With any luck we'll get broiled hen meat. I just hope we get cider and not two mugs of troll piss.'

The food arrived and with relief Brighton found chicken under the breaded layer. It was tougher than his sergeant's exam, so he decided to drown it in the steaming brown gravy that accompanied it. Eddie didn't say anything until he'd had a few bites.

'You're more game than I thought,' she said. 'Never know what's in goblin gravy. You can have mine if you like. I'm sticking with the chips.'

At that point Brighton didn't care. He felt like he hadn't eaten for days, and he discovered that the cider was the perfect accompaniment to wash his meal down. Brighton looked up and noticed a barman scanning his every move through a single yellow eye.

'What's up?' said Eddie, noticing that he'd stopped eating.

'The barman is staring at me.'

As Eddie turned to have a look, the barman motioned to someone in the crowd and ducked behind the bar and out of sight.

'You're as subtle as that waitress,' he said, 'I think we should get out of here.'

'Don't be silly,' said Eddie, 'We're cops. No goblin would be game enough to try anything.'

As if on cue, five of the patrons turned around to face them, each armed with a Heckler & Koch submachine gun.

'You were saying?'

'What are those strange weapons? Are they from your world?'

'Yes. Be careful.'

A horned, muscle-bound goblin lifted itself up from one of the chairs, growling as he towered over his men. Three eyes glared at Brighton who remained seated and surprisingly calm.

'You must be Glitch,' he said, staring at the fearsome looking goblin.

'Ha! You dare say my name?' said Glitch as he walked through the crowd, 'How would you know anything?'

'Your weapons gave you away. When did Billie give you those?'

When Glitch heard Billie's name all three of his bulgy eyes narrowed.

'How do you know about Billie copper?'

Brighton decided to bluff him.

'He's told me all about you. I know you work with Zaliel and I know all about the guns. But I don't care about that, and I don't care about Billie either. That's her problem,' he said gesturing towards Eddie, 'I do care about the missile you stole though and I'm going to give you the opportunity to give it back before there are dire consequences.'

This amused Glitch and he let out a big, forced belly laugh. The rest of his crew followed suit.

'What are you going to do human?' said Glitch, drawing a huge axe from behind his back. Raising it high in the air with both hands, the terrifying goblin gangsta came charging at Brighton.

'I'm going to turn you into...'

'Get down!' said Eddie from behind Brighton.

He ducked just in time, watching as a big ball of energy burst from her wand at Glitch, sending him barrelling back into the crowd and scattering the goblins like frightened Meerkats.

Grabbing his Asp, Brighton struck out at the first goblin he found with a submachine gun, knocking it out with an agonising thump to the back of its neck. He grabbed the gun as the goblins regrouped and returned fire at them, turning the thick oak table over, hoping it would give them enough cover.

The gunfire was too much for Eddie. It hurt her ears and scared her a bit as the bullets smashed into the walls and bystanders around her. Still, she kept going. Building a shield around them, which kept the bullets at bay for now, but not for long. Her energy levels rapidly depleted and she knew that she had to find another way to stay in the fight.

Brighton fired in three round bursts. He had not engaged an enemy for a long time, and not one that used swords and bows. There were so many of them, and they didn't seem to care about having their brains blown out.

'Watch out!' said Eddie.

Brighton ducked back behind the solid oak table just in time to avoid the black feathered arrow that flew past where his head had been. Another two hit the table, followed by knives, daggers, throwing axes, bottles, and plates. A flurry of anything that could be picked up and thrown. Either the goblins had run out of bullets, or they didn't know how to fix weapon jams. From the corner of his eye Brighton saw one of the trolls armed with a huge knotted club sneaking up behind Eddie. He turned and fired over the top of her, hitting the troll, with a neat line across the chest before it collapsed on the bloody floor.

Glitch got up from behind the bar.

'Attack!' he yelled at his men, before running out of the Rotted Ewe and off into the dark.

Brighton had a nasty feeling that he was going for the missile.

'We need to go after him.'

'Really? What do you have in mind?' said Eddie ducking as another spear came thudding into the table.

'Fire at the roof and bring it down on top of them. When it gives way, we'll jump down that chute. There must be a way out from there.'

'That's madness! What if we're trapped down there?'

A burst of machine gun fire chipped the tabletop above their heads.

'Just do it! It's the only way out of here and I'm running out of ammo.'

More spears and arrows joined the fray, chipping through the table as the hardened little crooks put everything they had into taking out the two cops. Eddie pointed her wand at the supporting beams above them, blasting them to ash. Brighton grabbed Eddie and jumped down into the darkness as the ceiling of the Rotted Ewe fell on top of them.

The fall was not as deep as Brighton thought it would be. But the chute had a steep incline, and their journey came to an abrupt end, pitching them forward into darkness. Eddie cursed as she tripped, landing on her bottom with a big splash. Brighton had the luck of grabbing onto the chute and was able to slow himself down. The air was thick, greasy, and hot and stank like kitchen scraps and rotting meat.

'Could we have some light please?' said Eddie, getting up.

Brighton shouldered his weapon and when he finally found his torch, he shined it in the direction he heard Eddie's voice and gasped. Behind Eddie was a huge strange creature that looked like a Lovecraftian octopus had mated with a pachyderm. Its brown furry octopus' body had elephant trunks instead of legs and rows and rows of giant razor-sharp teeth.

'Eddie, I want you to walk to me please,' he said, 'and whatever you do, don't turn around.'

Eddie showed her distrust and turned straight away, looked at the creature, shrugged and turned back to Brighton.

'What's wrong with him?' said the creature, 'Haven't you seen a food critic before?'

'I'm glad I found you Mr O'Corra, said Eddie, 'We were getting worried.'

The creature looked at her, it was not impressed. It spoke, with a strange deep hysterical braying noise like a disturbed donkey.

'If you were so concerned, then why did nobody come to Goblin Towne sooner? I've been here for days!'

'We thought this place was beneath you.'

Is she brown nosing him? Brighton thought, just glad that he didn't need to fight for a moment. He was happy to take a breath and watch the two speak. Whatever she was doing worked and soon Mr O'Corra was onside.

'How long have you been down here?'

'Oh, I don't know. It must be a week or more, or so I imagine. One minute I was reviewing the most awful Mon Cat pie and the next the ogre from the kitchen must have found out about my notes, because I had a sharp blow to the head and have been living off the scraps ever since, which might I add, was still far better than that bloody pie.'

The ceiling made creaking sounds as the rafters strained under the weight of the collapse, making Brighton just a tad anxious.

'Any suggestions on how we could get out of here?' he asked.

The creature looked at him and sniffed a few times.

'Are you human?'

'Yes I am.'

The creature backed off and glowered at Brighton, its fluffy tentacles rearing up, ready to strike him down.

'Your people murdered my ancestors. If it wasn't for...'

'Hey, do we have to do this now? We need to get out of here.'

His abruptness stunned O'Corra who snarled at him.

'Yes, we must do this now. As I was saying, your people murdered mine.'

Brighton blushed and felt bad about the calamari and chips he had for lunch when they took Emily to the seaside last year.

'Look I'm sorry for everything humanity did to you, and I'm glad you survived and that you're here. Now can we please get the hell out of here?'

'My you're so...'

'What? Arrogant? Self-assured? Cocky?'

'Miles off. I was going to say loathsome you horrid human.'

'If you two are quite finished, I think I've found our exit,' said Eddie.

Brighton shone his torch to where her voice came from and found her sitting on a stone step.

'This looks like it leads up and out.

'No chance I'm afraid,' said O'Corra, 'I've tried, and it won't budge.'

'We'll see about that.'

Eddie waved her wand at the door, turning it into toothpicks with a violent fiery blast that sent Brighton sprawling into the huge furry octopus, and landing with it in a heap on the floor.

'Get a room you two,' she said, rolling her eyes at the hapless pair before running out of the cellar and into the dawn.

After searching for goblins to question and finding nobody about, Brighton and Eddie sifted through the wreckage of the Rotted Ewe looking for survivors. There were none. Most of the former patrons were flattened. In return for freeing him, Mr O'Corra helped as much as he could. His strong trunks lifting beam after beam, casting them aside as if they were weightless. When he moved on, Eddie and Brighton dug around the powdery plaster and splintered wood. Brighton found a number of bodies still gripping submachine guns. He salvaged five clips of ammunition and now had two hundred and seventy rounds, which made him rest easier.

'Over here,' called the powerful food critic.

Brighton scrambled over the debris and looked down at the waitress as Mr O'Corra lifted the heavy timber from her squishy play doh like cleavage. She looked up at them and wheezed, trying to breathe and talk at the same time.

'Thanks.'

'Don't mention it,' said the polite Cephalopod.

'Do you know where Glitch is?' said Brighton.

The waitress laughed until she wheezed blood and burbled.

'He's long gone.'

'We know that. Do you know where he went?'

'Why should I help you... pig?'

That was the first time anyone from this land had called him anything remotely porcine and while he found the term offensive it gave him hope that there might be some bacon somewhere in this desolate shithole. I could murder a butty, he thought, looking at the dying wench and trying to think of what to say.

'Look, I know you're dying, and you don't like me, but there are others here that you like. Aren't there?'

'So what?'

'So, if you don't tell me where Glitch is, then I can't save them.'

'What you on about?'

'He's going to destroy this world. Your friends will get sick and die and nobody alive can save them.'

That must have done the trick because her eyes widened.

'In the Forbidden Mountains. You will find him in Croagh Marbh with the wizard,' she said. Her big fake eyelashes closed like curtains as she breathed her last rancid breath.

'Great, that's all we need,' said Eddie.

'Why?' asked Brighton, 'Is it far?'

'Of course it's fucking far! It's bloody miles from here and how are we supposed to get there?'

'Didn't you say goblins don't like daylight?'

'Everyone knows that silly. They hide and come out when the sun goes down.'

'Well, I'm thinking that he hasn't gone that far then has he? Considering the sun's up.'

Eddie smiled.

'I never thought of that. If only we had a way out of here. Mr O'Corra?'

Turning when there was no reply, Eddie saw that the food critic had left them and almost made a clean getaway, but she caught a glimpse of his tentacles as they shifted out of sight down a nearby alley.

'Come on' she said and charged down the debris after him. 'Mr O'Corra? Mr O'Corra!'

The octopus froze and then turned around on his tentacles and looked at her. He knew what was coming next.

'Mr O'Corra,' said Eddie, 'You didn't happen to fly here, did you?'

'Obviously. You didn't think I walked to Goblin Towne, did you?'

'Of course not. That would be silly. Only I was wondering if you could...'

'What? Fly you to Croagh Marbh? Sorry my dear but that's out of the question. I have an important review to do!' he said straddling a dirty looking old couch.

'Don't you understand?' said Brighton, flustered at the Octopus' refusal to help them. 'It's the end of the world.'

'Precisely. That's why I must get this review in. This could well be my last one!'

Before they could say another thing, he tapped the couch three times.

'Alto!' he commanded, and the old couch went bouncing up vertically into the air, shooting over the roofs of Goblin Towne and away into the distance.

'You might have stopped him,' said Brighton.

'And how was I supposed to do that?'

'I dunno. Use your wand or something. In England we can requisition a vehicle if there's an emergency.'

'What are you suggesting? That we took his couch? Do you have any idea how much trouble there would be? That food critic has powerful friends. Aldercy for starters.'

'Well it's better than doing nothing. What are we going to do now?'

'There's nothing for it but to walk there. It will take ages, but we might get a head start on Glitch if we keep moving, and it doesn't rain.'

35

They walked for hours through a blinding fog, interrupted by an intermittent downpour, and back through the forest where Brighton encountered the pixies. When they found a path through the pines and elm trees, their journey became a little easier. The path was well trodden and looked like something from a fairy tale. Brighton imagined Little Red Riding Hood being watched by a big bad wolf but there was no telling what was out there.

He heard a terrified bleat in the woods to their left. His gut told him something bad was going to happen and he just couldn't allow it, so he left the path to investigate.

'Where do you think you're going?' said Eddie.

'Didn't you hear that?' he called as he descended down a steep muddy embankment.

'So what?' Eddie yelled, 'We don't have time to muck around.'

'You go on. I'll find you.'

'Fuck. You are impossible! You know that?'

From the swearing behind him, Brighton knew she was tagging along and felt relieved. What was he thinking? He found himself surrounded by old oaks and rocks in dense vegetation. Using the embankment as a path, he ran towards where he heard the noise. He heard it again. Louder, calling for help after what sounded like a whinny. Cradling his submachine gun as he ran, he was ready for anything. The bleating came from a small white winged horse. One of its hooves was wedged tight between two large mossy rocks and it was well and truly spooked.

Running up to the colt, he tried to calm it down while pulling at the rocks that trapped it. When he heard the growling behind him, Brighton realised he wasn't the first passer by attracted by the pegasus' cry for help, only the other party had no intention of rescuing it. The wolf circling them under the cover of the strange tiny oak trees looked much bigger and badder than any Grimm creation.

'Get back,' said Brighton, levelling his weapon at the predator. The wolf looked at it and then Brighton and laughed.

'Ha! That thing has no blade! Where's your sword or your dagger? You'll need more than that thing to beat me!'

'I somehow doubt it,' said Brighton with an air of confidence, flicking the fire mode selector to automatic.

The hungry wolf growled, licking its sizeably sharp pointy teeth as it edged closer and closer to Brighton. Not knowing what to make of the strange device the human pointed at him, the wolf saw an opportunity to have an upsized meal and wasn't backing down. Brighton stared at its hungry bulging yellow eyes.

'What big eyes you have,' he said, not being able to help himself. What a stupid bloody thing to say, he thought. Anything to try and distract it though.

'What are you?' said the wolf, baring his teeth, 'some kind of freak?'

Brighton tensed his trigger finger. He'd never killed an animal in his life, but he wasn't going to allow the wolf to harm the trapped colt. Not on his watch. Focussing on his opponent, he was ready for anything. Well nearly anything.

'Hey!' said the voice of an irritated elf from above. 'There you are. Thanks Brighton! Now I have mud all over my...'

Brighton didn't have to guess what Eddie had muddied. The momentary distraction gave the wolf the advantage it needed. Propelling itself into the air like a marlin, the wolf launched itself at Brighton, baying for his blood. Brighton reacted in seconds. Falling backwards, he cut the wolf down with rapid fire rolling to his side as its lifeless body thudded onto the smooth rocks.

'Bloody hell,' said Eddie landing nearby. 'Are you okay? Sorry about that, I didn't know we had company.'

Brighton was not okay. He was shaking as he thumbed the safety back on the weapon, but he wasn't going to admit it.

'I'm fine thanks,' he said, turning his attention back to the colt that'd calmed down now that the wolf was dead. Can you help me get this little fella free?'

Eddie nodded and together they heaved at one of the rocks until it finally gave way. As soon as it could, the little horse shot off into the air, leaving its rescuers in a flash.

'Typical,' said Eddie. 'Come on let's get back on the path. If we're lucky we can go a few more miles before it gets dark.'

But no sooner were they back on the path when there was a commotion in the sky. Looking up, Brighton saw a herd of huge white flying horses swooping down at them like dive-bombers, and in moments the pair were surrounded and outflanked. One of the larger horses walked towards them with purpose, glaring at them with anger and hostility.

'You! You dare to try and take Prince Silvermane? My son!'

'Never,' said Brighton, 'You've got the wrong end of the stick.'

'Stick! What do you plan to do with that? Whip me? I'll thrash you myself!'

Eddie flew in front of Brighton and pointed her wand at the king with wings.

'Stand down. I'm an officer of the law.'

Brighton didn't think that this would help them much, but he was surprised when the pegasus held back.

'What is the meaning of this? Why did you upset my son?'

'We freed your son. We never wanted to harm him. This human risked his own life to save him. He killed a wolf.'

The King reared up, pawing his front hooves like a boxer.

'I don't believe you.'

'Look, Your Majesty, the wolf's body is down there in the embankment. Send one of your subjects to go and take a look. They'll also see the huge rock we moved to rescue the Prince.'

The huge horse flicked his flowing white mane at one of its followers. The older horse respectfully nodded and flew off.

Brighton was still in awe of the flying horses.

'Stop staring at them Brighton or you'll get more than a dwarf's foot up your ass this time.'

The detective stopped looking at the majestic creatures, but it was so hard for him to do. He'd seen a few strange things in his life, but a talking flying horse? What happens if he does not believe us? he thought to himself. They have us surrounded so we can't run into the trees, and I could never shoot one even if I wanted to. There must be a better way. Brighton didn't get time to think any further before the older horse flew back to them. Thudding on the ground near the King, it bent both front legs as if to bow.

'She speaks the truth my lord,' he neighed 'I found the dead wolf and I found rocks that were moved as well.'

The huge horse nodded and walked towards Brighton, his big brown eyes no longer angry dark shards but deep pools of tranquil melancholy. He walked all the way over to face Brighton, who stood still with his hands at either side, trying to keep his shit together. He felt the warm breath of the horse on his forehead.

'Thank you for saving my son, human. I have told him not to go off playing on his own especially there. But he never listens. I was wrong to doubt you.'

'You're welcome Your Majesty. It was our pleasure.'

'Pray what can we do to repay you?'

'Oh please,' said Brighton, being polite, 'I wouldn't dream...'

'Don't mind him, Your Lordship,' said Eddie interrupting, 'But we must get to Croagh Marbh urgently. Would it be possible for one of your followers to take us there?'

The big horse frowned.

'You mean for us to fly with you on our backs? To Croagh Marbh? That's a vile place. We don't go there. We won't go there for you.'

'Then take us as far as you can. There's no harm in that. We will walk the rest of the way if you're too scared.'

'We are not scared little woman, but you ask too much. I will not risk my herd.'

'Let me take them then sire, on my own,' said the old horse. 'I can manage the distance, and the fairy can fly most of the way.'

'No Seven Skies. It is far too much for me to ask of you.'

'My Lord, I beg thee. I am not young, and I would like nothing more but to have one last adventure before going to pasture.'

The powerful king looked at his faithful follower and nodded. He turned to Eddie and Brighton.

'Seven Skies will take you on your way.' He whinnied and shot into the sky, and in a flash his herd followed him. As the dust settled, Seven Skies sank to the ground and motioned to Brighton.

'Climb on human.'

'Brighton. Please call me Brighton, Seven Skies,' he said as he climbed onto the pegasus.

'Just hold on sonny,' said Seven Skies and without warning he did a full vertical take-off that made Brighton glad he'd not eaten since dinner.

'Wait for me!' Eddie shrieked, flapping furiously to keep up with them.

Once he felt certain that he was completely alone, Glitch came out of his hiding place in the hollow of a dead oak. He was surprised that the pigs had managed to catch up so quickly and now they were hot on his trail. He swore to kill the source of their knowledge. But he knew what they were up to and felt lucky that he'd stayed back purposefully and overheard everything.

Now he decided to make a few plans of his own. Few knew Croagh Marbh like he did. Its name translated into the *Mountain of the Dead*, and for those unfortunate to visit, it lived up to its reputation. He drew a circle with an oak branch with six sigils around it, chanting as he went, each word getting louder and louder.

Adonay Adonay Adonay!
Ecce ego ad Croagh Marbh, Ut ad me Croagh Marbh!
Ego præcipio tibi! Ego præcipio tibi!
Ecce ego ad Croagh Marbh, Ut ad me Croagh Marbh!
Adonay, Adonay, Adonay!

Soon after he shouted the last word, a green cloud rose from the ground, covering the goblin completely.

Flying on the back of a winged horse may have been a little cramped for Brighton, but it was not as uncomfortable as his last discount airline flight from Stansted to Brescia. Flying on Seven Skies took some getting used to, but he liked the feel of the wind in his hair and enjoyed the freedom of his steed who made his rider's stomach light with excitement as they flew with the currents swooping up and down over the purple clouds.

Eddie on the other hand wasn't doing as well as she'd hoped, and Brighton saw that it had been a while since his colleague had done any strenuous exercise.

'Wait up' she panted, and so Seven Skies glided long enough for Brighton to assist her to clamour onto the horse's rump.

She grabbed on to Brighton's back as they soared upwards. She'd never ridden a horse before, never mind flying on one, and her face turned green in moments like a sick kid on a rollercoaster. Her chunky projectile vomit just missed Seven Skies' left wing, as it fell out of her sight. Gasping for air, Eddie gripped onto Brighton's jacket for her life as the pegasus flew on.

After a long while, Brighton noticed that Seven Skies had commenced his descent and as they dropped down through the clouds, he saw their destination. So that's Croagh Marbh, he thought. It was the most horrendous natural occurrence, barely looking like any of the mountains he'd ever seen. There was no grass and aside from a few dead trees, it was bare and devoid of all life. The mountain was formed chiefly from shiny black obsidian. Sharp jagged outcrops like smiling crocodile teeth formed a grim rocky landscape with huge slippery round boulders that reminded him of the seaside in Cornwall, only instead of sea water, lava rose from the depths, splashing the obsidian walls with an abstract intensity.

Seven Skies flew around for a moment, landing at the safest point that he could, below the huge outcrop that stretched above the outskirts of Elfhame.

'Do you know where you need to go?' asked the pegasus.

To the left of the outcrop Brighton saw the entrance to a cave and thought about it. If he wanted to cause as much damage to Elfhame as he could in the shortest time possible then that's where he would put a Trident missile.

'I think we're here Seven Skies,' he said.

'Thank fuck for that,' said Eddie, still looking sick.

Brighton dismounted and helped Eddie down. He walked to the front of the brilliant creature.

'Thanks for the ride, Seven Skies. I need to ask you a favour. Could you wait for a moment while I have a look in the cave? Elfhame may be in danger, and your herd may be too. If there is a bomb in there, we need to raise the alarm.'

'I know not what you speak of human and though I grow hungry, I shall wait as you ask.'

'Thank you. Hold on I may have something for you.' Digging around in his bag Brighton found an apple he packed for emergencies.

'Here you go,' he said, holding the apple to Seven Skies mouth. The pegasus sniffed it cautiously and gave it a small bite.

'This is delicious,' the pegasus said. 'Thank you Brighton!'

The detective held his hand under the hungry horse's mouth until the apple was gone. He was tempted to pat him and stroke his mane but decided against it. Who knows how Seven Skies would react? Instead, he wiped his hand on his jeans, turned his torch on and followed Eddie into the cave.

The cavern felt hot and steamy on his skin, the air heavy and difficult to breathe as they followed the recently mined shaft directly into the heart of a huge ridge that towered over Elfhame. As he turned a corner Brighton came face to face with a thirteen and a half-metre missile. Just as he feared.

Eddie looked at it with her usual scepticism.

'Is that it?' she said, wondering what the fuss was all about.

'Yes. Come on, we have to warn Aldercy.'

'It's just a tube Brighton.'

'You've no idea, have you? This could take the whole mountain down and destroy Elfhame in the bargain. That's not all. If the wind carries its poison, it will kill everything in your land one way or another.'

'Alright alright. You bored a dying goblin with this before. So, it's dangerous then?'

Brighton tried not to roll his eyes and say anything he'd regret. It wasn't easy.

'Yes. It's dangerous.'

'That's all you needed to say.'

'Let's go and tell Seven Skies,' he said, but as he turned to walk back down to the cave mouth, an explosion ripped through the roof of the cave, knocking Brighton off his feet, and showering both he and Eddie in rock and dust. His torch was knocked from his hands, sending them into darkness. Eddie came to the rescue. Lighting the surrounds with her wand as she zapped Brighton out of harm's way seconds before the ceiling collapsed on top of him.

They sat on the cave floor gasping for air and coughing until the dust finally settled down. Brighton looked at the mess in front of them and saw that the explosion had blocked any chance of leaving from the same way that they came in. There had to be another solution. He walked over to the missile to find that there was just enough room to squeeze past it.

'Come on Eddie,' he said edging along with his back to the wall.

Eddie wasn't so sure, she had her wings to consider. She flew up to the roof, there was barely enough space to fly over the missile and wait for Brighton at the other end.

'Brighton' she said, 'You should have a look at this.'

'Okay I'm coming through. I'll be there in a minute. Don't touch anything.'

'As if I would,' said Eddie rolling her eyes. She was getting tired of the human treating her like she was an idiot.

A few minutes later, Brighton emerged and walked over to her.

'What was it you wanted to show me?'

'Oh, this thing. It's probably nothing.'

She pointed to a metal casing that had been removed.

Looking inside, Brighton saw something he did not want to see.

'Shit!'

A maze of wires had been introduced to the control panel, each connected to a battery and a central timer, ticking down from ten hours. Somehow the goblins had rigged the Trident to be detonated, and he had no experience working with bomb disarmament.

'Get back,' he said, stepping away from the time bomb.

'Why? What's wrong?'

'Well, the goblins have added a heap of wires to the control panel and rigged it to a timer that's set to explode in ten hours.'

'Pah,' said Eddie 'I'm not afraid of this silly thing. Why would I be when I can do anything. I have my wand, remember?'

'Don't point that at the bomb' said Brighton, 'One blast and you could wreck the timing mechanism, and nobody lives happily ever after.'

'Happiness is overrated anyway. Who on earth wants to be happy for all eternity?'

'Remind me to introduce you to the producers of East Enders,' said Brighton. 'You'd be great writing on one their Christmas shows.'

Eddie looked at him. She had no idea what he was talking about. Brighton loved the show and wondered what Dot would make of all this if she came back. She'd probably say I was away with the fairies, he thought.

'Well, I'm going to give it shot,' Eddie said, ignoring him and pointing her wand at the control panel. 'Rimilty dee rimilty mee thou strange device oh I command thee. Rimilty row, zazzle and dazzle turn thy life force into frazzle!'

Her wand surged a glowing sky-blue light at the panel, but it deflected and ricocheted away from the missile, zapping the wall. Eddie looked shocked.

'That's not supposed to happen. Someone's put an anti-magick charm in this device, my wand is useless. What are we going to do?'

Before Brighton could answer, there was another explosion and their only exit became a wall of rocks, trapping them with the bomb. That was not their only concern. The place on the wall that Eddie zapped, was for want of a better word, waking. Brighton watched as the wall heaved and stretched as if something below its surface had been stirred from an endless slumber.

'Eddie. What's that?' he said watching a huge form moving with fluid movement through the rock, like a great white shark swimming in through the obsidian in rippling cold calculated movements, circling them slowly with menace.

'I don't know. Do I look like an expert on all things fairyland?'

Brighton ignored her and thought hard. He didn't want to chance staying in the cave with a nuclear bomb, never mind with a creature that could eat him.

'Why don't you try and blast through the rock?'

'I'm not sure if it could do it. The wand is only made for short bursts, it's meant to capture and duel with criminals, not to smash rocks.'

'Let's try it anyway. It looks like we have company.'

Sure enough, three creatures were now circling them in unison. Eddie nodded and pointed her wand at the pile of rocks blocking their exit. She focussed and glared at the wall, summoning all the power from her mind that she could muster. A big thick bolt of energy flew from the wand and hit the rock pile, but the obsidian deflected it, making it ricochet around like a laser blast in a garbage compactor, narrowly missing the Trident before slamming head on into the body of one of the creatures. Uh oh thought Brighton as the creature stopped and the wall heaved and swelled with anger under the surface. Shit, he thought, moving away as it grew bigger and bigger. The others also stopped moving and began expanding. The walls crackled and popped.

'What are we going to do?' shrieked Eddie as she lost the plot.

Brighton didn't need this. He closed his eyes, trying to keep calm.

'This is all your fault,' she said.

That was all he needed, but he supposed it was true. After surviving angry pixies, gangster goblins, a hungry wolf, and nearly being incinerated by a dragon, Brighton never guessed that his fate was to become a rock monsters' dinner. He felt like a failure for not rescuing Emily and freeing Kerry from Zaliel's curse. He wanted to hold them in his arms and be with them more than anything, instead of spending his final moments trapped in a cave with a frumpy grumpy lesbian.

Then he heard a new sound. A steady heavy thudding from the other side of the collapsed tunnel. It was getting closer and became frantic. The banging reminded him of the sounds from the neighbouring room at a cheap hotel he stayed in on a surveillance operation. The more the creatures ballooned, the more the rock gave around them, chipping away like they were hatching from the walls. He gripped his submachine gun and hoped that the creatures were not bullet proof. Rocks fell from the collapsed tunnel until eventually there was a hole big enough to squeeze through.

'Is anyone there? shouted a voice from the other side.

'Yes. There are two of us. Go on Eddie get out of here.'

Eddie nodded with relief and climbed up to the hole. Brighton had his back to her, scanning the wall for life. As she popped through the hole to freedom, a huge reptile hatched from the wall. It stood on four legs supported by a long fiery tail that lit up the cave as it swished back and forth. Its long neck swayed with the hypnotic effect of a cobra as it glared at Brighton with cruel black eyes. Its bright red tongue hissed annoyance.

As it edged towards him Brighton pointed the Heckler and Koch at its chest and flicked the selector to full auto. The burst he fired was enough to take out a room full of German bearer bond robbers and sent the lizard thing sprawling out on the floor. To his relief the creature lay still.

As he began climbing up to the narrow hole in the wall, he heard an enraged screech. The other two had popped out of the walls and found their dead friend. Brighton crawled through the hole as fast as he could, not daring to look back. He felt his arms being grabbed by one of his rescuers who pulled him out through to the other side like a loose tooth, hoisting him high into the air just before another creature's head popped through and lunged at him. When the creature saw his rescuer, it squawked and retreated back into the cave.

Looking down, Brighton saw that his rescuer was a troll that was bigger than the ones he encountered at The Rotted Ewe. Its menacing tusks glistened in the torchlight as it lowered him to the ground with care.

'Good work Droit,' said a dwarf wearing a red outfit that looked more at home in a classic fairytale.

'Thanks,' said Brighton.

'Pah. Thank Droit human. He's the one who insisted we should save you.'

Brighton looked up at Droit and held his hand out to shake but Droit took one look and frowned at him.

'Are you suicidal Brighton?' said Eddie. 'You never shake a troll's hand. They don't like it for starters, and you never know where they've been.'

Bet you're regretting rescuing her Droit, thought Brighton, lowering his hand.

'Thank you, Droit.'

This amused the assortment of dwarves standing behind him, who leant on their picks and shovels and made snide little laughing grunts.

'What are you people doing here and why have you woken up the rock dragons?' said the dwarf dressed in red.

So that's what they are, thought Brighton. He was seriously thinking about writing a memoir of his adventures once this was over now that there were dwarves and two kinds of dragon. He hoped that his book would attract the attention of a famous New Zealand film producer, best known for making people pee their pants in the cinema while they tried to hold on through his brilliant, yet exceedingly long movies.

'We came here to find the bomb.'

The dwarf frowned.

'What the hell is a bomb?'

'It's a weapon that will destroy this mountain and this world.'

'And did you find this bomb you speak of?'

'Yes, it's in there,' said Brighton pointing to the hole he'd just crawled out of.

'You have got to be shitting me.'

Before Brighton could say anything, the dwarf skidded up the rocks and took a sneaky peek through the hole. He slid back down the rock pile and the dragon's head came through the hole again, but this time it didn't retreat, it sent a burst of fire down at the dwarf, narrowly missing his stubby little ass before it ducked back in.

'Did you crap your pants Grumley?' laughed one of the dwarves, a little ginger with a ZZ Top beard.

'Careful Paddy, or I'll stick that pick axe up your ass crack sideways,' said Grumley, marching back to Brighton.

'Okay I believe you. Now who put that fucking thing in there?'

'Ahem,' said Eddie. 'Would you mind telling me who gave you permission to mine obsidian in here of all places?'

'Aldercy did. He owed me a favour as it so happens. But he figured nobody would be stupid enough to mine on the mountain of the dead. So, tell me who put that fucking thing in there? It's disrupting our operation. Do you have any idea how to get those dragons back to sleep?' he said to Eddie.

'No, but Aldercy will. He knows everything.'

'Yeah right,' said Grumley. 'I know a few things myself.'

'Do you know who Glitch is?' said Brighton.'

Grumley laughed.

'Do I know who Glitch is? What a daft question. Everyone's heard of Glitch he's a fucking menace.'

'Well, he put the bomb in here, and it's going to explode before the day is over if I can't shut it off.'

'Okay what do you need from us?'

'Well first we need a way out of here.'

'Follow me,' said Grumley, leading them to a flight of stairs to the left of the mine. 'This leads out. We'll wait for you and try to clean things up.'

Brighton thanked him and ran down the stairs with Eddie in tow.

They looked for Seven Skies, but the pegasus was nowhere to be found.

'He must have gone for help'

'Saved his own ass more like,' said Eddie, sitting down to catch her breath.

They were both getting used to the quality of the air again outside of the mountain of the dead, even with the lava fumes it was much cleaner than being inside.

'Here he comes,' said Brighton, pointing at a dot in the sky flying towards them.

The pegasus was back, and he'd brought help. Flying alongside him were Aldercy, Kip, and Vera, the witch that flirted with Eddie at the station. Their reunion was brief. Aldercy told them that he knew all about Goblin Towne after O'Corra came to see him. They'd been back and it was completely deserted. Glitch had done a runner and not even a powerful Find Me spell could locate him.

'I take it you found the missile?'

'It's a bomb now,' said Brighton. 'Do you know the difference between the two?'

'Of course I do!' Aldercy snapped.

'Good. Then you should know that we have just under ten hours to find Glitch and get the code. How many hours is that in Earth time?'

'About five days. Why do you ask?'

'Well, we might not know how to find Glitch, but I know someone who may back in my world. I could go and find him.'

Aldercy thought about this.

'Hmm, I'm not sure about that.'

'It's the best plan we have. It's the only one.'

'If you don't find Glitch or this code then our world as we know it will end. Close your eyes,' said the elf, pointing his wand at Brighton, 'This may sting a bit.'

It stung quite a lot, and he preferred the unicorn pee experience, but the magick worked. Rubbing his head, Brighton found himself in a cleaner's storeroom and when he opened the door he saw he was back in the police station. Lord knows how he smelt or looked but he gave his coat a quick dust and went to brief Hayley Sharpe.

36

'Are you stupid?' said Billie, glaring at Brighton from across the table in the interview room. 'Hey! I'm talking to you!'

Brighton in turn didn't even look at him, not for a moment, refusing to acknowledge his existence and only speaking to his brief, the ever-present Bulldog.

While Brighton had no conclusive proof about The Bulldog and his links to Sid Fields and a corrupt copper, he decided to let the lawyer stew. This was Brighton's strategy, and long before walking in he'd briefed Sally the prosecutor and DS Dunbar. The tactic was simple. By ignoring Billie Brown there was a high chance of him overreacting and Brighton was counting on it. He needed a quick win before Elfhame and the rest of the fairy realm became a nuclear wasteland, and who knew what consequences there would be for his own world if the radiation skipped through a portal. Then there was Emily. He had to get her out of there.

'Advise your client that we have evidence that he has conspired with an individual known as Glitch.'

At the mention of Glitch's name Billie reacted exactly the way Brighton wanted him to. He folded his arms and became defensive.

'As of midnight last night, this individual has been registered on the official terrorist register. As you are aware Mr McGregor, associating with known terrorists is a serious offence and can lead to charges of high treason.'

That made Billie's jaw drop and Brighton smile. He'd wasted no time after speaking to Hayley. The first call was to Armitage who had the contacts Brighton needed to put Glitch and Zaliel on the terrorist register. Unlike his client, The Bulldog didn't move a muscle.

'This all sounds fascinating DI Brighton. Do you have any proof of this alleged association?' He leaned back in his chair, looking as cocky and confident as ever.

In his mind the only weak link, the only possible evidence, was a witness testimony from Helene, which he knew he could either get struck out or attack. He was not ready for Brighton, who motioned to Dunbar.

'DS Dunbar is leaving the room,' said Dunbar.

Now The Bulldog did not look so cocky. What were they up to? he thought. What could they possibly have on his client?

Dunbar returned carrying a large box of evidence bags and set them on the floor next to Brighton. Brighton fished through and pulled out the AK47 assault rifle that Jeanie found and put it on the table.

'I'm now presenting exhibit one, an illegal rifle found at the ambush site where Glitch and his gang stole a Trident Missile.'

The find was pure gold. After he saw goblins at the Rotting Ewe throw their weapons when they jammed, he wondered if they had done this at the ambush as well, and so he had Dunbar and the team sweep the woodland around the crime scene. They found three more. All of them were dusted for prints and one had a crisp set of Billie's on the magazine, the trigger guard, and the handgrip.

'Has your client seen this weapon before?'

The Bulldog sighed, his contempt obvious as he turned to Billie.

'No comment.'

'So, he is neither affirming nor denying that he has seen this weapon. Is that correct?'

'I said no comment. Pig.'

'Mr McGregor. Please advise your client that the weapon has been fingerprinted and the evidence has been positively matched with his fingerprints.'

That wiped the smirk of The Bulldog's face.

'DI Brighton this weapon may indeed have been handled by my client but this alone in no way makes him an associate of a terrorist.'

Thanks to Helene, Brighton had brought in another member of Billie's gang, Bryce Schroder, and his spotty lover Malcolm Somersby. Malcolm cried like a little girl when he was implicated in a gun smuggling operation. A deal was struck, and the curly ginger spilled his guts. Malcolm knew more about Glitch than he should have. He had times and dates of meetings and where they were held. He was a vault of information.

'I am now showing exhibit two. A witness statement that not only puts your client with the gun, but states that he showed Glitch how to use it.'

That threw Billie over the edge and before The Bulldog could calm him down, he slammed his fist on the table.

'I'll kill the bastards.'

'We don't really care about the weapons Billie' said Brighton changing tact and speaking directly to the accused. 'All we want to know is where Glitch is hiding. Is he with his friend Zaliel?'

Brighton saw something strange when he said the wizard's name. The Honourable Tim McGregor flinched. Just briefly, and for a fraction of a second, but he flinched. That little gesture told Brighton that The Bulldog knew who Zaliel was. Now he knew why the solicitor had taken Kerry's keys and had stolen the evidence from his home. The Bulldog was in league with the wizard. He decided to keep that little gem to himself for now.

'As of yesterday, Zaliel was placed on the terrorist watch list as well. Have you had dealings with him? Either of you?'

That made both of them squirm.

'I don't...' began Billie before The Bulldog shut him down.

'I request a few minutes with my client,' said the solicitor whose ego and confidence were deflating by every second.

Brighton wasn't sure whether Billie was more alarmed at the implication of his outburst or what his lawyer would say to him. Either way he couldn't care less. Fifteen minutes later, The Bulldog announced that

Billie wanted a deal. He wanted immunity from prosecution for the information that Brighton wanted, and he put someone else on the chopping block to sweeten the deal, his pal Darren.

A part of Brighton didn't want to give Billie anything. He was morally repulsed by the idea and felt it was making a mockery of the law and everything he stood for. He didn't sign up to let scumbags like this slip through his fingers. On the other hand, he had no choice, and The Bulldog knew it. Sally was equally furious, and Brighton had to adjourn to walk out of the room with her.

'We don't have time for this Sally,' he said, 'The DCI wants a result, and we are dealing with a national incident. MI5 will be all over this soon and if we don't get that information they will.'

'I still think this is crazy DI Brighton. If this deal ever gets quality checked, questions will be asked.'

'We'll cross that bridge when we come to it. In the meantime, we have a missile and a terrorist to find. That's more important.'

'Okay, I will do as you say, but I want it on record that I am extremely reluctant and that I am doing this under duress.'

'That's fine with me. Just get it done.'

He and Dunbar went to grab a coffee. On the way back, Brighton couldn't resist stopping at the cell where they kept Darren Rocco. Rocco stared at Brighton with his cold green eyes and asked for his phone call. Brighton told the custody sergeant about his request on the way out and agreed to it, a mistake he would soon regret.

With the deal signed and sealed, Brighton cleared the room, telling his colleagues and The Bulldog that he and only he could have the information. After feigned protest from the lawyer, the others left the room.

As soon as the door closed, Billie said 'Look, I don't know how you know about Glitch, but you have to believe me. He's not human.'

'Oh, I know Billie. I've been to Goblin Towne.'

'Are you serious?'

'Yes. I ate cat at the Rotting Ewe.'

Billie's face told Brighton he knew that he was on the level.

'Not bad that cat. Don't mind it me self. Watch out for that gravy though.'

'Look, that's not why we made the deal. Tell me where the bastard's hiding. Does he have a place that nobody knows about?'

Billie thought for a moment.

'Yeah. He does. Took me there once. There's a valley with a big lake in it and an island in the middle. That's where his place is. He has these magick doors that take him anywhere he wants. A door here, a door to the Ewe, there's a few of em.'

'How did you get there? Do you remember?'

'No idea. Through a door. You go through the door. Close it and bang! You're somewhere else.'

Brighton's heart leapt. What if there was one that went to Zaliel's wandering tower? He could save Emily and Jeanie. He didn't wait around to ask. He thanked Billie and walked out of the interview room.

'I want protecting copper' called Billie after him.

'See to it,' he said, walking past Dunbar and out to the carpark.

37

Brighton went home and prepared for battle. He dressed for the occasion in a dark navy-blue t-shirt, baggy jeans, and his beloved Australian Blundstone Boots which were steel capped and good for kicking in a shin or two if need be. He still had his webbing rig from his brief time with special operations. He'd use it to store the spare Heckler and Koch magazines for the MP5 he'd left with Eddie for safe keeping. Over the top of everything he wore the battered brown leather trench coat he'd found in an op shop when he was at Hendon an age ago, knowing it would keep him both dry and warm.

He stowed his ASP and looked around for Thundershack but the brouny was nowhere to be seen, so he walked down to the door in the hedge, not knowing if he'd ever see the place again. As he bent down to open the gate, he felt cold metal touch the back of his head.

'Going somewhere Brighton?'

Raising his hands he turned to face Sid Fields and the grinning Eric Grimsby who held a Beretta 9mm pistol just inches his face.

'Don't try anything,' said Grimsby, 'or I'll water the hedge with your brains.'

'Armitage already knows you've been in town Sid. I told him after we brought Eric here in. So, if I get hurt or go missing, he'll be the one knocking on your door.'

The old crook laughed in his face.

'This ain't about you Brighton. If I wanted you dead, he would have pulled the trigger, and we'd already be in the car. The geezer I want brown bread is the bastard who killed my daughter, and we heard that you might just have a lead on him.'

Crap, thought Brighton. Darren must have called Sid after he knew that Billie was about to send him up the river and this was his parting gift.

'Look Sid, this is not the best time.'

'I don't give a monkeys. I want him gone and you're going to help me. Understood?'

Brighton knew he had no choice, and there was no time to explain to Sid that the man he wanted dead was a wizard who lived in a wandering tower in another dimension.

'Okay you can come with me, but you have to promise to do as I say.'

'I ain't promising jack shit,' said Fields, 'Now open the fucking gate.'

Brighton obliged and the three followed the path all the way into the ancient oak forest until they reached the orange mushroom circle.

'What now?'

'Follow me,' said Brighton stepping into the circle and walking around to the mushroom with many little chunks taken from around the cap.

He broke three pieces off and gave one each to Grimsby and Fields. They were not impressed.

'Is this a fucking joke Brighton? Do you think I want to sit around and eat bloody mushrooms?'

'He's lost the plot boss,' said Grimsby. 'I say we do him in now and cut our losses.'

'Sid, if you want to find this guy, then you're going to have to trust me.'

Brighton closed his eyes and ate his piece of mushroom.

'You first Eric.'

'But Boss.'

'Just fucking do it. I know where you live.'

Sid followed suit when he saw Eric gulp his down, and sat down in the circle. He didn't close his eyes at all and nearly shit his pants when he saw Brighton starting to melt away like a snowman in Jamaica. Grimsby shrieked, and as he began fizzing Sid joined in. They all fizzed like lemonade into the thirsty earth.

Brighton woke up in the tunnel system. He thought about ditching Sid and Eric but who knows what they would get up to without an escort. He turned on his torch and nudged the two crims awake. Sid woke frantic.

'Where the hell are we? Where'd you bring us to?'

'This is another world Sid. We're not in England anymore.'

'That's bollocks and you know it,' said Grimsby. 'Take us back.'

'I can't do that Grimsby. I don't know how. But I know someone who does, follow me.'

Brighton walked down the tunnel with the two crims in tow. They walked past the little blue doors carved into the side of the tunnel, to the set of steps leading out and opened the door in the oak tree. Fields and Grimsby looked around, blinking in amazement at the strange forest and the pale green sky.

'Watch him a minute, will ya? I'm going for a piss.'

As Sid slunk into the nearby bushes, Eddie walked into the clearing and joined them.

'Oi! Brighton! Where the hell have you been?' said the grumpy fairy, 'I've been waiting here for days. Who is…?'

Turning around, Brighton saw Eddie and before he could warn her Grimsby pointed his pistol at her.

'Hello, hello. Who's this chunky little girl then?'

'Who are you calling chunky, fuck face?'

Grimsby didn't like that one bit and levelled his weapon at her.

'Watch out Eddie. That's a gun in his hand.'

Eddie looked at Brighton and wondered why he was stupid enough to bring other people into the Magical Wooded World. She rolled her eyes.

'This is a total security breach. Now I have to tell Aldercy and he's going to be well pissed.'

'Shut up you.' Who is she anyway?'

'This is Eddie. She's a fairy.'

'And I'm David Beckham.'

'Eric, I told you. You're in another land and seriously she is a fairy. Show him your wings Eddie.'

'But I hardy know him,' she said blushing, and extended her wings. Grimsby looked even more starstruck than before and had to slap himself on the face a few times, but not as hard as Brighton would have liked.

Sid crept up behind her and pressed his pistol in her back. That startled her and she whirled around and backed away.

'Ere. No funny business you. Where's your wand? Hand it over sweetheart.'

'Like fuck baldy.'

Brighton could hug her for having the guts to say that. She would have said exactly the same thing without any regrets even if she knew what an asshole he was. At the same time Sid didn't like being ridiculed, especially in front of his number two. He walked up to her with his palm outstretched ready to slap her in the face. She flew up, with every intention of zapping him in the balls but before she could grab her wand the old gangster grabbed her and held her like a python in his grip with one hand and levelled the pistol at her face.

'I said no funny business.'

'Let me go, Let me go!' said Eddie, struggling as Eric joined his boss and patted her down. He found the wand and gave it to Sid.

'Get over there,' he said to Eddie, motioning to where Brighton was.

'That's better,' said Sid, 'Now how are you planning to get to this geezer?'

Brighton didn't want to answer. He understood why Sid wanted revenge. He would want the same if anything happened to Emily, but at the same time he didn't want to compromise her safety. What if Sid killed Zaliel and Emily was trapped in a magickal wandering tower that nobody could find?

I understand, said Eddie telepathically, startling him for a moment. He pretended to swat at a bug to avert suspicion.

Should we help him?

We don't have a choice. Unless you want a bullet in your head like Glodprog. Let's just pretend we are on side and escape as soon as we can, okay?

That's fine by me.

'Well?' said Sid

Eddie looked at Sid's eyes and saw the great pain he tried so hard to mask with anger. A pain she felt and only knew too well. She felt a bit sorry for him.

'Come on then' said Eddie, 'I'll show you.'

She led them to a small meadow where Seven Skies stood waiting. He looked up and neighed when he saw them. As the pegasus walked towards them, Brighton shook his head. He didn't want Fields or Grimsby knowing Seven Skies could understand them. They were blown away by the fact he was a flying horse.

'Is that what I think it is?'

'Yes, he's a pegasus. We're going to ride him to the location.'

'I ain't going on a bleeding flying horse boss, said Eric. 'I don't like it, and I don't like heights neither.'

'Eric. Do you remember what happened to the last person that said no to me? I'm pretty sure you do since you poured the cement over him.'

The threat was enough to transform Grimsby's attitude.

Fields looked over to Brighton.

'So where are we off to?'

'I don't know. The description wasn't that good.'

Brighton told them about the place that Billie described.

'Hmm' said Eddie. 'That sounds like the Ebwarrod Ranges. It's close and there's definitely a lake with an island.' She looked up into the distance. 'I can see a storm coming. We'd better decide what we're doing.'

'Let's go and have a butchers,' said Fields.

They climbed onto the huge silent pegasus. Eddie sat first, Brighton second. Behind him sat Fields and at the back was Eric who shivered as the pegasus strained under their weight as he took flight.

Brighton closed his eyes and hunched forward as Seven Skies steadied up and flew into the wind of the violent approaching storm. He felt Fields' arms around his waist and said nothing. He was probably as terrified as Brighton was about riding a flying horse with no safe way of holding on, and being at the mercy of the elements. He felt the pegasus lurch from side to side and then up, adjusting for the jet stream. Despite being larger than a Clydesdale, Seven Skies wasn't used to carrying so many passengers and it showed. After a good while, Brighton felt confident enough to open his eyes.

He found they were surrounded on both sides by the huge purple mountains of the Ebwarrod Ranges. Looking around he saw snow on several peaks through the rain. How high up were they? They must be flying at least above three thousand feet. Seven Skies tried to get above the storm but struggled. Lightning struck like a frenzy of iron swords into the mountains above them. Rocks exploded, falling around them with dangerous precision, sending Seven Skies weaving about like an out-of-control rollercoaster.

Brighton was too busy watching out for the lightning display to see the threat drifting above them until it attacked. For a moment he thought it was another dragon, but it was five times the size of the creature that Zaliel flew upon in Elfhame and it had feathers. Swooping down, the huge bird screeched as it grabbed Eric Grimsby with its massive razor-sharp talons, ripping him from Seven Skies' back and instead of flying away, it pursued them, with Eric still screaming and writhing about in its claws.

Eddie looked terrified. 'Roc!' she screamed.

Brighton hoped that they could outmanoeuvre it. Seven Skies banked hard left like a Spitfire with a bandit on its tail. He galloped on the side of the range and jumped off into thin air in a seamless move that Tony Hawk would be proud of. Brighton looked in awe at the huge bird with its gorgeous pink and purple plumage. He didn't want to kill something so amazing, but then he remembered that he killed a rock dragon without a moment's thought. Why should this be any different?

Behind him, Sid fumbled for his Beretta and fired a burst between the surprised roc's eyes. Brighton and the others heard Grimsby's screams above the roaring wind as he and the lifeless bird plummeted to their doom.

'Good thinking,' said Brighton. 'We could have been breakfast if she'd caught us.'

'That's alright,' said Sid, without a care in the world for his fallen comrade. 'How'd you know it was a she?'

'We flew over her nest. I saw three hungry mouths the size of dragons.

Don't you watch anything? This place is crawling with them and that one was pretty small compared to others.'

Sid went pale and decided not to put away his gun just yet. Brighton enjoyed his captor's discomfort, but he was worried about the literal ticking time bomb.

The extra payload and the roc attack had impacted on Seven Skies' energy. His growing exhaustion evident as he slowed down and Brighton wondered if he had enough strength to get them to the island. How on earth were they going to get back to the defuse the bomb in time if he was too tired to fly?

Before he could start to think about other options, Eddie tugged on his jacket sleeve and pointed down. Through the thinning clouds he saw a lake that stretched for miles like a faded rocker's spandex collection. As the pegasus began to descend, Brighton made out the form of the island and hoped that Glitch was down there.

Seven Skies barely had the juice to do a perfect landing and all but collapsed.

'Thanks Seven Skies,' said Brighton as the great winged horse rolled on long wet grass.

He wanted to say something but knew Sid was watching and so he did something unexpected. He winked. That threw Brighton. Was that a message that he was just fooling about being tired while all the while he still had his mojo? If he is acting, thought Brighton, then he's doing a better job than Mr Ed, as he watched the pegasus lay on its side and close its eyes.

'Finished playing with your pony?' said Sid, 'He'd better be alright when we need him or it's off to the glue factory like my last nag.'

Brighton didn't bite. He knew that was what Sid wanted and just ignored him.

'What now?' said Eddie.

'Any ideas?' said Sid.

Eddie had a great idea involving the union of her size ten boot and his wrinkly old testicles but held back for the moment.

Brighton shook his head.

'Come on. One of you must have a clue.'

'Okay,' said Eddie. 'Let me fly over the island. I'll have more of a chance of finding him quickly on my own.'

'What's stopping you from taking off as soon as you're in the air?'

'Well... There's Brighton for starters.'

'Ha! Don't give me that. I know enough about people to know you couldn't give a toss about him.'

Eddie shrugged. 'True. I just want my wand back.'

Sid laughed. 'Thought as much. Off you go then. Chop, chop.'

They stood and watched as Eddie spread her wings, flying up into the air and out of sight. The sky opened up and Sid ushered Brighton under the cover of a large oak tree that stood on guard in front of a dense bush. It absolutely pelted down as the heavens opened. Only Seven Skies enjoyed every moment of it. For him it was like hitting the showers after a rugby match.

Minutes passed and there was no sign of Eddie. Brighton kept his mouth shut. He had nothing to say to Fields. Deep down he resented the gangster for burning his home to a crisp. He was only here because he had to move. If he hadn't moved, they'd never have gone to his mother's old home, and Emily and Kerry would still be with him. He missed them terribly and yet here he was, standing next to the man responsible for all his misery.

'What's up your ass?' said Fields. 'Is it because I broke your nose?'

'No. Have a good think and tell me Sid. What do you think you've done?'

His rage surprised the old crook, who leered at him.

'Why don't you enlighten me, you muppet.'

'Well because of you I lost my kid and my wife.'

'What are you on about? I never touched them.'

'You didn't have to. We had to move here after you blew up our bloody home!'

'What are you on about Brighton? I never blew no house up. Nothing to do with me.'

'Oh come on Sid. You knew where I lived, and you knew all about the patrol car. As soon as my security was moved, you blew my home up.'

Sid clenched his fists. 'I told you. I had NOTHING to do with it. OK!'

'I don't believe you.'

'I don't care.'

'You're a gutless asshole Fields and a fucking liar. You know that?'

That tipped Sid over the edge. He dropped his gun on the ground and turned on Brighton, laying in punches. The old man was good, but Brighton was better.

Fuelled by his anger he stepped around, blocked and belted Fields around the head, cutting his eye and his lip. Fields grabbed Brighton's arm and bit it, locking his jaw before Brighton grabbed his Santa sack and pulled it down like a church bell rope for Sunday mass.

The two fought a long overdue heated battle that was more street than Queensbury rules, ending up in a heap on the ground, rolling and punching and jostling for position. Sid straddled Brighton and punched him in the face once before Brighton lifted his legs around the gangster's neck and pinned him back down in a classic commando move. He raised his fist, but before he could bring it down, he heard the cocking of the abandoned Beretta behind him.

'That's enough human. Get off him. Slowly. You are our prisoners.'

Brighton stood up and raised his hands. Sid stared at the newcomers as he dusted himself off. Both goblins had MP5's, wore poorly fitting old armour and rusty horned helmets. He'd never seen anything like it.

Brighton didn't need to turn to know that there were goblins there. He cursed his luck. Of all the places to take shelter, they must be standing close to the entrance of Glitch's hideout. He turned and looked at their scrawny captors. They may have been half his size, but their weapons were intimidating enough. They looked unsure of what to do next.

'We should take them back,' said one, 'Glitch will want to see them.'

'No let's shoot them now,' said the other, 'Glitch will want to eat them.'

'Why don't you take us back and then kill us after?' said Brighton. 'That way everyone is happy. Only I wouldn't eat him, he's old and he'd be tougher than the cat pie at the Rotted Ewe.'

That made the goblins laugh.

'Hey! Watch it Brighton,' said Fields.

'Why? What are you going to do? Kill me? Blow my house up?'

The two guards were completely distracted by their prisoners' argument, which is exactly what Brighton wanted; otherwise, they'd have seen Seven Skies inching towards them. As soon as he was in range, the pegasus lashed out at the hapless goblins with his mighty front legs as hard as he could, knocking them down like a pair of whack a mole's. Brighton sprang up and disarmed his former captors, who lay writhing on the ground clutching what was left of their little balls.

'Good work!' said Fields getting up, but froze as Brighton pointed one of the MP5's at him.

'Hold it Sid. I want you to give me the wand.'

'Okay, okay, just don't point them things at me boy. Do you know what I done to the last man that pointed a fucking gun at me?'

'I dunno. Did you blow his house up?'

'Aww not the bloody house again,' said Sid, taking the wand from his belt and placing it on the ground. 'I told you, that wasn't me. I know who it was though.'

Brighton raised his eyebrow.

'Why didn't you say that before?'

'You never asked,' said Sid, rolling his eyes. 'A few weeks before Anna Bell was murdered, this strange woman set up a meet with me. She wanted me to kill you and suggested that if we blew your place up, we could take out you and your kid. I was interested but I didn't need the heat, so I turned her down. But I know she went and had a chat with Solly...' He paused long enough to kick one of the goblins that looked like it was recovering.

'Solly who?'

'Solly Parsnip.'

'The mad safe cracker?'

'The one and only. Mad Sol himself. Heard he charged her twenty grand down for the privilege.'

Brighton was happy for the lead and nearly inclined to apologise. But he didn't.

'Did you get her name?'

'No idea. She didn't say. All I know was she was young, but she was smart. She was dressed like she was in business, and she spoke well. Had a funny mark on her arm. A brand or something.'

'Brown hair?' said Brighton, 'All tied up?'

'Yeah. How did you know?'

'Let's just say we're not strangers,' Brighton said.

It all made sense now. Cecilia had sabotaged him by refusing to change the lock, searched through his place, and had introduced him to The Bulldog. He wondered if they were in it together and pondered another potential link to Zaliel.

'Glad I could help.'

Speaking of help, Brighton remembered that someone else deserved thanking.

'Well done Seven Skies,' he said reaching into his pocket and putting a couple of sugar cubes on his hand.

'You're welcome Brighton,' the old pegasus said, 'What's this stuff?'

'It's sugar.'

Seven skies sniffed and licked both cubes up in a single lick.'

'Mmmm that was delicious. Got any more?'

'Yeah sure.'

Brighton gave him another three. He looked over at Sid who was still coming to terms with goblins and a flying horse, only now it was a talking flying horse.

'How did you get Mr Ed here to talk?'

'Who's Mr Ed?' said the curious pegasus pacing over to him and finding it strange that the unnerved gangster was stepping away from him.

Brighton found it amusing.

'What's wrong Sid? Haven't you heard a talking horse before?'

'What were those mushrooms we ate?' said Sid looking alarmed.

The whole thing was getting too much. The strange world, the roc taking Eric, goblins, fairies, and now a talking flying horse.

'Do they last long? I want to come down. Please. I want to come down.'

'What's wrong with him?' said Eddie back from her scouting patrol.

She landed next to Brighton and looked at the gangster who pleaded with Brighton to take him home. Eddie picked up her wand and zapped him and the two goblins into a deep sleep. Brighton took his handcuffs out and cuffed one of Sid's wrists to a thick tree branch with a bulbous part that would stop the cuffs from getting past it.

'I think a nap will do him good you know,' said Eddie, 'Where did those two come from?' she said pointing to the goblins.

'Dunno. Not that far.'

The big horse sighed and rolled its eyes.

'They came out from that door in the tree,' said Seven Skies, 'It's around the left side, don't you people see anything?'

'Let's go,' said Eddie.

'Hang on,' said Brighton. 'Seven Skies could you fly to Elfhame and bring back reinforcements? Like you did last time? I think we'll need them.'

'Okay. But I want more sugar.'

Brighton fished around in his jacket and found the rest of the sugar cubes he'd brought with him. They were gone in a lick and blink and so was the flying horse.

Brighton and Eddie looked for the door and had no trouble finding it. He opened it with care, trying not to make a sound. In front of them was a flight of stairs leading straight down. They crept in, shutting the door behind them. Brighton found a stair rail and Eddie held his shoulder as they descended into darkness. Brighton found it difficult because he could not see a thing and put each foot down slowly, touching ahead for the next step. It was harder for Eddie and when something wet and slimy touched her neck she screamed, whirled around, and lit the stairwell, startling the goblin below them with her wand.

The goblin ran down the stairs with Brighton and Eddie in hot pursuit. They followed it through a thick wooden door and into a long stone corridor with many doors on either side of it. The goblin opened one of the doors and when he closed it behind him, with a spark and a puff of green smoke, the door exploded like the one Jeanie went through. Brighton found himself staring at stone brickwork behind it.

'Magick doors,' said Eddie 'We'll never catch him now.'

Another goblin came around the corner, carrying a tray with a small piece of bread and an earthen jar. It saw them, dropped the tray, and ran back where it came from. Brighton and Eddie chased after it.

'Faster' said Eddie as Brighton ran out of puff.

He redoubled his efforts and ran past her, and as he went to turn, his instincts told him to duck down. As he did, a nasty looking rusty pike was thrust where his neck had been. He came drifting around that corner like a new Maserati, smooth, low, and sleek with both MP5's blazing at the hapless goblin that nearly killed him and wounding several running to help him. The goblins saw the imposing man with the guns and legged it.

Brighton thought he had won, but in moments the tide turned as more goblins came around the next corner running towards him with a stunning array of weapons that would impress the Kiwi armourers of Middle Earth. There were many more behind them and they weren't afraid.

Brighton and Eddie worked together. His MP5's sent arcs of semi-automatic fire into their ranks, sweeping back and forth low and lethal with Eddie covering him with her powerful protective shield from the arrows, laser blasts, bullets, and crossbow bolts. Three magazines down and Brighton saw he was running out of ammo fast.

'We need to run,' he said.

'Where?'

'That way,' he said, pointing at another flight of stairs. 'Can you hold them off?'

'I'll try.'

Ducking behind her, Brighton ran down the hallway. But just ahead, he saw more goblins scurrying up the stairs. He fired at them as he looked for a way out and chose a big thick iron door.

'In here,' he said to Eddie as she tried to shield herself from both sides.

Brighton focussed on the stairwell and gave her enough cover fire to make it to the doorway. He pulled her in, shut the door and bolted it without a second to lose. It was unusual to find a door that had so much security, and it didn't make much sense at all, but it would keep the goblins out for the moment.

'Brighton,' said Eddie in a soft tone that barely disguised her discomfort. 'You need to see this.'

He turned and saw something that made his stomach sink. The room was quite big but there were no other doors or way out. They were trapped. In the middle of the room was an operating table. It may have been clean once, but it was filthy and bloody, whatever they did here it certainly was not performed under sterile conditions.

The room was heated and lit by the dull embers of logs in a small fireplace. Next to which Brighton found a bucket full of long slender branding irons. His attention moved from the fire to the pile of rags on the floor in the corner of the room. As he moved closer the pile jumped up and grunted at him. At first he thought it was a monkey, a dirty monkey in rags chained to the wall by the neck on a short leash. There was something familiar about her and he gave the rags she'd been lying in a closer look. When he saw a faded pink track suit jumper lying on the floor he drew away in shock.

'Annie Bligh? Are you Annie Bligh?'

Annie was the first missing children cold case Brighton had worked on, years before the others, and so he hadn't linked it. Still, he had not given up on her and looked at her file every day when he came to the office.

The creature in front of him blinked in a confused daze when he said her name. She was at least eighteen now and no longer the little girl that had disappeared off the face of the earth all those years ago. Her long hair was now cut short and raggedy. When the goblins banged on the door it set her off in a panic. She tried to yell something but all she could do was howl. The banging grew louder, but Brighton felt the door would hold for now.

'Eddie, could you please shine your light over here?'

Eddie shone her wand in his direction and bathed Brighton and the teenager in a soothing pale-yellow light. He recognised her eyes. They blinked in fear.

'There's nothing to worry about,' he said. 'I'm DI Brighton. I'm a police officer. I promise you won't get harmed. Can you understand me? Nod once if you can.'

The girl nodded and cried with relief.

'Is your name Annie Bligh?' She nodded again.

'Why can't you speak Annie? Have they put a spell on you?

Annie shook her head and opened her mouth. Her tongue was missing. That wasn't all. She had been branded on the right wrist and Brighton recognised it at once. Cecelia Lemon had the same mark. He didn't know what to think, but he knew what he needed to do. He looked at the heavy chain around her neck. It had an iron lock on it.

'Eddie, I don't suppose you could...'

Eddie clicked her fingers, and the chain sprang off. Annie ran to Brighton and hugged him, relieved after finally being found. Outside the thudding stopped all together.

'Hey pigs,' said Glitch outside the door. 'Don't know how you managed to get out of the caves, but I promise you that the only way you're ever going to get out of here after we get you and eat you, is if someone takes a shit outside.'

Charming, thought Brighton.

'Well come in and take us Glitch,' said Eddie, 'I'm not scared of you, you ugly stupid goblin.'

'Tell me fairy pig. Did you stop my toy from ticking? I don't think so. You don't have much time left. Tick tick tick tick. Soon all your friends will be dead, and I will be the king of this world.'

'There won't be much to be king of Glitch. Didn't Billie tell you? That bomb will kill everything and everyone in this world. It will poison all the food, all the water and everyone here including you.'

Glitch was silent. Was he having second thoughts? Did anything that Brighton said have an impact on him? Glitch's laugh echoed through the corridor.

'We shall see. As for food and water you have none in there. You are my prisoners. There is no escaping this time. When you come out, we will get you and then I shall punish you pig. And as for you fairy, I can't wait to fry up your wings for my breakfast.'

Another wicked laugh and silence. Glitch must have left and there was no doubt in Brighton's mind that he'd posted guards outside. What were they going to do? Eddie was silent and looking around the room for anything that could save them. Brighton inspected the fireplace hoping that they could climb through the chimney but when he looked up, he found it was too small, and a metal grill blocked the way up. The only way out was through the door. Annie flopped back down on her rag bed near the wall and began to cry.

'Hey,' said Eddie, 'It's not over yet. We'll get you out of here.'

'It's not like you to be optimistic Eddie,' said Brighton noticing a change from when they'd been stuck in the cave.

'Shut the fuck up Brighton.' said Eddie with a smile, sitting down and making herself comfortable.

'There must be something we can do.'

'Yes. We wait. Seven Skies will be back soon with Aldercy. That's if he made it past the Rocs.'

'Is there any way you can let them know that we're trapped?'

'Absolutely. I shall conjure up a messenger for you that can fly through the...' she stopped mid barb as something dawned on her. 'Sure. I could do that. My friends and I used to send messages to each other when we were small, and I'd forgotten all about it. It's one of the first spells I learnt.'

Brighton watched as she closed her eyes and focussed. Holding her wand close to her ear, she glowed a translucent blue. Gradually moving the wand back, Eddie extracted a long thin bright white light. Opening her eyes, she cupped it in her hands and blew the curling light towards the fireplace where it drifted up the chimney disappearing from sight.

'What was that thing, Eddie?'

'That was a message for Aldercy. I told him we were trapped and to get a bloody move on.'

'Will it find him?'

'Yes, it will. What I don't know is when.'

She was interrupted by a noise outside the iron door. It sounded like the goblins were dropping bundles of sticks on the stone floor in front of it. Load after load clattered on the ground and then smoke slithered in from under the door.

'Quick! Find something to block it', said Brighton as the smoke wafted into the room.

Eddie looked around.

'Sorry Annie', she said, taking the rags on the floor. She bunched them up us as best she could and plugged the gap under the door. It worked for a moment, until the rags caught on fire. Smoke rose.

Brighton grabbed one of the branding irons, raked the ashes out of the fireplace and onto the floor where he stamped them out as best he could.

'Over here you two', he said.

There was just enough room for Eddie and Annie to crouch in front and breathe any air from above them. It wasn't the best solution, but it was all he had.

'What about you Brighton?'

'I'll be fine Ed.'

As the room began to fill with smoke, Brighton lay on the floor and searched his webbing until he found his bandanna. He packed it to use to attract attention but now the bright yellow cloth would save him in another way. Putting it around his mouth as a makeshift filter, he closed his eyes, hoping that help was on the way.

Soon he could barely breathe. He snuck short breaths, holding them for as long as he could but it was making him sleepy, and he was afraid of falling asleep. He fought to stay awake. Willing himself on for Emily and Kerry. He had to save them. This was no time to think about dying in a goblin laboratory.

After lying there for ages, a gust of cool air passed over his face, making Brighton open his eyes. He saw a long swirl of strange blue smoke gusting down through the chimney, breaking off into strands as it approached the doorway, turning into a wave of water that put the fire out on the other side. A force sucked the smoke out of the room, and back up through the fireplace like a vacuum cleaner. He filled his lungs with grateful relief.

'They're here,' said Eddie. 'We'd better help them.'

Eddie pointed her wand at the crack in the door and sent a bright burst of cylindrical orange smoke under it. There was a shriek from the other side and the brief sound of submachine guns before an agonising cry.

'What did you do Eddie? A snake spell?'

'No smartie pants. It was a fire salamander.'

Brighton had no idea what that was and wondered why she hadn't used it before, but there wasn't time to ask. He removed the bolt and forced the door open pushing away the damp branches that Glitch meant to kill them with. There was nothing in sight other than the dead goblin sentry. Brighton picked up the goblin's MP5 and removed the nearly full magazine, stowing it for later. He turned and gave Annie his water bottle and a bar of chocolate he'd brought along for emergencies.

'Stay here and bolt the door', he said, 'We'll be back for you.'

Annie grabbed the chocolate and slammed the door behind her.

Brighton heard a huge blast from up the corridor, and it sounded like Aldercy and his police force were making a move into the stairwell. Remembering what happened to them earlier, Brighton turned and covered the stairs near the laboratory, to stop anyone from coming up. Eddie put her shield up at the end of the passageway where the goblins had surged from last time. They didn't have to wait long before the place was swarming with goblins. Brighton used the stone corner as cover and sprayed the stairwell every time he saw movement. Eddie held a surging force at bay with her energy shield, it was weakening her, and she lost some ground as the horde began to push forward. Brighton was careful with his ammunition, but the goblins were becoming more suicidal.

He heard Glitch yelling at them and urging them on as if they had super strength. Unlike the henbane taken by berserkers, it was more likely his machine gun toting goblins were high on Billie Brown's meth. Their eyes glowed red with anger and none cared if anyone next to them was shot. Brighton wished he had a Franchi Spas shotgun. He needed something with more power.

'I can't hold them much longer,' said Eddie.

'I'm nearly out of ammo' said Brighton turning a charging goblin's legs into sinew with a fiery burst of German efficiency.

But the goblin kept going, trying to aim its weapon at Brighton as it hobbled towards him on bloody stumps like a zombie. Brighton breathed, waited for the goblin to come closer and grabbed him from around the corner. Holding it down, he ripped the submachine gun from its arms and fired two rounds in its angry green face.

He recommenced his defence of the corridor as Aldercy and his reinforcements rushed to join them. Aldercy looked down the hallway and saw that his daughter's wand was running out of power. He held his wand high in the air, circled it around his head and brought it down hard like a stockman's whip. He pointed it straight at the goblin horde and bathed them in a deep purple light as the energy beam went through and turned the corner. As they ran towards them the goblins began to change and after a few steps they transformed into a peaceful forest of giant mushrooms.

'Beautiful,' said Eddie, admiring Aldercy's spell.

When the goblins down at Brighton's end saw that their companions were shiitake, there wasn't much room for bravery. They turned and ran back down the stairs. Eddie's mates zapped the stragglers as they joined Brighton in pursuit. Brighton was on a mission. He had to get Glitch and quick. Who knew how much time was left before the bomb detonated.

As he swung off the bottom rail, he saw the remaining goblins running through a door and jumped through it before blinking twice. The door ported he and the others back to the corridor of magick doors and he saw that the goblins were making good use of them. The fairies zapped a few of them but most escaped, slamming the doors shut and filling the corridor with a rainbow of coloured smoke.

Brighton didn't think Glitch had escaped, so he went looking for him with his ASP at the ready and found the corridor full of mushrooms. What is with these people and their obsession with mushrooms? he thought, as he navigated his way through them. Who designed this world anyway, the Grateful Dead?

Brighton followed the mushrooms around the corner, and down another passageway, which emptied into a central chamber. Judging by the gaudy furniture and the imposing metal throne, he guessed it must have been Glitch's space. There were two doors in the chamber on opposite walls. Glitch ran out in a hurry, carrying something struggling in a sack. The huge imposing goblin stopped in his tracks when he saw Brighton.

'You again,' he said, drawing a thick nasty nail studded club from his belt. 'I'm going to beat your brains into porridge.'

Brighton stayed silent. We'll see about that, he thought, as he sized the goblin up. Glitch ran at him, swinging the club like a frustrated golfer. Fending him off, Brighton blocked the goblin with his ASP as Glitch struck at the detective again and again with vigour. When the goblin paused for a second Brighton took the offensive and aimed at his legs, swiping Glitch off balance. He dropped the ASP and grabbed him, rolling on the ground and using his strength to pin him by the shoulders with his knees.

'Give me the code,' he said, smashing Glitch's face methodically with his fists.

Now it was Glitch's turn to be silent. No blow would loosen his tongue, so Brighton grabbed Glitch's neck with both hands. He was desperate to get the code, save the world, and save his kid in the bargain. Whatever it took.

'I said give me the code.'

Glitch looked fearful as the pressure from the stony cold cop started to hurt. He knew Brighton meant business.

'Okay pig!' the goblin cried. 'I'll give it to you. The code is 19017941.'

Brighton had what he wanted. He didn't need Glitch anymore. He lifted the goblin up and proceeded to frogmarch him back to the fairies. Glitch had other ideas. His free hand found the magick charm Zaliel gave him.

'Snicker snack,' he said, and Brighton flopped on the floor like a stunned mullet. Laughing, Glitch kicked Brighton in the guts and stepped over him to the other door, he opened it revealing a spacious round room.

Brighton saw his daughter standing in the doorway. She looked frightened.

'DADDY!' she screamed, trying to run through the door, but Glitch shoved her out the way and slammed it shut.

Brighton tried everything to get up and by sheer will power he stumbled for the door just before it closed.

'Emily!'

But as he opened the door it burst into flames. The doorway evaporated in a flash covering him in green smoke. Emily was gone. He nearly had her. Knowing how scared she was made him feel miserable.

'Guv is that you?' called a muffled voice from inside the struggling sack Glitch had abandoned.

He opened it and found Jeanie all tied up and relieved to see him. He freed her at once.

'Thank God you're okay. I'm so glad I found you.'

'Me too! I don't know where he was taking me, but it wasn't nice.'

'I'm sorry you were kidnapped Jeanie. I didn't think that there'd be any stragglers.'

'That's okay. I've had quite an adventure and discovered that years of quantum science training was a load of old bollocks. Those doors are amazing! Could you imagine what they'd do for travel back home. No more discount airlines. No more tube either.'

'Do you know where that one went? My Emily is there.'

'You saw her? That's amazing. I don't know where it goes though. Only that it goes to Zaliel. Glitch was going to take me there because he thought I might be useful.'

'You still can be useful. We've found the missile.'

'I know. What's the code for?'

The code! In the excitement Brighton hadn't written it down. It was gone.

'You didn't hear it by any chance, did you?'

'He screamed it out so of course I did. Don't tell me you forgot.'

Brighton nodded.

'I did. I was too busy trying to get to my daughter.'

Jeanie gave him an understanding look.

'It's 19017941.'

'How did you remember that?'

'Once it's in here it stays in here,' she said, tapping her head while Brighton cut the thick bonds around her legs.

As Brighton cut the final rope, Eddie joined them. Jeanie stared at her with amazement.

'Woah. Are you a fairy?'

Eddie looked her up and down and up again. She blushed.

'I might be. Who are you gorgeous?'

'Come on you two,' said Brighton to the smitten pair. 'We've got a bomb to defuse. You can get acquainted at the Wilted Toadstool later.'

38

Aldercy and his team had been busy in their absence.

'Ah there you are,' he said in the room of doors. 'I see you've found your missing friend. Please tell me that Glitch gave you the code before he escaped?'

How the hell did he know that, thought Brighton, but then he remembered that he was addressing a very powerful fairy.

'Yes, we have it.'

'Excellent, let's go shall we?'

Aldercy opened one of the doors and ushered Brighton, Jeanie, and Eddie through. Brighton looked around and when he saw that they were back at Croagh Marbh he was happy because he was still sore from their last flight.

'There you are!' said Grumley, looking up from the fire where Droit was cooking something that suspiciously looked like a tin of baked beans.

The door had conveniently opened next to their camp. Grumley led them back to the cave where the bomb was.

'Are the rock dragons still there?' said Brighton to Grumley, when they stopped where the hole was that led to the chamber.

'Nah they left. Paddy was supposed to check it a while ago.'

'Where is he now?'

'Dunno. Probably gone for a look around. He's one of those inquisitive types.'

Brighton took Grumley's torch and hoped Paddy hadn't been anywhere near the Trident. He climbed up the rocks.

'Come on Jeanie,' he said. 'The rest of you wait here.'

Grumley looked somewhat relieved. He had no intention of following Brighton into that room. Brighton squeezed back into the chamber and hoped Paddy's observation about the rock dragons was true. Looking around the cavern, he saw that it appeared to be empty and made a beeline to the Trident.

'Wow' said Jeanie looking at the imposing missile.

'Do you think you can disable it?'

'Oh yeah, I think so. You're lucky I did that bomb disposal course for my performance agreement. Let me have a look.'

Jeanie squeezed past and looked at the maze of wires leading to the timer and keypad. She breathed a sigh of relief when she read that they still had three minutes on the green screen of the timer.

'What's the code then?' she joked.

Before she could tap in the numbers that would save them all from destruction, Jeanie felt her legs being knocked out from underneath her by the swish of a tail from under the trailer.

'Help' she screamed lying in heap as she came face to face with the surviving rock dragon.

'No one can save you,' said the rock dragon. 'My brothers will have their revenge. I just hope that you taste better than my last meal.'

As the dragon neared, Brighton looked past and saw the remains of the ginger dwarf scattered nearby. He looked for his ASP and realised he'd left both it and his empty gun back in Glitch's hideout. The dragon looked satisfied at Brighton's fear as it slinked closer to Jeanie, and she squealed when its sharp pointed teeth were almost in biting range.

'Ad lava' said the voice of Aldercy peering under the trailer.

The dragon shrieked and writhed around as it turned a glowing red before oozing into a pile of smouldering rock.

'Hurry. There's no time,' said Aldercy.

Jeanie panicked as she lifted herself up to the keyboard. She had twenty-five seconds. What was that damn code again? She stared at the screen struggling to remember and then with rapid strokes she keyed in what she thought the numbers were, hitting the enter button just as the clock went to three seconds, and watching it freeze at two.

They'd done it. Not only had they saved the world, but in a way, they'd saved Emily as well. Now Brighton could focus all of his energy on finding and rescuing her.

∼

There were no celebrations. The less the folk of Elfhame knew the better, because if they learnt how close they'd been to certain oblivion there was a likelihood that heads would roll, and Aldercy declared that he liked his where it was.

When they arrived back in the city, he brought everyone to a hush, hush meeting in his office and made them all swear to complete secrecy about the missile on pain of death. Seven Skies also agreed to stay quiet, although his deal included a regular sugar and apple allowance. When the meeting ended, Aldercy asked Brighton to remain in his office with Eddie.

'That was a little too close for comfort,' he said, 'Next time we shall need to work faster.'

Next time? Brighton looked at Aldercy, just a little confused. Did he hear the fairy correctly?

'What do you mean next time? I thought that if I helped you with this that you'd help me rescue Emily and that would be the end of it.'

Aldercy smiled at him.

'Ahh yes. Now about that Mr Brighton. You must appreciate that this is a rare opportunity that has never presented itself in the history of our worlds. One that we should build upon.'

'What do you mean?'

'Without your help our world would be no more, and without our help, your government would never have been able to recover this powerful weapon. A weapon that I hope will never be used.'

'Yes, but it's over, isn't it? I mean we put a stop to Glitch's plans, haven't we?'

'Ahh but we haven't completely stopped him. Even now he will be fuming and planning his next move to reach out to your world and find something he can use to his benefit and gain here. It will only be a matter of time until he does, and when this happens, we shall need the help of your police. Well, your help at any rate.'

This sounded like the Aldercy that Thundershack didn't trust.

'Look Aldercy. You promised me you'd help me find my daughter. You didn't say anything about continuing the relationship.'

'That was then,' Aldercy said with a thin smile, 'things have changed.'

'You bastard. Thundershack said you couldn't be trusted.'

Eddie gasped. Nobody had ever stood up to her dad before. Aldercy looked offended.

'I'm sorry you feel that way Mr Brighton. Would you still like our help, or would you like to see your daughter in the same state as that girl you found? Branded and with her tongue missing?'

Brighton felt his anger rising at the fairy's betrayal. He had no choice but to comply.

'Alright. I'll help you. Now when do you propose to find Emily? Could you make a magick door to Zaliel's tower?'

'Do you think it's as simple as waving my wand and making her appear? Zaliel is a powerful wizard. His tower is warded from magick and it's on the move. That door was made by Zaliel himself, and now it's gone.'

'So, what do you propose to do then? Surely there must be a way to find her. There has to be a way.'

'I will try my best to find her Brighton. That's all I can promise. Wait for my word.'

Aldercy looked away and down at the papers on his desk. The meeting was over. Brighton could not believe it. After all he'd been through, Aldercy had tricked him. He probably never had a clue how to find her in the first place and knew that from the first meeting. Instead, he'd strung him along like a pirate captain, promising treasure and reward to his crew in return for their obedience.

He wanted to punch him in his smug little face, but Eddie's quick thinking saved him from committing anything he'd regret later.

'Come on Brighton,' she said, calmly touching his shoulder. 'We should get going.'

It took several spells, and trial and error to move the Trident from deep within Croagh Marbh to the gateway at the bottom of the hill, ready for transporting back to where it came from.

Annie Bligh refused to leave the Magical Wooded World. Her rags were gone, and she'd been given magickally altered clothes to wear from lost property. She hadn't seen her parents for over a decade and became distraught when Brighton told her that her mother had died from an overdose of sleeping tablets after succumbing to depression after five years. Her father had a new family now. Like a young desert farm boy, there was nothing for her in her old world anymore and she wanted to move on.

Besides, she had a score to settle with Glitch and had asked about joining the police force. That matter was in Aldercy's hands, and until then, Eddie offered to put her up at her house. Brighton didn't blame her and decided to let her stay even though it went against all protocol.

When they were ready to leave, Sid Fields was brought in handcuffs from the station dungeon, an experience that made him even more numpty.

'Is that a fucking nuke Brighton?' he said looking at the Trident as Seven Skies and several heaving fairies wheeled it to the portal gate.

'What's happening now?' he said 'Afternoon tea with the fairies? I want to go home!'

'Eddie, could you do me a favour?', said Brighton.

'With pleasure,' she said, and zapped the gangster, perhaps a little more forcefully than she'd planned.

'Teach me that sometime please.'

Eddie grinned and together, she and Brighton picked Sid up and put him on the Triton's trailer.

'That should last for a few hours.'

'Thanks Eddie. Thanks for all your help as well. I appreciate it.'

'You're welcome' she said, reaching into her vest pocket and taking out a small orange stone the size of a two-pound coin.

'Aldercy wants you to take this. It's so that we can communicate with you if Thundershack's not around.'

So that he can keep tabs on me more like, thought Brighton, as she handed it to him.

'It does other things as well. It will heat up and turn yellow if someone's lying to you. If you put it near someone that's been cursed, it will turn purple, and it will bring you here if you need to get here in a hurry.'

'Thanks Ed' he said, looking at it in the palm of his hand and thinking it might help with his normal work; mainly the lying part, though he doubted it could be used as evidence in court.

Someone like The Bulldog would have a fit. He remembered The Bulldog's little tell in the interview and figured that the stone would come in handy indeed.

'Ahem' she said, interrupting his train of thought. 'The portal's open. Are you going or what?'

Brighton nodded, and he and Jeanie followed the trailer with the Trident through the gateway to his own world and into the oak tree forest. To Brighton's relief the portal opened up on the side of the small country road as he'd asked. That took a little tinkering on the fairies' part, but he knew that the army would otherwise destroy the ancient forest in the national interest to retrieve it.

'Thanks guv,' said Jeanie, 'That was a real thrill.'

'I guess. We nearly got killed a few times.'

'True, but we got to use portals, see magick, and meet goblins and dwarves and a pegasus.'

'And Eddie. Don't forget Eddie.'

'Not likely!' she said with a playful wink.

Brighton wondered if they'd done the fantasy equivalent of exchanging phone numbers.

He turned his phone on, rang Dunbar, and waited with the excited jabbering forensic scientist and the snoring gangster until his offsider arrived. He wasn't on his own. Four patrol cars came with him, then Hayley Sharpe.

'I don't suppose you can tell me how you managed to find it?' she said.

'Everything will be in my report ma'am.'

Well, not everything, he thought, wondering how on earth he was going to find an explanation.

'Why is that man handcuffed?' said Hayley, pointing to Sid who was starting to wake up. 'Is he involved with all this?'

Brighton was tempted to include Sid in the mix. The idea of a gangster being involved with the theft of a nuclear warhead in this day and age was entirely feasible.

'Where are we Brighton?' said Sid as he woke up. 'Are we still in fairyland?'

'What's he taking about Brighton?'

'Am I happy to see you,' Sid continued. 'This man took me to fairyland, and my mate was taken by a bloody giant bird while we were on a flying horse that could also talk!'

'Is he high?'

'Yes guv, I believe so. I'm pretty sure that earlier this afternoon he took several potent magic mushrooms. I found him wandering around in a daze. He may not be involved with the Trident, but there's no doubt he was involved in the attempt on our witness's life.'

'Bollocks. I ain't on magic mushrooms. I only took them to go to fairyland. You tell her then. Go on. Set her straight for God's sake.'

'With your permission ma'am, I'd like to escort this gentleman to Mortlake House for psychiatric evaluation.'

'Psycho what?' Field's face exploded with rage as Dunbar hauled him away.

'Good idea Brighton. I'll take care of things here. You know, the press and the military, and those TV crews.'

Brighton didn't care less. After everything he'd dealt with, he was tired and wanted to see his wife. DCI Sharpe could have all the credit she wanted.

'And DI Brighton,' she said, as he climbed into Dunbar's car, 'I want that report on my desk first thing in the morning.'

He nodded as Dunbar drove off to drop Jeanie at the station and then stop by Mortlake House. On the way they passed a truckload of soldiers led by a relieved looking General in a jeep.

After Sid was sedated and processed, Brighton quickly checked on his wife. Her doctor approved the impromptu visit and walked with him to her room, where they found her sitting on her bed staring out the window.

'How is she doctor?' he asked, as they stood near the doorway.

'It's hard to say Mr Brighton. Kerry has good days and bad, but not as bad as your last visit. She responds to treatment at times but not as much as we would like her to. I simply don't understand. After a traumatic experience like the one she has been through, the patient usually calms down and starts being more responsive. Your wife has barely been coherent since she arrived. It's almost as if she's under a spell.'

Brighton tried not to flinch.

'Can't you do something about it? I need my wife doctor. Are you doing any more tests?'

'At this stage no. She needs time and as much rest as possible. I'm afraid she won't be leaving us just yet.'

Brighton thanked the doctor and promised that he would not be too long. He wanted to check something. He'd been thinking about Kerry the whole time on the drive over. Feeling around his inside coat pocket, Brighton took the little bright orange stone out and walked over to her.

'Hullo love,' he said, and sat down next to her.

She sat silently like a lone tree on a hill not acknowledging him in the slightest. He reached for her hand, touched the stone on her, and watched as it turned purple in moments, his fear confirmed. Thundershack was right. His wife had been cursed, and he wished with all his heart that he could break the spell with a kiss.

'Don't worry love. I'm going to get you out of here, and I'm going to get Emily back. Just you wait and see. We'll be a family again soon. I promise.'

After his visit Brighton took a cab home and picked up a curry on the way, hoping that Thundershack would appreciate a spicy chicken jalfrezi washed down with a couple of cans of Guinness.

He arrived home to find Cecilia Lemon with a locksmith who was trying his best to open the front door.

'What's going on?' Brighton said, wanting to arrest her on the spot, but he knew he needed to get a lot more evidence. For now, she would just be an inconvenience.

'You haven't returned any of my calls for days. I was worried, and so I came over to check and found that you've replaced the locks after I specifically told you not to.'

'That's strange, I haven't had the locks changed. In any case, if you were that worried why didn't you call the station?'

'I didn't want to get the police involved.'

Bollocks, thought Brighton. He didn't need the sting from the magical stone to inform him that she was telling porkies.

He reached for his keys and tapped the door three times just as the brouny had told him to. The door opened fine.

'See? Now look at my keys,' he said, holding them out to her. 'They're the same as the ones you gave me. They even have the labels on them. Now if you don't mind, my dinner is getting cold, and the microwave is on the blink. Oh, and get a plumber over here tomorrow, will you? The cistern upstairs is blocked. It wouldn't be the only thing to be streaming shite around here.'

His dismissal sucked the wind out of her sails, and before the entitled little harpy could open her mouth to protest he walked inside, swung the door closed in her face, and locked it shut.

Ignoring the feverish rapping of the doorknocker, he walked into the kitchen. The kitchen door put a second barrier between them and was thick enough to block the exasperated lawyers knocking. She'll give up soon, he thought, as he put the food down on the table to go and grab a couple of plates. When he turned around, he saw that Thundershack had joined him.

'Perfect timing,' said the brouny, as he opened the nearest can of Guinness. 'I just ran out of pork scratchings. Did you tell her lairdship about the upstairs bog? She's been trying to get in for days. Even tried throwing a brick at the back window but it bounced off and nearly smashed her little face. Scared the crap out of her.'

'I'd like to have seen that.'

Thundershack eyed off the takeaway dinner and sniffed.

'Mmm this looks amazing lad. Go and see if that woman's gone, will you? I have something to show you.'

Brighton peeked through the lounge room window. Cecilia and the locksmith were nowhere to be seen. He walked back towards the kitchen wondering what the brouny was going to do next.

'She's gone.'

The famished detective entered the kitchen and froze. His smile replaced with a frown. Sitting across from him at the table was someone he thought, and wished he'd never ever see again.

'Hello William,' said Anna Brighton as large as life.

CAN'T WAIT FOR MORE BRIGHTON?

Sign up to our newsletter and receive updates on the next Brighton novel...

Bound by Magick

Out soon!

www.twhowis.com/subscribe

facebook.com/twhowis

instagram.com/twhowis

www.ingramcontent.com/pod-product-compliance
Lightning Source LLC
LaVergne TN
LVHW041959060526
838200LV00039B/1293